MAX ABADDON AND THE WILL

A Max Abaddon Novel

Book 1 By Justin S. Leslie

J.S.L

Copyright © 2019 Justin S. Leslie

All rights reserved. No part of this book may be reproduced or used in any manner without written permission of the copyright owner except for the use of quotations in a book review be it right wrong or indifferent.

This is a work of fiction. Names, characters, places, and incidents either are the product of the author's imagination or are used fictitiously. Any resemblance to actual persons, living or dead, events, or locales is entirely coincidental. Or I had too much to drink while writing and just forgot.

Hardcover ISBN 978-1-7331873-2-9
Paperback ISBN 978-1-7331873-0-5
Ebook ISBN 978-1-7331873-1-2

Contact information for publication

Abaddonbooks@hotmail.com
Facebook @Maxabaddonbooks
www.justinleslie.com

"We know what we are, but know not what we may be."

WILLIAM SHAKESPEARE

PROLOGUE

A dull drizzle pattered the windows on the fiftieth floor of the Mags-Tech headquarters building as the city lights looked like hazy blotches of noise below.

Ezra Hevel shook the glass in his hand as ice tinkled the sides, followed by a long sigh. After hours of long meetings and the unexpected cancellation of his flight out of town, the man stood resolutely, overlooking the city. A city that he knew was shrouded in a dark curtain of plausible deniability.

A buzz from his desk cut through the reflective moment as the female voice of his assistant flowed through the large mash-up of phones and various other communication devices on his desk.

"Sir," the stern yet firm voice called out. Ezra placed his glass on his desk, sat down, and yanked his tie, loosening it from its exquisite home under his gleaming white collar.

"Go ahead, Melissa."

"The night security detail has just arrived. Are you staying in the building, or do you need an escort home?"

The reality of his position afforded Ezra a penthouse suite on the top floor of the building he had worked so hard to secure and the business he had built. Taking a deep breath,

Ezra leaned back, glancing at the decanter of whiskey on his desk.

"No. I'm staying here tonight," Ezra paused, looking at the glowing clock on his wall. While new in style, it still held a timeless elegance, much like the rest of his office. "Looks like the night security team was running behind. Everything okay?"

"Yes sir. There was a delivery that kept them at the loading docks before checking in. They are set in the lobby, and I was about to send up your team," Melissa stated, not sounding concerned.

"Very well. I'll stop by and see them before I go to the penthouse. I'm still in my office. Melissa, take the rest of the night off and go home. I'll be fine," Ezra replied, smiling for the first time in hours. The rest of his night would include a few calming cocktails and some peace and quiet, followed by a possible movie.

"Yes sir," Melissa again replied, not putting up a fight. She would usually stay in the building if Ezra did. This was a point of contention with her boyfriend, but it was offset by the massive salary and house afforded to her by the position she occupied.

Over the past several days, Mags-Tech had been working on a breakthrough with the military, as well as its massive profit implications. Leaning back in his leather chair, Ezra took another sip from his drink.

Grey eyes shifted back to an angry red as the figure now standing in the communications room of the main executive offices cleared his throat. The once-present female voice of Melissa shifted back to a deep, growling grunt. Taking his lightly glowing hand off a control panel, the usual traffic of a massive building started to fill the empty room with random voices.

The ominous figure had also given Melissa the night off, sounding very much like Ezra Hevel. Sounds of the indeed delayed night security detail clicked as the man entered the executive elevator.

Ezra stood up smiling as the elevator dinged, letting the man know the night security detail had arrived. He would say hello to Burt, a long-term employee and what he considered to be a friend, if there was such a thing for someone like him, then retreat to the penthouse.

A piercing stare quickly replaced Ezra's smile as he shifted to smack the alert button installed on his desk. Thinking he had already done so, Ezra was confused as he glanced down at his hand hovering inches above the button.

The dark figure waved his hand as Ezra shifted back to his desk, flattening out his hands not of his own free will. Whatever he was doing was not allowing Ezra to activate the panic button or move.

"What do you want?" Ezra asked as the figure walked out of the shadows into the office.

Sharp features and a shadowed face were offset by a distracting set of glowing red eyes, now bearing down on Ezra. While he could see the figure's face, for some reason, he couldn't make out its features, only seeing the man's burning eyes. He was better than this. To date, he had never been caught off guard like this.

"What do I want?" the figure's deep voice drawled out, letting the question roll off his tongue. "Information. Information that you will be giving me."

"We can be reasonable. What do you want to know?" Ezra asked, thinking of Mags-Tech's latest project. Even though he was strong-willed, he also knew when he needed to be smart. Being dead never helped anyone—at least anyone he knew.

"The Vale project."

Not expecting this, the color drained from Ezra's face. This was something different. Something dangerous and something not known by many outside a select, extraordinary circle of trusted confidants.

Ezra didn't reply. He knew the man standing in front of him would know if he lied.

"I see you understand," the figure growled, stepping closer as he pulled out a gleaming silver object. Knowing what this was, Ezra took a calming last breath, knowing he was about to die.

CHAPTER 1

One of Those Days

There are always those crucial times in every person's life where, without warning, everything changes. One wakes up and soon realizes that all the monsters under the bed one always dreamed of as a kid were, in fact, very real.

That random Tuesday, as I nursed one of the worst hangovers of my life, just happened to be the start of one of those times.

My head throbbed with vague memories of the night before—yes, I had gone out on a Monday and was paying for it—and as I looked around my small beachfront apartment, only two things were going through my head. For starters, the lines of sun shining in on my wall through the slats of my cheap, dusty blinds signaled that it was roughly one o'clock in the afternoon. Second, as I went to push the button on my coffee maker, I quickly realized I hadn't put any coffee in it..

The overflowing pile of dishes in the sink were oddly clean for once, though.

At first glance, you might think I was some type of minimalist slob. My apartment was fairly dark and empty; a chair, dresser, mattress, kitchen table, TV, and couch were all the furniture I owned. On a positive note, the rather pleasant scent of honeysuckle hung in the air from the candle my mother had given me some four months ago, which I must have left burning overnight.

The amazing view of the Atlantic Ocean on the other side of my window was enough to excuse what the rest of my apartment and life had become.

As I began desperately trying to scrape the last of the coffee grounds out of a clearly empty can, my phone rang.

"Is this Maximilian Sand? Maximilian Abaddon Sand?" asked the oddly soothing, monotone voice at the other end of the phone.

"Yes, and I absolutely paid my rent this month," I replied.

"Max, this is Edward Rose. I am your late grandfather's attorney, and I'm calling to set up a meeting."

The past month had been a tough one. My hard-chinned grandfather had recently passed away at the ripe old age of seventy-five, and it had felt like life was on pause ever since. My gramps had been an interesting man. He always had something funny to say and seemed to know the answer to everything. There had been an air of mystery surrounding Gramps that made people want to know more about him and keep their distance at the same time.

Gramps would disappear for months, even years at one point. We never knew where he went or what he was doing, but one thing that always remained the same about his trips was that he always came back with gifts for everyone and looking as if he hadn't aged a day.

Being around him was like standing in one of those wood-paneled offices in an old estate or sitting next to the fire of a perfect camping trip. His clothes smelled of burnt hickory, and he always dressed to the nines in a rugged manner. It was almost as if he was from another point in history, and his wardrobe was either catching up to the latest fashion or too hip for anyone to realize it was the next big thing.

He'd had a rough man's face. Everyone had always compared him to an older version of Harrison Ford at the end of his career.

When we found out about his death, it had bothered me a little that my parents had taken it so well. My father had said it was just Gramps time. Mom, as always, had just shaken her head, smiled, and asked if I wanted something to eat. Maybe she'd just been acting strong for me, but being that Gramps was her father and my last living grandparent to boot, I'd have thought they would be a little more distraught.

Edward Rose cleared his throat on the other end of the phone line, waiting for my response. "Let me check my calendar to see when I'm available for a meeting," I sighed, knowing full well I had nothing to do for the next two weeks.

Well, let's just say I didn't have anything to do.

Sitting at my kitchen table with the phone in my hand, I absently stared at the closed window, thinking to myself that Gramps surely must have realized that leaving me his cat, Oscar, would be a bad idea.

"It looks like I'm free all next week," I finally told him. You could hear the static hum in the phone as Edward took a deep breath.

"How about you come to my office tomorrow at 1:00 p.m.? I'll text you the address. It's not far from the beach." Before I could reply, Edward ended the call not caring about my schedule.

I remembered that my grandfather had spoken a few times about a buddy of his who was a lawyer in St. Augustine. I assumed this was the person I'd just arranged to meet. It made sense.

Looking back on this moment, I'd had no clue how

drastically my life was about to change. My thirtieth birthday was coming up in a couple weeks, and for some reason, I felt energetic. Maybe it was the fact that I had recently gotten out of the military after five years of basically figuring out how to show up on time, or maybe it was the idea that I needed to find a job.

I took a deep breath, figuring only one thing would make this day any better—a trip to the Fallen Angel, FA's for short, for a drink and a taco.

CHAPTER 2

The Will

I woke up the next day with a strange feeling in my stomach. Perhaps it was just the fact that I had something to do today. I couldn't remember the last time I'd had a meeting planned. Then again, perhaps it was the hangover.

I donned my favorite pair of well-fitting jeans and a trusty old T-shirt for the best band ever, Planes Drifter. It always reminded me that I used to be cool once upon a time.

Looking in the mirror, I reflected on how I had often been told that I looked like a younger version of my gramps, albeit a little less like a movie star. My hair was fairly short, thick, brown, and wavy. Since getting out of the army, I had let a light beard grow, keeping it up in a neat style. It covered my hardened jawline and the deep dimple in my chin.

I was strong from years of sports and exercising on the government's dime; however, I had enjoyed my time since getting out, packing on the freshman fifteen just like in college.

Jumping into the Black Beast, my old Dodge truck that had seen its fair share of parking lot buggy fights, I headed south to St. Augustine, Florida.

While driving, thoughts went through my mind of what

Gramps had left me; was it something from his travels? I hadn't really thought about what he had left my parents and never thought to ask.

As I was growing up, it was clear he was wealthy; I just wasn't sure how much. *Strange* was the best descriptor for Gramps. I had only been to his house a handful of times, the last being when I was fifteen. He would always come see us.

What I did remember was it being a secluded two-story house attached to a much larger facility that I couldn't clearly recall. I never really paid much attention to it.

I could remember the wooden walls of his office and the collection of weird things he kept from his travels. It always felt like going back in time, and the house felt older on the inside than it looked on the outside. The house smelled much like him—of rich, burnt wood—and was immaculate. It was like going back in time to a classier era.

But hey, who am I to judge what's classy? I think a Taco Bell staying open after midnight is a class act.

Arriving outside the law office of Rose & Vendal, I felt a strange pull deep in my chest, almost as if I were about to meet a high school bully behind the dumpster after school. I'd won that fight but still didn't win the girl. That'd always been the one thing that got me in trouble: standing up for others when they couldn't. I hated bullies, and for some reason, I felt like I was about to meet one.

Reaching for my keys, I noticed that my hands were sweating, and the keys were cold to the touch. All I could think about was getting back home and maybe stopping for a few beers, followed by some computer surfing looking for my future.

The building had the typical downtown St. Augustine old-style front, with a small hanging sign letting people know that this was, in fact, a law firm and not a tourist stop for trinkets or cold drinks.

Since I lived in Jacksonville, trips to St. Augustine happened every couple of months. I had even dated a girl who had gone to Flagler College at one point before I joined the army, but I had never been to this part of downtown, even after all my adventures.

There was no real front, just a buzzer, a gate, and what looked to be a walkway to the front door. As I reached out to touch the buzzer, the door opened. A gentlemanly figure stood in the doorway.

"Hello, Max, I'm Edward, an old friend of your grandfather's and executor of his estate and will. Glad you made it on time," Edward greeted, putting out his hand to gesture me through.

"Funny," I said. "You don't look like an old friend. You look about forty-five, and my Gramps was as old as it gets."

Edward was roughly six and a half feet tall, having a strong yet thin frame. My eyes were at mouth level with him, me being six foot and some change. He was dressed in a modern gray suit with a bright white shirt and thin black tie. It looked comfortable and like you could actually move in it.

His hair was light brown, parted on the side, and close cut with plenty of product in it, making him look like a politician. No man was that cleanly shaven without careful consideration. The barely noticeable lines on his face hid the story of his life. He was well groomed to cover up a life of fighting and hardship.

He was serious, his face lean and hard, with an edge that said you weren't getting the whole story. With all that said, he still had an inviting air around him that made you want to sit by the TV and drink a beer with him.

Edward reached out, shaking my hand with a firm grip.

"I'm glad you're here. Follow me inside, and we can get started. I have a feeling this is going to be a long day. Hopefully, you are rested," Edward spoke. His voice was flat and very old-fashioned. I couldn't really place it.

Walking through the door, I felt a light pull in my chest, making me stop. Ed, as I had decided to call him, looked back.

"Are you okay?" He paused looking curious, smiling at me for a quick moment, losing his cool composure after seeing I was fine. I had been in the intel world in the army, and I had picked up some knowledge about reading people.

"I'm good," I replied before continuing through the door.

To say that the office was interesting would be an understatement. Looking around, a few things stood out. The lobby was posh, with red crushed velvet chairs and cherrywood everywhere, and a sweet, floral aroma which I couldn't quite place. While not completely classic in style, it had a timeless elegance, much like gramps's place. It was fitting of a law firm which represented only the top of the top.

"Take a seat while I get a few things arranged in my office. It's been a busy morning, and I've been catching up on last night's murder of the CEO of Mags-Tech. It has demanded much of my attention," Ed indicated before he walked through the door to the left of the receptionist's desk.

I took a seat next to the desk, sinking into the expensive cushions.

"Hello. Can I get you anything to drink?"

I looked over at the receptionist. The name tag on his desk simply read "Frank."

What could I say about Frank at first glance? Overly thin, pale, and dressed in a completely black suit. Oddly good-looking in that goth kind of way the ladies loved in the late nineties. His cheeks were sunken in, and you could see the muscles and veins in his face.

"No, I'm good, Frank," I answered almost as a question. His eyes didn't move, and I felt as though he was a little more than an administrative employee. I knew a fighter when I saw one, or at least the look of one; the wiry strength and arrogant, youthful intelligence.

The door opened again, as a smiling Ed asked, "You ready?"

"Sure." I stood up following him.

The room was just as plush as the lobby, but cozier and more lived in, with well-read old books, more cherrywood, and oddly enough, a fireplace, which was always a big, red warning light in Florida, signaling a Northerner or someone who was just crazy.

I was a true Floridian—anything under sixty degrees warranted a field jacket and a real fire, and not the type of fire you put in a box in the wall but one that very well may cause the evacuation of a small neighborhood. I may have set the yard on fire at one point as a child; however, with my parents, the true identity of the culprit was still up for debate.

"Max, please sit down. What I am about to tell you is going to be hard to take in, so I'll go one step at a time," Ed started, settling down behind his desk and leaning forward over an organized set of papers.

"Look, Ed—if you don't mind me calling you that—this is all nice, but your boy Frank out there looks like he wants to rip my face off, so let's get this done with. I have somewhere to be later," I interrupted him impatiently. "I have not seen Gramps in a couple of years. If he left me Oscar, I'm not a cat person."

"He probably does," Ed muttered with a slight look of concern. I somehow don't think he was referring to Gramps. He continued. "And I know you're free for the evening. Look, hear me out for a while; we'll go through this in order, and I'll let you ask any questions you have as we go through Tom's will."

"Ed, seriously, Gramps's will? So you're saying he really left me something other than the cat?"

Ed leaned back for a minute, looking at me. "Max, I'll start simply; we don't know if Tom is truly dead," he said, lightly clearing his throat.

"What?" I asked, shaking my head in confusion, thinking I had to be in a bad reality TV show at this point.

"Max, this is not a reality TV show," Ed stated flatly.

"I didn't say that," I replied in a low tone, tilting my head slightly back and crossing my arms over my chest.

"You thought it, though. Look, Max, you know Tom traveled, and at times, no one knew where he was, so he left explicit instructions that if he was ever gone for more than a year before your thirtieth birthday, we were to consider him dead and issue his will."

"Why would Gramps have any interest in my thirtieth birthday?" I asked, starting to feel warmth flowing through me.

"Well, when people from a certain bloodline turn thirty, they usually start to change. Have you noticed any changes lately?"

"Look, Ed, I went through the change over two decades ago, give or take, and I have the back hair to prove it. I've been a little off lately and keep getting hot and cold flashes, but that's one I'll chalk up to age," I said. Uncrossing my arms and putting my hands on the chair to sit up straight, I went back to the topic I was interested in. "You don't know if Gramps is dead?"

"Tom was a special person, much like myself and Frank

out there. Honestly, there are not a lot of special people out in the world right now, but that is changing. There is a change coming." He paused, tapping his index finger on his chin, obviously a habit he had when carefully putting his thoughts together. "Max, what if I told you magic was real, and that all the things that made you scared to sleep at night were loosely based on reality?" Ed asked.

I sat there for a minute as a smile came across my face. "Bullshit; this is a prank. Tell you what, can I get that drink now since this is getting interesting?"

All I could think about was that this, being cryptic and weird, was typical of my gramps, so a stiff cocktail was needed. This Ed guy was so full of shit, and likely taking part in some crazy will performance my gramps had orchestrated.

I looked up then to see Ed smiling. "Frank, can you get Max a drink? Preferably one to take the edge off. And please don't eat his face," he called out. I noticed his voice always seemed flat when he spoke but wore his emotions on his face, his eyes speaking his feelings.

It happened before I could react. There was a rush of cool air and the sound of something crunching on solid wood.

Looking over at the entrance, I saw Frank hanging next to the door. The fingers of one hand were digging into the wall while the other held something. I never saw his hands under the desk outside…let's just say I wouldn't want to get him around a chalkboard. His feet were pushing against the grain of the wood paneled wall.

Ed cleared his throat, forcing me to glance over. He was too calm for what had just happened.

You see, Frank had brought my drink while crawling up the side of the wall, and he was now handing it to me while hanging upside down from the ceiling, smiling with that look on his face still there. He didn't move after I took the drink; he just hung there and stared. I noticed his eyes were now pitch black.

After a minute, I blinked. Neither one of us had taken a breath, and as soon as I exhaled, Frank looked over at Ed. I could smell that sweet scent of flowers coming from Frank so strongly that it was nauseating.

"Thanks. I'll let you know if Max needs anything else. You can go now," Ed told him.

"You're welcome, Max," Frank said like a little kid who was hiding a secret.

"Uh…thanks," I repeated.

Frank jumped from the ceiling to the door in one smooth motion.

This couldn't be really happening, my military mind was telling me. But what I had just witnessed was telling me differently.

"Max, well played. I can tell the manners your mother drilled into you as a child are paying off. You didn't even flinch when Frank popped in."

"Th…that…happened…what the hell was that?" I stammered, having much less color on my face than a few minutes ago and sitting up much straighter in my chair.

"Okay, if that's your question. Frank is a receptionist getting you a drink," Ed replied, leaning back with a smug look on his face.

"Look," I spoke sternly. "I'm not playing any of these games. What is Frank?"

"A Vampire on work release; he's doing great. He got into some trouble before. It happens," Ed explained.

"Vampire…like, bloodsucking, immortal, all lovey-dovey?" I asked, thinking that if this was the opener, the rest of the show was going to be a ride.

"Yes to a point, not completely what you think. They like blood, mainly the synthetic type these days, and are only as immortal as they want to be. I can fill you in later on what they really are and where they came from. It's more of a condition that started affecting a certain group of people from long ago. As for the last part—let me guess, you saw or read some cheesy Vampire stories."

Ed paused, giving me a minute to inhale; I was still holding my breath.

"They are about as normal as it gets unless they aren't tied to the Council. There are cases where they revert to old habits, much like an addict, and it has drastic effects on them. Frank was in that boat, but he's been doing much better. Not to mention there hasn't been a new vampire in over ten years. Well, not until recently, but that is for another time, depending on if you decide to accept what Tom has left you. Which reminds me, we need to get back to the will."

I opened up the old brain, sat back, and let Ed start. Watching him, I could tell that he was being honest, so I decided to calm down and see where this went. Oddly enough, as soon as the thought crossed my mind, I saw the tension in Ed's shoulders leave.

Am I crazy, or does he know what I'm thinking?

"Ed, do you know what I'm thinking?" I asked bluntly.

"You mean the part where you are ready to see where this goes? Yes."

"Okay, what's next...wands?" I chuckled nervously. Ed let out a flat laugh and smiled.

"No, this is where things get interesting for you, I believe. Max, this will is what we call binding. Tom bound its words to you and me, so we must follow it if you indeed decide to sign. Let's just say that once you do, things that we won't be able to stop will be put in motion. Questions?"

"Like a magic connection?" I asked.

"Exactly. Now you're getting it. Let me start by handing over this letter which Tom wrote for you; it explains a lot. He asked me to guide you through it and answer any questions you have. Let's get started."

Ed handed me the letter. I opened the envelope and started reading the contents.

Max,

I hope this letter finds you well and not too confused.

Edward has by now told you to some extent that magic exists. While it is real, it is not as widespread as you may think; at least, it wasn't.

As you approach your thirtieth birthday, you have probably noticed some odd things starting to happen to you. Things may be off. You may feel cold, hot, or have thoughts going through your mind that do not seem to be yours. It can be anything. But one thing is for certain: you are my grandson, and you will experience it.

The only reason I am not there to tell you myself is that I am either dead or lost. Hopefully, over time, it becomes clearer. However, with me gone, you are now the steward of the Atheneum, if you choose to bind with the will. You will soon understand what this position entails. The Atheneum is a repository of knowledge. It is very old and holds many things, mainly information and the Postern, a room you will learn more about.

Phil works at the Atheneum. He will be your partner in all things that relate to the day-to-day operations of the facility. He is trained and certified by the Stewards' Guild specifically to work with you. Edward is my most trusted confidant and, at one time, my partner. I am sure he will do everything to help you take everything in, and will slowly integrate you to the team and this world.

There is also an Ethereal Council. "Magic Court," if that makes more sense to you. It consists of regular governments, the Earthborn Mage community, and Ethereal representatives from different groups. It's called on paper the National Council of Traditional Sciences, or the NCTS, as it's officially known.

This Council represents the population of Mages and other creatures, and has four representatives in North America. It is the main overseeing body of the Atheneum. I worked for the Council as the liaison between the non-Ethereal (nonmagic-practicing) population. The Council Services Agency (CSA) is the global organization I report to. Edward will discuss the US representatives when the time comes. There are only a few civilian officers who work on cases or issues that are considered Other than Natural, OTN.

Normal people, as I am sure you are aware, are not cognizant of any of this; however, things are changing. There has been a surge over the past ten years of people gaining the ability to practice magic without explanation, which means that there is an imbalance somewhere. Incidents are starting to become harder to explain and/or address to the general population, which is the reason why the Council has all but decided to release the knowledge of the Ethereal and Magical communities to the general population. It is causing a huge power struggle.

There are people born on Earth who have magical abilities, and then there are the Ethereals, beings who came from the Plane who are not from Earth. We believe that the Ethereals living on the Plane are worried about the human population and the Earthborn Mages having more combined power at the end of the day.

Just as there is a guiding Council, there are also those who do not follow its rules, which is what I have spent my entire life managing, or at least helping others manage.

Lastly and most importantly, you need to know you will become a Mage. It's in your blood. Right now, you only have low levels of Etherium—the basis of magic—in your body, but this will change. The team will explain more to you when you meet. You have to train and learn to become sanctioned by the Council to practice magic, and for that, you will have to find a sponsor, and soon.

This process can be complicated, and you only have a year from your thirtieth birthday to find one, or for one to find you. I already asked Edward to take on this role if it becomes necessary, of which he declined; not having a sponsor could expose you to the other side of the Mage community, the ones not tied to the Council, and while not all bad, it could be an issue. However, I'm confident a sponsor will present to you in due time.

You have to learn to harness the power you will undoubtedly have. Every person who has some level of Etherium has the power to work magic, but it affects every practitioner differently, pushing a dominant trait forward. Edward, for example, can read minds. He's really good at it. He will tell you, when the time is right, about mine.

I know this is a lot to take in

Your grandfather,

Thomas Gabriel Sand.

"Well?" Ed asked, cocking his head slightly to the right while taking a sip from the glass on his desk.

I let out a low whistle. "I think that's the craziest thing I've ever read, while also making some kind of irrational sense," I answered, slowly nodding my head.

"Right," Ed started as he leaned forward and let a slight smile skim his lips. "Let's get started and see how far we can get."

Over the course of the next two hours, I asked Ed every question I could. It was clear he knew what I was going to ask before I did, giving some Captain Obvious answers that still satisfied my curiosity.

He even made it a point to have Frank bring in coffee from time to time, knowing he wanted to mess with me, which of course he did in various uneasy ways I'm guessing only a Vampire could manage. My favorite was his second trip in with a drink and some notes. While handing me the glass, he made sure to cup my hand, showing me that his body was frigid and clammy to the touch.

Ed had gone over how important manners were with the magical crowd, so after I had said thank you, and asked for some hand sanitizer. It became quickly apparent that was not an acceptable request in front of a Vamp.

Ed was already chuckling under his breath even before the words came out of my mouth, and I watched Frank storm out of the room with a quick spin and a slam of the door. So some of the stories were true; Vamps could be a little moody.

Ed explained that Frank had the temperament of a person in rehab, and that it was important to respect him while in his office. He was an untethered Vampire with no house. This was nothing more than the new, politically correct way of saying he didn't have a master.

After years of watching Vampire movies, I had some preconceived concepts of how they should be and how they fed, but apparently, there was a whole industry that produced synthetic blood which treated Vamps much better mentally and physically. It even helped to combat all the myths we learned about as young moviegoers, and now I was missing the movie about a male secretary Vamp who was in rehab.

After digesting most of what I'd heard, I took some notes and asked some other questions. I found out which companies supported the magical world—Mags-Tech heading the top of a list about a page long—but I was here, at the end of the day, to go over Gramps's will.

Ed looked over. "Max, I think it's time we focus on what we came to discuss. I believe you're in the right frame of mind now. Shall we?"

"Sure, can't be any weirder than this," I sighed, knowing that it probably was. By then, I already needed more than one drink.

"Let's go over the main parts and work through the details later," Ed stated. "Tom left you as the main heir to the estate and his property. You are allowed to move to his house; however, his room is to remain sealed in case he comes back. It happens. The building is truly not the family's property but a duty of sorts. The Sand family has been with the Atheneum since…well, let's just say a long time. This first section describes the details of the property management and the rights and responsibilities you have with the staff who themselves are part of the Atheneum."

"Hold up," I interrupted, cocking my head to one side. "You mean *if* I take a go at this. I just want to be clear."

"As I was saying, if you choose to accept. Since I know you don't have any valid questions at this time—"

"Wait, I do."

"No, you don't. Stop being stubborn. The Fallen Angel will be there when you are done, I promise. Though might I recommend that I go with you? It may change your perspective on the place."

"Sure," I agreed, knowing there was more to it. He wanted to spend time with me. In my head, I could hear the immortal words "young grasshopper."

"As I was saying, the second section is a release form for the NCTS. Since you're former military, that part should be easy. You're going to find that you'll have access to many new and, at times, powerful things. Please read this section closely," Ed requested.

It was basically what Ed had just laid out minus all the "You are responsible for your own life." It ended with: "Always remember casting/magic/spelling/charming can help protect you, but a bullet is a bullet. It can still have the same effects."

The documents were basically liability waivers making sure I understood that if I got hurt, it was absolutely my own fault.

"This is really a job interview of sorts, isn't it?" I muttered, slowly starting to realize what was happening.

The next section that Ed went over as monotonously as possible was simply a title for the house and the Postern —whatever that was—which strangely had several pages missing.

"Those pages went missing at the same time Tom did. They're notes on the Postern and what the room truly does. I don't really know what they stated or what many of the gates in that room do. You'll just have to see for yourself."

Great, I thought to myself. *A crapshoot of details I'll never go through before I end up signing. Just like with my first car which ended up having a twenty-nine percent interest rate.*

After that explanation, I followed up with a round of questions on the room and the gates, only to be told those should be directed at Phil when I finally met him.

Ed showed me another stack of paperwork to review, as

well as a few items. More deed papers and more documents to fill out with my personal information. I felt like I was joining the army all over again, minus having to bend over for an old man. Well, hopefully not…

Apparently, I was also left with a trust fund. As Ed described it: "You'll never run out of money for tacos, unless you live long enough."

"Max," Ed said sternly after I finished reviewing the paperwork. "The item I'm handing you was very important to your grandfather. It was his life's hobby to look for mythical places and artifacts. This was his Fountain of Youth journal. He claimed it was given to him, and only a blood relative can open it. It's probably worth a read."

Next was a Mags-Tech release form for what looked like a computer and new phone, paperwork for a set of keys to a vehicle Ed didn't actually have a clue where it was, more forms for keys to a gun box with a five-page disclaimer actually calling the gun the Judge, and another for a sword named Durundle. Man, everything had names.

At some point, my questions started to sound like I actually knew what I was asking. "So blended or charmed means it has power in it, like Etherium, to make it do something specific, and bound means it ties something together or connects things?" I asked.

"Close. Depends on who is doing the work, and the intent," stated Ed almost in a proud, fatherly tone.

Finally, we reached the last page.

"Max, this is the page you must bind with if you accept these responsibilities. It's a simple binding. You see that circle on the bottom? All you need to do is put enough blood of your own free will to create the binding and read the script."

"How will I know it works?" I asked.

"You'll know. I'll be there with you, as Tom requested. I'm giving you this document for now so you can review it today; it's important you carefully think about it, as the binding needs to happen tomorrow if you agree to move forward. I'll give you a carry bag, and we can secure it for now.

"Now, shall we go get that drink?"

CHAPTER 3

Time for a Drink

I picked up the leather carry bag with the papers neatly tucked inside, leaving the other items behind. The bag was made of old leather, the type you knew was handmade, soft, and carried by people who had a taste for finer things. The buckles were solid silver and dulled with wear, smelling strongly of leather and spices, reminding me of sitting with my father as a child in the barber shop while the barber sharpened his razor on a leather strap.

Throwing it over my shoulder, I could feel the weight of many important papers being carried in it over the years.

"Frank, take the rest of the evening off. I'll see you in the morning," Ed indicated as he ushered me to walk with him out the door.

"It was nice to meet you, Frank," I said, looking him square in the now gray eyes.

Frank smiled and responded in the coolest voice he could, showing his perfect glossy white teeth. "Sleep tight, Max. I'll be seeing you soon. Oh, and next time you stop by, do you think you could throw on something more appropriate?" Still smiling, Frank stood up and started arranging his already neat desk.

Ed was already out the front door, forcing me to take an extra step to catch up. He started talking over his shoulder while passing through the front gate.

"You know, Frank is a great guy. He's a huge music enthusiast and, just between you and me, is a huge Planes Drifter fan. You have to understand that everything you know about Vampires is nothing more than a marketing tactic designed by the original Ethereals. All the movies and books are a smear campaign to make people scared of them," Ed explained as I caught up with him.

"Especially in today's climate, there are people who don't like competition and consider Earthborn Mages and Vampires as less than desirable, and over the centuries, they have made sure that others see them the same way as well. Pretty convenient that almost everyone knows how to kill a Vampire, right?" Ed noted as if it was something everyone was aware of. I couldn't help but think Ed was saying more than I was understanding.

As we turned down the dark, humid alley, the smell of food hung heavily in the early evening air. Ed changed his demeanor visibly more relaxed as he smoothed his hair back and smiled.

"Ed, I have to ask, what about Werewolves?" I wondered, smoothing my T-shirt out with my sweaty hands, wondering how far this fantasy world actually stretched.

Ed chuckled. "Max, things are not always as they appear to be. You see, they are really called shifters, and they are highly intelligent and extremely loyal. By the way, never call them animals; in most cases, they shift to larger, more aggressive forms. The stronger shifters can actually take on a human form, keeping a good amount of their traits. It's kind of odd as they are extremely loyal and in human form keep a good amount of their traits right, wrong, or indifferent. It can seem funny or offensive at times."

I started thinking about all the odd people I had met before. Was my ninth grade teacher a horse? Was my girlfriend in college a witch?

Ed, sensing this, kept on talking.

"Much like Vampires, they too have been part of a long-term smear campaign. Again, funny how everyone knows how to hurt them. Imagine what would happen if the Ethereal and Magical community came out and everyone had these predetermined notions. Most Fae, for example, consider Vampires and shifters impure, since most Fae are pure Ethereals directly from the Plane."

"Wait, Fae like fairies?" I interrupted.

Ed took a deep breath and sighed. "Yes, like that." He continued, "The general population would be scared of them and treat them like monsters. Many worry they would be hunted down. Hollywood has been doing an okay job lately of making them appear more human in an effort to counter the damage already done. Wolf shifters, who do like to call themselves Werewolves, tend to be the more vocal of the bunch."

We turned the corner roughly a block away from the office by way of a cobblestone path, and there was another FA's tucked between an old dusty-looking bookstore and an abandoned building.

It sat there just like the one at home with the same heavy wooden door and sign that dully glowed. At first glance, anyone would think FA's was a dive and would not chance it. Me, on the other hand, craved the small, quiet hole in the wall, having been oddly drawn to it as soon as I moved back to Florida.

"After you," Ed stated with a smirk on his face, like he knew something I didn't. He probably did, considering I spent most my time trying to catch up on the latest trends in online dating or what the local taco joint was going to have on their menu this month.

Ed was a serious guy who you could tell enjoyed watching people figure things out. I really liked him and could see why Gramps had too.

The age thing was eating at the back of my mind, but I supposed I would have to figure that one out later. *Damn*, I thought, *I bet he knows I'm thinking about him.*

Looking over, I saw the smile only he could pull off.

When the old wooden door swung open and I walked through, I felt a familiar pull in my chest, the same as when I'd walked into Ed's office. Several things hit me all at the same time. First, the smell; it was just like the FA's back home. Fresh dirt, freshly cooked steak, and the aging tang of copper set me immediately at ease.

Secondly, the place was identical, from the dark marble floor to the large, curved hickory bar with plush tables and chairs arranged in groups. While I did always say FA's looked like a dive on the outside, the inside was another story.

One thing that always stood out was the ceiling. These days, restaurants and bars had metal-looking ceilings that were nothing more than plastic tiles, trying to fool people into thinking the place was more upscale than it actually was. Not FA's; the ceiling was made of solid copper paneling with real designs etched into the tiles, generating a unique smell. The walls were dark and covered in classic paintings that I always assumed were high-dollar knockoffs painted by art students out of Savannah.

And last but not least, there was Trish, the faithful bartender who was always on shift. Tall and strong with dark-brown skin and brown eyes that never missed anything, she was always wearing a genuine smile. After a few conversations, I knew I was not going to get anything past her or, in any case, neither would anyone else.

I'd asked her once where she was from, and she had told me from an old patrician family, which I had no idea what it meant. One thing that stood out was that she never wore any kind of jewelry. If you looked at people closely, you'd notice they almost always wore some type of accessory: a watch, earrings, necklace, ring, bracelet—but not her. Not even a tattoo, which was rare these days for a barkeep.

"My God, look at the odd couple," Trish greeted with a grin that could light up a dark cave. "Out of all the people I expected to see you walk in here with, Ed, Max was not one of them."

"Ed. I knew it! You are an Ed," I blurted out, grinning back at Trish and feeling like I had won some type of contest.

Ed smiled. "Trish, be careful what god you ask to join us for a drink tonight. How are you doing? Max and I are here for a drink and some light conversation." Walking up to the bar, he ushered me to join him.

I just stood there taking it all in, not moving an inch.

After a moment, I sat at my normal seat, dead center of the curved bar where I could see the large mirrors behind and the ever mysterious serving window where, if you looked close enough, you could see movement behind pushing out some of the best food I had ever tasted.

Trish looked at us both and let out a deep breath. "Ed, why are you with Max? He is a regula—"

"Wait, Trish," Ed interrupted her. "Max, yes, this is in fact the same FA's you frequent back home." He glanced at her. "Sorry, Trish. Max was about to walk out and back in to make sure he is not losing it."

Trish started back. "That's fine. It's been a while since you've been in here, and I always enjoy watching you make people feel dumb. So I'm taking it Max is not just a normal sensitive as I thought he was? I knew he was about to turn thirty per his ID, but I wasn't sure what level of Mage he was."

She turned to me. "Max, you see, only people with a certain gift can make their way in here. That is, unless someone inside opens the door and holds it for someone walking in off the street. You've done that a few times."

"Trish," Ed spoke up, looking at her. It was then I figured out he could not read her mind. "I heard the news today about the CEO of Mags-Tech being killed. Ezra Hevel was a very powerful man, and I know he came here from the New York location from time to time. Has there been any updates on your end?"

"I knew there was more to your visit. No, only that the police and onlookers alike are baffled at how the shooters escaped from the thirty-eighth floor without notice yada… yada… The CSA has no comment since the investigation is still ongoing, no suspects have been arrested, blah, blah, blah. It has people a little spooked with everything else going on," Trish said as she set a blank laminated menu in front of me. "Oh, Max, I think since you walked in here with Ed, it's time you ordered from the big-boy menu."

Glancing at Ed, I saw him place his hand flat on the menu in front of him, and it came to life, filling the pages with items. So I did the same, except nothing happened.

"Max, think about everything you have seen and discussed today. I know you are at your limit, but concentrate on the menu putting a little more effort," Ed guided.

I sat up straight and placed my hand back on the paper, imagining the menu appearing.

Just like that, it morphed into something different. My hand felt warm on the laminate, and I could smell a waft of ozone as I pulled my hand away.

"Yeah…that just happened," I said, startled.

It had most of my favorites listed with slight changes; the Mango Tacos were coolly labeled Fae Honey Tacos, and there was a fairly odd list of additions to the staple menu. But hell, I was here for a drink, so I flipped the page over, only to reveal a list of drinks I had no clue about.

Beers—Vamp Amber, Aegir, Ogre Stout, Fae Lager, Elf Juice…*really?* Mead, Honey Mead, Mage's Brown, Abby's Number 1, Planes Wheat, and the menu went on like some kind of funny list of gag drinks. Liquors—Magnus, Ambrosia, Ogoun, Aged Terrum. I knew one of these: Ambrosia, better known as the nectar of the gods. Things were about to get interesting…until I saw the price.

It was about that time that Ed cut me off from ordering.

"Trish, can you get Max a Vamp Amber? Something that he can stomach for now. I need him thinking clearly the next few days, and no, these are not gags, Max. Some of these drinks can have a very specific effect on you if you are not careful. Vamp Amber is the most popular, since it is fairly normal and has a great way of not making you feel groggy in the morning. I'll take a Magnus, neat, please," Ed told Trish as he pushed the menus out of the way.

One thing about me is that I'm not shy. As Trish handed us our drinks, I looked at the bottle in my hand while also glancing at Ed's black drink in a highball glass.

Vamp Amber. Made in Romania. 15% ABV. Imported by the Vlad family brewery.

"Vlad, really?" I noted before turning the bottle up to my lips. I was instantly in love with the silky-smooth texture; the almond and chocolate flavor was amazing. "Hello, where have you been all my life?" I groaned in a low, rumbling tone as if the love of my life had just kissed me. I let go of my long first pull. "So, Vlad as in the movies?"

Trish laughed out loud. "You mention that to Ana Vlad, and she is likely to have you put on a stake. I am sure that Ed has discussed the whole smear campaign by now, and Ana will be the first to prove you wrong. While her brother is a bit of a jerk, to put it mildly, she is one of the best brewers in the world and is at the forefront of funding research to eradicate hunger in Third World countries. She's a real softy with a bite," Trish said as she leaned in closer to Ed. "So, what's Max's story?"

"He's Tom's grandson," Ed replied, leaning back in his chair and taking a long sip of his drink.

Trish looked at me with eyes so intense and deep I could feel them looking for answers in mine. "I...I can see it now, in his eyes. My God, you are Tom's blood. Ed, what's going on? Why are you with Max? And Max, I understand you might not have known any of this, but if I had known..." she trailed off, staring at Ed in a manner that looked hurt and surprised at the same time.

"Trish, relax. This is day one for him. I brought him here to make sure you two were formally introduced; I know Max frequents FA's. For now, I need him to understand you are a friend, not only of mine but of Tom's. Max, we have all known each other for a very long time, and Trish is a well-informed barkeep. Someone you will want to keep by your side if this all works out."

Ed quickly finished his cocktail before starting back up.

"Max, Trish, I think it's time to call it a night. Max, if you walk out the door and think about your home, you will find yourself a block away from your place at the FA's you know. Your truck will be fine till tomorrow. In the morning, when Trish opens up for lunch, come back in and grab a bite to eat. When you are done, walk out again, but think about coming to my office, and you will hopefully be there. Takes some getting used to."

Ed stood up and shook Trish's hand. Watching them, I could tell they interacted with each other in a way only old friends did.

"Good night. And Max, sleep on it," Ed said before he walked out the door.

Standing up too, Trish walked around the bar and gave me a warm, short hug. "Be careful, and I'll see you tomorrow. Don't be a stranger, and whatever Ed talked to you about, take it very seriously. I have not seen him this happy in a while, and it worries me a little. Good night."

I stood up and grabbed my bag, noticing a few other people had trickled in. I was tired, and as I trudged to the door, all I could think about was lying in my bed. I would either wake up and this would all have been a dream, or I would find out what the prize was behind door number two.

Pushing the door open and looking around, I could see the familiar scene I was accustomed to of the ocean, the salty smell of the beach, and the sidewalk leading home.

CHAPTER 4

Home Is Where the Heart Is...

"What a day," I sat up in bed and said out loud to no one, looking over to the carry bag on my dresser.

"Yup, that was real…" Rolling over, I put my feet on the cool floor; I knew there was only one thing that could get my day started: coffee, the miracle that actually convinced me that there was a God. Well, at least a few, by the way things were looking.

Luckily, I had grabbed some prior to my trip to Ed's office.

Thoughts of the night I met Sarah at FA's a few days ago started filling my mind. She was the reason I had been out on a Monday. I still couldn't remember the entire evening, even though I hadn't had much to drink. She had insisted on coming over to my apartment after a walk on the beach, being that she was from out of town. Most of what happened after sitting at my kitchen table having a cup of coffee was a soft blur of conversation. I wasn't even sure if she was real, with everything I had just learned.

Maybe I should talk to Trish about it later, I thought as

I pushed the glowing red button on Chester Coffeepot. Yes, that's what I had named my coffee maker.

The rest of the morning, I went through the usual routine of any respectable ex-military person: coffee, more coffee, and a steaming hot shower. Standing under the stream of water, I walked back through everything that had happened the previous day.

Looking at the small, steamy mirror I used to shave every couple of weeks, I caught myself talking out loud, asking myself questions, and answering them in Ed's flat voice.

The smell of mint and lemon was strong in my bathroom, doing its job of reminding me that I needed to go outside and face the day. Then it hit me: my truck was in St. Augustine. I was still in a light form of denial and was slightly apprehensive about going back to FA's to walk through what I found myself calling the other side of things.

The other side of things…things that are on the other side… other sidey? Is that a word? Anything to not say *Ethereal* out loud.

The term "Other than Natural" seemed too abrasive for a discussion with someone not in the know—*look at that, I'm in the know now*—so I figured if I was going to keep people from thinking I was crazy, I needed to approach it as "the other side of things."

Gathering up what I had left of my common sense, I grabbed the carry bag after a couple of hours of looking over the documents, and headed to FA's.

Remarkably enough, the sun was still the sun, my grumpy neighbor frowned as always, and the door opened the same way it always did. As if on cue, my phone chirped with a text from Ed, asking to bring him a cup of Trish's finest on my way through. Was it always going to be like this?

As I wandered into FA's, Trish already had a cup carrier in her hands, accompanied by a huge smile and some old rock playing in the background.

"Morning, sunshine," Trish greeted with an ear-to-ear grin, handing me the cups. "This will get you going this morning. Tell Ed to take it easy on you today."

The thing about Trish was that no matter what time of day or night, she always looked refreshed, not like someone who had shut a bar down and conducted last call six hours earlier, or whenever she closed.

"Thanks," I said, smiling back. "Trish, what were you guys talking about yesterday, about an assassination or murder or something?"

"I really don't know the details, but I have a feeling you will find out soon enough. Ed did explain to you what you are going to be doing, right?" she replied, guiding me toward the door in that subtle manner a leader does when convincing someone of what they should be doing.

"Kind of. I know I have a job, and that's great. Maybe I can now afford to keep coming in here. Seems like some kind of consultant, investigator job?" I stated in the form of a question.

Trish had a way of doing that, same as any good bartender does. Making you state the obvious while also making you feel like you had accomplished something.

"Sounds about right. Now, Max, take it easy. Here's my number; I forgot to give it to you yesterday. If you need something, give me a call." She pointed at the cups. "That's Fae honey, if anyone asks. Also, here's a little something for Frank; it's on the house today." She handed me a small bag and then ushered me out the door and into the steamy St. Augustine morning.

When I strolled up to the gate at the law office, it opened

without warning. Much to my surprise, Frank was standing on the porch in the morning sun and not melting or something to that effect.

"Good morning, Frank. So I take it you're not going to burn?" I asked, genuinely curious. Frank chuckled slightly.

"No, not exactly, Max. Hope you slept well," Frank said, seemingly in a rather good mood. "Look, I wanted to catch you before you went in. I didn't mean to freak you out yesterday, but Ed asked me to crank it up a little if you started getting skeptical, not to mention it was a long day for me. When I get released from the property in a few months, maybe we can get a few drinks." He looked me up and down. "And for the love of the gods, do you have anything else other than Planes Drifter's T-shirts to wear?"

"Nope, that's it, Frank. Old logo shirts and my four favorite PD T-shirts," I replied, handing Frank the bag Trish had given me for him, smelling the strong scent of roses.

"All right, A-plus for music taste, high D for fashion, and extra credit for this bag of scones Trish sent with you. I can smell Fae honey in that coffee; she must really like you. You know that stuff's about $300 a pop, right?" Frank told me, turning after grabbing his bag and walking inside.

A bag of scones was not what I thought a Vamp would like. Maybe a liver or something, but nope, orange scones. Seemed like Frank was a fairly normal guy and really was there to get his act together.

Maybe I would hear the whole story at some point. From what I could tell, he had pretty much eaten someone. *Well, at least he did it in style*, I thought to myself. *I bet all Vamps are fashion critics*. The movies had one thing right: from what I saw with Frank, they must all look like models.

"Max, coffee...ahh, is that Fae honey I smell? Trish must be in a good mood this morning," Ed said, more relaxed than pretty much all of yesterday. "I'm just catching up on the news; I suggest you do the same later. Once we get wrapped up here, we are going to the Atheneum. I know you heard us talking yesterday about a recent murder. Needless to say, you might be getting your feet wet sooner than planned." He pointed to a chair. "Have a seat. I will get the papers, and we can get this wrapped up."

"I'm guessing you already know I'm in." I smiled back at Ed as he nodded and turned, leaving me holding the other cup of coffee.

Ed's demeanor had changed. He was not the robotic lawyer I'd dealt with yesterday but rather more informal, almost like we were a pair of colleagues at the office. I still hadn't figured out the full scope of what I'd be doing, but it was slowly becoming clear that Ed's law practice was more of a hobby or afterthought.

The next hour went as I thought it would. Papers were laid out, and believe it or not, there were actual candles involved; intricate candles with iron and wood, one even set in a metal sphere, and all having distinctive smells, the type of scent that stuck to you.

Ed spent a few more minutes going over the details of the ritual, explaining that once we began, we had to finish, adding a few side comments such as "Don't move too much," and "Don't say anything that is not written down in the instructions."

Lastly, Ed made it a point to explain the order in which a ritual took place was important, and that I should never reverse it. *Yeah*, I thought, *like I know what I'm doing*.

Lighting the candles in order, Ed mumbled in a low voice the inscription on the paper in his hand. Once that was complete, Ed pulled out a knife. He cut both our hands, and we pressed them into the paper. The smell of ozone wafted into the air as Ed smiled..

"That's it, Max. Welcome to the team! How do you feel?" Ed asked, wiping off the pitch-black blade before putting out the candles with a bell-shaped cup.

"I feel warm and a little dizzy, but otherwise good. Fingers and toes are all still here," I joked, turning to Ed. He had an odd look on his face that I had not seen before.

"Max, you turn thirty in about a week, correct?" he inquired with a puzzled look on his face, leaning in to take a pull of his still piping hot coffee, which strangely never lost its temperature in its paper cup.

"That's right," I replied back.

Ed just shook his head and continued putting things away. Once he placed the last of the papers in its folder, he spoke again. "Ready to go to the house and see the Atheneum? Phil is excited to meet you. I think he needs a friend."

The smell of ozone still lingered in the air. I had seen enough craziness over the past two days to make me anxious of going anywhere else.

"Frank!" Ed yelled packing up. "We are going to the main house and won't be back today. Keep an eye on the NCTS feed and stay here tonight. We need to keep a close eye on things until I or Dr. Simmons get word from the CSA."

"All right, boss," Frank yelled back. "Not like a good-looking person such as myself had any plans tonight. I'll let you know if I hear anything on my end. It looks like they are going to replace Ezra in the next couple of days, according to the latest post. Oh, and tell Jenny I said hello. She owes me that drink she has been working on, and if she wants, I would be more than glad to take her out to dinner."

"Frank," Ed interjected, walking by. "Dr. Simmons is not interested, as she has made clear by not dating anyone. But

I'll remind her about the potion. Last I heard, she was moving along nicely with it."

Ed looked at me and stopped to explain for a minute. "Max, the NCTS feed is like a social media forum for our community. Very much like police computers but much more streamlined. It also covers normal and OTN cases as well, all thanks to Mags-Tech."

"So, like, you have to power it with magic?" I asked.

"No, Max," Ed stated in a low voice like he was talking to a child. "You log in like any other computer. You just have a fifty-fifty chance of seeing anything."

Saying goodbye to Frank, we walked out the door.

"I'll follow behind," I told Ed as we walked through the gate. "Sounds like I'll be spending a good amount of time there and will need the Black Beast to grab a few things."

The Black Beast, as lore has it, had survived the great buggy wars of 2019; it had even held its own in several one-on-one fights, as I liked to call them. I'd had her for ten years, purchased used from a neighbor that Mom had insisted was crazy.

Three wrecks, countless dings, and an awesome stereo to boot later, she was a beastly thing of beauty. The type of truck that made a statement. *Go ahead and cut me off. I don't care. I'll either win the fight or not lose any pride.* The interior was immaculate, though, unlike the outside. Black cloth and vinyl all polished with cleaner.

One thing I always took pride in was keeping the interior of my ride super clean. It was a habit I'd picked up from my pops, and as a matter of fact, it was one of the many things I used when figuring people out, much like how someone treats their animals.

Hey, I had some standards. I was a how-clean-do-they-keep-the-interior-of-their-vehicle type of guy. You see, that could tell you a lot. It doesn't matter what you are looking at from the outside; it's what's inside that matters and tells the true story of a person. Do it next time you're in someone's car. Messy? I bet they are often late on bills and have trouble figuring out what to wear, plus have a disaster for a bedroom. Told you so.

"Max," Ed stopped me. "I took the liberty of having your truck moved to the Atheneum last night. It will be there when we arrive. I'll drive."

Turning the corner, there sat a jet-black Continental, not a speck of dust to be seen. The engine was growling in a reserved manner, letting you know that, if required, you could go very fast.

"Look at the name, Max. CTL-MT," Ed exclaimed proudly. "The MT stands for Mags-Tech. It's a special edition with a few extras on board. There is another car manufacturer that caters to Ethereals and Mages; however, the NCTS will not pay for one. Something about a long-term partnership contract which probably results in cheaper pricing. "

As I slid into the front seat, the smell of fresh new leather and rich tobacco smoke immediately filled my nose. My hands went directly toward the radio, only to be smacked by Ed.

"Not all of us want to listen to Planes Drifter this early in the morning," Ed stated as he turned on the '80s pop easy-listening channel. I learned something about Ed then and there: he was never allowed to touch the radio in the Black Beast. She would never forgive me.

The Atheneum was more tucked away than I remembered. The drive took roughly thirty minutes through back roads. Nestled somewhere between I-95 and the beach was the inconspicuous turn down a sandy road, the kind of turn that if you didn't know it was there, you would miss it.

Ed took a deep breath, then began explaining. "The gate and property are glamoured. I know you probably can't remember much of this place from when you came here as a child. If you were not here by invitation or for a specific reason, you would not see a thing past the gate, just more road which eventually came out through the same entrance you came in. It's a little bit of a parlor trick.

"An adventurous teenager in a jeep once figured out when cutting through the woods that the glamour only hid the Atheneum. Needless to say, we had a Council member that could manipulate space come in and make it a little harder to get around once inside. Not to mention the landscaping. Pay close attention; you don't want to be in those woods if you can avoid it. The underbrush can be a little hard to traverse. Ahh, here we are. The gate."

We drove up to a gate that was no less than twenty feet tall, made of old wood and iron. The doors were attached to large stone walls that seemed to melt into the surrounding forest.

Coming to a stop next to an intercom sticking out of the ground, Ed reached over having his watch scanned. The blinking red light turned green, and the gates smoothly opened. The door system, while looking old, must have had a newer, top-notch gear-and-piston system. Did I mention I was good with machinery?

As we pulled through, the doors closed behind us. I could tell Ed was being quiet to see what my reaction would be. He was not going to win today, as I was not going to give him the satisfaction of seeing my jaw drop. A quarter mile down the overgrown path stood the main property, and attached to the far left end was Gramps's house. My jaw dropped.

How to fully describe what I was looking at?

Well, first you had to start with the facility itself. It stood like a stoic, medieval version of the Biltmore House, shaped like a massive H, with a large circular driveway. To the right, facing the house, was a garage that had rooms above it with turrets. It easily could have held dozens of cars. To the left was Gramps's house. The whole thing came together like some type of classy, medieval Floridian castle. Did I just make that up? *I sure did,* I thought as I smiled to myself.

The massive building looked slightly out of place, with palm trees peeking around the edges of the house. The round driveway had a large water feature in the middle, and there in all its glory sat the Black Beast, dwarfed by the size of the house's entrance.

True to form, the house was appointed with a large, wood-and-iron entry door. Some of the windows were stained glass works of art, and others were there to serve as paths for light to soak the inside of the massive house.

It was at that point that I noticed an odd figure standing at the large front door smoking a cigarette. I was still questioning if I was going crazy, as I paused for a moment, trying to figure out if it was real.

Ed looked over, smiling. "And that's Phil. I know this is a lot to take in, but you will have plenty of time to learn your way around. Just remember, this is a special place, and not everything in it is safe. Take it easy for the first few days and let Phil show you around. Doctor Simmons should be here on time for dinner. She and I are partners, though I find myself following her lead more often than not. Due to Ezra's murder, I'm sure we are going to be getting an assignment sooner rather than later. In fact, I am surprised we haven't already."

There was only one way to describe Phil: hipster. Tight jeans, a button-down shirt with the sleeves rolled up, a slim fit vest, and a pair of black boots. Phil's most striking feature, however, was his shoulder-length, jet-black beard and undercut hair, leaving it hanging down to his hardened jawline.

I was pretty sure if you called Phil a hipster, though, he would—without a doubt—place one of those boots directly in, on, around, or through some part of your body. Phil's arms and neck were covered in intricate tattoos of Celtic designs, and as we approached, he flicked his cigarette out on the ground, then bent down to pick it up and put it in his pocket. Was he a military guy? He was definitely a fighter, evidenced by the way he tensed up as the car turned off.

Ed had pulled up right next to Phil on purpose to see if he would open the door. He didn't. After a twenty-second pause, Ed grinned and got out, and I followed suit while Phil stood there.

"Max, I'm Phil. Heard a lot about you over the past three months, bruther. I'm glad you're here so Ed can finally calm down. I bet he was playing Hanson on the radio on your way over. He has been like a pregnant woman nesting before giving birth waiting for you to come along," Phil grumbled with a strong Southern, Irish drawl that I placed somewhere between Texas and Ireland.

He broke form, and a smile appeared from ear to ear as he reached out pulling me into a firm handshake. Phil had on a large brown leather and silver watch that was hard not to look at.

"Phil, same. It's good to meet you. Apparently, you have a lot of showing me around to do. I'm sure we will get some time. And yeah, I think it was something like Hanson. Ed said you also live here?" I asked, pulling out of the firm shake.

"I've been here a few months, but I spent a lot of my youth here, so I know my way around. Once you get settled, we can go over to your place and get some of your gear. Come on, let's show you around," Phil indicated as he answered his ringing phone. "Yes, Dr. Simmons, yes, he is here. No, I didn't. Yes, I will." He hung up the obviously one-sided conversation huffing, "Let's go."

I could tell Ed was pleased with how Phil and I interacted. It was like he had gone to great lengths to make sure we met and got along with each other. I instantly liked Phil. He smelled like Irish whiskey and sweet cigar smoke.

He obviously didn't take himself too seriously; however, you could tell he had a switch that if flipped, could turn ugly or fun pretty fast. Ed had explained that Phil was basically my partner for everything related to the Atheneum. He managed the laboratories, evidence room, and morgue. I wasn't really sure what this all meant but figured I would listen to him for now.

Heading in, Ed started talking about the entrance, as I started zoning him out taking it all in.

The main door was a massive work of craftsmanship, inlaid with various family crests. Stepping through, I could see the house showed its personality. There was another water feature in the middle of the entrance hall with a stone ball rolling around the center.

To the left sat an electronic security panel, and to the right a coat room—for visitors, I guessed. Further past the fountain was a set of stairs on either side reaching around the main hall and meeting at a catwalk that overlooked the hallway past the foyer. Past the catwalk and staircases were several sets of closed doors, all in a row. The doors were crafted with the same type of material as the main entrance, but looked a little more modern.

The floors were black marble without a shine, almost like black stone. The walls were dark and a mix of large stone pieces in some places and shiny dark wood in others, all pulled together with that timeless elegance that flowed to make a work of art. The fragrance of wet moss, old books, and lavender lingered in the air.

Ed explained that the facility had been recently undergoing several modernization projects and was roughly fifty percent complete. You could tell the attention to detail. The updated lighting still captured the original mood of the building with a warm yellow glow.

The celling went up no less than forty feet, and the massive chandelier was made of what looked like iron. It probably was. I could not tell if the lights were candles or electric bulbs.

The place was grand, and I had only seen the entrance. It didn't look this big from the outside, I thought to myself. Then I realized something: Ed had not cut me off since we'd completed the binding. I'd have to ask him what was up.

"Max, are you listening? I said to not drink out of the fountain," Ed repeated when he realized I wasn't. "You will have access to all these rooms; however, we need to get you keyed to them. You are only keyed to Tom's house and office at this time."

"Thanks, Ed," interrupted Phil with a wry look on his face. "Let's get over to the house, and we can get Max set up with his gear." Everyone seemed to call Gramps's old place "the house."

"Jesus, this place is massive!" I exclaimed, looking around, letting everyone know the initial shock had worn off. "I don't remember seeing any of this as a kid, and I am sure I would have. What's that room over there with the cracked door?"

"It's a bathroom, Max. And for the love of the gods, take it easy on the names you say out loud," Phil deadpanned, giving me that *come on, dude* look. "Not everything in this place is crazy. A lot of work goes on here, and it can seem like there's always someone doing something at all hours. But I can tell you for a *fact*, listen to Ed. I went on a bender one night and drank some of the water in that fountain. *Huge* mistake, bruther."

This time, I could hear the pure Irish in his voice. I had a feeling Phil and I were going to get along just fine, but he still needed to pass the drink test. Did I mention I liked to test people?

Heading up the stairs, we took a left toward Gramps's old place. "Hey, guys. Why wouldn't we just go through the front door of his house?" I asked, trying to map out every last detail. I finally realized it would be too much and decided to just take it all in.

Phil started before Ed could. "I'm supposed to be giving you a proper tour. At the end of the hallway at the top of the stairs, take the other set back down to the first floor. The back door to Tom's place is attached to the Atheneum at the end of the hall. It goes into the kitchen. The old servants used it to take meals back and forth. It's also fairly tucked away and a great way to come in and out of the Atheneum without everyone knowing you are running around. You can also get to the Postern through here. According to Ed, it was the main way Tom used to come and go, as it was the closest to his office."

"That's right," Ed stated as we walked down a staircase into a hall that had a door at the end and one on either side. "The door on the left goes to the old service hall; that's what Phil mentioned. To the right is one of two paths to the Postern—that's the room with the gates we discussed. It actually goes underground and back under the stairs toward the main house. It comes out beside the Postern in an alcove that is rarely used. There will be time to go there later."

Stopping at the end of the hall, Ed held out his wrist with the watch, as the door slid open. It was nothing magical, just a new, self-opening operator, the latest in door technology.

"Max, when you get to the office and set everything up, your watch will be dialed into you and act like a key. You will soon find that the watch you are given will impact you greatly. It's more than just a timekeeper, but I would rather Doctor Simmons explain," Ed suggested, stepping into a kitchen.

Gramps's kitchen was medium sized and showed that it had seen its fair share of wannabe cooks over the years. They had obviously not updated it. Once we left the kitchen, I saw Gramps's place was pretty much the same as the main house, just on a smaller scale. In the foyer was another water feature and a set of stairs leading to a small catwalk.

As we walked upstairs to the office, I noticed several pictures of people hanging on the wall to the left.

"Who are these fun-looking individuals?" I asked, making sure they understood that I thought the look on their faces was over the top.

"Those are pictures of past stewards," Ed explained. "Mostly men and one woman. Some passed away in war, others at the hand of a love gone wrong, or while protecting the Atheneum and its keep. Jane there lost her life helping the Vamps find a stabilizer and partial cure, one of the reasons they are so protective of humankind these days. They are cast out cursed, diseased Fae. The human race helped them from being wiped out when they crossed over from the Plane, cast out and diseased, and gave them a life after the Planes' war. But that story is for another time and was in another place."

Ed looked sad and as if he could spend the whole day talking about these people. He knew them in the literal sense, and there was a slight pain in his words that you could barely pick up on unless you were looking.

"Ah, here we are, your new office," Ed cheered as we walked into Gramps's old personal office.

Going in, I immediately remembered this place as

somewhere I had been the few times I'd visited Gramps. I could smell him in the air. A welcoming feeling filled the space. Much like Ed's office, it was full of books, trinkets, and artifacts. Some items sat on shelves whiles others adorned the fireplace mantel, a few simply hung from the walls.

His desk sat facing the front door, large and black with iron inlays. I had always remembered this desk. You could tell it had stood the test of time. The question was how much. Behind the desk was a window made of stained glass thick enough to soften the color in the room but light enough to see clearly through up close.

The tall leather back chair stood looming behind the desk. The floor was covered in Persian rugs and had a few chairs and a table sitting in front of the fireplace to the left, facing the desk. Just past that was a door holding a small guest suite equipped with a bed and bathroom. *Jackpot!*

"Max, those will be your quarters when you are here," Ed informed me, clearly back in the zone of reading my thoughts. "Your equipment is in there too, as well as some other paperwork. Tom's old room is sealed."

"Max," Phil interjected. "Take some time in here and get settled. I suggest you go through the gear in the room and get your castor on…you know, your watch. We will set it up later and go over its uses. Doctor Simmons is bringing dinner; she'll be here in a couple of hours. I suggest you take this time to make peace with the past, but don't get too emotional. Rooms like this can have personalities.

"When you're done, just come back to the main hall. We will be in the first set of doors to the left past the stairs. It's the dining room, though it usually turns into the briefing room. Lastly, your new email account and system access are turned on. The logins are written down on the pad on the desk—oh, and one last thing, bruther." Phil walked over to the wall to the right and, smiling, opened the doors to one of the large bookcases, revealing a mirrored bar full of bottles. "You might need this, but don't get too attached. We may have work to do later."

"Phil, where have you been all my life?" I exclaimed, marching over and admiring the old collection of bottles.

"That's an even longer story, bruther. Over a drink later if we can." Phil's phone started chirping. He answered as the muscles in his jaw tightened. "Ed, there's been another one; this time in London of all damn places."

Ed looked up from reading a message on his phone. "This isn't good. Another influential Mage has been found dead. This tour will have to be cut short. Phil, let's head down to the crucible room and see what else is coming in. Max, that's the working office in the actual Atheneum located before the archives," he explained. "Most of our workstations and main communication equipment is there. Kind of like a war room. It's the door all the way at the end on your right."

With that, Ed and Phil headed out the door at a quick pace, talking all the way.

I decided to go sit in the desk chair, look around, and get a perspective on the office.

Some offices face out a window. These are for daydreamers, people who want to be somewhere else. Some offices are small—people who want to interact closely with others. Some offices are large, as the owners want to show their status. Some offices were places of reflection and determination. Gramps's office was the latter.

As I sat in the chair, I could see memories everywhere I looked. Everything was set in place with a purpose. The chairs and table were well used, and the books well read. It felt like home. This was Gramps's safe place in the world.

After a moment of sitting quietly, I started opening the

drawers. In the middle was a bunch of basic office supplies, including pens, paper clips, and pads of paper. To the top right, the drawer was full of what looked like color-coded flasks, obviously for drinking. That being said, the one thing I'd learned today was that if I didn't know what it was, I shouldn't drink it, taking my cue from the fountains.

The drawers on the left were all locked. I would find the key another time. On top of the desk sat a large leather pad with all my login information, a landline phone, and a computer monitor that was obviously a hookup for a laptop. The lamp on the desk was a Tiffany that had to be worth a small fortune. It radiated steady, solid light that I could tell had been Gramps's companion many a night.

It was time to go into my new room and check out this gear everyone kept talking about. Hey, new stuff! You can't go wrong. I figured I was somewhere between a supernatural US marshal and a bookkeeper. While it wasn't completely clear, I had a feeling that was all about to change.

Going into the bedroom, I noticed it was small, organized, and just like the old trailers I stayed in while deployed, making me feel right at home. Everything was within hands' reach if you were standing in the middle of the room, minus the contents of the closet.

On the bed lay a laptop, a watch box, a big-ass sword oddly enough, a cell phone box, and lastly, what looked like a gun box with a set of identification papers on top. Yep, the only question was if I would look cool after a few cocktails walking into my first meeting wearing the sword.

CHAPTER 5

Phil Me Up

"Max? You in there? It's time for chow," Phil yelled as he loudly knocked on the door with knuckles that sounded like stone hitting solid wood before he pushed the door open.

Phil was obviously here to make sure I was on time for dinner. It was apparent that Dr. Simmons was someone not to be left waiting. Great time for another evening of guaranteed confusion for me.

"Hey, man. Yeah, just going through all this new stuff. I turned on my phone, and you would have thought I was the most popular guy in town. The damn thing won't stop beeping with messages. A bunch of these are just nonsense, not even words. I guess the phone had some messages backed up," I said, also glancing down at the new silver-and-blue watch on my wrist, looking for Phil's approval to ensure I wasn't t making a fool of myself.

"Look at you, all ready to go. Leave the sword; it makes you look like an ass, and I'm sure you're going to have plenty of chances to do that later. Were you standing in front of the mirror checking yourself out?" Phil ribbed as he grabbed my wrist to look at my watch. I had noticed earlier when I was talking to him that he had no issue invading a person's personal space.

"Man, that's a nice castor you have there. One of the nicest I've seen in a while. Ed must either really like you or he had too much to drink when he got mine. Either way, that's your lifeline for now; I'm sure you'll have to sit through a class or something.

"I grew up in a half-Fae household, so I actually have another one. They are priceless and will help you focus your energy. I know Ed explained the birthday thing, but did he tell you that Doctor Simmons is the person who actually figured out the exact time it takes to have the Etherium activate in your body as an Earthborn Mage? Kind of easy to tell if someone is lying about their age, to say the least."

I had absolutely been checking myself out in the mirror —just saying, a sword could make about anyone look badass.

While lingering around office for about an hour going through everything before getting ready, I had even had an unannounced guest. Ed had pointed out when reviewing the paperwork that Gramps had an administrative assistant who "may or may not" be around, but hadn't mentioned anything else.

Leshya arrived roughly five minutes after everyone had left and asked what I needed. She was slender, roughly five foot tall, and had grayish blond hair with absolutely no distinguishing traits, even dressing plainly. Leshya had a ghostly beauty, one that did not need much to stand out. The type of face that was innocent and also full of curiosity at the same time.

After asking, she simply stated she was there to care for the house. I was pretty sure Leshya wasn't fully human, and I was also surprised no one had mentioned her more.

"Phil, I had a guest while you all were gone. Called herself Leshya; said she worked here?" I asked in the form of a statement while I took the sword belt off, setting it on the desk and taking one last glance in the mirror at the open bar while Phil stood there impatiently.

"Huh, she actually popped up?" Phil commented as if he did not fully want to believe me, but had to. "Leshya is what's called a craft. It's a controversial topic for some, but she's not really a person. You see, many times there are things and jobs magic folks don't want to do. Doctor Simmons and Ed have a much more technical explanation, but crafts are really nothing more than a construct made to run errands and stand in when the crafter doesn't want to be present.

"Stronger Mages can actually bind spirits to them, so always be careful on blind dates with witches, mate. The Fae like to keep crafts around almost like pets. Makes me sick, in all fairness. Leshya has been here a long time and is probably the only craft I know with a name. She's not been around much since Tom left, but we figured she was wandering around the Atheneum somewhere. Glad to hear she is back. Oh, word of advice: don't eat her cooking," Phil warned as he strolled out the room.

We walked down the stairs and through the kitchen to the main house, hearing a noise coming from the hallway past the fountain. It sounded like Ed was on the losing end of a conversation. On the left, the double doors were open. Just as described, it was a formal dining room where Ed and, I assumed, Dr. Simmons stood.

While classic in style, the room had also been updated and looked like the type of dining room where more work got done than eating. The ceiling was high and covered in some period art, and the walls were draped in worn tapestries that moved slightly. The room smelled like roasted chicken and pine, and was lit by several newer-style lamps hanging on the walls that had obviously been made to look old.

Ed looked over. "Max, I would like to formally introduce

you to Doctor Simmons. Doctor Simmons, Max Abaddon Sand," Ed presented, walking to the other side of the table to usher us in and close the door.

"Max, it's a pleasure to finally meet you. I've heard so much about you. I feel as though we have already met," she greeted in a sharp voice with a genuine smile that reached her eyes.

"Doctor Simmons, great to finally meet you as well. So, can you at least tell me I'm not crazy, doc?" I asked as we shook hands. I felt the warmth in her hand.

She let out a slight chuckle. "Call me Jenny. You have a very warm handshake. I would like to spend some time with you and look into it a little more. As you are aware, I am a doctor, but I specialize in transitioning Mages," Dr. Simmons said, still wearing her smile. She probably knew by now from Ed that I had a warped sense of humor. I let out a slight chuff.

"Hey, hold on, lass. You told me to call you Doctor Simmons; never Jenny," Phil interjected, trying to look emotionally scarred but not pulling it off very well.

"Well, Phil, the first words out of your mouth when we met went something like, 'Hey, baby, want to go get a drink and see where this connection goes?' A-plus for effort, D-minus for execution. If memory serves me correctly, you had just drank half a bottle of Magnus. Just saying, it's all about first impressions." Dr. Simmons took a seat and started unwrapping takeout Chinese food.

You could tell their relationship was close. The type you got in the military or with cops who had been on the same hardened beat for years. Playful yet cordial, almost like siblings who actually respected each other but had to get in their jabs when they could. I could tell that the team in front of me was a tight-knit group of people.

Ed looked over and sighed with a wry smile, probably

having heard that exchange more than a few times. "Now that that's out of the way, Dr. Simmons—sorry, Jenny would like to go over some news she just picked up from the box."

"The box" was the term used by the team to describe the terminal computers connected to the NCTS feed tied into the federal law enforcement database in what they called the crucible. It was also connected to the CSA, meaning it was a type of dispatch for OTN cases, or Other than Natural. I found out later that the civilian population would tag a case or evidence with that acronym, and it would automatically feed into the box.

Thank God for my time in the army allowing me not to lose my mind with all these acronyms, I thought, shaking my head slightly.

Dr. Simmons was very elegant in her movements, light of touch, and very articulate. Her eyes conveyed intelligence, and after what I'd heard about her, I was pretty sure she was the smartest person I had met in a while. That is, besides Ralph, the local beach bum who lived under the pier near my apartment. That guy, let me tell you…genius. He had it figured out.

Dr. Simmons had straight, pitch-black hair and wore thick-rimmed glasses that stated, "I'm smart, but I don't recommend you get too close." She had thin lips, and while she was talking, she never took her eyes off of you. It was clear Jenny was analyzing everything and everyone around her at all times. I respected her immediately; she had an air of confidence about her.

Ed might have been the boss on the books, but I think Jenny here ran the show.

She capped her look off by wearing dark slacks and a long sleeve top that was form-fitting but covered her almost completely.

Jenny cleared her throat, causing Ed and Phil to look up from their already half-eaten trays of fried rice. "As everyone is aware, Ezra, the CEO of Mags-Tech, was murdered a couple days ago. Needless to say, we suspect it was a hit. The initial reports suggest high levels of magical activity. The scene has been sealed and is awaiting further investigation. As luck would have it, that would be us. Jayal, from the NCTS New York office, suspended the location in a containment field awaiting our arrival. From what I hear, the issue is that it has already been gone over by a few other CSA agents. I am working to find out whom exactly."

Ed looked up, raising an eyebrow. I sat there, still thinking I should have brought the sword or anything else to distract me from the events of the past couple of days.

Jenny started back up after her pause. "Ed, I'm sure you are aware nothing has been entered into the system. In front of you is a folder with the details and initial pictures taken. As you will see, the person—or persons, as reported, who did this were not worried about leaving behind his body in rather poor shape. There are also initial reports of a ritual taking place on-site, but they aren't sure of those details, which is why we're being asked to come in. The civilian authorities are staying clear, and the head of federal law enforcement is sitting this one out, it being election season and all."

She continued after a brief pause to take a sip from her drink and look at me. "Max, before you ask, the regular authorities are staying on the margins because the general population has no clue who Ezra is—was, or how much power he held. The timing is bad due to the discussion on dates for the Balance. The Council has decided it's a good idea to let the regulars fully know about us, simply put. They are still figuring the best way to market it."

Jenny went on as Ed and Phil kept eating. "As you are finding out, there is a power struggle between some pure

Ethereals and the Earthborn Magical community. We know that the Council is basically split down the middle between both groups right now, and Ezra's murder reeks of foul play due to the influence he had over the process for the Balance. But while he may have pulled some strings, Ezra himself was not part of the Council, which is making the CSA think someone from the outside was involved. We have been asked to see if we can find any clues as to why and who."

Phil was cramming what looked like two egg rolls in his mouth at the same time, making a slurping, crunching sound that was obviously annoying Jenny.

"Politics," I said, trying not to focus on the noises Phil was making. "Sounds like the folks from the Plane don't want the normal people on Earth teaming up with the Mage community here."

"Pretty much," Jenny responded. "But not everyone from the Plane is power hungry. Most of the Fae already on Earth support the Balance. We believe that both groups are working to accelerate whatever agenda they have."

While it was a lot to take in, I was starting to understand that my background and acceptance of this new world was no coincidence. In fact, this had me hook, line, and sinker. I was in; this was it. I had found that future I was looking for.

Ed spoke up. "Thanks, Jenny. I think we need to plan and send the team. Getting to Ezra was a feat unto itself. Phil, Jenny, and I will go to the scene while you get acclimated, Max. I intended to give you more time before we got you into the fold, but the best we'll be able to do now is a few days to get you sorted."

He turned to Phil. "Phil, I'm going to need you to get the gear ready for tomorrow while Jenny and I try to figure out who was on-site. At this point, my main concern is spillage. This already has people worried, according to Trish, which means we should be too."

I stopped taking notes as Ed continued. "Max, I'll need you to get into the box and start looking for anything that is OTN in the NY area. Your laptop is connected to the system; however, it won't have access to the full database. I want you to do some research on Mags-Tech, see if you can find anything they may have been up to or reports of stolen E-Tech. This should keep you busy until we can get some training behind you.

"We will gate into the city and go on foot," Ed told the other two. "I don't want to draw attention to us being in the area just in case. Phil, I would like a V present. Call Angel; she will be able to control herself on the scene. I'm afraid Frank is not ready yet to do fieldwork."

"You mean Frank is part of this?" I asked, looking over at Ed. I suspected that V stood for Vampire. I was still making a lot of assumptions, but I was starting to get that feeling I used to get before going out on patrol.

"Yes, Max, we have a few trusted Vs that we like to get involved from time to time. As we have discussed, they are very handy in a pinch and have a nose for picking up things we often cannot. Frank is with me for a reason, but that's for another time," Ed said as he looked around the table for any objections. "Phil, anything from you?"

Phil must have been fairly new, but at this point, what was new? Ten, twenty years?

"No, let's get the shenanigans started. I have a few things I was planning on doing this weekend, and they do not involve any of you lot. Well, maybe Max if he can keep up," Phil joked, winking at me.

That was a drinker's wink. Phil needed someone to hang out with and was banking on me. I smiled back and gave him a slight salute, sealing the deal for an adventure at FA's this weekend. I hate to stereotype the Irish, but my man Phil was not letting me down, and I could not be happier.

Since leaving the army, I hadn't met more than a handful of people, and unfortunately, none that I could see myself hanging out with. There was that evening a few days ago with Sarah that was still an odd blur.

"All right, it's settled," Dr. Simmons interjected quickly. "Max, I see you have your watch on. We call it a castor. It's used to store and harness Etherium, and to focus abilities—those will soon become clearer. With that handshake, I'm pretty sure it won't be much longer. That castor must now be a part of you, much like putting on your pants or grabbing your phone. It will become even more important in a couple of weeks when you hit thirty. Based on my math, you should already be feeling the changes."

She was right, and I had figured out a way to explain the feeling to myself: it was like when you took an extra scoop of pre-workout powder and your skin started to crawl for about thirty minutes afterward. That was the feeling, but for now, no magic. Heartburn, yes; magic, no.

"Jenny," I figured that was the correct way for me to address the doctor, "I get it. All this stuff is somehow magical. I understand you guys are some type of team that works for the good guys and that I'm some kind of intern who happens to be related to Gramps and got lucky enough to get his house.

"But know that I don't like sitting on the sidelines when there is fun to be had, even if there's not much I can do outside of drinking a ton of beer and holding my own in a fist fight. I'll work on this computer and see what I can find. Jesus, this is like being back in the army doing intel work," I sighed, feeling as if I had been sidelined.

"Hey, mate, J-man is not involved in this; give him a break before he shows up for a chat," Phil warned with a smile while Ed and Jenny chuckled. I wasn't getting the joke, but guessed time would tell. I had started growing impatient with the whole conversation and needed to get a drink.

As the group stood up, I shook hands again with Dr. Simmons and nodded to Ed. Looking over, I saw Phil was giving me the head nod, and I knew that meant only one thing: time for a drink. We walked back to Gramps's office to partake of his bottle collection.

Standing in front of the bar, Phil poured us two drinks out of an unlabeled brown bottle.

"Here, bruther, take a few pulls off this; you look like you need it." He waited for me to do just that, then continued. "Listen, you need to take everything the doc and Ed are saying and take it to heart. They truly have a good amount riding on you; don't bang this up. I can tell you want to jump into this, but trust me, you are not ready. Just wait, the shit will hit the fan soon, and all that normal bollocks you know will be a distant memory."

Taking a drink, I noticed how smooth the whiskey was. Top shelf.

"Phil," I started. "Why are you here, and why does it feel like I know you?" I looked around the office at the bookshelves.

"I'm here because I want to be. I have a bone to pick with a few people. I met your grandfather several years ago while he was helping my father, and I told him that I owed him. Well, Tom collected, and I was glad to oblige. My father was a pure Ethereal Fae and my mother a red, white, and blue Texas woman. She had no more knowledge of this world than you a few days ago at first. That changed, and now both my parents are dead.

"The person who killed them is from the Plane, a place you will get to know. Tom helped my folks; he was a good man. One of the few out there who tried to get involved when he didn't have to. He was an idealist, you see. Always wanted the folks from the Plane and Earth to work together. Tom was part of the initial team that worked on the Balance and such. That's why he liked my parents.

"There are good and bad types everywhere, and the Plane is no exception. The thing is, there are a few people on the Plane who have real, no-shit power, not like you or I. The type that crumbles cities and makes people obedient. Those are the types of people I am here to sort out," Phil declared in his thickest Southern Texas/Irish accent.

"Fair enough," I replied, feeling almost guilty I'd asked. "I'm here to take this on and I'm all in. Ed called you a steward earlier. What is that all about?" I took the rest of the drink down in one gulp.

"Ah, the Stewards' Guild. You see, I'm a mix of two worlds. Not fully a Fae and not fully human. When Tom came to me, he offered me a slot in the Stewards' Guild. It's a school for people like myself who want to work with the Ethereal community but aren't as old as dirt to help manage the spaces in between and train through the Council's newer ideals. Some type of new age attempt at training people to work jobs in the Mage community. It is a more specialized approach to manage places and-or things. For me, it's the Atheneum. Mate, this place has more knowledge than a hundred supercomputers. Much of it is in old texts, but nonetheless, very old and very powerful."

I stood up and poured myself another drink, finally relaxing. Phil had a way of explaining things that made sense to me.

He looked over, shaking his glass, and I filled it up as he started back up.

"They are working on digitizing it all. While we are not as cool as the CSA agents who are in the field all the time fighting bad guys, we are the middlemen, so to speak. We collect, analyze, and at times, get involved in fieldwork. Your boy Ed was in the war, and damn...let me tell you, don't let that suit and pretty face fool you. I damn near think he is the oldest Earthborn person I know, Tom excluded. He was around before medieval times, I know that much," Phil said as he downed his third drink.

I was starting to get tired. It had indeed been a long day, and I wanted to get some rest to again make sure that today had really happened. Usually, I would stay up draining the bar, but tonight was not one of those nights.

As we wrapped up and said our goodbyes, Phil shook my hand. Much like myself, I could tell he had not made many friends over the past few years. I was not getting the whole story, but I was still satisfied with the evening. Not the completely satisfied feeling you got after listening to a new album for the first time, but the type of satisfaction you got after eating a pizza knowing you would run it off in the morning.

CHAPTER 6

Home Alone

A full day had passed without me learning the world was coming to an end or something along those lines, and I finally had a chance to get settled in. It was bothering me that I had still only seen a small portion of the place.

I had gone back to my apartment and gathered a few things, opting to take the battlewagon instead of going through FA's to try and remember the normalcy of a couple days ago. After a few calls to my parents, where I decided to keep most of this to myself, I could finally spend some time getting my thoughts in order.

Everyone was busy, so most of my time was spent talking to Phil about what was going to happen on my birthday. He stated the same things as Jenny and Ed; stuff along the lines of "You will find out when it's time," and "Your castor is there in case things get out of control," whatever that meant. He also added I would probably get a cake if I hadn't run off by then.

I knew there was more going on, but I could not help but feel that the Magical community was not as large as I had made it out to be in my mind.

"Max, we will be back shortly," Ed said, looking at me while acting like he was addressing a group of kids, not singling out anyone to hurt their feelings.

"All right, all right, all right," I grumbled, trying to get a laugh out of him. "I know, no parties, no girls in the house after dark, and turn off the lights when I go to bed."

Looking around, I saw the only person with a grin on their face was Phil. To be honest, I truly didn't understand what they were going to do other than look at a murder scene, which, according to the pictures, was less than appealing.

Standing in the main entrance, Ed took out a small amulet and walked toward what I had deemed as the coat closet, muttering something under his breath. As soon as he did so, the door to the room started to shimmer, almost like it was one of those cheap waterfalls at the entrance of a midrange Chinese buffet trying to convince you that they were a high-end joint. The door shimmered into a clear, moving reflection of the door.

"Right, everyone," Ed spoke, looking around. "We are first jumping to Eighth Street then walking a half block toward the building Jayal has contained. As we discussed earlier, we are in and out. Since we have not been able to identify who was on the CSA crew there before us and due to the sensitivity of the scene, we are going in under the radar. The NCTS and federal marshals have asked us as much, namely Bert and Kim.

"In full disclosure, I think there is more going on here than first thought, especially since the civilian authorities want this to get cleaned up quietly. Stay frosty." He turned to me. "Max, the radio we gave you will link you with the team; you'll hear us while you dig around on the box. Head back to the office once we are through. If things get out of hand, call Bert and Kim immediately. Their number is on the desk. And yes, you will know if things get out of hand."

Looking at them, it was clear the team was ready. I nodded to everyone as they walked through, the door hardening behind them, and I headed toward the offices in the main house. I had still not gone much further than my new space and the dining room. That tour had been cut short.

It was odd how the entrance was so large yet closed off, with all the sealed doors that were not open to me yet. In most cases, I would feel left out, but at this point, I was good with just getting some time to myself. While I was driving up A1A the other day, I could feel my body having fits trying to figure out the temperature. I was absolutely going through something, and it was not a hangover for once.

The locks to the doors past the entrance all took actual keys. The upgrade team had not made it to those yet. Turning the key to the working offices, as Ed called them, I wandered into a room that was fairly modern, with hints of long hours and stress painting its walls.

There were four offices on either side with their own door, glass wall, and name tag. In the middle of the room stood more modern-looking workstations with desks that were probably used by transient people coming to the facility. Old books were stacked up on a cart beside the door, and two of the workstations, I noticed, showed signs that a regular squatter had claimed them. Each had a monitor and plugs for a computer.

To the far left of the room was what they had called the crucible room. It had two large monitors on the walls which appeared to be displaying some type of dispatching map of Northeast Florida, showing small glowing spots in Jacksonville. To the left of the monitors was a smaller screen showing some national news channel. And there, in all its glory, was the box I had heard so much about, sitting on the obvious main desk facing the screens.

I decided to come back in a few minutes. The smell

of stale coffee was coming from the end of the hall, next to another heavily secured door with a reinforced lock. *That must be the break room*, I thought, smiling to myself. Everyone knew that distinct smell of coffee that, while frequently made, was also often left to burn in the pot.

"Bingo," I whispered lightly to myself. With an overused coffee pot on the counter and a fridge that looked as if it had seen better days, the break room had been found.

Anyone who knew me from the army could tell you that if it didn't have your name on it, it was fair game. Opening the fridge's door, I saw four separate groups of snacks and drinks with, I am guessing, Phil's at the bottom where a half-drunk six pack of European Pilsner sat.

"Thanks, Phil," I declared out loud grabbing one.

For some odd reason, there was a note attached to the freezer, warning people not to take anything out of it. It looked like Ed's handwriting. Even stranger, I was feeling compelled to open it and check the freezers contents out. Not only because he said not to, but because I literally was feeling compelled to do so. I of course opened the freezer.

There, in the middle, was a chunk of ice about the size of a basketball. At its center, you could barely make out several small shapes. For a second, I felt the urge to pick it up and smash it on the floor.

Funny thing was, as I lifted the Pilsner to my lips for a pull the weird sensation to further explore the freezer stopped. *Man, is this really where I am now in life?* I thought to myself. *Getting weird over chunks of ice?*

After finishing the drink, I decided it was time to actually get some work done so I could make a real paycheck. To be honest, I still wasn't a hundred percent sure if I was getting paid. I needed to talk to HR. If there was one.

Sitting down in the crucible room, I turned up the radio Ed had given me and clicked on the computer at the same time. "Ed, can you hear me?" I asked, realizing that we should probably have some super fancy call signs.

"Max, loud and clear. We are moving toward the next jump site. I'm going to put the radio on continuous feed so you will be able to hear us talk," Ed replied in a strictly business manner.

The radios they were using were some serious tech. Even in the military, I had rarely seen this quality of multifunctional radio, a mix of satellite and shortwave including everything in between. The radio was attached to a strap usually worn on the waist with an earpiece and receiver that ran under one's clothes to your head.

I used to geek out when I saw these types of radios, but never got to work with one much. Yup, that's right; I nerd out to stuff like this. It would come as a surprise, since I bet they already knew that I had a habit and reputation of being a little bit of a wild card on missions when I was in the army, blurring my role and that of the door kickers just for fun.

That was one of the reasons I needed a drink, to calm my nerves, and admittedly why I was also feeling left out. Dammit, I was going to find something on this computer if it killed me.

After going through the main interface, I found the box was very user friendly. It had a search engine much like any other platform; however, it was tied to a federal database that included terms not usually meant for the non-Magical or un-Ethereal communities. I had not checked my personal or new email in a couple of days, but decided now was not the time for that either.

I started with a few searches while scratching my beard —magic accidents, OTN, Mags-Tech—and I got more data than I could process. One thing, however, stood out more than the rest. There had been a recent theft of several Mags-Tech servers in the same building where the murder had occurred. The official report from the NYPD stated that the servers contained sensitive project information and was to be considered OTN. *Gotcha!*

After I looked at a few other reports, it was easy to see when something would be considered OTN and flagged. Another indicator was the names of the people that the OTN cases were assigned to. The same civilian law enforcement that I'd been told to contact in case of an issue: Bert and Kim.

Doing a cross-reference search, I found Kim was located in Jacksonville, Florida, and Bert was based out of Los Angeles. I'd bet there was one person for the East and one for the West Coast, again telling me this world might not be as big as I had first imagined.

Much like the team, Bert and Kim were there to bridge the gap between both worlds. Ed had explained that with the Balance on the table, things had recently escalated, causing an avalanche of work for the teams. I sat thinking, *Why would anyone mess up a perfectly good arrangement?*

A few minutes later, I had finished taking notes and was simply listening to the radio, which had been eerily silent for the past ten minutes, when all of a sudden, it snapped to life. I could hear the conversation happening on the ground.

"Right, we are close enough to jump into the field. Everyone stay close. The field is not as large as we would like, so it may be tight," Ed stated as they walked through the next gate. As they did, the radio made a muffled, squelching sound. Not enough to bother you, but enough to know that it was getting some serious interference. Soon as it cleared up, I could hear a throaty, gagging noise.

"Oh God, the smell," I heard Phil saying under his breath. *"It's like someone made a wet copper and rotted seafood*

sandwich." His words were followed by a retching sound.

At the same time, I heard the silky-smooth voice of a woman who I could only guess was the V they had mentioned would be meeting them there. *"Classy as always."*

"Angel, you okay?" Jenny asked. You could tell they were at the scene.

"Yes," came the smooth, buttery voice. *"Someone wanted to send a message with this. Too sloppy for one of ours."*

Ed started to divvy up orders, even though I could tell they already knew what to do.

"The e-meter is showing large traces of mind magic, and the body seems to be warded, or it might have some type of spell on it. Something is not right about the body," Jenny said. I could hear a beeping sound in the background. *"Whoever came here before us must have tampered with it. The spell and the Etherium underneath the body is much fresher than the traces on the victim. Ed, look at this, can you see his skull under that mess?"*

"Jenny, that's a Mind Eater's cut. I haven't seen one of those in a long, long time; not ever since the practice was outlawed," Ed explained in a calm, practiced tone that revealed it was indeed not the first time he had seen this. *"It's outdated and barbaric compared to today's tech. Why make this mess and go to these lengths unless they wanted to make a point? Or maybe something went wrong, and they had to skip the pleasantries and read his memory the old-fashioned way. By eating it."*

"Look, I'm going to lose my lunch if we stay here much longer," Phil interrupted. *"Let's just wrap up and get out of here. By the looks of him and the fact that someone else was here before us, I'm starting to get the feeling that we are being watched,"* he said with a hint of seriousness that I hadn't heard until now.

"My understanding before coming here was that we are probably being watched already. I'm betting whoever did this or

got here before Jayal could set up the field wanted to know who the NCTS would send out to investigate. We'll need to go to the field office in Jacksonville before we go back to speak with Marshal Kim Kinder.

"Phil, I want you to go back to the Atheneum and go over what Max found, and maybe show him around a little more—sober, might I add. I'm not sure how long we are going to be. Angel, lightly nudge our late friend Ezra there. I want to see how long it takes before Jayal gets a read that someone is trying to jump here. Jayal, you get all that?" Ed indicated as if giving marching orders to the offensive line of an experienced football team.

"*Yes,*" came a strained voice over the radio with a strong South Indian accent. I assumed this was Jayal. He must be working on the field thing that everyone kept talking about. Speaking had clearly taken some effort, so it's no wonder why they hadn't been talking to him.

Sitting there, I started to get excited; moving in my seat, sitting straight, making sure the volume was all the way up. I noticed my hands were warm to the touch, and when I grabbed the radio, the slight odor of heated plastic made its way to my senses.

Ten seconds later, I could hear the radio light up with noise, and I assumed Angel had nudged the body. "*Ed.*" Jayal was now on the radio in full rhythm, obviously no longer in his Zen mode. "*Whatever just happened, there are multiple inbounds to the area. They won't be able to gate in for the next thirty seconds, so you need to move now.*"

"*Time to go,*" Ed declared before I heard that same squelching noise over the radio. It was clear that Ed was already working his way out and that the night's work was done. After a minute of silence, the radio came back to life.

"*Jayal, we are clear. We already gated to our second stop to make sure we are not being followed. You there?*" Phil asked. I could hear a rapid conversation between the doctor and Ed in the background.

"Yes. That was a team of Mags-Tech security, and not the ones to stop shoplifters. They had a gate inside my field. I had my field approved by—" Jayal started before being abruptly cut off by Ed. Jayal was the type of guy who probably spent a lot of time behind a desk, and you could feel the excitement in his voice.

"Jayal, thanks. Yes, we know the field was approved, but I do believe we just found out who got to the body before us. Thankfully, it wasn't another CSA team working for a lone-wolf Council member. Good thing. I know the Mags-Tech board wants to keep this quiet, however…Jayal, thanks again for the help. We will be in touch." Just like that, you could tell Ed was, essentially, hanging up on him.

"Max, you still awake?" Ed asked next.

I was literally clutching the radio in my fist not to miss anything. I leaned back to help calm myself. "Yup, still here and standing by. How's everything on your end?" I said, trying to not act concerned and show my excitement over the radio. Truth be told, my heart was racing.

"Glad you are still with us. The doctor and I are going to be a little late getting back. Phil will gate back shortly. Hopefully the house didn't burn down," Ed joked.

I could tell he was playing off the day's quick ending and probably knew I'd been holding my breath the whole time listening. There was also an edge of distant worry in his voice, almost as if he were trying to work out a puzzle in his head. Honestly, I had no clue about most of what he'd referred to; however, I felt that was about to change.

Had I mentioned I needed to check with HR on getting a paycheck and, at this point, some vacation days?

"We will debrief you all when we get back."

CHAPTER 7

I Don't Think We're Supposed To Do This

I made my way back to the break room, brewed a cup of coffee, said hello to Leshya looming in the main hall, got a key from her, and headed to the front of the house where Phil was just walking through the gate. As soon as Phil arrived, Ed turned all the radios off remotely.

"My God, did you hear that mess? Ed could have gotten us all mangled with his 'Hey, Angel, nudge the warded or enchanted body. Phil, be sober' rubbish. He always does this; knows more than what he is saying. A damn demon could have popped out of Ezra's arse and had us for lunch.

"Anyway, I need a drink. Later we can get you into the main library that we never got to, and, hell, the Postern. Ed doesn't want me opening that door, but he can piss off after that. We just have to find the key. You know what, he knew nothing would happen and about gave us a heart attack; minus Angel, she doesn't have one," Phil ranted all in one breath while looking oddly happy at the same time.

I think he liked to blow off steam after his adrenaline spiked. "Hi, honey. Glad you made it home safe. Was the traffic bad?" I teased in my best woman's impersonation which came across more like fingernails on a chalkboard.

Phil tilted his head back and started to laugh. "You are going to fit in just fine here, lad."

Moving back to the office I had been in earlier, Phil walked into his little slice of the room and started unloading gear. Wandering behind him, I noticed a weapons rack and what looked like a dresser full of various types of armor.

His office was organized without being too sanitized. You could tell he came in here often and kicked his feet up on the desk. There was an overflowing ashtray on the desk, a defiant message stating, "Go ahead and tell me I can't smoke here." Phil was a hipster's worst nightmare, being the real deal who happened to have had his style hijacked by bleeding-heart young men with tattoos, overly groomed beards, and who could not change a flat on a car if their life depended on it.

Phil reached under his desk and pulled out two room-temperature bottles.

"Here, try one of these. They come from a connection I have on the Plane. Rare, and pack one hell of a punch. Be careful; it's cold," Phil warned as he handed me the room-temperature bottle. As I opened the cap, it was like a cool breeze came flowing out of the bottle, wrapping around me.

I slowly brought it up to my lips for a pull after watching Phil take his first, lean back in the chair, put his feet up on his desk, and let out an "Ahhhhh" as he lit an unfiltered cigarette. *Man*, I needed to work on my style. I thought I was smooth. *Maybe I'll go get the sword later.*

The drink was indescribable. Cool, minty yet not, carbonated but again not. It had a flavor that changed as it moved around the inside of my mouth. Bubblegum, strawberry, grape, mint? I could not place it.

"Phil, what is this?" I asked, already feeling a nice,

warming sensation.

"It's the nectar of the gods, bruther. Ambrosia. Let's just say I usually have one tucked away for when I get back from doing fieldwork that got my blood pumping. That seems to be happening more and more. I used to get away with a couple bottles every few bloody months. It's hard stuff to get your hands on, much less afford. Usually, only Ethereals drink it, as it's easier to get on the Plane. I, however, have an inside connection that owes me a huge favor, mate, and when I say huge…I mean it. The kind that keeps on giving. Issue is, at this pace, I'm going to be owing them," Phil finished with a genuine look of concern.

All I knew was that the drink was living up to its name as I took another light pull.

"It basically becomes your favorite flavor, including your desired temperature. It will also put a little pep in your step, all while curing you of what ails you," Phil said as he followed suit, taking a light pull.

I could see why this stuff was as rare and expensive as Phil made it out to be. I was already buzzed yet wide awake and alert, and could feel its grape-flavored energy flowing through me.

"Hey, man, before you got here, Leshya stopped by with the key to the Postern. I keep hearing about that room, but Ed said we weren't to open the room without everyone here. Something about monsters. You serious about what you said? We going to check it out? I need a little excitement after sitting on the sidelines," I said after the drink worked its way through my system. With all the excitement, I'd almost forgotten she'd handed me the key before Phil had gotten back.

"I still can't believe she is just showing up now out of the blue. She gives me the willies, but Tom held her in high regard," Phil admitted. Wiping some drops off his beard, he smiled and chewed on the cigarette still hanging from his mouth. "Ah, hell, we will take some guns with us. Grab that sword of yours, just in case. Let's check out the Atheneum on our way. The fastest way to the Postern is through your office at the house, but there is another entrance in the Atheneum itself."

Running back to Gramps's office, I grabbed the sword and hooked it on my waist, checking out my badass self in the mirror before heading back to the main entrance. Well, I just looked like a guy in a T-shirt and jeans wearing a sword.

The sword looked simple, yet had intricate details once you took a closer look. It had a long handle you could use both hands to manage, like a broadsword but shorter. It was the type of sword a knight would proudly hang off his armor for show and tell, then run through you after you mistakenly spilled mead on his gauntlets. Why did I always imagine knights as big, mean dudes?

I remembered the name of the sword from a book my mom had on the shelf when I was a kid. Durundle had once been owned by Charlemagne and could cut through anything, plus it was indestructible. I had yet to test that out; however, I had decided to give about anything a chance.

Leaving the office, I went downstairs through the kitchen and out into the hallway attaching the house to the Atheneum. Entering the hall, I came upon the ever-present Leshya. Her head was leaning forward, with her hair covering her face except for one eye, which was staring blankly through me. Standing there, she looked like one of those Japanese movie apparitions that would even freak out a ghost.

"Hey, Leshya, thanks for the key," I said, trying to calm myself. When I got closer, she moved back disappearing into the shadows of the hall.

Note to self, always turn the hall lights on in the future. I had a feeling I would be seeing that image in my dreams later, but hey, I had a sword! Or, as I was dubbing it, a BASS, which was short for Big-Ass Scary Sword. Hey, another acronym couldn't hurt at this point.

"Max, let's get going. I want to get in and out before the rest of the team gets back or this Ambrosia wears off," Phil prompted, all while having a Sig hanging off each hip and an honest-to-God fully automatic shotgun with a drum hanging on its bottom napping in his arms. Yup, that summed Phil up perfectly; he was the muscle.

"The ammunition's not standard load. It has a little extra something in it for the ghoulies. Mr. Goolsby, a local heavy who's not exactly on the straight and narrow of things, supplies it. He's kind of the equivalent of a local mob boss," Phil explained as we walked in step.

"Sounds like an interesting character," I said, curious to hear more.

"Marlow Goolsby runs a group called the Order Society, more or less a shifty organization that rides the line between normal and not so much. Stay clear of that lot for now if you can," Phil finished just as we arrived to the large double doors at the end of the main hall.

The room was at the very end of the entrance hall, on the part of the house that the Atheneum was named after. If you turned around, you would be looking at the fountain in the main entrance just a quick jog away. A moment later, Phil turned the key with a satisfying clunk. What lay before me was breathtaking and one of the most eclectic yet intriguing spaces I had ever laid my eyes on.

The room was massive. When you walked in, the first thing that hit your senses was the smell of books, teakwood, and smoke, the kind you got after you blew out a good-smelling candle. The ambient lighting that filled the room was soft and warm, coming from various areas without giving away its location.

The main area itself had to be the size of two football fields, with two other parts, one on each side, looking to have similar dimensions. From what I could tell, the area formed a cross. Overhead, the ceiling went up fifty plus feet, with a second-floor wraparound balcony and a few other small two-story alcoves in the middle of the room poking out above the rest of the shelves. Phil called them the stacks. It stuck out to me how there seemed to be random three-story alcove sections of books and other items in random places.

There were aisles of books as far left and right as I could see; walls filled with knowledge. A few aisles within eyeshot appeared to have a card filing system. Lining the walls were tapestries again slowly moving without any wind, same as in the dining room. In other spots, glass display cases held artifacts or strange books in them.

At first glance, you would think this was some type of museum. It took my damn breath away. I was sure that someone in a hat and snapping a whip was about to come around the corner so we could start off on an adventure. The room didn't exactly line up with the size of the space I saw on the outside. The house hid this place a little too well. That, or maybe I'd had one too many rum punches before I went outside to take in the property with Phil earlier.

"Well?" Phil asked, looking over with a grin. "I said the same thing when I first saw it: not a damn thing. I just stood here and stared. Let's take a left then head toward that alcove. You'll start seeing doors on the sidewalls; we are heading to the black one with an iron dragon on it.

"You see that alcove to your right that sticks up out of nowhere? It contains a door that will lead you to the labs and evidence rooms below. The one further over goes down to the training rooms and storage. The one on the far end, if you can see it, is where all the really sensitive stuff is kept.

Books that are outlawed and artifacts that, in the wrong hands, could cause some serious problems. There is also a terminal in there and a safe that holds some very sensitive information regarding the old gods and Terrum, where the Ethereals are originally from.

"Tom was the only person I know who could get into that safe. Ed is the only person I know with access to that room itself. I have never been in it. Probably for the best. The locked room in the back of our offices you were at today leads underground and links up with these rooms."

"So there's really a room with magic books and evil artifacts? This keeps getting better," I said with genuine interest and childlike ignorance all at the same time. "This place is something else. I can see why you don't just let anyone in here. Some of these books have to be worth a fortune. So those doors go underground?" I asked, starting to get my bearings and pulling my thought processes together.

"I'll tell you, a man can get lost down in those spots quick. Quite frankly, I have no clue where some of these doors go. Also, I would not touch the display cases. Always seems to get Ed and Tom excited. Glory-day trophies, maybe? Who knows. They're not the dangerous or really powerful stuff, I'll tell you that much.

"Oh yeah, and as mentioned, we are working on digitizing this whole collection. There are some workers from the NCTS who come in and work on it over the weekends. I don't think it will ever be done, but they are taking a go at it. If you see a yellow tag on a shelf, it means that section has been scanned.

"They're also updating some of the older files. They have people's names and old papers. Remember, a lot of the folks you are going to meet have been around a long, long time. You can access most of the digitized files on your laptop," Phil explained, stopping in front of a black door with a dragon on it.

It looked like a family crest, and an old one at that.

Looking over, I could see Phil tensing and getting set. He was really concerned there might be something on the other side of the door. As he lifted the key, he looked over at me. "Get that sword out. If Durundle is at the ready, not much is going to get to you, lad. Plus, I read your file. You have a mean streak and a moderate ability to back it." He lifted the shotgun.

"Wait. You're telling me this is really Durundle, the sword from the fantasy books? I remember the story, but that's just a story, right?" I asked, taking a minute to realize how crazy of a situation I was in.

I was in a mansion, in a massive, creepy library with a sword out of the medieval ages that guaranteed victory in my hands and a tattooed hipster pointing a shotgun at a door with a dragon on it. A guy could get used to this. To think I hadn't even been out with the team and there was this much fun to be had back home.

"It is. Let me tell you, Tom obviously left it to you, but don't let anyone know you have that. People would do a lot for something like that. Kill…lie…whatever it took. That is not a gift; it is a responsibility," Phil said as he leaned down and turned the key, catching the latch with a loud clunk.

A strong blast of cool air and two small, red winged creatures the size of Barbie dolls went flying past us as the door opened. Phil had tensed but kept his cool and I…well, let's just say I almost swung the sword. Phil and I both stood fast, still looking into the dark room beyond.

"We'll have to find those at some point, lad," Phil noted about the small, red creatures. "Those things can be a headache. We have a couple frozen in the freezer back in the break room. I bet those are some of their mates."

Made sense as to why Ed didn't want me touching anything in the freezer. While I didn't get a good look at them, they were humanoid, had wings, and were red as a tomato from head to toe. Now that I thought about it, they looked like they had armor on.

"Max, their presence in the room is good news for us. Those Pixies have probably been waiting for a long time. Anything that was in there with them is dead; if you are not careful, they can be rather deadly. We should be fine. They had their kits on—red is their tribe color—so they are ready for a fight, but I am pretty sure they don't know what happened. Probably think we let them out to help them. I bet we are now some type of heroes. Although that will change as soon as they find their buddies in the freezer," Phil said in a more professional manner than I had heard him use before easing back on the cannon in his hand.

"So you're saying those little things—I mean, Pixies could possibly have killed something bigger than they are?" I asked, chewing on the inside of my lower lip.

Phil responded with a throaty, "Yup," as he pulled the door the rest of the way open and waved his hand, lighting several candles instantly.

Neat trick, I thought to myself, making a mental note that it was one I wanted to learn.

And while this was all very theatrical...I looked over to see an old light switch on the wall and flipped it up to reveal soft, electric lighting in the rest of the room. *Score one for the seminormal guy*.

The space was just as eccentric as the rest of the house. The difference was the smaller scale of the room and its overall unique oddity. I liked some weird stuff, but this room made no sense to me. The rest of the house had some type of flow. This room was another story. It was rectangular in shape, about fifty feet wide and forty feet deep. Along the three sidewalls, not including the entrance, were doors...or, as I was soon to find out, gates.

All the doors were different in design and material, plus the frames, in many cases, sat at odd angles. In a few cases, some were not even flush with the wall. There were four on the back wall and three on each side to the left and to the right. In the middle of the room was a large Persian-style rug with a table and a few chairs around it.

On the entrance wall, there was a cabinet on each side. One was obviously for storage and the other for documents, maps, and by the looks of it, other reference material that was often taken to the center of the room for review. No bar. *Bummer*, I thought to myself.

While the main house was warm and full of earthy smells, the Postern was musty, owning a cool breeze that added an edge to the room. Almost like an open locker-room shower in December, cold and making you shake your head no, all while inviting you in for a nice, hot shower to steam the place up.

"Looks like other than our pals out there, no one has been in here for a good while. Ed has a key, but we couldn't find the other one. Guess Leshya had it. There was a ward on the door that kept us from opening it. Apparently, it was one of the last things Tom did before he left. We thought he may have enchanted the door. I believe Ed tried to get in through a gate but couldn't, which means it had been warded. But as soon as you bound with the will, it unsealed. Bloody complicated," Phil said, looking around with a questioning expression.

"What's up?" I asked, starting to feel like we probably shouldn't be in the room. It meant that the drink was wearing off or something was out of place.

"Nothing…it's…I just realized I have no clue how to use these gates or what they all do. I'm not too sure anyone else besides Tom, and partially Ed, does either. I know Ed can use that first one on the left with the wood panel and hook handle. From what I understand, it can gate to any location it's linked to.

"I'll let Ed explain all that mumbo jumbo. Something about ten stones and ten locations, and that it can move. Not a normal gate, like the one in the front of the entrance hall. That is a set gate, limited on where it goes to and what gates to it. Takes an act of the Council to get a gate tied to it. Plus, Space Mages—or Fae, if they are feeling up to it. Takes a good while to get them tethered to each other," Phil explained, walking to the table in the middle of the room.

I learned later that most normal gates, if you could call them that, only went to and from one specific location.

"There was some stuff in all the paperwork about these gates, but there were some pages missing. Ed seemed a little stressed about it. It will probably take some research to figure this place out." I turned toward the entrance. "Phil, thanks for the time showing me around, but we should go now. Ed was pretty explicit about not coming in here. Hell, I bet he already knows we are in here," I said, starting to walk back while taking in the oddity of the different doors in the room.

Phil started to head out as well, still wearing a slight look of concern on his face.

"So what's Ed's deal?" I changed the topic, looking over at Phil and hoping now was a good time to start digging.

"Ed's a super strong mind reader with slight limitations of distance and how he's linked to someone. If you are on a phone or radio, Ed can some damn way work his way through. He can only focus on one person at a time, though, I think, but he can switch between people very quickly, within less than a second. The fact that he hasn't tried to reach out to us tells me he's occupied elsewhere," Phil further explained.

Walking back to the main house, we discussed what

had happened on their mission. Phil said that Ed wanted to meet us for lunch to go over his and Jenny's meeting with the civvies, and I also ended up getting most of my HR questions answered, because there really wasn't one, though we had some administrative relationship with the local federal marshals office.

And guess what? I was going to get a paycheck starting the first of the month. Life was looking good.

CHAPTER 8

Breadcrumbs

A few days had gone by before the rest of the team got back to the house. I was grateful for the time to get adjusted and explore. I had spent the day after our walk around the house reading back over the initial paperwork for details on the Postern. By that point, I was determined to figure out that room, also keeping a keen eye out for our little red friends.

My birthday was coming up, and the hot flashes had started to become normal. I even woke up with small scorch marks on my bed, and they weren't from a hot night out on the town.

Leshya and I had about as many conversations as our first few encounters. She was starting to come around more and being less creepy as the days passed. That, or maybe I was just getting used to it, like owning a cat and finally admitting you could not smell how bad your own house stunk, taking it as normal. She still freaked Phil out a little.

Several hours of my time had been spent going into the main Atheneum and looking around. I had settled on calling it the library. Fancy, I know, but I always had a knack of breaking things down to what they really were. I also got in a workout for the first time in over a week, cranking out the new single by Planes Drifter "A Night at the Gates" on repeat. It was a crushing ballad that made your body move while also making you pick apart the message. It cleared my mind, and it allowed me to reflect on everything going on.

I had already finished the report in the box; however, I hadn't submitted it per Ed's guidance. He had called once to check in and let us know he would be a few days.

My biggest find had been in the old paper files when I'd looked up Ezra. There had been a wealth of information, including the fact that my gramps and Ezra had served in the same unit together in the army during World War II.

I had mostly gotten used to the fact that most of these people were hundreds of years old. They had been fast friends, and there was a picture in his file of them, both men toasting with large mugs, smiling after a long day on the front lines. There was also a couple of recent entries in Tom's handwriting that noted some recent meetings on the Balance. That was Gramps—old-fashioned.

Phil had also made sure that I knew my birthday was coming up and that we had to put something together. He was absolutely the muscle but by no means the party planner unless it involved getting smashed. I wasn't complaining if that was the plan. It had been a while.

Actually, before meeting Ed and all the craziness that started, my list of friends had been fairly slim since leaving the army. Frankly, I'd liked it after years of being on a dependent team, but I was starting to realize I needed to get back into the fold.

"Phil," I started as we sat in Tom's old office that I was starting to dub as my own. "Ed just sent me a text. He's on his way and wants us to go down to the dining room for a debrief. You guys know there is a perfectly good conference room in the main offices, right?"

"Don't ask me. I said the same thing when I got here. Ed replied some scuttle about it being private. Something's up, mate, mind yourself. Ed doesn't usually spend this much time with the marshals—*if* that's in fact where the bloke was," Phil warned as we both stood up and headed to the dining room.

Phil and I had gotten comfortable around each other. We had even gotten into a short-term routine of having a drink in the evenings. He lived in the main house directly across from Gramps's house, in a loft above the garages. I had not gotten the invite yet to see it but had a feeling it was Spartan at best.

The research I had completed was apparently up to scratch. The stolen servers had, in fact, included some very sensitive information on new Ethereal tech that Mags-Tech was going to release during the Balance. Also on the server was information on a very old and powerful artifact. After some digging, I learned it was called the Genesis.

I found a reference to it in the main stacks, but it ended up referencing the alcove Phil had mentioned; the one with all the secret squirrel stuff in it that only Ed had access to at this point. The book did state that it had a certain transferring ability; no clue on my end what that meant. Phil seemed to think it was some type of enchanted artifact that could transfer things. Again, not sure what.

I'd looked on the civilian or, as I like to call them, civvies' online search engines and found several different versions of what the Genesis was, but I didn't want to guess which one was the real deal. I figured some of the crazy tinfoil hat–wearing people on the Internet were actually onto something—with everything I had been made aware of, there had to be spillage somewhere—but sifting through it was the problem.

As we slid into the dining room, Ed stood there drinking a cup of coffee. We both fully expected to be scolded for our trespass into the Postern.

"Gents, Jenny will be back tomorrow," Ed started. "She's going to the Council to debrief the CSA. Have a seat; we have a lot to go over. And no, I'm not mad about you two knuckleheads' little trip into the Postern. I understand that Leshya gave you the key. I'm starting to think Tom might have given her some instructions. I need to talk with her soon. When we are done, I would like to discuss what you found in there. I also heard we have some rogue Pixies in the house," Ed finished in a professional tone.

"So we are not grounded? Great!" I exclaimed, relaxing my shoulders. Ed had that effect on you. He was in charge and could make you feel like a dog being scolded after you had chewed up the sofa cushions by just stating what you did.

"Max, I can see you being a smart-ass didn't change while I was gone," he declared. "Look, we stayed in Jacksonville to view the body. They brought it down after our little run-in with the security team. Here is what we know: someone cut a hole in the front of Ezra's skull and ate his memories, a very old, dark form of magic that has been outlawed for some time. While sloppy, it has its advantages, as you can actually relive close to thirty days of someone's life after you do the ritual. In theory, the thing or person who did this basically just took a hard drive of live feed from a very important person, but it will take some time to review it," Ed explained.

"I have not heard of this happening since the seventies, and even then, it was a rumor. Why not just get a Mind Mage or a diviner to figure out what they needed?" Phil asked with his elbows on the table, leaning toward Ed.

"I asked myself the same thing. That's where something's not adding up. The practice, from what I understand, has only been recorded as done by a pure Ethereal, not any Mage that I could find or think of. I once saw a body in the exact same condition, when we went into Germany during the war. Those freaks had an appetite for stuff like that.

Sadistic. When I say eat, I mean it. Jenny gave our target a name. The Eater..

"There is a lot I'm leaving out, but they are looking at Vestulie Kaspar as the person to replace Ezra with. There isn't a lot of info on him, but he's the one who set up the beacon in an attempt to see if anyone came poking around before the CSA or civilian police arrived at the scene. He knew there was a field holding the area in suspense, and that's my issue—if he knew, why would he tag the body? Vestulie came down to answer some questions. Friendly guy, but very serious. He was the CIO and next in line, which gets me to my next bit of information. Max, regarding the reports you found on the stolen drives, his team was responsible for them, and he himself called in the theft." Ed stopped to sip his coffee.

"The drives, as you noted, were located on the same building Ezra was found," Ed started back up after a long sip and a light glance at his notes, acting like he was looking at them while really, he was just going off memory. It was obviously another one of his habits.

"I don't believe in coincidences. Someone somewhere knows more. Max, good work on the report. We could have found the link easily, but you went into a lot of detail that we would have glazed over. I want to see you in the field next time. I'm still not sure how you pulled out what was on the drives." Ed stopped, looking at me with a questioning twist of his thin lips and narrowing of his eyes. He was genuinely impressed.

"I just pulled the cloud data that was transferring at the time of the theft. That computer system you have is very close to the one I used to use, but on steroids. If you know how to use it and it's tied to a system, you can get about anything. It took a little extra keyboard work, but it pulled through. In these cases, it's not the hardware being stolen; what's on them is usually the prize. Appears like the drives were unplugged mid-download," I said, enjoying being back on the hunt.

It had been a while since I had returned from deployment chasing leads and identifying targets for the army. Sitting there, I realized that I missed it. Not to mention, I used to go on the missions on the back end, getting me in trouble on more than one occasion. So I was bragging to Ed and could not stop myself. He knew it and was letting me.

"Good thinking. That's what you need in the field. Needless to say, Max, not all Mages are computer geniuses. Plus, computers often disagree with them unless it has e-tech built in. Which brings me to my next two points. This was too sloppy for an inside job. I get sometimes things are set up, but this happened in a rush. But I still think someone within Mags-Tech knows more than they are telling," Ed finished before looking over at Phil, knowing there was a question coming.

"Look, bruther, from the minute we set foot in New York, it felt wrong. Manufactured. I could feel the bad magic in the air. I could smell it like your cheap aftershave. We should be able to figure out where that spell came from," Phil said, stroking his beard and chewing on an unlit cigarette.

Phil had explained his dominant trait was Earth magic. In other words, he was very strong. I had done some research on this as well. While everyone had a dominant trait, they could still work general spells. When it came to casting—basically making something happen with nothing—the dominant trait came in. It took a little more thought to do spells than, say, Ed reading my thoughts.

I had also learned that items were often enchanted. The slang for it was "blended." So if you had a blended item that had been made, for example, to track someone, you didn't have to do much other than put a little Etherium or will into it. This basically meant charging it with the energy in your body.

Both Phil and Ed were looking at me. I must have been wearing my thoughts on my face. I had a habit of doing that, which meant I spent most of my time with a dumb look like I was trying to figure out funny cat videos. You know the one.

"That's another issue. The e-meter didn't store any of the data. Max, the e-meter reads Etherium like DNA, and it's almost as accurate in identifying people. Jenny said she stored the data, but admitted that in the rush it may not have completed before we gated out. If it was not fully stored, gating will sometimes dump or pull out the Etherium to power itself. The doctor, needless to say, is not happy, and I wouldn't recommend bringing it up," Ed warned, leaning forward and changing his tone to a more bothered cadence as if he was explaining to his in-laws how much he really wanted them to come over for dinner. He sighed.

"My last point is the murder that happened in London. Max, you remember the text we got when you first got here. A few people from the Met in London are coming to visit." As I looked up, my face must have shown I had no clue what that meant. Ed went into grown-up-talking-to-a-kid mode. "That's the Metropolitan Police. They are sending a couple from the MIT section."

Again, I made a face, and Ed continued. "The Major Investigations Team. They have a subgroup that handles OTN cases and are, oddly enough, called the AI—Abnormal Investigations. Our new friend, the Eater—as named by Jenny—has been at it elsewhere. Pictures came through yesterday. We are not being pulled in yet, stress on the *yet*. Ezra's body is going to be stored at the morgue downstairs until the Council can plan the funeral. We're going to see if there is a connection between the two murders. This one is not as high profile, though it's just as important. He was the assistant to the London Ethereal Council magistrate. Magistrate Winston is not just a normal judge; Cage Winston is *the* head judge. His assistant had access to a lot of information. The case is being kept fairly quiet for the most part."

"Is this normal? The coordination and bringing bodies

here?" I asked, truly wanting to see how far the tentacles of this operation reached. Phil sat back in his creaking chair while Ed stared at me with a blank expression on his face. I had noticed he had done this a few times; he was having trouble getting a handle on what I was thinking.

"No, it's not," Ed replied. "This isn't a normal time or a normal string of murders. Someone wants to know what two very connected people have been up to for the past month. The data that was transferring may be nothing, but we need to look into the Genesis more. I'll grant both of you access to the secure alcove in the stacks. Max, Phil already knows this, but we don't get many magic-related murders happening in public. The civilian authorities rarely get to see this. This usually happens in private."

He stood up pulling on the bottom of his suit coat.

"Now, for a change of subject, I hear we have a birthday dinner this week?" Ed stated with a smile. "Phil, you suck at hiding things. I already stopped by FA's. Max, I took the liberty of letting your folks know. You're welcome."

"Wait, my parents don't know about any of this; at least, I don't think they do. Are they okay going to FA's? I mean, I have seen the people in there, but Mom?" I asked, thinking about my mom sitting next to Frank while he licked his lips.

"They'll be fine," Ed waved off. "I've known your mother for a long time, and she can handle herself. Anyway, Trish is holding a section for us, which means that if someone starts acting up, and if Trish doesn't deal with them herself—which let me tell you, she can—her cook, Amon, will come out. And that, Max, would be very, very bad news for everyone. The place is heavily warded, so most people couldn't even cast an offensive spell if they tried. So I think your mother will be fine."

"Great, only one more day. I would be lying if I said I wasn't anxious," I admitted, standing up as well. "I'm going to head to the office for a minute, then the stacks to see what else I can find. Ed, you said you would give us the key to the secure alcove?"

"Absolutely." He patted his pockets, then pulled out a key. "Here it is. This will give you access to the room and the station inside. The safe is not to be accessed—not that you would be able to get into it anyway. No one outside the people in this room and Jenny is allowed inside. Am I clear this time?" Ed remarked, handing the key over to Phil and making him the adult in charge.

Phil grunted, looking over at me. "Hey, bruther, I'm going to get a few things sorted out. Let's meet back at the alcove after dark."

"That's settled," Ed declared. "I'll be in the lab the rest of the afternoon if you need me. Max, take some more time to look up what you can on the Genesis before going to the alcove. You may still find something. Phil, I know you have a few things to do. Come see me when you're done."

Dismissed, I thought to myself, walking back to the office. I realized that I had spent over a week at the Atheneum, with only one trip outside to Jacksonville. I was starting to get the feeling they were keeping me here until my birthday. In all fairness, I could appreciate that. Coming to grips with everything was still a challenge. It was like going back to school after graduating and realizing you never really went to class in the first place. I hadn't even gotten smashed yet, stress on the *yet*.

"Halt," demanded a small, high-pitched voice as I strolled into my office. I put my arms up in front of me to throw a punch, but by the time I had my hands up, there was already an eight-inch-tall Pixie in my face with a flat, long sword pointed at my eye not an inch away. If I sneezed, it would be *goodbye, left eye* and *hello, year-round pirate costume*.

He was small yet strong looking. His hair was jet-black and in some type of intricate ponytail. The armor he was wearing matched the others, looking as if it had served its purpose on several occasions, but it was no longer red.

"Is this the Wiz that put us in the freeze?" the Pixie asked his three other friends floating about two feet away. They also had their swords at the ready, minus the one holding a small dagger and wearing a smirk.

They must be the pair I had seen hauling ass out of the Postern. They were all, in fact, wearing leather body armor. I was guessing the other two were the ones from the freezer. Their wings looked like those of a hummingbird. You could barely see them, though I knew they were there, moving at a lightning-fast pace. Looking at them, I thought the odd part was the light glowing dust that surrounded their blurring wings.

I let out a light chuff, thinking to myself, *Pixie dust, really?* The Pixie closest to my twitching eyeball backed off and lowered his sword.

"No, this is the savior," he continued in his high-pitched voice. They all lowered their swords and cheered.

By this point, I was pretty much sure I wasn't going to get poked to death, so I sat down at the desk to be eye level with the motley-looking crew. "Hello? I'm Max, and you are?" I greeted in my best trying-to-be-cool voice.

The tallest of the group spoke up in a slightly deeper—though still high-pitched—voice, working to take charge. "You are the one who my brothers said opened the freeze jail. Then you came and let us out of the gate room. You saved us all. We owe you a life debt four times over. I am Bosley, this is Treek, Gran, and the dagger carrier is Petron. He is why we are here."

It was obvious they were all very excited, evidenced by their rushed way of talking. Everything was one big, fast sentence. I noticed Petron was the only one who acted calm as he sat there picking his nails with his dagger. They looked like Ken dolls, with chiseled features and long hair tied back, obviously to keep it out of their wings. Though again, Petron was different. He had short hair in an undercut style with long hair on top folded over.

"Nice to meet you, guys. So, how did you get in the freezer, Petron?" I asked.

"Yeah, that was Treek and me," Petron started with a more distinct high-pitched voice than the others. "Well, you see, the mind reader Wiz had his car parked out front, and I was here with permission from the Plane Pixies, and I decided to check it out. He did not like me checking it out, and next thing I know, Treek and I are in the freeze jail."

"What does 'checking it out' mean?" I asked apprehensively.

"You know, take the engine apart to check it out. We like to take things apart to see what makes them tick. I was about to put it all back together, but nope, into the freeze jail. You know, it was cold in there. That Mind Wiz is strong. We didn't even have time to move. We heard a snap of his finger, and that was it," Treek spit out at lightning-fast speed.

"Hmm…I see, and now I understand why Ed has a new car," I muttered, chuckling barely loud enough to be heard. "You guys are all right in my book. Just don't take my stuff apart, please."

"You have a book of names? Scary. No problem, boss, we owe you, and we have decided that Petron will stay here to protect you from the Mind Wiz. Petron loves Earth anyway, and is why we are here. He wanted to come see Earth. There are Earth Pixies that came from the Plane a long time ago, but we are not those; we stay on the Plane. Petron has always wanted to come here and see what happens. He is brave and wants to be here anyways. Will you accept?" Bosley asked, as was the norm, in rapid pace.

"Ahh, look, guys, I don't know. This seems like a big responsibility," I said. Having an eight-inch bodyguard would be a little odd, but what hadn't been over the past few days?

At that point, Petron spoke up. "You will not know I am here unless you want to. I have already found a place to live in the wall. Look, I have a caller charm. It's a blended item. Just hold it in your hand and say my name. I will be there, boss. Come on. I will smite the Mind Wiz. I also heard Earth Pixies are easy, is that true?"

"I really don't know, Petro, if you don't mind me calling you that. If you stay here, you can't smite people." I paused for a second, considering. "Look, if you found a place to stay in the walls, go ahead. You have a deal. Here, hand me that; it will fit on my silver chain. Just one thing, Petro. I see you got into my Gramps's bar. No more, my man. We have a deal?" I said, going along with the whole ridiculous situation.

"Yeah. Boss, count on me. I'll be like a ghost but not a ghost. I'll be real. Oh, and I will help with spelling and give you as much dust as I can spare, and we can go to the movies and..." Petro started rambling until I cut him off.

"All right, guys, it's time to go. How will you get to this Plane I keep hearing about?" I asked.

"We are Plane Pixies. Not Earth Pixies. We have a gate key we can use. It's easy for us to get here. That room you saved us from has strong magic. It stopped us for some reason, but seems fine now. We will go. Petron, we will check up on you soon; you know how to reach us. Be safe, and make good stories. Goodbye, hero, we will tell our kids stories of your bravery," Bosley declared before he took flight with the others, and they took off out the door and into the main house.

Just like that, I was sitting there looking at Petro as he

slowly got up and flew out of the room. "I'll see you, boss. Wow, a lot to do, a bed to get. Just say my name and hold that charm in your hand. I'll be there, boss," he told me as he flew out of the room, armor flapping in the wind, with me calling behind him into the air, "Call me Max."

The rest of the day was full of the same routine, including Phil and me enjoying a stiff drink in the evening. I had spent most of the day trying to wrap up going through the stacks before getting into the secure alcove, or as Ed had renamed it, the restricted section. Even though Ed was old-fashioned in manner, he was working to modernize the facility and his methodology; the renaming of the secure alcove was part of that effort.

Reflecting on this, it dawned on me that Ed was doing this to prepare for the Balance.

I was set on getting more information on the Plane, and when this murder mystery wrapped up, it would be on the top of my to-do list.

Our research in the restricted section had been fruitful, and we had found several references to the Genesis.

The room itself was much like the rest of the stacks; however, it had a more formal feeling to it. The room was immaculate. Come to find out after a visit by Leshya, this area was where she spent most of her time. It would take a few days to sort through the notes. Phil had insisted on following up on a book that referenced the Genesis being used when the first Ethereals left Terrum to go to the Plane and eventually to Earth. It was apparently a tool used to ensure a god stayed a god when they traveled.

After a few more hours of work and another cocktail, Phil and I went our separate ways. Lying down to sleep, I had almost forgotten that tomorrow was my birthday.

CHAPTER 9

Happy Rebirthday to Me

Waking up the next morning was like peeling my head off a sticky vinyl seat in a hot car—don't ask. My head was pounding, and my body was like a furnace. If this was the big change—hot flashes in my early thirties—it wasn't going to work.

The day before, Phil and Ed made sure to tell me to put on my castor in the form of a watch as soon as I got up. If the face changed color, it meant that whatever was supposed to happen had occurred.

Throwing my feet over the side of the bed, I reached over and pulled on the currently blue-faced diver-style watch. As soon as it touched my skin, my head immediately stopped thumping, and the face of the watch turned bloodred. Talk about a high-dollar mood ring.

The sensation that went through my body was hard to describe. It was like running a mile in a hundred percent humidity in the middle of August in Florida, then immediately walking into a cool, refreshing room and being handed an ice-cold beer.

"Ahhhhh," was all I could let out. It was then I realized, over the past several months with all the hot and cold flashes, I had actually been fairly uncomfortable. This was the first time in weeks that I felt, well...normal.

Along with the cooling sensation after putting on the watch, I felt energized. Sitting there in my briefs and no shirt, I looked over to the mirror at the side of the bed and noticed my eyes looked two shades of blue lighter. About the time I was going to stretch, Phil started knocking on the door.

"Hey, wake up, bruther. Did ye wet your bed last night, lass?" Phil called in a blustering loud tone only suited for the dead and possibly annoying door-to-door salesmen.

"If I did, I'm sure the whole world would know by now. Let me get some clothes on," I yelled back, standing up and getting the morning stretch out of the way. I felt good.

The small living quarters attached to the office had a small, working bath. The actual house had a master suite and bath, but as mentioned, they were Tom's and had been sealed after he left.

With my military background, I actually liked the smaller, more personal spaces. Not to mention it reminded me of my apartment. It was the kind of space where if you took a hot shower, the whole room warmed up and the mirrors fogged, leaving the smell of soap lingering for when you came back in later.

Walking over to the closet, I settled on today's uniform which, you guessed it, was a nice, dark pair of jeans, a T-shirt, and reasonable boots. I wasn't ignoring Ed's request to get some working clothes, and I would need to get something more suitable to wear soon, but hey, it's my birthday, and I can throw on a Planes Drifter shirt if I wanna.

Opening the door, Phil was right there leaning on it. He barged in grabbing my wrist, looking. "Damn. Red. And just not any red—bloodred. Mate, few options with this, but I think you'll be leaning on the Fire Mage side of things."

I suddenly realized that Ed and Dr. Simmons were also in the office, walking toward me. It was obvious they had all been out there waiting for me to get up. I was starting to think this was either for everybody's safety. It was just odd, as I really didn't know these people that well, but I could tell their genuine interest; everyone was festive and excited, a huge change from the brooding talk the previous days.

"Max, old boy, happy birthday, and from us, happy rebirthday," Ed exclaimed, arms outstretched, reaching for my wrist. "Let's see…bloodred. Exciting! We don't see that often. As a matter of fact, I have not seen bloodred in many years. You, my boy, are going to be a strong Fire Mage. Well, if you become a Mage, that is. Lots of work to do first. How do you feel?" Ed asked, the smile stretching from ear to ear, something I hadn't seen much from him.

"I feel great. I was expecting to wake up with another arm or something, but I feel great. I'll need to call Mom soon, or she will be knocking on the door," I replied, looking around. Not a second later, I started to hear text messages going off on my phone. It was the tone I had set for my parents. *Too late.*

Jenny walked up behind Ed. "Max, sorry I missed you the past few days. The plan was for us to do some tests prior to today, but here you are. All in one piece and in tip-top shape. This is from all of us," Jenny said warmly as she handed me a wrapped package.

Leshya had creeped around the corner and was giving me a flat smile. Huh, I thought she was a craft and not able to really have any skin in the game. No real emotions. I decided to store the thought for later, mainly because no one else around me seemed to care. Minus Phil—I could tell she still freaked him out. Maybe even more than me.

It was like these people had known me my whole life, and I had just woken up from a coma not remembering anyone. I understood they had been keeping tabs on me, and that Tom must have spoken about me more often than I imagined.

"Thanks, everyone. This is nice," I admitted as I sat at the desk and opened the package. "Oh, and I fixed our little Pixie situation," I added as I looked down to see a deep navy-blue corduroy blazer. The coat was the type you wore out but not always to a meeting. It was dressy but not enough to look off when wearing it with a pair of jeans and a T-shirt. The inside was silk, soft to the touch. You could see the light touch of silk through the outside lines of the sports jacket.

Putting it on, I immediately noticed two things. First, it was featherlight; I didn't feel like I had anything on at all. Secondly, I could tell this was not an ordinary blazer. I could feel it almost take ownership of me. It moved slightly and adjusted to my form, with the two buttons on the front in a perfect line.

"Please tell me you didn't strike up a deal with them," Ed groaned, still smiling. He shook his head. "Anyway, the blazer is not a normal jacket, as I am sure you can tell. It's a blended and enchanted item. It actually has two special properties—the good doctor called in a few favors to get it done. It will neither make you hot nor cold—perfect for Florida and other places you may need to go to. You can also now carry a sidearm without it being noticed. You will want to start carrying a few other things with you too, and as we discussed, look presentable.

"I'm sure you noticed it is formfitting to the point that it will move with you—grow, shrink, whatever—giving it the ability to be a fairly good form of light armor. While I wouldn't go around testing it, I'd think small blades, possibly low caliber pistols, and minor spells should be dulled by this property. My jacket is very similar."

Best gift ever—a magic blazer.

The jacket was great. These people were growing on me by the minute, plus Phil and I had already locked in our "bruther" status. I decided to remain vague about the whole Pixie thing for now. For all I knew, I had messed something up.

"So am I supposed to start being able to do magic stuff today?" I asked.

Earlier in the week, I had realized I needed to open my mind up more. Asking these types of stupid questions while everything was still so new to me was exactly what I needed to be doing. Ed had even picked up the difference between me being a smartass and asking questions that I didn't truly know how to ask.

Jenny looked over, getting approval to answer back. In retrospect, she was really telling everyone to shut up while she talked. "Yes, to answer you directly. The issue is you don't know how. There are a lot of ways to use magic; the Etherium in your body can do many things, it just needs to be guided. I think we're all on the same page that you'll be working with fire. You wear that castor to regulate it until you can control it."

I looked at the shiny watch on my wrist, shaking it around and feeling its weight on my arm.

"Let's just say, you don't need to lose your temper or try anything stupid for a while till we get the training program started. It's not like you see in the movies—people being born with the ability and going to special schools. That's more along the lines of something an Ethereal would experience on the Plane. Earthborn practitioners start later in life, in most cases," Jenny continued as the group let her do her thing.

"The process is more open to fit the needs of the person, though some guidelines are still in place. Like a driver's license, in order to be sanctioned, you need to get through the program. We can discuss this more a little later down the road, once we get a handle on where you are with things and get you a sponsor.

"We need to get you some time in the lab and in the practice rooms. Work a few spells, a couple castings, maybe even try to blend a small item or generate a ward. All of these present their own challenges and have various levels of difficulty. For example, blending an item is not something you learn overnight."

The doctor had a way of explaining things that was clear to me. Oftentimes, I felt like Phil and Ed assumed I knew what everyone was talking about.

Her quick explanation made me think. Maybe it wasn't a good idea to go outside and wave my hands in front of a tree screaming random words to see what happened.

Ed chuckled under his breath. It started to make sense why they had kept me in the house for the most part, and I was starting to realize it had been more for my own benefit. Ed and Phil treated magic like something that was romantic and mysterious. Jenny, on the other hand, was mathematical and scientific about it. I had a feeling it was really a little bit of both.

I had noticed that they dubbed it my rebirthday. It turned out a rebirthday was a bigger deal than I thought. It was a celebration for everyone.

After the gifts, we walked out of Tom's old house and into the main Atheneum. I had yet to take off the blazer, as it had already grown on me. I loved it. Plus, it perfectly hid the flask I'd snagged from Tom's old desk. As a matter of fact, it seemed like the pockets on the inside could hold a little more than they appeared to without showing on the outside. Needless to say, I had been sipping rum all morning. Rebirthdays were my new favorite.

The plan for the evening was to leave in Ed's new Continental—the four horsemen going out for cake—but for now, I got a chance to test out the charm Petro had given me.

Holding it in my hands, I whispered his name into it. Not one minute later, he came screaming out of nowhere, fluttering around me then landing and striking a pose.

"Hey, birthday boy, what's up?" Petro asked, proud that I'd used the charm to call him.

"Works like a charm," I said, chuckling lightly at my joke.

"Because it is there, killer," Petro countered, wearing a smile on his face and enjoying the banter.

"Look, we have a few hours before we leave. We spent some time in the stacks looking up stuff on the Genesis, and while we found a few things, I figure you may be able to hunt this stuff down a little faster, being that you don't have to get a ladder to reach the top shelves," I told him.

Within ten minutes, I had a pile of old notes and books from the stacks in front of me. I didn't know how and didn't want to know, but there it was.

Petro was true to his word, and I had a secret that the others didn't need in on. I wondered if Ed would figure it out. The cost for his help was only a few sips of rum and an old John Denver CD. He had apparently gone through Gramps's old CD collection. I honestly hadn't seen a CD in years. They had become as classic as vinyl. It was all followed by a thorough inspection and several very nice comments by Petro about my new blazer.

* * *

As we got in the car, I asked the one question that had struck me as odd. "Ed, why are we not gating to FA's? I thought we could gate there from here."

"Good question. While gating is great, it doesn't always agree with one's body. I know Jenny isn't the biggest fan of it. I think her scientific background has her focused on not how good it works, but how bad it could go," Ed replied as he turned the key and gestured to the radio. "Here you go, rebirthday boy. You can run the radio for a few. I'll just drive very fast."

"He's right," Jenny started. "If you gate enough, it can have some rather less than desirable effects on you. I used to think it was the distance, but it's not. The act itself pulls Etherium from you to power the trip. It's a major issue if something is wrong on the other side—your trip may be cut short, even ending up at the wrong gate. This could be problematic if you need to get somewhere quickly, not to mention you are in for a long ride home—if you even know where you are. That is, of course, unless you dematerialize and get lost in what we call the warp.

"We believe it's part of the Plane," she continued. "The area that allows you to cover hundreds of miles instantly. It's actually relatively safe if the gates are well known and kept up. The gates in the Postern are some of the most stable gates in the world. That's one of the reasons the room is so important. There is a rumor that the tenth gate, which has been sealed for as long as I or anyone else knows, goes straight to the Under and Over, or even to Terrum. Gating to the Plane is even more problematic for Earthborn Mages and is not often done, but Tom had a knack for it."

"That's Heaven and Hell, bruther, in case you didn't pick it up. Despite knowing a few gods, the good doctor is an atheist," Phil said with a grin, kissing the silver cross he wore around his neck.

The trip was relatively short, and was full of conversation with no mention of the murders. I had called my parents, and they were waiting at Ed's office for us. Mom had insisted on bringing my gift and that I was to come to the house next week for my home-cooked meal. Funny thing was, I didn't know when I would have another day off.

My birthday had seemed to shut everything down, but I had a feeling that it was about to get busy. Not to mention the upcoming visit from the London AI group on the second murder.

When we pulled up, my folks were standing outside their car, smiling. My mom held a box, and Dad, as always when he was forced to leave the house, had a firm look on his face. Ed pulled up beside their sedan, and everyone started piling out.

"Mr. and Mrs. Sand, pleasure to see you both this evening. Thanks for coming out," Ed greeted my parents as we all stood in front of them. I had noticed my dad had his arms crossed in front of his chest and was acting more distracted than usual. My father didn't like much anything that involved leaving the warm confines of their home, and this evening looked to be no exception.

"Evelin, you look amazing as always," Ed said.

My mother walked over to him and, oddly enough, hugged him closely, smiling. "Ed, so nice of you to invite us. It's been years since I've seen you in person," she replied, looking over at me next to Pops. "Oh, dear, I brought this for you. Happy birthday."

"Thanks, Mom," I said, starting to feel the ice forming on my dad's shoulders. "I'm sure it's perfect like always."

I had been drinking most of the day, and with my new blazer and friends, I was not going to let anything throw me off tonight. I *did* notice my mother's instant warmth toward Ed, and realized immediately that they knew each other better than I thought.

As we started walking to FA's, Ed took my mom's arm, and I stepped over to nudge my dad. "Hey, Pops, not feeling it tonight?" I asked. Besides lightly shaking hands and throwing up a fake smile, he was not being open to the idea of a birthday party.

"Max, I'm fine," he swiftly responded, then muttered under his breath to where only I could hear, "This isn't really my crowd. I'll get a few drinks in me and relax. Maybe you can come over later, and we can have a home-cooked meal."

Was that it? He just wanted some father-son time? I wasn't buying it. I had a hunch he knew Ed as well. I remembered his text: *Did that Ed guy get a hold of you?* Usually, calling someone "that guy" was not a term of endearment. *Note to self, maybe it's time to have a talk with the folks. Let's get some drinks in us first.*

As we stepped into FA's, the place was packed—*more so than usual*, I thought to myself. Phil had gone ahead of us and was at the door with Trish waiting to walk us in. There were people mingling at the bar, plus couples and groups eating at various tables. You could hear glasses clinking and the murmur of loud conversation filling the bar.

The lights must have been on a dimmer, as the ambience was set for a night on the town; not too light, not too dark, but dark enough to soften the lines of people's faces. This wasn't the usual scene I was used to at FA's. Then again, I wasn't even sure who or what most of these folks were.

Trish walked us past the entrance and tables to the other side of the bar, to a room that had written on it in neat letters *Reserved for Party*. Hell, maybe I was going to get some tokens to play video games. I always liked that growing up, but I noticed the general lack of electrical devices in the place.

When Trish opened the door, I saw that the room was just the right size. Not too big and not too small. A space where a small group of close friends could hang out with the feeling of being in a busy nightclub. The table in the middle of the room was set with food overflowing from plates and drinking flutes that a few people in the room were already enjoying. In the background, techno harps were playing low enough to fill in the quiet gaps in conversation.

Finally walking toward me, Trish shook my hand, sneaking a glance at my wrist. "Oh my, someone's had a fun day. Happy rebirthday." She handed me a gift. "Here, this is for you. Don't open it until you are alone; just read the instructions," she said as she reached up on her tiptoes and gave me a quick kiss on the cheek. Too bad it wasn't the type I needed. The peck made it clear we were in the friends zone.

Frank was there with a cup in his hand, smiling at me. He waved, then shook my mother's hand. *All right, thirty seconds and he hasn't tried to eat her. Maybe I can calm down.*

Two people I didn't recognize were in the room: a short gentleman of Indian descent who immediately after hearing his rambling voice knew was Jayal, and a tall man with striking features with straight blond hair to his shoulders. He was dressed in a perfectly tailored hunter green suit.

A month ago, I would have predicted dinner at my parents' and drinks by myself. Now, here I was—a bunch of new friends all looking to have a good time and a magic blazer to boot. I had actually planned on calling a few buddies of mine from the army; however, most of them were still in, and I'd heard through the grapevine they'd be out on a training exercise for a few weeks.

In the corner sat a table with a couple gifts on it. I walked over and set down Trish's package, noting to not open it until later. There were two others. One looked to have been quickly wrapped and was probably off the shelf of a twenty-four seven pharmacy. The other was ornate and wrapped in silk paper, probably worth more than the clothes I had on. I was betting the blond had brought that one. Time to meet the new guy.

I started walking over as Ed cut me off. "Max, before you meet Nuadha Danann, or as he likes to be called, Ned—you need to know we did not ask him to be here. He is the highest ranking Ethereal in the area, one of the Council representatives for North America. He is a Fae from the Plane, or used to be.

Do *not* make a promise you cannot keep; he is not human," Ed stated quickly and to the point. Then as soon as he got that out, his mood changed, and the smile reclaimed his face before he led me over to formally introduce us. Presumably to not give me the opportunity to mess up.

"Ned, hope all is well. Surprised to see you this afternoon, nonetheless, perfect timing. I see you brought a gift. This is Max. Max, this is Ned Danann. He is the regional Ethereal representative for the Council. Your grandfather was his peer on the Mage side of things before he got wrapped up with the Atheneum," Ed said with an emphasis on the gift. Come to find out, you never accepted a gift from a true Fae unless there were no strings attached. Making a promise or a deal with the Fae and breaking it could apparently have dire ramifications.

"Ed, lovely to see you," Ned greeted in a silky yet manly tone. "The gift is at no expense to you or Max, so please take it freely. I think you will like it. I knew your grandfather well," he told me. "I didn't always like him, but I respected him. Now, believe it or not, gents, I was sent by the Council to pay our respects."

I could not get a read off Ned, but I noticed Ed relax when he noted the gift was at no expense. Ed explained later that if he hadn't made that statement, then it meant he was not being straightforward with us, a dangerous thing when dealing with a Fae and politician.

While I felt comfortable around Ned, I had a sense that it was a forced demeanor. Like he was going out of his way to act normal. It clicked later in my head that he had the same forced bearing as Frank, which made sense since Vampires and Fae were one and the same—or at least once upon a time, before the curse and virus that had created the V's. I did notice them standing on the exact opposite sides of the room, not looking at each other or talking that evening.

Hey, Frank's a good guy. He was the only V I had met so far, and he hadn't eaten me or my parents, so we were good as far as I was concerned.

Ed didn't leave my side while we were talking with Ned. The conversation was light. Ned, like the others, discussed training and finding a sponsor, and he of course assumed I knew some of the same people, which I didn't. He spouted out several recommendations, only to see Ed coughing up his drink after hearing a few of them.

My dad had cheered up slightly after Angel joined us. She was keeping him occupied with a drink and talk about the upcoming playoffs. Angel had to be one of the most sensual, drop-dead—literally—gorgeous women I had ever laid my eyes on. Oh yeah, and she was a Vampire. My mom didn't seem to care about the attention he was getting, as she was knee-deep in conversation with Jenny, discussing baking recipes from what I could tell.

The evening was turning out nice. I had started making it a little game, really trying to nail down what the differences were, but not finding many.

Then like clockwork, Mother Nature called. That's right, magic folks needed to use the bathroom too.

When I walked into the bathroom, Phil wasn't far behind me, obviously having followed me out of the party. "Bruther, damn, thought I would never get out of there without being noticed," he complained, holding out a small bottle, the size of one you got on a plane with your drink.

"Phil, if we keep meeting like this, people are going to talk," I joked, laughing as we both lined up at the stalls. "All right, what's in the bottle?"

"It's a little concoction my old lady used to make. I still have a few lying around. Didn't want to give it to you in the room; Ed or the good doctor might become party poopers and not let you have it." We both backed up going to wash our hands.

"Phil, old lady—you married? I had no clue," I said, not thinking that it might not be something he wanted to talk about.

"Max, another time. Let's just say, you drink that, and things might get interesting. Just don't tell anyone. And no, it isn't drugs," Phil finished as he tapped the tip of his nose and strolled out, singing some Celtic drinking song.

I opened the small bottle and drank the contents. The flavor was sharp and tangy. I immediately felt the urge to go out and be sociable, so walking out of the restroom, I went to the bar quickly ordering a Magnus. That was the drink Ed liked, right? It was time to turn it up a notch.

The bar was busy, and Trish had help tonight. The woman behind the bar was moving at lightning-fast speed and handed me a Magnus without me even ordering it. Man, I loved this place.

"Damn, would you look at that?" I said to myself. At the end of the bar sat Sarah, the mystery woman I had run into prior. While usually my feet would plant on the ground, something was driving me to get up and talk to her.

As I moved, a crowd of people stood up and started talking loudly. "Excuse me, pardon me, nice hat," I said, pushing my way through. Getting to the other side of the crowd, I knew it was too late. She was gone. Or had she ever really been there? Who knew? Looking at my glass, I saw I had already polished off half of it.

Magnus was strong, clean, and to the point. It was jet-black and smelled of leather and oranges, but the taste was hard to place. It was a drink you sipped on, and I had just downed half a glass trying to reach Sarah. That had been her; I was sure of it.

Standing there, I saw Ed marching toward me with Phil in tow.

"Max, let's get back to the party. Here, drink this." He handed me what looked like a water bottle. I had a feeling Phil had been busted. Instinctively, I slammed the rest of the Magnus, letting out a full body shake afterward. I wasn't sure what Phil had given me, but I was feeling lucky.

Walking back to the room, the Magnus started kicking in. I took a pull from the water bottle, looking over to again see Sarah at the far end of the bar. As soon as the liquid hit my throat, she disappeared into the crowd, and the feeling of luck floated away into the distance.

Phil had given me a potion that would make me lucky. We deduced later that my luck was Sarah deciding to come to the bar that night. The unlucky part was Ed being a mind reader. Come to find out later that the true luck had been not making it over to her.

Back at the party, the buzz started to really kick in. It was time to talk to my mom; I had decided now was better than never. Walking up, I put my arm around her shoulder and headed over to the presents table. Dad was still talking to Angel, and everyone else was wrapped up in a story about Jenny almost accidentally walking into the kitchen at FA's once. Must have been a funny story from the laughs it was generating.

"Mom, hey, I've been meaning to talk to you about everything going on the past couple weeks," I started, gauging her mood. To my surprise, she lit up with the same smile she made while cooking.

"Max, you do know Tom was my father, right? I didn't see a lot of him growing up, but I *did* have a set of eyes and ears. I have known Ed and Jenny for years; those two age at the pace of a turtle," Mom said, leaning in with a whisper. "I know they are a little different and that you are in that house they all work out of. You don't have to say anything. We're not jealous that you got the house and some much-needed new friends to boot. He left us plenty."

"What about Dad? He acts like he doesn't like these people, and you seem to know them better than I thought," I asked, leaning toward the table, digging for her to let something slip while I picked up the large, ornately wrapped box.

"Your dad has always been like that toward my father and his friends, or should I say, coworkers. Look, he thinks they are all weird, and the aging thing has him stumped. Remember, darling, I grew up around some of these people. I'm sure they all have secrets. That was the nature of what my father did for a living, some secret spy or something. I used to always dream he was off saving the world. Who knows?

"And I saw you looking at Dad and Angel talking. Truthfully, I have only met her once before. She, according to your father, knows more about football than ESPN. Plus look at her. To have those curves again…hey, if talking about football will get him to relax, fine with me," Mom finished, not really giving me anything solid.

That was enough digging for one evening. Half of what she just said contradicted itself. Did she know? Time would tell. I set the box back down and decided to open them at the house.

After I'd stuffed the last few shrimps in my mouth and said goodbye to my parents, Jayal, and Trish, we made our way back out to the cars. FA's had calmed down an hour after we arrived. Trish let us know there had been a house party close to another location that spilled over after it was shut down. *Hell of a party*, I thought.

The crowd had been eclectic; however, as I was learning,

it hadn't been much different than everyday people and life. Ned had also left a little early. He'd told me to enjoy the gift and handed me a card with his contact information.

As we piled into the car, Jenny handed out bottles of water and slapped Phil, who had already started to snore, on the leg. My head was foggy. Looking over, I saw Ed start the car.

He woke up Phil and scolded him again over the potion. He looked at it as a prank.

"Oh, Max," Ed started, pulling out, finishing his water. "Tomorrow we are going down to the lab and the training rooms. Time to get started." I noticed that Ed didn't have a drop to drink all night, minus the toast we did.

Sitting back in the passenger seat, I tilted my head back and turned the radio on. This was now a favorite pastime of mine: annoying Ed and making Jenny laugh. Happy rebirthday to me!

CHAPTER 10

This Is Really Real...

Waking up the next morning was an easier task than I thought it would be. The night before had been fun. New friends, family, and gifts I had yet to open still sitting on the dresser across from my bed. At some point before I went to bed, I had taken off my watch, setting it on the nightstand.

My nightstand had the typical items on it: a bottle of water, phone, watch, wallet, loose change, a random magazine, Gramps's journal I still needed to read, and a dull lamp. I swung my legs over the side of the bed to start my day, and then I decided to break from routine and open my presents. I also noticed a note someone had slid under the door.

Was it normal for people to come into the house and just walk around at night taking liberties? Maybe it was from Leshya? Either way, I figured it was something I could ask Petro. Since he lived somewhere in the walls of my house—I had pretty much triangulated his location to the kitchen—he might know. Hell, he might have delivered it.

Going over, I grabbed the packages and sat back down on the bed, taking a deep breath while making adjustments to my manhood. The coffee pot started automatically. I had it on a timer for 8:00 a.m., and it filled the air with the strong smell of morning. I'd forgotten to discuss if taking the watch off would have any effects, so I slid it back on, immediately feeling a flood of warm relief go through my body. It was like jumping into a hot shower after a cold day. It felt good to have on.

First, I opened my parents' gift. It was wrapped in brown parchment paper and oddly shaped. Upon opening it, I found myself holding an old-fashioned alarm clock, the type that was brass and had a windup gear on the back with two bells on either side of the top. I could tell this was from my mom. She was eclectic like Gramps.

Growing up, she always had strange-looking antiques on shelves. Now I was thinking those vintage pieces may have had a little more meaning to them. Either way, I settled on her thinking I needed one when she found out I had a job, but was there more to it? After our conversation last night, maybe we still had more sorting out to do.

Next, I opened Trish's. Much to my disappointment, it wasn't a lifelong free-drink card. It was a perfectly round, small gray stone that was cool to the touch. Attached was a note that simply read, *"In case of emergency, throw in water. P.S. it's a one-time thing, so don't waste it."* I had accumulated a small bag of goodies to carry around with me. Thankfully, the blazer helped slightly with all the new trinkets, though I was thinking I should have a utility belt. I heard charmed fanny packs were back in style.

Hey, maybe that was inside box number three.

Finally, I started to unwrap the gift that Ned had brought. After some strategic unwrapping, I found myself holding an intricately detailed walnut case with silver inlays in the shape of a tree. It was amazing craftsmanship. Figuring it was basically an immortal who gave it to me, I was guessing the value was something that could not be measured. It was the size of a square shoebox that would hold a pair of size tens.

Inside were neatly organized containers, most with colored powder, plus a few with what looked like stones and gems. On the inside of the lid was a handwritten note in real parchment. The writing was cursive, neat, and written with real ink and quill. Someone was old fashioned and detail oriented.

Max,

Please accept this meager gift from a family friend at no cost to you. This kit will help you get started with your spelling and is a great starting point for any new up-and-coming Mage. It includes pure minerals and several elements only found on the Plane. Some of these are hard to find, so make sure you keep it close. It will give you a little head start on a few things.

Respectfully, Ned.

Behind the letter attached with a wax dot was a catalog of the ingredients, listing several elements and gemstones. Nice, and to think two weeks ago, I just wanted a new pair of running shoes. Hopefully, I would be learning soon. *Oh yeah...* I thought to myself, *I'm supposed to start training today.*

After my thirty-minute routine of steaming up the small room and getting dressed, I picked up the note under the door. It was from Jenny and simply stated that after I got something to eat, to meet her in the dining room to get started.

I was sure Petro was living in the kitchen, so I was going to give him a shout to see if he wanted to join me for some food. Picking up a few things and placing them in my bag, I quietly whispered into the charm hanging from my neck, "Petro, breakfast time."

He came flying up the stairs before I could get the door closed behind me. I'd give it to him—he was living up to his word. I planned on testing how fast he could get to me over a distance in the near future.

"Hey, boss—I mean, Max. What are we eating? Bugs?" Petro asked, landing on my shoulder with a light dusting.

"Morning, Petro. I was thinking more along the lines of some cereal. You ever tried Golden Grahams before?" I inquired, seeing the excitement in his face.

"Golden Grahams? Are they golden? This must be food fit for gods!" he exclaimed, rubbing his hands together.

"You could say that. Let's get to the kitchen, and I'll set you up," I said, acting natural while he perched on my shoulder like a parrot along for the ride.

As I poured Petro a small coffee mug full of milk over a handful of cereal, he started hovering around the food, looking like a tiger about to pounce on its prey. "Oh boy, oh boy, oh boy. This is going to be great," he declared, finally landing beside the cup, picking up a milk-covered piece, and eating it violently.

After a minute, he was done, leaning on the cup with a wry smile on his face. "Oh, that was amazing...my new favorite." He looked up at me with a quizzical look. "Hey, you trying to bribe me here? Why aren't you eating the golden food? Oh, and yes, that was amazing...my new favorite."

"You got me, Petro. It's the least I could do."

I had figured out after the John Denver CD episode that while he swore an oath to me, something I had said made it a two-way street. He was here for me, but when I asked for something, there was always something given in return. I also learned that when I'd told him he couldn't smite Ed, it'd changed the initial deal he offered. Ed said to be careful with Pixies. In all honesty, I think he knew and was letting me figure it out on my own.

"Alright, Petro. Do you know who dropped off that letter to my room?" I asked, pouring myself a bowl.

"Sure do. The gray lady with no soul. Leshya, the smart lady calls her," Petro stated, putting both hands on his obviously full belly. "She came early this morning. The smart lady stayed at the house last night. There was a really bad fog on the property, and no one could travel, plus the gates were acting funny. Strange, if you ask me."

"Hmm…" I let out with a mouth full of cereal and some milk dripping on my chin. You ever had Golden Grahams after a night out? Don't judge me. "Also, let's work on some of those manners. I was about to call for help watching you eat. Take your time; no one's going to take it away from you."

"There's more, as long as you promise to have more golden food," Petro said, slowing down and talking at a more normal cadence.

"You bet. I'll get an extra box just for you. So what else happened?"

"So last night, I looked at your castor—oh man, that's a nice one. We don't have those on the Plane; no need for them. It smells funny, like it's confused. It helps to hold some of the Etherium in your body in check, and Mages use them to cast spells and whatever else or just store energy. Not like a Pixie or Ethereal…we are magic. The smart lady seems to think we are all the same—maybe she is not so smart. Anyways, what I meant to say was you have a lot of power flowing through that castor for a rebirthday human. You need to keep it on," he breathed out in one long sentence.

This little guy was smart. I had learned more from him in a short couple of days than anyone else. I leaned over and poured a few more flakes into his cup. "Petro, thank you. Can you do me a favor while I'm in the labs today and tell me more about the box Ned gave me? There's a note in it about making potions and spells. I would like to know more about it," I stated, getting up and gathering my things.

"Sure thing, boss—Max, I'm on it. This is great; we are like a team. Maybe later we can watch a movie, and—" I cut him off again. It was time to go. If I let him go on, he would, and I would probably end up owing him more than I apparently already did. He wanted to go to the movies, that much I knew.

Walking into the dining room, I saw that everyone was sitting around the table in various stages of eating and checking their laptops. While yesterday had been a break from everything, today looked to be all business.

"Ah," Ed said, looking up from his bagel. "Just in time. We were about to wrap up here. I just confirmed our visitors will be in later tonight; looks like they are staying in the guest house. Jenny will be seeing to them when they arrive—I don't think they will be in much of a mood to hang out. Also, a quick update from Jenny now that everyone is here."

Doctor Simmons looked up from her keyboard and took a sip of what appeared to be tea. "A few things. Ezra's body is now in the morgue for further examination. Bert and Kim had to pull some strings to get it released, which is the reason for the delay in getting him here. We also confirmed the name of the magistrate's assistant who was killed in London. Sir Luke Pendleton. Apparently, he was knighted some years back and had just gained the position. He was about to test for full Wizard."

Phil cut her off abruptly. "Old Penny? What the hell is this? I was at the academy with old Penny Duster. Nicest guy you would ever meet and super smart. He was a great Space Mage. We lost touch after I left. If memory serves me right, he also had a rather influential family. Great folks. Dammit," Phil cursed as he slammed the lid on his laptop closed.

"Interesting," Jenny said. "We need to figure out some more of his background. Phil, maybe you can go and meet his family and friends, if time permits. Chloe and her boss Richard Holder are coming."

I spit out the coffee I had just taken a sip of.

"Something funny, Max?" Ed asked, again not being able to read what I was thinking. I noticed the others picking up on it; it must not be a phrase Ed used often. It seemed to come and go when he could pick up on my thoughts, unlike the constant connection he'd had when we first met.

Plus, I was the only one laughing.

"Sorry," I said, regaining my composure. "That guy's name is Dick Holder." I was hoping that at least Phil would back me up here, but the mood from yesterday had obviously shifted. I decided it would be a good idea to keep the rest of the jokes to myself.

"Cute," Jenny deadpanned before she cleared her throat. "As I was saying, Richard and Chloe are coming later tonight. As you all know, Richard can be a little hard to deal with."

I could feel a tear coming out of the corner of my eye after her last sentence. It took all I had not to say, "I bet he is."

Jenny continued. "Also, we know that either Bert or Kim from the marshal's office will be getting involved again at some point. They have been notified of the visit. I don't believe Kim and Richard have ever met—Ed and I have spared even Phil from that pleasure. Inspector Holder doesn't like Mages or anything else they can't explain away due to some type of drug use. That includes not being able to fix something with anything other than a bullet. They are, nonetheless, good, clean officers. I have been able to find some common ground with them both due to my rationalization of magic. I just use big words to make them think it isn't Ethereal in nature.

"The next bit of information, before I forget, is on our friend the Eater. The job in London was not as clean as Ezra's. They actually have some Etherium traces from the scene. It's not enough to make a tracker; however, we can at least narrow down if a suspect or suspects were present at the time of the ritual."

Ed spoke up. "With that update out of the way, we need to give Max as much time as possible in the lab and on the test range today. Max, you'll be going with Jenny to the labs for some blood work. She will explain more on that. Afterward, I'll be going to the range with you. It's underground and close to the labs." He turned to Phil. "I also have a little update for the group. As of this morning, we are officially in the books on this investigation. We've been asked to do fieldwork on this one."

Phil groaned. "Max, that's like being on call and not getting paid for it. I'm not complaining, but it's extra work. Ed, any idea why, mate?"

"I had a feeling you would ask," Ed said flatly. "The Council liked the way we handled the scene of Ezra's murder. The fact that it has not yet been leaked out to the media that his brain was scooped out with a spoon got the attention of a few people. With everything going on and the fact this was so public, I believe they are keeping the pure Mage or Ethereal teams off this. Additionally, we actually get along with some of the federal authorities thanks to Jenny, which has us now in the mix."

You could see Jenny blushing slightly, though not enough to draw attention.

Ed and Jenny had an odd relationship. It was like the odd couple you would see out. They could just as easily be dating as be father and daughter. You know the type. Walk up and comment, "Oh, your wife looks so amazing," only to find out it's his daughter. Either way, you could tell their relationship was one of pure respect. Ed was protective of Jenny. He was also old fashioned and probably, like me, still liked to open car doors for his date. Jenny, on the other hand, didn't need protecting.

"All right. It's settled. Max, follow Jenny to the labs. Phil, let's go to the crucible room and see what we can find on your old friend. Jenny, when you are wrapped up, shoot me a text, and I will come down. Even though our guests are arriving tonight, we won't be getting started till the morning," Ed finished, finalizing the day's plans.

Walking out, Phil nudged me with a grin and showed me a drawing he had been doing. It was the best offensive depiction of Richard Holder I could think of. He'd liked my joke after all. See, even Mages had good taste in comedy.

Jenny and I grabbed our belongings and headed toward the stacks. The labs were as described—underground. Funny thing was that I thought there was nothing but sand a few feet below ground level in Florida. After entering the main Atheneum, we took a right and headed toward an alcove on the far wall. Jenny explained that the door at the end of the offices led to the labs and underground.

Going over to the light mahogany door, Jenny opened it with a click. We strolled into a dim, moist corridor that, much like the rest of the building, looked like it belonged in a medieval castle. It smelled like moss and fresh dirt.

Again, this building made no sense to me. The walls were made of stone, with columns that stretched to a ceiling roughly nine feet tall. We had already taken two right turns and walked down two spiraling sets of stairs. I estimated we were at least two stories under the main building.

When we got to the bottom, the corridor looked more modern. There was a set of stairs at the end going up to what I guessed were the main offices. On each side of the passageway sat a pair of industrial double doors, contemporary looking both in fit and finishes. The doors on the right had obviously been updated recently, maybe in the past five years. Above the doors hung a sign that simply stated "LAB" in capital letters.

The doors on the left side of the hall were less defined.

Above them was a sign in older script stating "Evidence Room." While not totally inviting, much like the main Atheneum, it gave a person the feeling of wonderment.

With an echoing click, Jenny opened the doors to the lab, and we walked in. The environment immediately changed. The room was warm and inviting, reminding me of Gramps's old office. It was slightly smaller than the Postern. The wall to my immediate left was covered in books, while the wall across from the entrance had a counter and various devices: monitors, computers, and burner stations. Next to the counter appeared to be a cauldron on wheels, followed by two fridges like the ones you saw in medical labs.

The wall to the right was what got me. There were shelf after shelf and rack after rack of what appeared to be ingredients for magic potions. Ever since Phil had given me that lucky potion, I had started to get the mental image in my mind of a witch with a bubbling cauldron. Interestingly enough, according to Ed, it was a moderately accurate image. Similar to the Halloween movies from my childhood, there were jars with liquids of assorted colors preserving various wormy-looking objects.

The room smelled like a bakery, but not one that made sweets. The smell was close to that of burnt bread fresh out of the oven and just right if you liked a hard, dry crust. In the background, as subtle as it was, I could also make out the light scent of bleach. In the middle of the floor and set into the stone was a copper pentagram about seven feet wide. *Note to self, it appears the doctor is not as scientific as she likes to pretend.*

"You like it?" Jenny asked as she closed the door with a motion of her hand and ushered me to have a seat at one of the chairs by the far wall. "This is my work lab. I'm sure you'll find out most Mages have a room like this. Some call it a lab, others a spell room or some other old romantic term. I spend most of my time working out the science behind what produces

Etherium or, as you call it, magic. Since we're Earthborn practitioners, I believe it's important to study what makes us the way we are."

She continued. "Your blood is valuable. It's yours and not to be shared or given freely if it can be avoided. With that being said, I'm going to take a sample for a few purposes. First, to study then destroy, and secondly, to make a tracking beacon for our team in case you're ever in trouble. Your blood will tie a blended tracker to you like a GPS. Do I have your permission?" she asked, already rolling up my sleeves and laying out the normal blood-drawing devices of torture.

Ed had said this was like being in the military; he wasn't kidding.

"Sure," I replied. "I have to ask. I get the scientific part you're trying to isolate here, but there has to be more to it than just elements and chanting, all jokes aside. Why go through all this?" I was wondering if this was the right tack to take with Jenny.

"I'm really glad you asked. Proves you were listening when we first met," she said with genuine enthusiasm while jamming the needle into my arm before I could react. "You've heard some of this already, and I get you may not have caught on to everything, but here it goes, as plainly as I can put it."

"The magic theory for dummies version works for me, doc," I joked, seeing if I could smoothly slip in a new nickname for Jenny.

"It's Jenny," she immediately corrected. "Look at it this way. Magic, as you call it, is roughly ninety-eight percent science and two percent, well…magic. You see, we can now figure out why humans are affected. Much like getting a skinny nose from your mom or dark skin from your father, possibly even a deformity or genetic abnormality, a level of what we call Etherium is passed on through breeding. It amplifies nature, in a manner of speaking. It allows you to make elemental changes in things. There are also different kinds. For example, I'm about to find out if you truly will be a fire dominant. The test is not exact, but it's close, and has been used to make technology we can use. In most cases, the type of dominant Mage you are can have drastic effects on technology due to the transition of amplified electro particles."

"Alright, you will need to dumb it down a little more after electro particles," I interrupted. I wanted to make sure I was truly comprehending the conversation.

"Of course," she continued. "The other two percent is what we cannot figure out. It's what makes the Ethereals from the Plane into basically gods. On the Plane, they are bulletproof, subject only to other Ethereals, but when they come to Earth, they lose some of that power. Also, that two percent is what makes us Mages able to cast spells, do castings, and make potions. The religious type will tell you it's our soul, though I'm not one of those, as you can tell.

"Funny thing is, I have met a few gods and even a ghost with Tom once. I've just never heard or seen a soul before. So you see, it's that small percentage that I'm chasing and trying to understand. It's like how a small change in DNA would have you flapping your wings—that's what I'm after. It's the key to figuring out what separates humans, Mages, and Ethereals. For example, I can heal people. Not bring them back from the dead or anything, but I can accelerate the healing process in living tissue. I can even explain how it works. Just not the two percent which allows me to actually do it. Good enough?"

"I think I get it. Some people are old-fashioned about it, and others are like yourself. Most people like Ed—or Trish, from what I've gathered—are old. I mean, really old, and they seem to be more along the lines of 'it's all magic.' On the other hand, I'm like you. I like to know," I said, feeling as if I was at least two percent smarter. I hadn't noticed until now how striking her intelligence made her look.

Jenny nodded toward the large cauldron. "This is the easiest potion there is to make: an easy energy potion. Here is the recipe. The ingredients are simple: coffee, purified water, air captured on a sunny day, and a bee preserved in honey. All you have to do is mix it all together and push some will into it while adding the air. There is an invocation word at the end. You'll always hear magic in Latin because they were the first to start putting it into words. You say *Excito*—in Latin, that means 'awake'—and once it turns light blue, you know it's ready. It will make one hell of a cup of coffee.

"There is science behind it, the caffeine for instance, but like I said, it's the two percent. Witches are really good at making potions; however, they aren't full Mages. The correct term for them is spellers. As for me, I don't understand the 'air captured on a sunny day' piece. I challenge you to try it with air from a rainy day; it should be moderately safe. As I said, I like science, but it's the—"

"Two percent," I interrupted, cutting her off so she understood I had it down. She had stated it three times like any good teacher to ensure it stuck in my memory.

A gas fire was lit under the cauldron, bringing the bowl to temperature. The first round Jenny made was perfect. I tried the potion, and true to its word, I was immediately wide awake. The taste was bitter, much like the potion Phil had given me.

On my first two tries, it turned purple and smelled of rotten cabbage. On the last attempt, it turned dark blue, smelling of strong coffee and fresh air. Jenny settled on good enough; however, she decided to throw my concoctions away. *Note to self, get someone else to make the potions for now.*

What I did get out of the whole lesson was how to project or push out my will. For me, it felt like being asked a very hard question while on a timed game show. Squinting your eyes, looking up, trying as hard as you can to figure out the answer while at the same time, making the skin on the back of your head bunch up or tighten until the answer finally comes and is blurted out, releasing the stress just in time to win the prize. That at least was my explanation. For all I knew, I was doing it wrong.

I walked Jenny through my thoughts on potion making after she asked, and she nodded in agreement with my assessment. Man, talking to smart people always made me feel inadequate.

"I think that wraps up my part of things. We should be able to take a look at your blood by tomorrow; it has to sit overnight. It was nice to get to spend some time away from these murders—they aren't pretty. The fact that the civilian authorities and Council are both involved makes it that much worse, putting us in the middle. Anyway, since we're finished, I'll shoot Ed a text. Let's head to the testing room, or as the boys call it, 'the range.' I'll drop you off."

We walked out the door and took a right, continuing to the end of the hall toward the other spiral staircase. It took us a floor down to a matching hall with two sets of doors, same as the floor above, on either side of the passage. This area, however, looked like it had natural rock for walls. The lighting was coming from bulbs hanging on the ceiling, a switch at the bottom of the staircase. The doors looked much older than the ones above. The one on the right was labeled Storage and the one to the left stated *The Range* in what appeared to be Phil's handwriting.

Walking closer to the entrance, you could hear Ed talking to Phil.

"Ah, Max, Jenny. We just walked in. How did everything go?" Ed greeted as he pushed a table to the far end of the room.

The room was basic. It had a few cabinets, and the stone walls had targets hanging up that had been heavily used. Phil had an armful of candles and was winking at Jenny.

"Everything went well," Jenny replied in a quiet voice. The room had an echo. It was also damper than the others. "Max made his first potion, and we are still alive. We will have his results in the morning. Now, I'm going to go get the guest quarters ready for our company; Phil actually cleaned the hall in front of his room. Leshya was walking around earlier, and she said she would help, so I might even get to go by my house for a few minutes to grab some things. I'm planning on staying in the guest quarters as well."

"You live close by?" I asked, realizing why Jenny had used a calmer voice. "The room has a lot of echo for a range, doesn't it?"

"It does. My house is actually on the property. It's a simple one-story house tucked away in the woods roughly a quarter mile from the back of the house, on the property line. Story goes when the Atheneum was moved here, the house was already on the property. It has been updated over the years. Ed's the only person who doesn't stay on the property. By the way, this room has some special qualities." Jenny picked up a rock and threw it at the wall. It bounced off, making no noise.

"The only thing in the room that will echo is your voice. We have tried to figure it out for years. Tom used to always laugh at us when we would talk about it," she finished.

"Thanks, Jenny," Ed spoke up, taking off his tie and walking over with Phil. "Let me know when our guests arrive. I understand they are flying in, as Richard refused to gate, so we can at least send the car and speed up their journey a little. I'm betting they'll want to go straight to their quarters. It's going to be an early morning. Chloe probably already knows we'll send the car, so they'll wait for us. She's a diviner," he clarified for me.

"Diviner?" I asked.

Phil cleared his throat. "Bruther, you think you hate Ed being able to read your old skull filler? Wait till you have a conversation with a diviner. They have a knack for seeing into the future, including what you are about to say. Ed here just knows what you are thinking. A diviner, a real diviner, can be lethal. Most are interrogators, as they never really have to do anything. Just stand there and divine what the person is going to say depending on what they ask.

"Most of them are from Europe, for some reason. They are trained to pick up on what you are going to do; try to get in a fight with that. My advice is to get good and drunk when you are dealing with one so they never know what you are going to do. Remember they can't read your mind, so think away. Just be mindful of what you are actually going to say or do."

"That's actually some good advice," Ed admitted. "Having a few drinks in you always seems to throw them off. All right, let's get started."

For the first few minutes, we set all our things down, and Ed explained the basics of casting.

"Your watch is, as you know, what we call a castor. It stores power like a rechargeable battery, which you can then use to cast. You can also use the power you generate yourself, of course, but it's more taxing on your body," Ed explained. For some reason, I kept getting it stuck in my mind that I should be using a wand.

The best learning point was when he asked for Phil's opinion.

"Well, mate, think of your castor and casting like this. It's like abstaining from rubbing uglies with the old lady. After a while, it builds up inside you and can cause all kinds of issues. The castor is a way to bleed some of the pressure off or save it for a rainy day," Phil added, deadpan serious. After his drawing earlier, I wasn't sure if I could read his humor.

"Phil, you put it so eloquently," Ed drawled. "Again correct. I prefer to say it's like static that builds up in one's body that shocks you when you touch someone or ungrounded metal. We are talking about this so you understand how to feel the power your body holds. After releasing a casting, it can take some of your energy, like a strong sneeze that can throw you off for a second. Or as Phil would say, you may want to take a nap after rubbing uglies too long."

We all let out a little laugh, being caught off guard by Ed's flat attempt at humor.

"A spell is basically just another word for a casting, but it often includes a physical object. A spell can release or channel a casting. Certain blended items are objects that have one simple spell contained within them, only usable one time, sometimes to devastating effect. To recapitulate, a casting comes from you. A spell is a casting that is channeled through something which oftentimes has certain desirable effects on the casting. Don't get too caught up in the language. I think you get the drift," Ed said as he lifted his left hand. "Now, we are going to work on starting a small flame."

He looked to Phil.

On the table, Phil placed a handful of candles. Ed looked at them and snapped his fingers, saying, "Flame." All the candles lit up at the same time.

"Being a Mind Mage means that, for some reason, I rarely have to speak an invocation; it took a few decades to figure that out. Most Mages who make it to full Wizard don't have to use invocation words either," Ed explained as he walked to the other side of the table.

I was betting Ed was just that good.

Phil was next. He waved his hand, saying, *"Breeza,"*

under his breath putting out the candles.

"You see, bruther," Phil started as he put his fingertip up to his lips and blew on it as if it were a smoking gun. "You can also use an object to do the same thing—yes, like a wand or even your castor. Use the power that's in it first before tapping the main fuel tank."

The next three hours were spent figuring out what the proper sequence was for me to start the candle. Ed finally landed on me yelling *Ignis*, Latin for "flame," and pushing out while holding my arms out in front of me, palms slightly up, with my fingers not touching.

After my third attempt, I raised only my right hand and in a growling, lower cadence, I yelled, *"Ignis,"* finally igniting the candles. You would think that after the show I'd just put on, the wall would have melted. It didn't. The candles wavered and lit. Ed was impressed that I didn't even melt the wax.

"I'm really doing this!" I exclaimed, excited, jumping up one time and clapping my hands together. "Magic man." When I stopped gloating, I looked over to see Phil and Ed smiling at me with faraway looks on their faces. The type you got when you were reminiscing about your first kiss—or first drink, in my case. They were remembering the first time they had done a casting.

Ed and Phil both started clapping too, coming over to shake hands and congratulate the newest candle lighter. I had just lit a candle across the room with magic. This was real. I was real.

That's when it hit me like a ton of bricks. "This is really real," I whispered, starting to shake.

"Max, here, take a sip of water." Ed suddenly handed me a bottle of water. "I think today was a success. It took Phil a few days to do a casting. Phil, let's close up down here and go grab a drink. I think a trip up to Tom's old bar is in order. Jenny just sent me a text; our guests will arrive in about an hour. Max, you good in thirty minutes?" he asked.

Fifteen minutes later, I was back in the house and in my office. I called Petro to get the scoop on the gift from Ned. Apparently, it was full of very rare potion ingredients, as was noted, and some hard-to-come-by recipes.

What Petro followed up with was even more intriguing. There was a lab under the floor. Gramps, according to Petro, had another lab, but it had been sealed along with his room. He'd found it in the walls when he was looking for a place to live, and it was warded.

Petro went over to the large black desk and zipped under the top, tripping a lever and separating the minibar from the wall. There was an honest-to-God staircase leading down to a lab behind the mirrored bar.

With everyone coming for a drink, I didn't have time to explore. Petro said no one had been in there in decades, and I quickly decided to keep the discovery to myself. *Note to self, ask Leshya if she knows anything.*

"Hey, boss, just push the lever and the mirror will close. Nothing special there, all old mechanical stuff," Petro said as he guided my hand to the switch. I walked over and clicked the glass door shut, saving the exploration for another time.

Petro was growing on me. In exchange for his exploring services, he only asked for a glass of red wine and a phone. I had to take a rain check on the phone, but supplied him with a small container full of red wine. He planned on using the phone as an entertainment system. I guess it would be like having a large screen TV for someone his size.

"Petro, before you leave. Have you met any other Pixies yet?" I asked, really wanting to have someone to talk to other than my new friends for some reason.

"Oh yeah, there are a few Earth Pixies living in the smart lady's place in the house in the woods. That's why I need the picture phone. If it's okay with you, I want to have them over," Petro quickly buzzed.

"That must be Jenny's house. Okay, sure, just let me know when they are coming over and stay out of the main house and this office," I agreed. "Time to go, company's coming over," I finished. Petro took off into the air and out of sight.

Ed and Phil showed up shortly after, proud of the day's accomplishments. "I believe a round of Vamp Amber is called for," Ed proclaimed as he walked over to the bar and opened the somehow always stocked ice cabinet. No one protested.

Over the next hour, we all sat in the office with a drink in hand. I listened to Ed and Phil tell stories of their first castings, and by the end of the evening, I was tired and feeling the weight of a long day. Ed, in classic fashion, could tell.

"Gents, it's time to call it a night. It's been a long day, and we have more coming tomorrow. We will pick up on your training after we meet with our guests in the morning. I can't stress enough that we are just testing the waters right now. We just want to make sure you can mentally handle what you may see and may be dealing with. The big stuff will come with time. It might have to wait until this is over and we get you a sponsor, since the immediate need is to make sure you can go out into the field. With your military background, you have sound skills. The magic stuff is just a plus. You will need to get qualified with your service pistol as well. Got to love the federal government."

After another round of nightly farewells, it was already too late to check out the hidden room. I planned on going through it tomorrow, and to get that phone for Petro. I bet they had some lying around. It had been a long day.

Did I mention I did magic today?

CHAPTER 11

The Visit

I woke up to the sound of fluttering wings and Petro hovering over my nightstand. It was early morning, and Ed had made it clear we needed to "get at it" as soon as we could. Ed and his old-timey lingo, I thought to myself.

"Hey, Max. There's a bunch of people in the house," Petro informed me as he quickly fluttered around. I hadn't left the door cracked, meaning he had gotten in somehow. The coffee was set to go off at 6:00 a.m., and just then began its trusty job of getting my day started.

"Petro," I barked as he flew back into view. "I thought you would only come around if I called for you. We had a deal," I said, remembering my conversation with Ed and figuring I needed to be more direct with the Pixie.

"Uh, yeah, uh...sorry, Max," Petro slowly apologized, holding the back of his neck and standing on my nightstand. "It's just the Mind Mage was walking around late last night and was in here with you earlier. I'm worried he may try to put you in the freeze. Also, you think I can get some of that golden food?"

"You know I wouldn't fit, right?" I replied. But I knew what this was about. He was hooked on the cereal; a man after my own heart. "Alright, alright, Petro. I'm going to set you up with your own box and small bottle of milk so you can help yourself."

"Really?" he exclaimed, jumping up in excitement. "Okay, I'll never come into your room without you calling again. This is going to be great. Those Earth Pixies will be so impressed with the food."

While going through my morning ritual, I started thinking about my old rules for figuring people out. In the army, my squad had come up with a set of guidelines for sorting out the new soldiers that came on board. We had a set of tests, and Petro had just reminded me of the one I had come up with. The cereal test.

You see, there are four types of people in this world. First, the type who eat their cereal by pouring the milk in the bowl, followed by the flakes. Mostly, they're supplying milk so they can drink the flavored goodness after finishing. This type of person appreciates the cereal but wants the full 3D experience. They're fine in my book; however, they can be wasteful and not take the time to appreciate things. Soggy flakes and flavored milk—not my thing. While these folks are still purists at heart, they can be easily distracted.

The next category, which I would fall under, is the type who pours the bowl full of flakes then adds milk, no sugar. This type of person doesn't like soggy flakes and appreciates the cereal for the thought put into it. Also, doesn't like waste. The type of individual who orders a real steak at a restaurant and when asked for a side just says, "Whatever," as they aren't going to eat them anyway but feels obligated. This is the way cereal was engineered to be eaten.

The third type pours the milk, followed by a moderate amount of flakes, then fifteen scoops of sugar. They're in it for the sugar rush, no appreciation for the cereal flavor or engineered experience. I'm usually wary of these types, and often skeptical of them. The fourth type are the ones who don't eat cereal at all; it's all eggs and meat for them. These types are too serious. While trustworthy, they're not the type who will stay up drinking beer and eating pizza with you all night.

It made me nostalgic, remembering better days of sitting at the kitchen table reading the back of the box, followed by digging to the bottom for buried treasure.

"No problem, Petro. I'm glad you're holding down the fort," I reassured him, noticing he was genuinely worried that I was upset.

I finished getting ready while Petro waited by the door. I didn't know what he was doing in my room, but I guessed he flew around at night. Walking out, I decided to get some answers about the previous day's findings. "Hey, Petro, that reminds me, what's in that lab under the office?"

"Oh boy, a bunch of stuff. I don't think anyone's been in there in a long time, or at least did any spelling in there. If that's your lab, you're one lucky Mage. There is a ton of stuff in there, even some magic items. If you want, I can figure out what they do. After you open the wall, just go down the small spiral staircase, duck your head, and go in. The room opens up after that. It's right under here, from what I can tell. You should take your new spell kit down there. I can help you spell. There's a big spelling pot and everything down there," Petro spit out in one long breath.

While he was still running his sentences together, Petro was trying to talk slower. I guess my mild Southern accent was rubbing off.

"All right, I plan on going down there later tonight. Meanwhile, check it out; you have my permission." *Like he needs it*, I thought to myself. "Help yourself to the golden food too," I finished. For some reason, I'd thought his small size meant I needed to get it for him, though I had finally remembered the little guy had taken Ed's old car apart.

"This is the greatest," he gushed, buzzing off downstairs with a light dust following behind him. He was excited. It was a welcomed distraction from everything else.

Getting to the fountain in the main house, I could hear loud voices and conversation coming from the dining room on the other side of the catwalk. *Time to earn the old paycheck*, I thought as I made sure my shirt was tucked in properly.

This morning, I had decided to actually look the part. While I was still wearing dark jeans and brown leather field boots, I'd opted for the nice button-down, wrinkle-free dark-blue dress shirt. Luckily, I had purchased one a month ago just in case it was needed for an interview. Funny thing was, I hadn't actually applied for any jobs and had basically purchased the shirt to make myself feel as if I was at least doing something.

Marching into the room, it appeared like I was the last one to the party. Ed and someone I assumed was Inspector Holder, as I'd decided to call him, were standing beside the table talking, Jenny had her nose buried in the screen of a laptop, and Phil including a woman I guessed was Chloe stood at the far end of the room drinking hot beverages while moving toward the buffet. Bagels, various cream cheeses, hard meats, and fruit that looked so good it seemed fake were spread on the table. Someone had set up a nice reception; Jenny must have had a little help.

While the house had a kitchen, this had obviously been catered. Come to think about it, with the gates, you could get about anything you wanted from anywhere. You were literally a minute's walk from a New York bagel shop. By the looks of things, this had come from the Big Apple. St. Augustine actually had several great eateries in the downtown and surrounding areas as well, not to mention a few distilleries and wineries that always lent themselves to a good evening.

The room smelled strongly of coffee and sweet bagels. *It doesn't get much better than this*, I thought until my brain caught up with the sight of Chloe.

She was breathtaking. Chloe had the type of look that would make a man do things they usually wouldn't. Roughly six foot tall, muscular but feminine at the same time, she wore the curves of her body well. Her skin was light brown, almost tan but a shade too dark. She must have either a black mother or father, possibly even second generation. Her hair was straight and neatly pulled back into a bun that kept it out of her face, minus one loose strand that she kept tucking behind her ear. Her smile was what got me, though. It was alive, electric, and lighting up the room.

As I shook off my initial awe, I noticed she was wearing a conservative pair of dark jeans, pulling off the women's version of what I was wearing. On her hip hung a service pistol and badge latched onto a thick leather belt. She also wore a good amount of jewelry. I noticed a delicate necklace with a cross that stood out as my eyes lingered on her bare skin. Chloe had on a castor much like mine, and on the other wrist was a charm bracelet like the one you bought your girlfriend and continued to add dangly charms to on an annual basis. I bet it made soft jingling sounds when she moved her arm.

Was I staring too hard? I thought to myself as I walked over to the table. Ed and Dick—I mean, Inspector Holder had barely noticed my entrance, minus a quick glance by Ed. Phil and Chloe walked up, both seeming to be in good moods.

"Morning, bruther," Phil said as he reached for a handshake. "I want you to meet Chloe, from London. We have a few mutual friends; we met when I was training at the Guild." He winked at me as she looked over, holding out her hand.

"Uh…hey, Chloe, nice to meet you," I greeted, feeling stupid that I was basically acting like a nervous high school boy talking to a girl for the first time. "Name's Max. How was the trip?" I asked, knowing that she had probably been probed a few times already and would have a nice, canned response by now.

"It was fun, actually. I don't fly much these days, with gates and all, but Dick over there doesn't believe in magic. Makes it a little harder to get to places that way," she said with a smooth, midrange voice with a crisp British accent. She called him Dick; I would laugh every time. "Phil was just telling me all about you. Sounds like you guys have hit it off smashingly."

When I realized I was still holding her hand and shaking it, I smoothly pulled back. "True. It's been a crazy couple of weeks, and Phil has put up with me most of the time. With everything going on, we've also been working a good amount together," I replied, trying to pull work into the conversation to get my mind off, well…her. Oddly enough, I think she was doing the same.

"Sounds like it," she agreed. "Ed and Phil both mentioned we should talk about the mentorship program if we have some free time. My rebirthday was only five years ago; I'm still a cub. I'd fancy some time to get a drink with everyone later," Chloe finished with a smile. I was guessing she already knew my reaction.

Ed reached over and tapped me on the shoulder. "Max, meet Inspector Holder." He put a strong emphasis on the "inspector" part. "Excuse me for a second. I need to top off this cup." Ed was clearly leaving the conversation with Richard and running for the hills.

"Oy, Max. I'm Inspector Holder," Richard introduced himself with a thick Cockney accent as he reached out a pudgy hand.

I took it and had to lean back to avoid him pushing into me. He had an aggressive stance and shake. I decided to drop the Mr. Holder and go with the easy out. "Inspector, nice to meet you. Glad you're here," I said, taking my hand back and quickly taking a half step away to regain some personal space.

"You're not another one of those nutters, are you? All witchcraft and voodoo dolls?" he bluntly asked.

"Not last time I checked," I answered, grinning to see if he cracked even part of a smile. He didn't.

Inspector Holder was five foot tall with a beer gut that he attempted to hide under a well-placed shirt and blazer. His brown trousers and plaid blazer didn't match, and he had a cheap striped tie on. It all came together screaming, "Look at me. I'm an overworked, past-my-prime cop." He had on a conservative leather watch and black shoes. These, of course, didn't match his brown belt. Just like Chloe, he hung his pistol and badge there.

Richard's most striking feature was his receding hairline. It was perfect for a toupee. I bet he wore one from time to time. He was bald on top, but only to a point. The hair at the sides of his head formed a perfect horseshoe, leaving empty real estate on top. His face was stern and rounded, much like the rest of him, and his nose was small and pointy, making him look like a small bird. He had an honest face, though, and I'd been told he was one of the good guys.

"Well, nice to meet you," he said. "I hear you live on the grounds. Chloe stays at the Dunn back home in London. Pretty damn creepy. Close to this place, but not as American, I suppose." I guess he was taking me for a normal guy. "Let's get on with it. I'll see you later. We might go for a pint if we have time."

"Sounds like a plan," I replied, looking over at Phil, who was grinning at me. I had a feeling that after taking one look at Phil, the good inspector had wanted nothing to do with him, and Phil was loving it.

"Right, now that the pleasantries are out of the way, we

can get moving," Ed spoke, about to start his normal cadence of doling out orders. "Dr. Simmons has been working on the basic details and has found a few new pieces of information she wants to tell the group before we all work on our separate assignments today."

Ed already had everyone's to-do list for the day. I had to admit, he was organized. I had seen his board with assigned work for various people in the house in the main offices.

"Good morning, everyone," Jenny said brightly. "Sorry, I was going through my notes this morning and wanted to make sure the data was correct. First, thank you, inspector, for bringing the e-reader data."

"Ah, that old beeping thing," Inspector Holder grumbled as if he couldn't care less about the meter or the readings it supplied. "Thank Chloe for that."

"Yes, thanks," Jenny continued. "The data indicates that the same person conducted the rituals on both bodies. Inspector Holder, we found trace amounts of the same chemicals at both murder scenes."

"Bloody voodoo witch doctors," Inspector Holder muttered under his breath. He absolutely didn't want anything to do with an explanation he couldn't give to a reporter.

Jenny started back up after giving him a moment to realize he was making the only other noise in the room. "The e-traces from Ezra's body were limited, mainly due to our quick exit of the scene. I have concluded that the Etherium was not, in fact, pulled out of the e-meter by the gate but was instead removed by Jayal's field. I never thought to ask him about it. If I had asked him to clear the gate, we would have gotten the reading. When we were leaving, his field grounded everything that we didn't bring with us; he's that good. Luckily, we had enough of a reading to extract a match."

"What does that mean?" I asked, wondering how

accurate this stuff really was. Jenny was on top form this morning. She even had a pencil pushed through the bun on the back of her head.

"The same person performed the same ritual at both sites, just in different time frames," Jenny explained. "I'm actually surprised there was any trace. Someone advanced enough to do this ritual should be good enough to cover their tracks. That is, unless the Eater, as we call them, is not worried about getting caught." She paused for a moment, then continued.

"Next, while we'll be looking at the bodies this morning in more detail, it's clear that Ezra's murder was fast and sloppy. Luke Pendleton's, on the other hand, was done in a secluded area. After looking at the reports, I've concluded that more time was taken on him. It appears the Eater got the information they needed from Luke right there because they left what they took out of his skull behind. At the New York scene, they took a portion of Ezra's brain with them, which we project means they ran out of time and finished the ritual elsewhere. Lastly, and I judge most importantly, the initial contact with both victims appears to not have been defensive."

"Meaning?" Chloe asked, obviously knowing the response.

"Meaning that the victims had some level of comfort with the Eater. My initial thought is these were two important people and the encounters could have been set up as meetings with the Eater. The only reason Ezra's security got involved is that one of the guards just happened to leave a notebook in the upper offices and came back to get it. Which brings me to my last point. This person knew that both victims would be alone. With that, I'll hand it over to Ed," Jenny wrapped up.

"The inspector, Dr. Simmons, and I will be going down and looking at the body," Ed started. "Max and Chloe, you need to go to the crucible room and see what you can find on the victims. Look for connections based on what we just heard. Chloe, I understand you brought an access point for your systems so we can cross-reference the two. Phil, see what Old Penny had been up to lately as only you can. If you leave the grounds, let me know," Ed stated in his flat tone. He was not giving away anything today. Strictly business.

The group split up and went its separate ways. Chloe and I took a left turn out of the dining room toward the main offices on the first floor. Phil headed to the gate at the front of the house—obviously, he was going somewhere else—and the rest headed toward the stacks.

As we walked toward the main offices, it was clear she was ready for work. I was trying not to stare too hard at her. She was intoxicating. Chloe smelled like that perfume you couldn't quite place but knew in your soul was your favorite.

We made small talk on our way to the crucible room, and I noticed that her being a diviner actually made the conversation very easy. Since she knew what I was going to say, she worked the conversation around that. To be honest, I still didn't have any idea what a diviner could truly do.

"Here it is, home sweet home," I said, opening the door to the room. The monitors were on with various flashing lights and the box sitting there waiting to be abused.

Chloe placed her laptop on the counter and opened it up. "Let's log in and do some keyword searches side by side to see if anything comes up. I hate that the governments don't let us connect our systems. You know the Council couldn't care less," she said, smiling and shifting in her seat as I sat down beside her. "Let's start with work-related searches."

"I was about to say the same thing," I mumbled.

"I know," Chloe retorted as she let loose a flurry of hard keystrokes on the keyboard.

For the next few minutes, we went through several keyword searches. It was easy to talk to Chloe, and she stated several times that we thought alike.

"So, what does a diviner really do?" I asked, wanting to let her do all the talking.

"It's much like what you used to do in the army—yes, we do have files on people, Max, before you ask. You see, Ed can tell what you're thinking in the current tense. I can do it in the future tense. I generally know what your response will be to a question before I ask it. Ed does it in real time. I'm just running a little faster than he is," Chloe explained without looking up from the computer screen but still smiling.

"So you could ask me any question without really asking it and see what I'm going to say?" I inquired, thinking of how great that would be while out on a first date.

"There are diviners who can. Let's just say they have been around for a very long time, and only the most powerful of my type can do that. I typically have to actually initiate something. It can even be a thought, or forming a question in my mind. I can see actions sometimes, which is a little different. It can come in handy in a fight. I do one thing, then something will happen," Chloe said, taking a break and looking at me.

"It's like you can travel in time. That's amazing. Almost like what you see can change. Something can happen that is out of your control, then you can shift to compensate for it," I said, thinking about that one movie, Butterfly something or other...

"Exactly. I can tell you, knowing what a suspect is going to say after you ask them a question allows for a quick change of course. It helps get the desired outcome in most cases. If I can ask one question, then see a handful of responses based on quick follow-up questions, I can figure about any regular person out," Chloe replied, slightly bragging.

I had a hard time keeping focused, as I was regressing to the old primal urge to show off for the pretty lady. I admit I was forming a little crush on our new associate.

Okay, so I had a crush on her from the moment I first laid eyes on her. Sue me. Told you I'm old-fashioned; love at first sight and all.

The funny thing was that she was giving off the same vibes.

"Bingo," I suddenly said. "I have a hit on Luke and Ezra." I jumped out of my seat. The software was the normal spider type that linked references and several systems. It was a key term on Chloe's computer which got the box to catch the link. "The Blue House, Riverplace Tower, Jacksonville, Florida. It looks like the two met there last year. The link is the receipts. They both paid for drinks at the same time on the same day. Gotta love credit card companies," I finished, looking over at her.

"Hmm...That place sounds familiar. Hold on." Chloe let loose another storm of finger strokes loudly on the keyboard. "That's what I thought. That place is a hangout for Mages. My travel notes state that no Ethereals are allowed in. The place must be warded to keep out certain types; I'm guessing Vamps and the like. It has a five-star rating. We must do dinner, you know, field research and all. I love road trips."

"I wonder if Trish knows about this place. I've walked by it a few times; from what I hear, it's a nice place. After reading up on these guys, it's no surprise they would go there. Let's get this information sent to Ed and see what he thinks. We have some local marshals that may be able to dig something up, possibly some security footage," I told her.

"Let me go freshen up a bit, and we can keep digging." She stood up. "Oh, and tell that little friend you're about to call that it's okay if he's around when I get back. Your secret is safe with me," she declared before walking out of the office, heading to the restroom.

"Gods and graves," I exhaled out loud, leaning back. I had read the phrase off Gramps's desk. It was carved in the wood under the leather place mat. As I grabbed the charm and said Petro's name, he came flying around the corner as if he had been waiting.

"Wow, man, do those come in small?" Petro exclaimed, referring to Chloe. The guy was not as politically correct as everyone else. I was guessing the Plane had to be that way. Man, I was starting to want to go there more and more, unlike everyone else who was at a steady "Nah."

"Hey, Petro. Why don't you ask her yourself? She knows you're around. She knew I was going to call you as soon as she was out of sight. For now, I need a favor," I told him. "Here is an address for a restaurant in Jacksonville. It's closed and reopened a few times, but the address has pretty much stayed the same. It's in one of the taller buildings in the city, and I do know they have a restaurant on a floor, but it doesn't go by that name. Go into the stacks and see if you can find anything. According to Chloe, the place is warded, and I'm sure there is something on it somewhere."

"Sure thing, boss," Petro agreed before he flew off toward the stacks.

I continued to search random files, but nothing came up. In all fairness, I was a little distracted. When Chloe walked back in, she smelled of fresh soap, and a cool breeze followed her into the room. I couldn't help but smile.

"Hey, hope your friend is well. Surprised you haven't told anyone," Chloe spoke with an air of curiosity around her.

"Yeah, about that. I'm not sure I did the right thing after apparently saving his life. He's from the Plane and is going to be staying here from now on," I admitted, laying it all out.

"Lucky guy. Not many apprentices get a Pixie to help them—they're the best at making spells. I can tell you, though, that you need to think very closely about whatever deal you made or things you said at the time. But truthfully, he likes you. I don't think you'll be walking around wearing an eye patch any time soon—they have a habit of poking out the eyes of people they don't like. I haven't met too many Pixies from the Plane. Maybe one that I can remember," Chloe stated plainly.

My phone chirped its cheery little jingle. "There it is," I said, looking over at Chloe. "Ed texted. He wants us to meet them in the dining room for dinner. I guess they are wrapped up."

"Looks like it," Chloe agreed as she leaned over and put her hand on my wrist to get my full attention. Her touch was warm, putting me at ease. "Your secret is safe with me about your little warrior. And I think we need to take a road trip to downtown Jacksonville."

I was melting on the inside, but couldn't let it show. "Thanks. I think you'd like Jacksonville," I said, standing up and logging out of the box. If there was one thing I had learned in the military was to always lock your computer; otherwise, you or someone acting as you might send an email to the Secretary of Defense professing your undying love of their bathroom habits.

Chloe, on cue, stood up, closing her laptop.

"You know something funny?" Chloe let out as if she had been holding it in. "I don't think Ed can read your mind as well as he can the others. I mean, he can't read mine. Diviners kind of scramble a Mind Mage's signals; kind of a cool trick. But I noticed that earlier. Thought you would like to know, being the new guy and all."

"Well, it did seem to change after I signed that damn will," I said, walking toward the door.

CHAPTER 12

Shrimp and Gates

Entering the room, the table had been set with plates full of seafood. Fresh Mayport shrimp prepared in different styles overflowed various bowls. How do you like your shrimp? I thought to myself. I could tell where it was from by the size; plus, it was in season.

For once, I actually saw Leshya walking down the service hall to the kitchen. Was she always the one setting the table? I didn't think so. However, it appeared she was working tonight. It was the first time I had seen her in the dining room.

"Ah, the dynamic duo," Inspector Holder called out, sitting in the closest chair while grabbing a bowl to fill his plate. He wasn't shy.

As always, Ed had class when he addressed people. "Max, Chloe, how did everything go?" he asked, pulling out a chair for Chloe. Jenny was at the head of the table with her face buried in a laptop. Man, I had to see what she was looking at.

I looked over at Chloe and put my hand out, palm up, giving her the go-ahead to brief the group.

"So we found one very interesting bit of information. Ezra and Old Penny, as Phil called him, met in Jacksonville at the Blue House a few months ago. They both had receipts in the system that opened and closed at the same time. Too much of a coincidence. Max and I would like to go check it out and see if we can find anything, if that's alright with everyone? Maybe they have CCTV or the bartender remembers something. Both receipts were bar tabs," Chloe stated, ending with a proud tilt of her chin in the air. As a diviner, she'd tried to answer everything up front. I was catching on. I could also tell why having a few drinks in you could throw them off.

"Oy, yeah…you just want to go get some pints with your new pal Max," the inspector said as he crammed a peeled shrimp into his mouth. He was a sloppy eater. Though, to be fair, no one looked graceful while eating peeled shrimp.

Ed looked at the two of us, wearing a little grin on the right side of his mouth, agreeing with the inspector.

"Sounds like a plan, but maybe for a later time. After talking with everyone, we want the both of you to take a trip back to London in the morning. I want Max to look at the area surrounding the murder scene. He was an intel analyst in the army and might see something the rest of us don't. He's proven to have a keen eye for details that aren't so obvious. Also, Inspector Holder will be leaving directly after dinner to catch a flight. Max, we will discuss your travel arrangements after he's left." Ed put an emphasis on *after*, so I took his cue.

I got it…no crazy talk in front of the inspector. It wasn't like we were sworn by some oath not to tell him. I believed he knew the truth; he just didn't want to accept it. That, or it freaked him out. *Smart.* To be honest, it scared the hell out of me too—but in a cool way, of course.

Phil was still out and would not be back till later.

Later turned out to be at the end of dinner, when he walked in drunkenly singing out loud. He did that when he was lit. Jenny shuffled him off as fast as she could while the expression on Ed's face shifted. Phil must have gotten up to speed on his friend Old Penny at a bar with some of their mutual friends.

The inspector pulled the napkin from his collar, slamming it down on his plate full of shells and messy remnants of dinner. He stood up and stoutly proclaimed, "Well, I have a plane to catch. It's been fun. I can't say I'm not going to miss you all, but it's time to go do some real policing. Have fun with all your witchcraft."

"I called a car for you about ten minutes ago," Ed replied courteously. "Your ride should be here in five minutes."

"Max, good to meet you. Tell your assorted friends no pints on the job before noon. You lot are all the same. I'll call the marshals on my way to the airport. I understand Kim wanted to be here today but was held up with other matters," he said, slipping his index finger off the edge of his nose.

As the inspector walked out of the room, everyone stood up and wrapped up the formal, see-you-later pleasantries. Looking at Ed, you could see him relaxing, his shoulders dropping about a quarter inch. Inspector Holder was one of the good guys, I could tell. He was a hard-nosed, grumpy cop out to get the bad guys. I actually liked him.

"Now that we can talk," Ed said, directing his attention to Chloe and I. "Max, I want you and Chloe to gate to London tomorrow. Since you haven't done it yet, you two can make a test run to Jacksonville tonight. Also, since you don't have your service pistol yet, you need to stay with Chloe. Leave for London right after breakfast and be back by dark. As I said, it's obvious you have an eye for seeing things others don't, going by your file and what I've seen, so I want you to check the area surrounding the murder. You two should be back before the inspector gets home."

As he finished, Chloe turned the volume back up on her smile at the same time I did. *Was gating considered a date? What do you wear when you gate?*

The funny thing was that Ed could tell what I was thinking and was trying not to smile.

"Alright. Max, I about lost my breakfast my first time gating. I had a fry-up that morning. Seafood is always a fun precursor to your first gate," Chloe teased as she looked down at her phone, obviously getting a message from the inspector on his way out.

"You get used to gating," Ed reassured me. "When you get back, we'll plan a trip to the Blue House. I didn't want to talk about it in front of the inspector, but the Blue House is a private club in Riverplace Tower for Mages and Earthborn Wizards only. They don't allow Vamps, Ethereals, or other creatures in there.

"When you want in, take the elevator. It will tell you're an Earthborn Mage and let you into the restaurant. It isn't a bad place; you just need to be on your toes. Warlocks and independent Mages frequent it," Ed said, talking to both of us. "It's owned by one Mr. Goolsby, if that helps explain things. I know Phil has mentioned him."

You could tell Ed and Chloe knew each other by the way he talked to her. I bet they had worked together before.

"I get it. Will there be an issue once we are in?" I asked, starting to get more interested in this place by the minute.

"No," Ed declared, looking like he had forgotten something. "You need to have your papers and badge on you. Kim, from the marshal's office, had your badge delivered a few days ago. We have to wait till you get the qualifications for your pistol, but I will give you the badge. The sooner you meet Kim, the better. When you leave this house, you need to have that badge on you, especially since you are officially on the case. If anyone asks, just show them the badge and state you're on official business like we discussed a few days ago."

Chloe looked over at me, raising an eyebrow and taking a deep breath while sneaking a glance back down at her phone.

"I want you two leaving shortly. Make sure it's not too late. Chloe is one of the star apprentices in the program," Ed informed me, "and by all reports has a knack for gating. If it's not going to work, she'll know, if you get my drift. Oh, and, Chloe, before I go, thanks for telling Max I'm having trouble reading his thoughts." With that, he turned and left.

Chloe's jaw dropped. "Shit, he surprises me every time. No way." She tapped her fingers on the table. I figured this was her thing to do when she was thrown off. "How did he know? I don't think he was getting that from you. I was sitting here thinking about it. You know, that ass was the one who taught me how to scramble Mind Mages."

"Chances are he knows about my little secret as well. He's a good man. Like the inspector," I said, chuckling a little and trying to ease the mood.

Even if Ed knew about Petro, it was my secret…well, maybe Chloe's as well until he wanted to say something, or I was ready to give it up. Maybe that wasn't the point, and Ed was seeing how I would react. I think the fact that I didn't freak out about it was a good thing. The only thing I needed now was a paycheck.

Chloe cracked a smile. "You're right. They both are. Inspector Holder is a good man. I thought he faked not having powers at first, but he really doesn't. He may look frumpy, but when you see him in action, it's another story. And Ed actually offered to sponsor me at one point, but I had to go with another diviner.

"The Dunn and the Atheneum have worked closely for as long as they have been in existence. From what I gather, they used to be one and the same. You know, pre-1776. That bugger has been messing with me the whole time. He likes to have the cards in his favor. You know, with the Balance coming in the near future, they are cataloging what all of us can and cannot do. He's been bluffing a little," she said as we stood up, wearing pride on her face while talking about both men.

She admired them, but you could tell it was for different reasons. "Let's meet in the entrance in fifteen minutes. I need a few to freshen up," Chloe concluded.

Setting out, I headed to the house to get cleaned up and grab a few things. I also wanted to talk to Petro for a minute. It was finally feeling as if I was a part of the team and not just interviewing anymore. Things were solidifying by the minute, and I could feel the weight of the work ahead bearing down on me.

On my way to the house, I started really thinking about what to bring. *Blazer, yup. No pistol...hmm, sword? Nah, too obvious.* I was starting to think I needed to carry everything with me. *Would a fanny pack be too much?*

Arriving at the kitchen, I called out to Petro under my breath. As I walked into the main hall, he came buzzing down the stairs, landing on the small water fountain.

"Hey, Petro," I greeted, seeing that he looked a little disheveled. "You busy?"

"Not much. Just getting things ready. I got two ladies coming over from the smart lady's house tonight. That's right, two. Lucky me," he bragged.

His voice had a way of projecting into a room, especially one as quiet as this one; the only other noise you could hear was from the water fountain, which wasn't large—about three foot by three foot with a globe on top and water slowly coming out.

"Hey, boss, how about that big screen?" he asked.

"Tell you what. You have room for a really big screen? It's

temporary, but it will do for now," I replied, thinking I needed to keep my promise.

I had a midsize tablet sitting in my room that I really didn't use much. It was hooked up to the amazingly fast Wi-Fi in the building. I wonder if I was paying for that.

"Sure thing, I have plenty of room. I'll come up with you and get it," Petro said, jumping off the globe and landing on my shoulder.

I walked past the fountain, heading up the stairs to the office and my room. He had a great sense of balance, and I noticed he hadn't landed on me until I'd put the palm of my hand up. I think it was some type of universal symbol for "it's all right to climb all over me."

"Hey, so I hear you're gating later tonight?" he asked, looking at me. "What do you have going on tonight? You hanging out with that pretty lady?" He had a little bit of smoothness in his voice.

"As a matter of fact, I am. Then tomorrow, we're going to London," I bragged right back, as I had no one else to talk to. "I don't really know how to gate, but I'm about to find out."

Petro let out a short laugh, sounding like a little kid giggling. "You know, gating is easy. You humans just can't do it a lot. Ethereals can, though. We'll see how you handle it. I know how to make a little something-something that will make it a little easier on you and also help you recover faster. If you don't mind, I'll take some ingredients out of your box and some old fairy dust and whip something right up. I'll show you how to make it too."

"Sounds like a plan," I said, knowing he was going to get into my stuff and do it anyway.

"That reminds me, I went to the lab today. There are a ton of old spell books and even a spot for what looks like a

Pixie workspace. It was meant to be, by the stars above!" Petro exclaimed, happy that he could help me out.

"See how fast you can throw that potion together. I want to know how it affects me first. I'd like to have it for tomorrow," I said as he hovered off my shoulder.

Walking into the office, I started thinking about the rest of the night. I figured asking Petro for dating advice would probably not go well. Grabbing the blazer, my wallet, and a few other items, I set my phone down to charge. It apparently didn't need much, as my body had partially charged it. I also started getting actual official emails.

Checking the phone, I saw an email from Phil. It was a picture. He was flipping me off with a bottle in his hand and throwing up some rock and roll devil horns, asking where I was. I replied with a simple *going to gate*.

Phil followed up with a frowning emoji. Did he not know that grown men weren't supposed to send each other emojis? I had a problem with that. He was a weird kind of guy, though, a man stuck between two worlds. I typed, *When I get back, I'll give you a shout*, knowing he would be passed out by then.

In my little bathroom, I checked out my hair and sprayed cologne on the shirt I had picked out for the evening. *This will have to do*, I thought. Tomorrow, it would be time to put my game face on. Tonight, it was time to do magic and hopefully not make a fool of myself. "Gods and graves," I muttered to the mirror.

Heading out of my room, I picked up the old tablet and walked into the office. I spent a few minutes showing Petro how to use it while he sat on the desk impatiently staring. It wasn't a phone, but as it was hooked to the Wi-Fi. Lastly, I showed him how to use a texting app in case he needed me. I had assumed correctly he knew how to write due to all his talk about spell books. Once I was done, he was rubbing his hands while flying in a circle.

"Petro, we'll catch up when I get back. When are these folks coming over?" I asked him, actually wondering if they would be loud.

"Way late. You'll be asleep. Pixies don't get out much during the day on Earth. They have stuff to do," Petro said as he grabbed the tablet and started rubbing his hands on it, making it light up.

"All good. When I get back, I'm going to the lab, and I want you there," I told him, looking over as I kept walking out the room, figuring he would get the tablet where it needed to go and had ways around the house that did not involve doors.

About nine minutes later and a few seconds to spare, I was in the entrance hall of the Atheneum. Chloe stood there looking as if she hadn't worked a full day. I kept forgetting that this trip was only going to take a few minutes.

Standing there, she explained to me the intricacies of going through a gate.

"Unlike lighting candles, as I hear you can do, gates have already been set up. They are tied to specific areas, so one really doesn't have to think much about it. I hear the Postern has a special gate that will let you go to and from about anywhere as long as you have a key there. The Evergate, I think it's called. There are Spatial Mages who specialize in making gates. It's actually considered advanced magic, and it takes skill." Chloe paused, waiting for my response.

"So how about these Ethereals I keep hearing about, like Ned?" I asked, thinking about all the new types of people and things I had recently learned about.

"Great question. Earthborn Mages are more tied to gates than others. Ethereals, for example, can pretty much gate anywhere as long as they know where they're going and if they're strong enough. In most cases, they can gate here, then it takes them a while to build up enough power to go back. That is, unless the location is warded, like the Atheneum," Chloe explained, pursing her lips.

"Sometimes, it's just like having a reverse ward," she said, breaking it down to a kindergarten level. "It depends on how it's set up. You push some of your will into it to activate the gate, but some are keyed for specific people. Also, there are registered and unregistered gates. These are registered. From what I understand, that's one of the issues with the Balance talks. They want to close all unregistered gates."

As noted, the gate at the front of the house was tied to only a handful of locations: the Dunn, Jacksonville, New York, San Francisco, and lastly, the Council halls. According to Chloe, you could only have so many locations go out of one gate before it became unstable. I really didn't understand, but nodded my head as I watched her lips.

"A gate is a transition point between locations that passes through the Plane. That's what makes the trip so short. Time to go," Chloe finished, the educational portion of the lesson over.

As we got ready to gate, Chloe held her hand up and whispered, "*Porta*." The door began to shimmer. She then raised her hand again. "*Prope*." Closing the gate back, Chloe explained that closing the gate was just as important as opening it. If you didn't close it, the gate would still close, just not as fast. "Your turn."

Raising my hand, I pushed out my will and loudly said, "*Porta*," flicking my wrist as the gate shimmered into life. I smiled. Looking over, I made a gun out of my index finger, blowing the fake smoke out of the barrel, earning another smile. She obviously knew I was going to get the gate to work.

"Lucky you. It took me two weeks to figure that one out.

Let's go," she said, a wry smile on her face.

Seeing someone walk through a gate and actually going through one were absolutely two separate things. It was like walking into a cold shower with no water running. Like cool steam, almost. The other part was a slight tug you could feel in your stomach, though not as strong as walking through the wards at the Atheneum. Those took a little piece away from you, same as the wards at FA's. You could see the opening as soon as you walked through, just a couple feet forward. I didn't stop to look around; just kept moving.

We popped out the other side of the gate under the Main Street Bridge. I fell on my knees immediately and, like clockwork, reintroduced my dinner to the world in a spray of seafood. Chloe took a quick step to the left, obviously knowing before we went through that I was going to lose my dinner.

I looked up. "Thanks for the warning," I said, wiping the rest of the mess off my chin, embarrassed. She was avoiding the scene of my dinner.

"You're fine. That was great. I remember, my first few tries, I couldn't even get the bloody gate to work. So, was it everything you thought it would be?" She beamed.

Smiling and blushing, I began to stand up, quickly realizing what everyone was talking about. You know that feeling you get fresh out of bed in the morning, when you have to stretch before you get going? The one where you could just as easily stay still and get another few minutes in before you got up to be fully recharged? That's how it felt.

Standing up, I stretched and straightened myself out. "It was great. Actually, that tall building on the other side of the river is Riverplace Tower. You could walk from the gate."

"The Blue House," Chloe confirmed as she started smiling, looking at the building.

"That's right. Looks like an easy walk."

"If you actually walk around the corner, the marshal's field office is about half a block away; it's tucked away over there. Let's head back for now. The gate is still open. Let's go," Chloe said.

Passing back through the gate, I thought, slowly shaking my head, that I always knew how to show a lady a good time. Chloe turned around and closed it behind her.

The trip back generated the same feeling as before, minus the food coming back up.

We stood in the entryway as Chloe looked at me. "How was your first time?"

"I don't know," I replied. "We'll have to do it again sometime. My head is spinning a little, and I feel like I need to go lie down and read that journal Gramps left till I pass out."

"Tom left you some reading material?" Chloe asked. "I know he used to talk about that Fountain of Youth journal all the time. I always wanted to see what he had found on it. If you get bored of it, let me know. I would love to take a look at it for an evening."

She was much like everyone else, interested in old superstitions and lost places. I had a feeling most of them had been real at some point, but most importantly, I had just found a conversation starter with Chloe.

She followed my banter faster than I could dish it out, always one step ahead of me by knowing my thoughts. "It's a date, then. Pick me up at ten tomorrow morning. I'll see you tomorrow," she said before she walked away.

I texted Ed that I was alive, minus the dinner. In Ed fashion, he told me that he knew I would do well and expected as much with the dinner.

I was truly tired and thinking about not going to the lab,

but with my lack of personal time lately, I decided if I didn't do it tonight, I wouldn't have another chance for a few days. After all, I was going to London tomorrow.

The entire episode had only lasted about ten minutes. I gave Petro the nod to let him know I needed his assistance, walking into my office. He still looked disheveled as he came flying out of nowhere.

"Petro, how's it going? You ready for your company later?" I asked, looking at him.

"Sure thing, boss. The TV is set up, and the golden food is laid out. Let me tell you, tonight is going to be a great night," he said at a normal cadence.

"You know you can call me Max," I huffed, finally figuring out he couldn't let "boss" go. I was starting to believe he looked at us as part of a working relationship. "All right, I have to get up early in the morning; however, I want to check this lab out," I told him, jaunting over to the desk.

"Sure thing," Petro replied as he disappeared under the desk, releasing a latch with a loud clank. "Man, that desk has all kinds of buttons and gizmos on it. Let's get a move on. I have places to be and things to do. You see my hair?" he asked, heading toward the small crack in the wall behind the bar.

The crack was about an inch thick. Looking at the bar, I thought about how much I needed a drink, but reminded myself of the risk associated with going over to see Phil. A good night's sleep was the better course of action.

As I pulled the door open with my hand, a damp, musty breeze came up from the spiraling staircase in front of me. It looked like a small fireplace that had been hollowed out. Two turns down the stairs, and there, right in front of me, stood the overhang I had to duck under. Petro was right. After that, the room opened up, and there it was…my own secret lab. All I needed now was a cat to sit on my lap and pet while I figured out how to take over the world. I couldn't help but thinking to myself how crazy all this was.

Petro flew in and yelled, "*Ignis!*" forcing the massive fireplace at the end of the room to ignite. Looking around, I realized Petro was right again. The lab was roughly the same size as the room above, with the fireplace in the exact location. *A two-story fireplace?* I thought to myself. The one upstairs was closed in. Being a Floridian, I had no interest in checking it out unless it got under seventy degrees.

Like many other rooms in the house, the lab looked like it was in the building but didn't quite fit. The math was not working out in my head. How did it fit under the office with the ceiling height under us and the entrance as high as it was? An inch here, a foot there, who knows? Maybe later I would solve the mysteries of the world and find out what the real, true meaning of life was besides a number.

Taking the rest of the room in, it seemed to not have electricity, and the walls had oddly placed candles. I decided to give it a shot, raising my hand up and saying, "*Ignis.*" The candles sprang to life with the quick pop of ozone. Petro and I used the same word. Everyone was different, but I guess we both liked Latin.

"Good job, boss. You're all over this stuff," Petro praised as he zipped over to the far edge of the room.

The fireplace was at the far end of the space. *The room is set up oddly*, I thought. In the center of the room, similar to Jenny's lab, was a large inlaid pentagram on the floor. On the right, where the desk would be upstairs, stood a tall working table with candles and papers laid out on it. The table also had wheels so it could be moved about the room. Petro had set my new box on the corner.

To the left, there was a small cauldron the size of a basketball with a gas burner under it. The fireplace also had a small cast-iron bowl hanging over the fire which you could slide over and easily access.

On the walls, there were cluttered shelves full of random books, canisters, and odd-looking artifacts dangling everywhere. There was just a general sense that someone came down here and worked, not cleaning up before they left in a hurry. If you've ever seen a picture of Einstein's desk, you'll notice nine times out of ten it was a disaster.

In the corner, true to Petro's word, there was a tiny table that stood by itself with a small cauldron the size of a softball cut in half next to a miniature cabinet full of small books.

"See, I told you, boss. Just my size. Gods above, this is a gift to us. It was meant to be. You should see some of the books in here. Some of the spells are straight from the Plane. I can't even read some of these. It's crazy no one has been using this place. It's a little spooky," Petro gushed.

There was a small pot boiling on his table with a blue glow coming from it. The room had an odd moldy smell to it, not the mossy, earthy smell the rest of the house had. There was obviously dampness in the air that was not supposed to be there. *Note to self...I need to come down and let the fire burn to dry out the air and clean up some. Maybe Petro would be game to help. I'll ask later.*

I went over to the large working table and noticed a chart of the Postern with a handwritten book of old notes on it, the type with a leather clasp. *Bingo*—notes on the Postern. I grabbed the book and rolled up the sketch. It was still throwing me off why no one had used this room in so long.

"Petro, you sure no one has used this room in...what, ten years?" I asked, starting to get suspicious.

"Yup. Pixies can tell the last time someone was in a room. Plus, the embers in the fire haven't been lit for at least as long," he said proudly. "By the way, the gate potion will be ready by morning. I'll leave it on your desk. Just drink it down, and you'll be good to go."

By all accounts, Tom's actual lab was in another room, warded and locked. Maybe this was his old laboratory? The house was very old and had had more than one owner, according to Ed.

"It's getting late. I got to get some rest," I sighed, heading out of the room and telling Petro to turn off the lights behind me while he stood there, resolute.

Petro had a way of getting around. Over the short few days of his companionship, I trusted he would close up shop. Getting cleaned up and lying down, I put the notebook on the nightstand, floating off to sleep listening to Planes Drifter.

CHAPTER 13

London Bridge Is Burning Down

"Good morning, Max," Jenny greeted as I walked into the offices and saw everyone busy at work. "We need to chat about your lab results when you get back. You're not dying or anything; I just need to run a few more checks."

"Good to see you too, doc," I replied, noticing Frank sitting at one of the empty desks in the middle of the room busy at work, beating the computer keyboard as if it had offended him somehow. "No problem, as long as I get back in one piece. Full house this morning, I see."

Jenny nodded and ushered me back to the conference room. Who would have thought they actually used it after all the time spent in the dining room? I walked to the back, hearing Ed and Phil's voices. Passing by Frank, I gave him a nod. "Morning, Frank," I said, apparently in too happy of a tone for Frank to handle.

"What's got you so happy, pretty boy?" Frank answered without looking away from his work, still typing at a furious pace. He was reading, typing, and talking all at the same time with no signs of movement. Vampires...what can I say? Creepy. "Everyone was in here early this morning, except you. The crew had a call in the conference room—something came in overnight. Your boy Phil looked rough. Good thing he had some clearing potion in his drawer," he continued, talking to me as if I were nothing more than an afterthought.

I walked past the crucible room with all the monitors and the ever-present box to where Ed and Phil were sitting in the conference room. The room could fit about ten people at the round table with one of those fancy call systems in the middle and dry-erase boards on the walls. The scent of freshly brewed coffee hung in the room like a dinner bell calling everyone home.

"Ah, Max, busy morning," Ed greeted as he looked over Phil's shoulder at a tablet.

Phil glanced up with a sluggish gaze. You could tell he was being driven by nothing more than coffee. "Morning, bruther. Sorry about the late text. Had a little bit of a reunion with some old friends to talk about Old Penny," he said in a low tone.

"No problem," I replied, already having had two cups of coffee. "To be honest, I'm a little jealous. With everything else going on, the only chance I've had to cut loose was on my birthday. I wish I could have been there," I said, reassuring Phil we would catch up later.

Ed looked over at me, all business. "Max, here's the deal. We actually received a lot of material from Phil's field trip yesterday, got some good information, and links to the Genesis have appeared again. I have reached out to all my trusted contacts; it's time to get a few members of the Council involved. We all need to be careful because we don't really know who is at play. Roots have been planted here by many powerful people, and the connection you and Chloe found makes me suspect this very well may be tied to something or someone close by. You see, there is a reason the Atheneum is here. It's called the 'First Coast' for a reason, and St. Augustine is the oldest city in the US. It's a hub for the Magical community in the US, for older families and, let's just say, *things*."

I didn't have much to say to that, so I decided to ask about the call. "Who was on the call? Anything I need to be in on?"

"Rubbish," Phil spoke up. "You're one of us, mate. You're already in on it. Kim wanted to speak with us this morning to discuss your find on the Blue House. She doesn't want any trouble in her city but can 'smell it in the air,' as she put it. That lass is smart, mind you."

"Yes, and that takes me to my next point," Ed interjected. "Last night, we received a message from the NCTS. Vestulie apparently requested Ezra's body, per company policy, and it was approved. They literally just left. That's why everyone was up; nothing to concern you. We had Frank come in from the practice to work out where they are going. Something isn't sitting right with me."

I started shaking my head, trying to digest everything I was hearing.

"Kim was furious. Not sure why, but I second the notion. Very odd. One more thing. Max, be careful in London. I don't expect you to be gone long, and for the love of God, stop giving Chloe the eye. She's a grown woman, and this isn't a bar." He gave me a warning look. "She's in the main entrance, by the way. Waiting," Ed finished.

Phil looked at me and smiled. "Max and Chloe, sitting in a tree, K.I.S.S.—" Ed gave him a sharp look, stopping the rest of the rhyme.

I had to admit, I was a little bit more spruced up than I usually was: the blazer, a dark pair of jeans, and the only other dress shirt I owned, sporting the badge on my belt, following along with the others. I had even put on a nice, shined pair of square-tipped cowboy boots. No sword, though; just the ball

Trish had given me in my pocket. I felt official and ready to make the trip.

Ed made sure to tell me that I should only be about five hours before I left. On my way to the exit, I downed the sweet potion Petro had left out for me, reading the note he had written stating that I would not be getting my tablet back due to technical issues. I guess I would find out later what that was all about. Saying my goodbyes, I walked out of the office, stopping in the break room for another cup of coffee.

"Morning, Max," Chloe greeted as I walked up. She was wearing an official-looking dark navy suit with her service pistol on her waist and her badge hanging around a chain on her neck. I guess the badge on the belt clip was considered business casual.

"Hey, hope you slept well. Looks like there was some excitement last night," I said, walking up and goofily reaching out to shake her hand. Of course, she knew I would and made it seem effortless.

"Yes, I heard. I know Ed wasn't in a cheeky mood earlier. He gets fired up quickly when he is told what to do. Either way, we need to get going. Hope you avoided leftover seafood for breakfast," Chloe teased, the radiant smile finally making an appearance on her face as she held her hand up toward the gate, willing it to life.

"Ladies first," I said, thinking she would know I wasn't going to lose my stomach contents again.

We both walked through the gate. Much to my surprise, I didn't feel sick at all. I didn't even have the sluggish feeling I'd experienced the night before. *Man, Petro, A-plus. You can mess up my tablet any day*, I thought.

Looking around, I saw it wasn't as eventful as I had built it in my mind to be. We had gated into the Dunn. The room looked more like a police station than the old castle we had just left.

Much like the one in the Atheneum, the gate appeared to be in the front entrance. Instead of a fountain, in the middle of the space was a working security desk with a few monitors, accompanied by a smiling older woman named Karen. She was dressed in a police uniform, a high-visibility jacket hanging from the back of her chair.

The entrance was large and had a cool, damp feel to it, almost as if someone was skimping on the gas to save a few dollars on the bill. The smell of fresh cinnamon hung in the air—not just a little here and there, walk to the other side of the room and get a little less, but a consistent, heady scent scattered equally throughout the space. The smell reminded me that I needed to talk to my folks when I got back. We usually had a big get-together during the fall, and I hadn't had much time to discuss it with them yet.

The walls and floor were old, albeit neat and orderly. This was a working facility, and unlike the Atheneum, I highly doubted anyone stayed here other than Chloe. It was more official.

The double doors behind the entrance desk had a sign stating *Employees Only*. The floor was comprised of off-white tiles printed with a black, classic, royal crest design. They looked extremely symmetrical, and I had a feeling if I had an overhead view, they would form some type of picture. The walls had wood paneling up to about waist level, where white tiles took over the rest of the space. The ceilings, oddly enough, were stone and had several supporting arches spread out in various locations, namely the second floor, which you could not access from the entrance. Employees only, I guessed.

"Morning, Chloe," Karen greeted in a thick Liverpool accent mixed with some type of American background. I bet she had spent some time in the States. "This must be Max," she said, cutting Chloe off before she could introduce us.

Karen was warm and friendly while also having a mother's caution on her face. I did my quick analysis and landed on liking her. "Hey, Karen, nice to meet you. Think they could turn the heat on for you in here?" I asked, shaking her hand and fighting off a chill.

"Right," Karen bellowed. "A man after my own heart. Dick had these new fancy thermostats put in that only run if the room is cold enough. Supposedly energy efficient. I think it's to keep us miserable and awake."

"That's Inspector Holder," Chloe corrected Karen in a dance for domination in front of me. "I know a little trick to get them to come on. Where's everyone?" she asked, looking around.

"Yes, they're all out for the morning. We had an OTN call come in from Spain. They headed to the embassy a while ago. It may be tied to our case. Ed sent a message a few minutes ago, telling me you two wouldn't be here all day. That reminds me. Chloe, Di—Inspector Holder wants you to stay here until they confirm what happened in Barcelona," Karen informed, correcting herself at the last moment.

Chloe thanked her, and we walked past the doors behind the desk into a long hallway that had names listed on the wall to identify the offices. The second door on the right was Chloe's.

"So what's Karen's deal? Is she a diviner like you?" I asked, watching Chloe get a pad of paper and a bulky satellite phone out of her desk and place them into a one-strap field backpack. The pack appeared to be no fuller than before. Man, I needed one of those the next time I went to a concert. I could fit a stash of beer in there.

"She's a good cook and one hell of a beat cop. Other than that, she is as normal as that pair of boots you have on. Her brother, on the other hand, was another story. He was a Warlock—I stress the *was* part—and not a very nice one at that. He got caught doing necromancy. Karen's a regular, but she grew up around all of this. One night, we showed up after we got a call that a Vamp had gotten a little crazy in Soho, and there she stood, like everything was business as usual. Karen explained she'd had to put him down before the other officers saw. She had no clue about us. Craziest thing I've ever seen.

"You know suicide by cop? Well, vamps can do the same thing. She single-handedly took out a blood-drunk Vamp. I couldn't do that at the time. When we got around to talking to Karen, Ed actually came and interviewed her. She told us about her family, and well, the rest is history. She's been here ever since. That was about four years ago. I was still a rookie," Chloe explained, heading to the door.

"Y'all seem to be more official than the team back home?" I said in the form of a question. "You are…real police?"

"We are, and so are you to a degree. Look, the Atheneum functions in a more advisory-type role. The issue is, with everything that has been going on, that role is changing. The Balance everyone keeps talking about is also challenging that role. Your marshals do a good job, but as you may know, there are only a handful of them. London is much older than the States, and we are much more integrated. Don't think so linearly. Remember, at the end of the day, we're all part of the Council. Say what you want, but we all report to the CSA. Plus, I think some people like Ed are probably older than the States and at one point called this place home. Get your head wrapped around that two-ton pile of confusion," Chloe concluded.

Leaving the Dunn, we got into a small, unmarked car that was as bland as my love life. Well, hopefully that would change. Nonetheless, it was probably the most boring vehicle I had ever seen.

We drove through London, heading to Victoria Park. Penny, as Phil called him, had been killed on the northeast side of the park behind a small bar and brewery.

"Can we gate there?" I asked Chloe as she slammed through the gears on the manual transmission of the small Ford.

"I didn't want to gate, as it may tip off someone that we are in the area, and getting there the old-fashioned way is better. Plus, you get to see some of the city. You'll learn soon enough that gating all the time will eventually catch up with you," Chloe warned, letting out some additional colorful words directed at a delivery truck that had cut her off.

Arriving at the park, Chloe and I left the vehicle in the main lot and headed toward Victoria Road to scout out the location. She seemed to be on edge about something, walking fast while constantly looking at her phone. I was starting to think she had a boyfriend. Maybe I just needed to focus on the fact that I was there to look at a murder scene.

"Penny for your thoughts," I said, making a joke of the victim's name that landed flat.

"Something doesn't feel right," Chloe replied as she slowed down, giving me a chance to catch up. "The murder and ritual took place in a shed over there, behind that building. I say we look around the park then head over. This place was combed thoroughly, so I'm not sure what Ed wants you to look for," she said as we walked behind the small brewery heading past a taped-off shed.

"For all I know, he just wants to get me out of the house," I joked, keeping in step. "To be honest, I think he wants me to think outside the box here and see what my gut is telling me. Ed was clear that he didn't want me worrying about the main scene, so that tells me he has plenty of confidence in you. Is there a gate close by or one of those unregistered ones?"

"I asked Karen to look into it. Other than the registered gate we use in the center of the park, there's only one other, and it's across Victoria Road near the school. It's tracked, and we already checked to see if it was used recently. No such luck. We also checked the CCTV feeds near Hackney, and there's no record of anyone using it around that time," she said as we continued walking into the tree-covered path.

I had a feeling she was looking at the near future.

Observing the tree line, I noticed that the path to and from the shed was covered and easily provided concealment for anyone waiting to catch a target by surprise. I also noticed the lack of any ambient noise. No birds, cars, dogs, nothing.

"Hey, Chloe. London is a loud, big-ass city. Am I the only one who notices it's as quiet as a library around here?" I asked, not immediately realizing that Chloe had her service pistol out and was scanning the tree line.

"Max, get behind me now. Something's not right. I can't see anything past a few seconds. Check your phone. Are you getting a signal?" she ordered in a serious tone.

My heart started to race, and my hands started to sweat. I grabbed my phone and confirmed the lack of signal. "No, nothing. I don't think I could even get a call out."

"Someone has us in a weird type of containment field. We need to run for it now. Follow me."

I glanced toward the tree line, figuring she could see the outcome of us running through her use of divination.

When Chloe turned to head back toward the building, I realized that we had walked far into the park, trees surrounding us on all sides. It was at least five hundred meters back to the brewery.

The air was stale, and the sounds of the city had all but disappeared. All I could smell was the light hint of my cologne and the aroma of damp earth that had recently seen rain.

"Get down!" Chloe screamed, pulling me instinctively as

a ball of solid water the size of a basketball went flying by at impossible speed, splashing into the tree behind me and making the bark fly off with a loud *whoosh* sound.

The air fizzled and hummed with power as the smell of ozone drifted from the now shattered tree.

"What the hell was that?" I asked as Chloe leveled her service pistol at the trees.

"That came from a strong Mage. It was meant to knock one of us out. Shhh…I'm trying to concentrate."

As soon as she said those words, another spell was released. This time, a glowing green sphere of hissing, dripping liquid that smelled like sulfur went flying to the right of us, slightly overhead. Flames immediately burst to life from the green liquid the ball had dropped, forcing us to move to the left.

As a former military guy, I knew that wasn't good. My hands started shaking; however, it wasn't from fear. I was burning up.

I heard another sound that must have been a spell being cast. Chloe opened up with her pistol, letting out a bark of hushed bullets, multiple rounds leaving in quick succession. The noise of the spells being cast sounded like a light flush of a toilet. I turned to see Chloe shaking her head.

"I hit him square in the chest; he's got a shield up. We need to go now. I knew I should have brought backup," she muttered a moment too late, as the second person that we hadn't seen behind us grabbed me by the right shoulder.

His grip was like a hydraulic claw, setting itself deep into my shoulder with no chance of release. The large man was well over six feet tall, as he pulled me up to my feet with no effort, freezing my body momentarily in place.

The few seconds he held me up felt like an eternity as I

took in his appearance.

He was a large, squarely built man with hard edges and bulk on top of natural muscle, the kind you saw in hardworking farmers after a lifetime of heavy lifting. He was dressed in a trench coat and had a ballistic vest on underneath. The man's face was stern, square and strong like the rest of him. Looking closer, I saw his eyes were black pools of nothing, lending to the hard, angular lines on the rest of his face.

Chloe rolled out from the bush we were using as cover and opened herself up to the other perpetrator, hoping to make them expose their location. The huge man holding me up went for my arms, so I grabbed his wrist. As soon as I did, a bloodred flame engulfed my hands, as I squeezed his forearm with everything I had.

Chloe threw out a bark as she lunged toward the other person, releasing the rest of her magazine. Several shots obviously landed this time around, as confirmed by several wet thumps followed by a low growl and the sound of retreating footsteps.

The smell of burning flesh was unmistakable, sweet and pungent all at the same time. The hair, the meat, the bones. I knew this smell from my deployments. Grabbing the large man's wrist, I pushed my will out as I had with the candles, but this time, directed toward the person.

The flesh melted away under my grip all the way to the bone within a handful of seconds. Looking in horror, I could see a steaming gap in his forearm with nothing but burnt bone connecting a normal-looking hand and forearm. As fast as it had happened, it was over, and my hand stopped burning.

The large man let out a loud howl of pain and dropped me, clutching the now charred remains of his forearm. Chloe had reloaded another magazine by then, and as soon as I was on the ground, she let out another round of silent barks from the pistol. It was a machine made for killing.

The man looked up with intense, glowing black eyes and disappeared into thin air, leaving the bullets to pass through and land in the tree behind where he was standing with a crack and whip sound. It was over.

Immediately after the large man left, the sound came back, with traffic and birds chirping filling the empty void.

"We have to go. Now," Chloe declared, as we headed toward Victoria Road.

We ran side by side without any regard to what might have been behind us. Making it to the brewery, Chloe pulled out a flat stone and threw it on the ground, immediately opening a gate that we, without hesitation or thought, both ran through.

As we caught our breath standing in the lobby of the Dunn, Karen looked up, saw our condition, and made a call before coming over to us.

"What the hell was that?" I panted between breaths. Chloe was already on her phone, talking to Inspector Holder, I assumed. She hung up after a moment turning to me.

"That was, from what I could tell, an attempt to either kill us or kidnap us. Someone knew we were coming. We didn't gate in, and only a handful of people knew of our presence. The inspector is heading back; we have another linked murder on our hands in Spain. What the hell did you do to that man?" Chloe asked.

I looked down at my hands, realizing they were smooth as if nothing had happened. In reality, I had just about burned a man's hand off with nothing more than a little anger and determination.

He was trying to do harm to us, I rationalized. "I don't know. I just grabbed him and got really pissed."

"That flame was bloodred. Like hellfire or something.

I've never seen fire that color. You melted that man's arm, Max," Chloe said, coming to terms with what she had witnessed pretty quickly.

I was starting to feel like Chloe was more in control of the situation than I may have thought, though I quickly dispelled the thought, as she was truly surprised.

"Max, you need to go back to the Atheneum. Something is going on; someone tipped those folks off. Plus, there was another murder."

As I started to respond, my phone chirped to life with a text from Ed calling me back. I was actually surprised the team wasn't coming here to check out the scene of the attack. *The bad guys seem to have a way of knowing where we are*, I thought to myself sighing.

CHAPTER 14

The Devil Is in the Details

"What the hell happened?" Ed demanded without giving me time to take a breath as I stepped out of the gate.
The whole crew was there, Phil with his pistols hanging off each hip and a lit cigarette in his mouth, and Ed and Jenny looking more aggravated.

"You know what," I snapped. "I just about got killed. Oh, and someone knew I was coming. You want to know what the hell happened? I'll tell you. Over the past two weeks, I've met Vampires, realized magic is real, started fire with my hands, moved into this creepy house, and almost got killed by a water-wielding maniac. Oh yeah, and on top of that, I grabbed a man and burned his arm to the bone. That's how the hell my day has gone so far. Oh! And before I forget, I have a Pixie working for me as well," I finished, letting out the day's frustration. I quickly passed the three standing there with their mouths hanging open.

It was time to go to the office to talk with Petro and get a drink. I could hear Ed and Jenny on my way up the stairs. "Let him cool off," Jenny whispered to Ed as they walked toward the offices.

Phil decided on another route to intercept me, catching up with me by the time I turned the corner upstairs to head to the house. He stopped me when we arrived at the kitchen door.

"Bruther, that was a little harsh; we've been worried sick. As soon as your phone signal went out, we could tell you were in a field. It set off all kinds of alarms. Karen called when you got back to the Dunn. Apparently, you and Chloe stood there for a few minutes getting yourselves together, which was enough time for me to grab my babies. Word travels fast. I was about to head that way when you popped up back here," Phil said with his finger in my chest.

He was becoming a good friend, and as I had learned in the army, good friends told you when you're being a jerk.

"All right, man. It's just, gods and graves, that was some real-world magic shit," I exhaled as I opened the door.

Phil was still chewing on a lit cigarette, putting it out as we passed through the kitchen. The guy could carry on a full conversation without taking the smoke out of his mouth.

"You have a Pixie? One of those blokes from the Postern or the freezer?" Phil asked with a slight tone of admiration.

He immediately walked to the bar, grabbing two Vamp Ambers. I had stocked the fridge with a few beers and hadn't had a chance to enjoy them. Phil grabbed one of the chairs, while I clunked down at the desk. We kicked our feet up on the table, both taking a pull from our beers.

The thing about fights was that while they seemed to take an eternity for the people participating in them, in reality, most only lasted a few seconds. I told Phil the whole story, while he sat there listening. Doing so was actually calming me down, and by the end, I had more questions than complaints. The only comment Phil had made was that everyone knew that Chloe and I were "making eyes" at each other, whatever that meant.

"So what about this Pixie?" Phil inquired as both of our phones started chirping with messages from Ed telling us to come down to the crucible room for a video conference in thirty minutes.

"Petro," I called out loud, figuring as long as I had the charm on, he would come. Now that I thought about it, I still needed to test the distance thing. Petro, painted all red, came flying out of the bookcase wielding a small scalpel-like sword.

"Let's go. Let me at them!" Petro yelled, stopping a foot in front of Phil's face, who slowly raised his arms in surrender.

"Easy, mate, I surrender," Phil said, playing along with Petro. Honestly, I think he was a little apprehensive. I think these little guys could really do some damage.

"Hey, you're the strong Wiz that let us out of the room and freeze with the boss. My apologies," Petro said, lowering his head as Phil put his hand out palm up, allowing Petro to land and sheath his sword.

"Apology accepted, little warrior." Phil nodded. Petro jumped down to the desk and scanned me.

"I heard the news and was getting ready to come get you, boss," Petro insisted.

"Thanks, Petro, you're a true warrior," I praised, watching him push his chest out at my words. "Why are you painted red?"

"It's so my enemies can't see if I'm bleeding. Most Pixies on the Plane get painted before they go into battle. The ladies love it," Petro explained, brushing the hair out of his eye. "Oh yeah, the tablet. Things got out of hand last night. The smart lady's Pixies didn't seem to like my smooth talk. I told one she was pretty and then the other she was prettier. It was all downhill from there—the Pixie dust was flying—and they left early. Earth Pixies aren't easy."

"Petro," Phil started. "The smart lady? That's Jenny. If those are the two Pixies that live in her house...mate, I don't think you're their type."

"What do you mean? They don't like my hair or Plane Pixies?" Petro asked. It finally clicked for me.

"You see, they like—" Phil cut himself off, obviously figuring Petro wouldn't comprehend they were a couple. "Neither one of them will ever take a husband, Petro. I'm truly sorry."

"Old maids. They must be widows of warriors," Petro said, still not getting the hint. "I can respect that. I got to go since there is no fight. Man, we got to talk later, boss. You should have taken me with you." With that, Petro flew out of the room.

Phil and I sat in silence for a few seconds before both of us started chuckling at the same time, leading to hearty, deep laughs. Petro was entertaining, at least.

"I like him," Phil declared.

"Yeah, he grows on you," I agreed. "He makes a great gate potion. I didn't get sick gating either time today."

"You may have to get the little man to make some of that for me. A Pixie in your service is worth its weight in gold," Phil said as he stood up. "Let's go, bruther."

"Thanks, Phil." I stood, taking the final pull from my beer.

Walking into the crucible, I saw Phil give Ed the all-clear nod. Ed and Jenny stood in front of a monitor while Inspector Holder's face appeared on the left screen. Frank smoothly slipped in behind us, standing in the corner of the room.

"Can you hear me?" Inspector Holder asked, looking tired and hard-chinned all at the same time.

"Loud and clear," Jenny replied.

"Right, it's confirmed that Eater bloke has been at it again. I can't bring myself to explain the rest, so I'll let Chloe do that piece while I go stare at the sun," Inspector Holder said, obviously not comfortable with the situation.

"Ed, it's Devins's son," Chloe spoke up. Ed stood up, snapping to attention. The temperature in the room must have dropped about five degrees, and Frank let out a slow, hissing sound which made the hair on the back of my neck stand up.

"This is bad," Ed muttered as he looked at Jenny then up at Frank before finally resting his eyes on me. "We'll talk more about the details later, as it's out of our jurisdiction. Chloe, was he in one piece, or did the Eater take any brain matter with them from what you could tell?"

"It appears they took some with them. The body had been dead for some time, so Circes—" Ed sharply cut Chloe off.

"Got it. I suspect that since we have some knowledge of our perpetrator, we'll be getting a visit from the old man himself." As Ed talked, Frank walked out of the room. "Right. Chloe, take care of yourself; we will be in touch. You should have a package in your office by now. Talk to you later. Inspector Holder, any guidance from the team in Spain?"

"None, other than they want to keep it clean. The government understands the implications, and preparations have been made, whatever the hell that means," Holder informed.

"Got it. Thanks for the call. We will be in touch," Ed finished, as the monitor went blank.

"Let's go to the dining room; we need to discuss a few things," Ed ordered. The group stood up, walking out without saying a word. "Jenny, call Angel and tell her the news."

Whoever this Circes guy was, his death sounded like bad

news because everyone looked upset. Frank was already in the hall, and Jenny was calling Angel. I was starting to think Circes had been a Vampire. I guess my near-death experience was not that important all of a sudden.

Ed looked at me. "No, Max, that's exactly what's important," he said as we walked together.

When we took our seats in the dining room, Jenny waved her hands, closing the doors, and started to speak. "All right, everyone, take out your phones and set them in this bowl." She pulled out a wooden bowl with a lid on it, giving hers up first. Once all the phones had been taken, Jenny continued.

"Only the team here, Chloe, and the inspector knew of your trip, Max. Not even the marshals really knew what you were up to. While you and Phil were off talking, Ed and I did some thinking. The only other way for someone to detect what we were doing well enough to set up an ambush that would throw Chloe off is if someone had access to our communication devices. It's been done before."

"You're saying someone is intercepting our calls or texts?" I spoke, again stating the obvious but doing it to make sure it sank into my thought process and future actions.

"Precisely," Ed agreed. "Let me throw something out to the group. The Mags-Tech CEO is murdered. He is a staunch advocate for the Balance. Penny is murdered and his boss was the magistrate, the same. Circes is...*was* also in full support of the Balance and kept his father, Davros, who tolerates everything human, in line, albeit lightly. Max, we all knew Circes. He was a hero many times over, minus one little incident, and probably why Frank stormed out. He's the equivalent of George Washington to the Vamps."

I let out a whistle, finally getting a clearer picture. "Let me throw this in there. All this tech is supplied by Mags-Tech, and it was just taken over by a previously fairly unknown CIO. I would bet they have backdoors to all this devices and their information. Kind of scary, if you ask me," I told them, looking at Ed, who was tapping his finger on his lips.

"Perhaps, but I don't think we should jump the gun on that aspect. The gate in the entrance can't be tracked, but anyone with access to the systems could find your location if they were smart enough using your cell signal; we're all tracked that way. If someone's line goes dead, not off but truly flatlined, we are all alerted. That's how we knew you were in a field," Ed explained, all of a sudden reading my mind like a book.

I sat there for a minute looking around the group. Ed took advantage of the pause to continue his thoughts. "Max, you were not bait out there this morning. I had no clue. It was a chance to get you out of this house and into the field for a few. While we are on this subject, let's hear everything that happened."

For the next thirty minutes, I relived the morning the same way I had with Phil, remembering more details about the attackers.

"One thing that bothers me," Ed interjected, "is that field. It was roughly fifty meters round and able to cut off signal and sound." He sounded like he might have a clue as to who'd set the field. "That's the second time we've had a field involved in something related to the case, and as you all know, I don't believe in coincidences. Phil, you and I are going to pay Jayal a little visit this afternoon. No one outside this room is to know—this is local CSA only.

"Max, one last thing. Good job today. I know hurting someone with magic is tough and can get you in a lot of trouble, but I look forward to hearing more about this hellfire, as you call it. Lastly, please be careful what you transmit over the phone. We can use this to our advantage, but we're still not sure if that's even how we are being tracked. I'll get some of the old-style communicators rounded up. I should have them by tomorrow. Relax this evening," Ed finished, standing up.

I had taken the hellfire phrase from Chloe, and I was more than fine with an afternoon off. That was some serious firepower I had witnessed, not to mention what I had done. I wanted to experiment, but tonight was not the time. I actually planned on doing some research on the laptop and spending some time in the lab to see if Petro could teach me anything new. I wanted to find out more about the types of Mages out there.

As the group broke off, Jenny came over and asked me to meet her in the labs at 9:00 a.m. tomorrow. I agreed and headed out of the dining room back to the office.

Funny thing about the past couple weeks was that I had learned not to let anything surprise me. So when I walked into the office and saw a lean, immaculately dressed man sitting at my desk, I kept my cool and walked over to the chair Phil had pulled up earlier and sat down.

"Ahhh, Max," the deep, throaty voice rumbled like a V8 engine. His voice was strong and soothing all at the same time. He was dressed in a suit so well-tailored it looked fake, deep black to the point that its shape was hard to distinguish from the lines of his frame, with a gray shirt and bloodred tie.

The man's hair was cemented to his head and pulled back, revealing a lean, strong, and chiseled face with a smile that was predatory and wide. His nose was pointed and sharp like the rest of his features, and his skin was a shade too tan to be artificial but also a bit red to make it look like the mild start of a sunburn on a person who had lived their life by the sea.

The oddest feature, however, had to be the strong smell of cracked pepper coming from him as he moved. "I thought it was about time we caught up."

"And you are...?" I inquired. His presence was crushing, and it threw me off. I had even lost focus as I was about to call for Petro.

"You can call me Devin. Your little friend is otherwise occupied at the moment. I brought him some company. Squirrely little guy," Devin said as he leaned back and widened his smile to a slightly disproportionate size. "Looks like someone had a long day. I hope it's better now."

"Devin, yes. I'm all in one piece. Can I help you? How did you get in here?" I asked, starting to get a sinking feeling in my stomach that whoever this was, if he wanted to kill me, I wouldn't have the chance to walk more than one step past the door.

"Nervous? I keep forgetting my manners. Old habit. Let's just say I'm an old friend of Tom's, and we had a little gentlemen's agreement which I'm hoping is void if he is, in fact, dead. Which oddly enough, has been a challenge to determine. Either way, I promised him on my honor that if he was ever to go away and you turned thirty, I would stop by for a visit. The terms of that piece of the conversation are vague and up for debate, but I owe him two favors and would like to no longer be in his debt, so to speak. I was hoping he was dead, but no such luck yet on confirming it either way."

Devin got up and poured himself a drink, not bothering to ask if I wanted one. Following suit, I stood up and did the same.

"Good to meet you. Make yourself comfortable. Did he tell you why?" I asked, remembering Ed's statement on manners. Whoever or whatever this was in front of me, he was, without a doubt, not human.

"Ah, smart boy. You must have learned your manners from your mother because Tom was not always as polite. I'm not glad you asked why. Look, I'm not technically supposed to get involved with things here or for that matter, anything you mortals like to convince yourselves of doing. Well, most of the time, at least. We all slip up. I'm here to give you a much-needed piece of information which happens to be something I'm very familiar with," Devin said, leaning back and sipping the drink.

"All right, I'll bite. What information?" I asked, mirroring his sipping pattern.

"Mmh, I tell you what. You give me the rest of that bottle of scotch, and I'll tell you two things, deal?" Devin bargained, sniffing the cocktail glass.

In all honesty, I had no clue how valuable some of the liquor in the bar was. I knew a few bottles were worth well in the thousands, but some were unlabeled. He had picked one of those, which, to his credit, was amazing.

"No other strings attached?" I pushed.

"Again, clever boy. Yes. I'll even let you in on a little secret: I was the one who opened the lab under this office back up. That was, unfortunately, another part of what Tom asked for. That's the old housemaster's lab. Tom used it for a while until he and I had a little disagreement and I closed it," Devin replied as if he were holding all the cards. I knew if I kept asking him questions, the answers would come with a price.

"All right, I'm listening." I sat back to let him talk. He liked to talk, and I had a feeling he didn't come around too much. He was probably from that Plane everyone kept talking about.

He let out a light chuckle.

"So you remember those people that you were investigating and found had been drinking together one night?" Devin prompted, starting back up to not let me interrupt his flow. "If I were a betting man, which I'm not, I would say there were five other tabs closed at the same time at the same place. Just saying it may behoove you to take a closer look."

"Dammit," I cursed, knowing that we should have cross-referenced other receipts. I think Chloe and I had been so caught up making googly eyes at each other that we had let that slip.

"I'm not done there, Maxxx." He let the *X* ride out into a hiss. "Look up the Vale Project in that little box you have downstairs. That little meeting may have had something to do with it. Use this code that I got from someone recently to gain access to the files."

He handed me a cream-colored parchment paper. His fingers were long with nails that came to sharp points at the end. They looked deadly yet civilized at the same time. "Please excuse the blood. Hopefully the information is still there. Tick tock and all," Devin finished with a satisfied grin as he pulled a book out of his blazer and checked off one of two empty boxes next to Tom's name, letting me see that he had done what he had come to do.

"Devin, thank you for the information, and consider it one favor down," I said, figuring that would make this more official. It didn't. He had already lost interest in the conversation and stood up.

"Oh yes, one other thing, Maxxx. My son, Belm, is running around here somewhere on your little rock. He may be looking for the same people—it's his mother Lucy in him. If you see him, he's not one of the bad guys. Please refrain from treating him as such. That could lead to issues," Devin warned, standing with the bottle in his hand.

I looked down at my notepad to make sure I had everything written down, and by the time I looked up, he was gone. All that was left was the scent of pepper hanging in the air.

"Shit. Petro!" I yelled as my heart started racing. Sure enough, he came flying out of the bookshelf.

He looked disheveled and had little lipstick kiss marks all over his face. He had a toothy grin and about as much swagger as an eight-inch man could muster. "Hey, boss, what's cooking? Let me tell you what I'm cooking," he said, standing there in what looked like a pair of miniature boxers.

"Petro, what the hell happened to you?" I asked, letting my guard down slightly after witnessing his condition.

"Whoever that friend of yours is—which, let me tell you first, he's an immortal—he's welcome over any time," Petro declared, looking down at his lack of pants.

"Let's have it. What happened?" I prodded, trying to hold back a smirk.

Petro went on to explain how he had spent the last ten minutes still not getting past second base. My company had brought a distraction.

A few days back, I had explained to Petro the importance of respecting lady Pixies on Earth, and the base system had been a good way of doing that. No third base on the first date, always be polite, and I had even explained to him the concept of dating. I guess Pixies had a different take on things. While not offensive, he just seemed very sheltered. I even had the feeling they were very monogamous, and Petro was right in the middle of looking for the love of his life. I think he may have recently viewed some videos that had skewed this perception slightly.

"You know who that was?" I asked.

"The nice lady Pixie he brought with him called him the warden or something like that. Who cares? I'm in love," Petro swooned.

"She has a name, Petro," I told him, reminding him that people and Pixies had names, not just the pretty lady, smart Wiz, and Mind Wiz.

It started to occur to me that I may have just been given the golden egg to crack this case open. I decided to head to the stacks and the crucible room to look up the code I had received and what I had just heard.

A quick pause to reflect on the day slightly altered my mood. "Get cleaned up, lover boy," I said to Petro. "We have work to do."

Did I mention I needed a night of solid nonstop drinking?

Hell with it, I thought and downed half a bottle of spiced rum, sharing only a little with Petro before heading off to the stacks. I hoped no one called human resources on me.

CHAPTER 15

The Fountain of Youth

"Wake the hell up, you bloody wanker. You went out on a bender and didn't call me?" Phil accused as he smacked my shoulders.

Apparently, at some point during the night, I had passed out in the crucible room. The beer cans that Phil had kept in the fridge were now strewn about on the desk, as well as a half-eaten bag of chips. Petro was gone, and my head was throbbing.

"Bloody hell, hold on. I'll get you something. The marshal is here to boot," Phil said. I could feel his footsteps in my head as he walked off. One minute later, Phil came back and handed me a small potion vial. "Drink this," he urged, playing the overprotective older brother role.

Not being in any condition to argue, I downed the potion, fighting back the urge to lurch up everything in my stomach. On cue, a cool, refreshing wave swept over my body, opening up my eyes. I now knew how Phil had been operating the other morning. The potion gave me a head rush, crawling over my skin, before finally resting over my body and making the hangover go away. Sadly, it didn't appear to fix anything else, like my disheveled disposition.

I had drool on my shirt, which had apparently served as a napkin the night before. My hair was sticking straight up, and I could taste the familiar tang of hangover in my mouth. I felt better, but my appearance was obviously telling another story.

About one minute later, Ed and Kim, the marshal I had heard so much about, came trudging into the room. There was another minute of them both taking it all in before Ed spoke.

"Max, what the hell is this?" Ed demanded, already knowing the answer.

"Uh…late night," I replied. My memory wasn't kicking in yet to digest what I had discovered last night and actually communicate it.

"Ed, I can see the new guy fits right in with your crew here," Kim Kinder drawled, lifting one eyebrow and tilting her head to one side.

"Thanks for the kind words, Kim. Max?" Ed prompted.

The gears in my head started to turn. The potion was taking hold, as my thoughts started to line up. All of a sudden, my head became clear as day as I jolted up from my seat. "I know what's going on," I exclaimed, looking the group square in the eye.

They were all judging me except for Phil. He was just pissed I hadn't called him to join in the fun. I was glad Petro was gone, as I didn't need to also explain him to anyone this morning.

"Oh, do you, Max?" Kim said in a sharp voice with the same look on her face as she had walking in, not showing any surprise.

She was roughly five and a half feet tall. Muscular and blonde, she wore a stern look on her face. Kim was pretty in a strong way that lent itself to endless hours lifting weights or being a member of one of those cult gyms where you did nothing but squats all day in skintight shorty shorts.

She was sharply dressed in a formfitting skirt to her knees and a blouse with a black, short blazer over it revealing her pistol and badge. She was obviously like Ed, critical of her appearance and absolutely putting me down in her book as a useless freeloader.

"Kim, hi, I'm Max," I introduced myself as I put out my hand standing up. Chip crumbs fell off my Planes Drifter T-shirt.

"Pleasure," she replied sarcastically, taking her hand back which would probably be immediately washed once she was out of sight.

"Enough of this grandstanding. Max, we'll talk later about this. Kim was just leaving. We went to visit Jayal last night, and now he's missing. I'm sure this is not a coincidence. She's agreed to put a notice out for him to see if anyone knows anything. Tell us what you have," Ed said, ignoring the others in the room.

The potion Phil had given me was forcing my mind to work on overdrive. "I think we need to go to the dining room," I suggested, figuring that if we had been compromised, now was not the time to let the cat out of the bag.

"Right. Kim, you have a few more minutes?" Ed asked, looking at her as she was sending a message out on her phone.

"No, I want to get the word out about Jayal. The sooner the better. The last thing we need is another murder related to this mess. I already have a sheriff in Jacksonville calling about some weird catlike animal walking around town," Kim informed. "Fill me in later today. I should be back in the office by five." She turned to leave, abruptly stopping to look me square in the face. "Don't come into my city and start trouble. We have enough of that. I'm not like other regulars. I know who and what you are."

Kim obviously was setting the tone for our working relationship, or perhaps she was that serious of a person. I leaned on the second half, feeling she had a lot on her plate.

"Got it," I replied, giving Phil a side-glance. Ed gave me a nod walking Kim to the front door.

"Damn, bruther, you look like horseshit. Let's go to the dining room, then get you cleaned up. The murder in Spain is all over TV. The spin they put on this one is a classic. I hope you're right and have something," Phil told me, patting me on the back as we walked to the dining room.

When we got there, Ed was standing with an odd, distant smile on his face.

"You're just like Tom. Up all night figuring things out while drinking your life away. I swear, you looked like him sitting there. Anyway, let's hear it," Ed said as memories of the past swept over his face.

Jenny trudged into the room. She was obviously taking it easy today—I hadn't seen her in a pair of shorts and a T-shirt before. I don't think the sun had either.

"This better be good," she said as two smaller female Pixies went flying off her shoulder into the house. I guess Pixies were a little more common than I'd thought. They must work with her like Petro did with me.

I had decided on not giving the source of my lead. "So I pulled the rest of the receipts from the Blue House bar. I didn't have to cross-reference them. Instead, I pulled them from the point of sale system. Anyhow, Circes was also on that list. There were also two others. The kicker is that they split a bill, so we know they were all together," I relayed. Phil let out a whistle, and Ed started tapping his chin and looking at Jenny.

"There's more. I did some more digging and found all their names tied to a project called the Vale. It was a research group funded by the NCTS to look for the Genesis." The potion was in overdrive at this point, and I was saying things I truly didn't remember finding but had written down on a paper and was regurgitating at lightning-fast speed. "I had some help looking up other details on the Genesis, and it's not an object, but a nickname for…" I paused, seeing the group on the edge of their seats. "…The Fountain of Youth." The group let out the breath they had been holding all at the same time.

Everyone leaned back in their seats, all in their own headspace thinking about what I had just said. Funny thing about this brave new world? I could say shit like that and not get sent off to the loony bin.

"You figured all this out while smashed?" Jenny asked, pulling out her laptop and firing it up. Ed pushed the lid closed, looking at her bare skin. He stood up, not saying a word for a minute, commanding silence in the room. It didn't last long, as I leaned over and dry heaved a few times before finally straightening out.

"I think so," I replied, looking at Ed still standing there.

"Does anyone else in here know what the Fountain of Youth really is?" Ed finally spoke up in a manner that told us he already knew the answer.

"Eternal life," Phil stated.

"Same," Jenny said, adding its location. "It's here in St. Augustine. It was brought to the new world by a Fae, an old god or something like that."

"Wrong. Well, for the most part," Ed corrected as he started pacing the room. "Tom would know more about it, as he went looking for it on several occasions. That story holds true if you're an immortal from the Plane or Terrum. The old gods. Story goes that if you are immortal or an Ethereal from the Plane and take a drink from the Fountain, they will have all their powers from the Plane here on Earth. I think most of us, minus Max, understand how that could be problematic. Especially with the Balance being discussed."

I looked at Ed, realizing I had Gramps's journal on my nightstand. A journal that would specifically only open for me. "The journal," I blustered out.

"Right," Ed said, turning to me. "We'll need to take a closer look at it. Make sure you have it secured. Tom had the thing bound to only open for you; he was very specific about it. It might just be the key to this whole thing."

Phil stared at me with wide eyes. "Bruther, a full-on Ethereal with all their powers on Earth could move mountains, start and end wars in minutes, and, my God, do whatever they wanted. It would take everything the Earthborns have to match it. Even then…" he trailed off.

"Max, when Ethereals come from the Plane, they lose a part of themselves. They're not as powerful as they are on the Plane. It's almost like Earth has one big ward around it. Mages on Earth are more than a match for them, and the Fae, Vamps, and others here on Earth are at odds with many of them. There is only a handful of full Ethereals on the Council, but they're different. They don't want to control the Earth. They appreciate the Balance," Jenny explained as everyone was obviously landing on the same conclusion.

"It makes sense. I think we know the motive now. Someone or something wants to come over with their full powers. Or maybe an army? And they want to do this before the Balance happens to ensure that they are in control. It would be a hard fight if they had to deal with mankind and the Magical community at the same time. Our combined strength would be a handful," Ed said thoughtfully, finally sitting down. "This is bigger than us. I need to talk to a few people. Jenny, grab the communicators."

Jenny pulled out a black, medium-sized waterproof case

and unclasped the side. "Ed believes we are being tracked somehow, and I agree with him. However, we don't really know how. Max, not everything is done through magic. It could be via our texts, calls, or a GPS signal," Jenny stated, turning the box around to face the group.

"Max, we have used these before when we needed to keep the conversation private," she explained. "These communicators are linked to each other and no other system. They fall into the 2 percent category. All you have to do is put it in your ear, touch it with your finger, and push a little will into it. You should get a small cool sensation followed by an open line of communication to the rest of the group. To turn it off, simply take it out."

"Bruther, don't leave it on and go out to the bar," Phil cautioned as the rest of the group chuckled at a joke I obviously didn't get.

"Right," Ed said, regaining his composure. "Those are wise words, Phil. Now, we need a simple sign to switch over to the communicators. Send a group text using three periods and nothing else. Everyone will then activate their devices."

We spent the next five minutes testing out the communicators. Much to my surprise, they were just as Jenny had described, right down to the cool sensation that followed activating it. After wrapping up the test, I walked back into the room.

"I need to get cleaned up. What's the plan?" I asked the group, watching them all huddled around Jenny's computer.

Jenny spoke up first. "That's fine. You can go. I don't think we'll be able to redo your labs with the amount of booze and that potion in your system. Which reminds me, Ed, I spoke with Frank, and he said a client stopped by the practice this morning, dropped off a letter."

I kept forgetting Ed had a law office in the city. He was,

after all, hundreds of years old. When I had gone back to bind with the will, we had discussed what he actually did at the practice, and it was fairly straightforward. He supported the Magical and Ethereal communities with legal representation either with the Council or with the civilian legal system.

Ed had told me, "*It always helps to have an understanding lawyer present when a Mage has a bad day and decides to set someone's house on fire.*"

I could even visualize one of those judge TV shows on during the day with two Mages suing each other over stealing the other's crystal ball, even though I didn't think they used those.

"That's odd," Ed replied. "I didn't have any appointments, and I rarely get visitors there. I'll call Frank and check it out." He turned to me. "To answer your question, Max, about what's next, we need to find those other persons on your list. Belm and Jamison Danann. Jamison's Ned Danann's son. I don't know who this Belm person is. We need to get a hold of Ned now—this needs to take priority over our trip to the Blue House. Phil, while Max is getting cleaned up, jump on the box and see if you can locate them. I don't think this is something we need to communicate to Kim just yet."

Everyone looked around in agreement. I was thinking of how to explain who Belm was, then decided to just tell the group.

"So, I believe Belm is the son of an immortal named Devin," I said, looking at the shocked expressions on everyone's face.

"Are you sure you're not a diviner?" Jenny directed toward me. Obviously, most of the information I had received the past few weeks had been supplied to me, but this gave me an air of mystery with the group, since they had been watching me prior to me coming to the Atheneum and knew I was ignorant to the world.

I all but knew that Ed and Jenny had figured out that I had a pixie in the house. The rest...that was for me to know and them not to find out.

Phil and Ed looked at each other with raised eyebrows, then Ed glanced at me, still trying to figure out my thoughts. "So now we are looking for an immortal's relative named after Lucifer's son? Great, this keeps getting better."

Had I shared a drink with the devil? *No way*, I thought. Ed was probably reading some of what I was thinking, but not clearly enough to make a call on it.

"Max," Jenny started. "Are you okay?"

I must have put a blank look on my face. "I'm fine. It was a long night, and I'm trying to process this information. For all we know, Belm is a fake name," I said, regaining my composure.

"I doubt it." Phil spoke up. "The others are all real names. I don't think we will find a one-off here. I'm heading to the crucible room."

"Right," Ed agreed in the tone he used to close up a meeting. "I'm heading to the practice to check on this letter. Jenny, let's plan on meeting back here in five hours to look at the next steps. Can you reach out to our Mags-Tech IT rep and see if they can find out if someone has been tracking the phones?"

Jenny nodded her head in affirmation. She had opened her laptop back up, much to Ed's displeasure, was already pecking away at the keys.

"Jenny, you do know you have the morning off?" Ed asked as he looked back over at me. "Max, I want you and Jenny to go down to the range, since she is obviously on the clock, and get your qualification completed. Everyone is to have their kits ready to go at all times. Once Phil does some digging and I talk with Ned, we will meet back here in about five hours. That should be enough time for everyone to get set. I have a feeling it's going to be an even longer night.

"Also, take the case Tom left with you to the range. That pistol is a little different, and I want you to know how to use the Judge. Lastly, we need to get that journal reviewed by someone a little smarter on the subject."

Phil had already headed out of the office as I stood up and walked to the door. For some reason, I stopped a few feet out of the room, no longer visible but still able to hear Jenny and Ed talking.

"How's he figuring this stuff out?" Jenny asked Ed.

"I'm not completely sure. It's obvious he's getting some help. He's so damn much like Tom—just shows up and has everything resolved, or at least a direction to go. I'm a little worried he may be getting some advice at a cost. We need to sit down once this blows over and sort this out. He's young and arrogant. Max believes this is a game. The incident yesterday hopefully changed that perception," Ed sighed.

"You're right. We all trust him, but it's like he doesn't trust us. Or maybe trust what he is seeing or hearing. This has been a lot for him. We all thought he would not be this easy to convince. And if his labs are right, we may have bigger issues on our hands. Ed, you know his tests will be the same. If he can summon hellfire without an invocation, he might be just as powerful at the other elemental powers," Jenny said in a concerned tone.

"I know…I know…" Ed rounded off. "Let's get to work."

I had listened enough. I headed off to the house to finally get cleaned up. On my way over, I started to think about what I had just heard. The team trusted me, but I didn't think it was a lack of trust that kept me from telling everyone the sources of my recent knowledge.

Walking into my room, I started to get the mess of clothes off and noticed that Leshya had laid out fresh clothes on the bed. Creepy or not, she had my respect. I still wasn't convinced she was a craft; the others had to have the same feeling. Turning on the water, I closed the door behind me to let the steam build up while I stared at my face in the mirror, watching it slowly fade in the mist.

Melting into the steaming hot water, I thought about everything that had happened over the past few days. The statement that Jenny had made about me possibly being able to control other elements started to swim in my mind. Was she right? I truly hadn't pushed myself, or even tried.

As the water ran down my face, I concentrated on the feeling of it hitting my body. I jumped as a quick puff of ozone snapped in the air, forcing the water to stop hitting my body. It turned immediately to steam while the rest hovered about an inch from my skin, rolling off an invisible shield as if it were hitting a wall.

It came over me as suddenly as the hellfire did in London. With a gasp, I stepped back and held up my hands, watching the water curl around them. Small beads moved lightning fast then turned to steam. I was doing this. Concentrating, my hands starting to glow red, generating even more steam.

Before I could push myself anymore, Petro came flying though the room, slamming into the wall, obviously disoriented from the steam.

"What the hell, boss?" Petro exclaimed. "The whole room smells like magic. It's so humid in here I can't even fly," he said, standing up and shaking off his soaked wings. I guess Petro was not good at flying in high humidity.

"Nothing, Petro. What's our rule about my room?" I

reminded him, not giving him too hard of a time.

"I'm leaving. I thought something was wrong, but you're just doing whatever it is you weirdos do in the automatic waterfall. The air felt wrong. Did you do this with your hellfire?" Petro inquired.

"I think so," I replied, forgetting for a minute I was standing there wet and naked as the steam dissipated. I had told Petro the whole story last night while we were working and drinking. "Let me get dressed. I was about to check up on you anyway to make sure you were good. Where did you go this morning?" I asked, trying not to show off my pride and joy to the Pixie.

"I came back to my room to draw up treaty papers for the Mind Wiz," Petro answered, sticking to his decision of wanting to get a treaty in place. While it was funny, he was serious, so I treated it as such.

"Good. I plan on setting it up this evening," I said.

"Stars above, I'm out of here. The steam is going away, and you are naked as a newborn." Petro stalked out of the room, taking flight when he got to the bedroom door and shutting it behind him.

I stood there, thinking about what had just happened. I had controlled water and fire at the same time. While doing nothing more than generating steam, I was fairly sure I needed to talk to the group about this. *No more secrets*, I thought to myself. *No more.*

Grabbing the pistol off my nightstand and the box with the Judge in it, I looked at the journal sitting there and shook my head. Was this the game that was being played? I didn't think a journal that had been sitting on my nightstand could make much of a difference.

As expected, it took all of twenty minutes to get my

qualifications, and Jenny promised to send the results to the marshal when she got upstairs so I could officially carry.

It was funny how much the Magical community was normal in many aspects.

The crazy part came with Jenny explaining the Judge.

"The pistol is Ethereal, from the Plane. Like its name, it's judge, jury, and executioner," she explained, holding it in her hands. "Tom rarely took it out. It has a mind of its own; you can shoot someone or something with it, and it'll make up its mind on how the bullet will affect the target. Sometimes, it will kill, while other times it'll do nothing more than knock the person out or even not fire at all, like a few years ago. It's not a blended item; it's like your sword, an enchanted magical item that was built by Ethereals and brought here from the Plane."

The Judge was bronze in color and resembled a revolver. It didn't have a hammer, yet chambered and rotated the round via a pull of the trigger. The barrel was medium length, looking like some steampunk version of a .357 magnum. The odd piece was the barrel stretched from the top to the bottom of the handle on the front, making it hang down below the trigger guard.

It was well balanced having silver neatly woven into the handle, forming a pentagram. You know, with all these cool toys, I might find myself at one of those conventions picking up women dressed like anime fighters in short dresses.

Jenny could tell I was daydreaming.

"Are we going to shoot it?" I asked as Jenny handed it over, putting its full weight in my grip and breaking my train of thought.

"No, the ammo is…well, let's just say it's not the easiest to come by. Max, before I go, I want to ask you about your little friend," Jenny said as more of a statement. "I think you need to be upfront with the team about him. My friends, I'm sure you know, had plenty to say about him. They actually like him; they had never met a Pixie from the Plane in order to understand how they are. I want to meet him as well."

"Well, perfect timing. He is drawing up a treaty to go over with Ed about the freezer incident," I said, not realizing I had a smile on my face.

"A treaty?" Jenny asked this time. "That means this is important to him."

"I told him I would set up some time tonight with Ed to discuss it," I replied.

"Good, it's important. I'll tell the girls they can be witnesses," Jenny said. "Pixies have a tendency to be old-fashioned about things like this. He felt he was wronged. If Ed agrees, then we may have another team member," Jenny added, returning the smile. "Max, one more thing. About your labs."

"I know. We need to talk. No more secrets. I think I can work water as well as fire. Not as well, but I can," I informed her, wanting to present the new and improved open Max to the doctor.

"Max. It may not be that simple," Jenny said. "The word's out that you may be able to use hellfire. It's very rare, if not impossible, for an Earthborn Mage to use it. You may get some unwanted attention with all this. Ed wants to keep this quiet until we know more."

I agreed with Jenny and decided to tell her about handling water in the shower without mentioning all the awkward parts. Jenny just stood there with a curious look on her face like she wanted to take me to her lab and run tests the rest of the day.

After talking a few more minutes about my powers and wrapping up at the range, Jenny sent a text ten minutes later telling me that my carry tag was on my desk in the office. I started to realize her little friends ran errands and, like Petro, were good at getting around.

I also took a moment to call Mom, and we spent about twenty minutes talking. It was the usual: *How are things going? Anything new? What about the weather? I think it's going to be a cool winter*…and it went on. I still hadn't gathered the courage to ask them about what they knew, so I wrapped up the call talking to my dad about coming over for dinner next week. Then something odd happened at the end of the call. My father handed the phone over to my mom, as I heard her click off the speakerphone they always used while talking to me.

"*Max, be careful. I heard about your trip to London. Next time you go, you have to bring me back a plate of the queen,*" she said before hanging up. She knew I had made a trip to London and back.

The thing that struck me as odd was that she didn't seem to think it strange that I had done everything in the span of two days. I think she was in on it and was trying her best to get me to open up. How did she know? I hadn't told her. Was she talking to Ed? That was it. My mind was set on talking to her next weekend.

With the call to Mom out of the way, I saw a text had come in while I was talking with her from Ed.

Max, get in your truck, grab Tom's journal, and head to my office.

CHAPTER 16

Mr. Marlow and the Unlucky Professor

The Black Beast is a thing of beauty. Its rumbling V8 and rough exterior always put me in the mood to take on the world. Jumping back behind the wheel reminded me of life only a few short weeks ago, driving around with not a care in the world and cranking Planes Drifter.

On my way to Ed's practice, I planned to do just that.

Before I could get the truck started, Petro came whizzing through the open window and immediately started pushing every button on the dash.

"Hey, man," I greeted. "I think you and vehicles are not a good match after what I hear you did to Ed's old ride."

Petro looked up, wide-eyed, while turning up the volume on the radio. "This thing is awesome. You could fight a war with it. Can I have it?" Petro said, deadpan serious, letting a little dust out on the seat.

Maybe I was giving the little warrior too many new things and he was getting used to it. It did put a smile on my face, though, when he started dancing to the music, flying around the cab.

"No, it's mine, buddy. Maybe you can go on a ride with me next time I go out. You know, after the treaty," I hinted, also letting him know it was time for me to go.

"Sure thing. See you later, boss. That was fun." Petro flew out of the window, admiring the truck as I left.

As I peeled out of the private drive onto the main road, "To Hell and Back" played at maximum volume. This particular ditty was from their first major label release, The Bridge to Nowhere, and was a crushing metal ballad reminding one that even though things got tough, they could always get tougher. The guitar screamed angst over emotionally driven drumming only meant to do one thing—make your blood flow and focus your energy on whatever lay ahead.

It had been a few weeks since I had driven the Beast with my mind in a place to crank up the music. My previous drive to the old apartment had been a solemn, quiet ride alone with my thoughts and the occasional out loud comment to myself.

Just like always, the Beast delivered.

I felt good about the day ahead, and even better, I got to beat the steering wheel and scream at the top of my lungs—I never said I was a great singer. By the time I walked into the lobby of Ed's office, it was clear that something had happened.

"Max. That was fast," Frank said as he walked over, shaking my hand with a firm, clammy grip. "He's in his office."

"Is everything okay?" I asked, looking at Frank's face, which wore some type of vague, concerned emotion on it.

"I don't know. Ed got here, looked at the letter that was dropped off, texted you, and stormed into his office. I haven't seen him like this since Tom was officially pronounced...well, you know," Frank finished, walking beside me to the office entrance. "I'll stay out here. I'm already aware of what's going on. Max, something has him fired up."

Entering the office, Ed stood in front of the fireplace, looking at a letter with a fire going. It was eighty degrees outside, so I wasn't sure about the reason for the fire, but I had learned not to question these types of oddities.

"Ed, is everything okay?" I asked, walking up beside him.

"No, it's not, Max. Dr. Freeman came to visit today and dropped off a sealed note about Tom's journal. The one in your hand," Ed stated flatly.

"Fair enough. I'm sure he was paying his respects," I said, knowing full well that Ed was working to put pieces of a puzzle together in his head.

"Max, I'm not going to sugarcoat anything here—I have a feeling you'd appreciate that. Tom was obviously looking for the Fountain of Youth when he disappeared. I didn't want to say anything today, as this is all news to me, but this letter confirmed it. It's not a coincidence Dr. Freeman showed up here and dropped this off. The journal is bound to you, and all this started around the time you got your hands on it. This is all tied together, but hell if I can figure out how, or at least who would be doing this. Here, read the note," Ed said, handing me a handwritten sheet of paper.

> *Ed,*
>
> *If you are reading this, that means Max is with you. The notes contained in the journal detail what I was working on prior to my death or disappearance. As you know, I have been working with Dr. Freeman throughout the years hunting for various items. The fact that this letter was delivered to you means that he has found the location of the Fountain, and it must be secured. The journal holds the key. My God, I'm sorry I could not let you in on this before.*
>
> *Your True Friend,*

Tom

P.S. There is a file labeled the "Vale Project" hidden in my office. Ezra gave it to me, and if he is alive, he is someone you can trust. When the time is right, it will make itself known. Take this file and give it to the marshals and our trustees on the Council. Send my regards to Max.

I stood there for a minute taking the note in, watching as Ed stared into the fire. Looking at this note was like reading a dead letter. During the two World Wars, letters were often sent home from young soldiers to lovers, wives, and family, only for them to arrive after word of their untimely death. These letters had drastic effects on people, sometimes leading them to do unexpected things. Ed just stood there with a lost look. I almost felt bad for how he wore his emotions so openly. He was still missing his old friend.

"Looks like we are going to be paying Dr. Freeman a visit," I spoke, cutting the thick silence.

"Exactly. He's at Flagler College. I don't know what he expected to happen, but according to this, he found whatever it was Tom was looking for. We need to go now," Ed said as he turned around and went over to his desk, reaching in the top drawer and pulling out a holstered pistol.

He secured it on his belt. "You know what, Max? I think it's time we went on the offense here. Someone is playing us, or at least I think they are waiting for us to go find the Fountain."

I stood there, feeling that familiar prickle on the back of my neck that told me things were about to get interesting.

"We're not going to let that happen. We're going to get that relic and smoke this asshole out of hiding. Finding out who and what we are dealing with is the priority, and I have a plan, but Phil has to find Jamison first. I don't want the team knowing about the importance of the journal till we are done talking to Dr. Freeman. Frank will let them know if we run into any trouble," Ed said, finishing his motivational speech. The letter had gotten to him.

We spent a few minutes discussing the journal, looking over its contents, and examining odd drawings that looked like traps and puzzles. The detail was amazing and showed years of work. I had a feeling that Ed was taken aback by the work Tom hadn't fully let him in on.

The college was only a few blocks away from the practice, so we opted to walk the stretch. Heading out, we gave Frank the details and instructions on what to do if he didn't hear back from us in one hour.

Ed was clearly in a reflective mood and decided to talk about Tom on the way.

"You know what Tom's main ability was?" Ed asked, already knowing I didn't have the answer. Ed liked to speak like this, and it was obvious that his ability to read people's thoughts was the reason.

"No clue," I responded.

"He was one of two voyeurs on Earth. He could talk to ghosts and see things others couldn't. This made him very smart and thirsty for knowledge. Ever wonder how someone died? Tom would try to find them and ask. For some reason, his ability gave him a direct line to the Plane. He could summon power unlike anyone I've ever met and could use other people's magic. Voyeurs can also go back and forth to the Plane like it's a simple gate. Part of me still thinks he's there," Ed admitted.

He shifted his tone to a more personal cadence, finishing up his thoughts. "Hey, so you know, I got a bit of what you were thinking earlier. No more secrets. I didn't want to talk to you about this until I thought you would understand," Ed said, looking down at his phone and responding to a text.

"Ghosts are real?" I asked, actually not surprised. This put a whole new layer on the world I had already been struggling to figure out.

"Oh yes. If you ever notice one, be very polite and do whatever you can to figure out why you can see them. Heaven and hell are just names for things that are, for the most part, close to as described from what I understand. Tom knew. The Plane, the old gods, all of this…it's not just some tale made up to explain the two percent Jenny always mentions," Ed replied as we rounded the corner, standing in front of Flagler College.

If you've never heard of or seen Flagler College, it's a very old and prestigious private school in the middle of downtown St. Augustine, Florida. In many ways, it looked like the Atheneum: old-world style with timeless elegance. It also screamed expensive.

"I get it. For some reason, I just get it," I said, wanting to change the subject. "You know, I have a Pixie at the house who wants to present you with a treaty."

"Yes, your little friend. I see you're not keeping him a secret anymore. I knew about him the minute we came back from our trip to New York. I've been able to sense him in the house," Ed commented, looking at me and taking a deep breath. "Right, when we get back, I'll hear his proposal. A Pixie from the Plane is a powerful thing. By the way, I'm sure he told you why he was in the freezer, so you must understand; we weren't completely sure if he was on the up-and-up."

Wrapping up our conversation about the meeting with Petro, we headed into the main gate after passing security and off to the back offices. Walking down the long hall, we finally got to the door labeled "Dr. Freeman." Looking through the glass window into the office, Ed immediately went in, ignoring the privacy a closed door often signified.

Dr. Freeman and his guest stood up, showing no signs of

emotion.

"Marlow Goolsby, this is a nice surprise. Dr. Freeman, is everything okay?" Ed asked sharply.

"Edward. Yes, Mr. Goolsby came in a few minutes ago asking about an acquaintance of ours," Dr. Freeman replied as he sat back down. Marlow Goolsby kept standing, reaching out a hand to shake Ed's.

The two exchanged unpleasant pleasantries like I wasn't even in the room. Mr. Goolsby, as everyone kept calling him, was at least six foot eight. His looks led you on a chase to figure out his age, finally landing on somewhere between forty and fifty-five. He looked strong, owning the type of strength gained through power and influence. He commanded the room.

Much like Ed, he was dressed to the point of exhaustion in an immaculate black suit with a bright white shirt. His blond hair was parted neatly, offsetting his brown eyes with a scar splitting his left eyebrow. Mr. Goolsby's face was angular and strong. His cheeks pulled in close to his jaw, showing off muscle, yet still soft enough to cover up chewing a two-hundred-dollar steak for dinner.

This was a man with power and confidence that he was exactly where he wanted to be when he wanted to be there. He smelled like fresh basil, an eccentric scent that mixed with a sweet orange tang. He was the kind of guy I immediately wanted to punch in the face but knew better than to do it.

"You must be Max?" Marlow, as I had decided to call him, asked.

"Yes," was all I summoned up, obviously making myself look less than important. I knew better. He had a presence that suffocated you. *Maybe I should call him Gooley and see where that goes*, I thought, settling back down.

"Much like your grandfather, I see," Mr. Goolsby said,

smiling and turning to Ed. "I was about to leave anyway. I believe my business here is concluded."

Ed spoke up, cutting Dr. Freeman off as he started to talk. "What business would that be?"

"I figured you would ask," Mr. Goolsby replied. "We have a mutual interest in recent occurrences. Before you think I'm not fully aware of the other murder, or your little friend Max's trip the other day, don't. It has come to my attention that your friend Max here has been looking into one of my establishments in Jacksonville. So I thought I would do a little investigating myself, which led me to the good doctor here.

"You see, Mr. Rose, I'm not the bad guy here. As a matter of fact, Mr. Ezra's untimely death has caused a ripple with some of my constituents. You know, the ones interested in pulling the curtain back on everything. I'm kind of banking on it. I want to see it happen. All this mess, however, is changing some of that. Not to mention it's in my damn backyard. Is that clear enough?" Mr. Goolsby concluded, not flinching.

Note to self, never play poker with this guy.

Ed glanced at me then back at Marlow with a look of understanding on his face. "All right, I believe you. Out of everyone I know, you wouldn't have anything to do with Ezra's murder. I guess that's something you and Max here have in common: important relatives. I know how you felt about him. However, I don't trust you. You being here is enough. I know you and others are looking to turn a profit on the Balance. I think it would be best if you left."

"Okay. I'll tell you what, let me give you some advice," Marlow started as he looked at me, ignoring the rest of the room. "If you show up to one of my establishments, namely the Blue House, please respect my property. The bartender on duty that night works from Thursday through Sunday. His shift starts at five. Yes, I know you have been looking at my billing system." Marlow looked at Ed, followed up by a nod to Dr. Freeman.

As he walked out of the room, the temperature went back up, and the mood, while still thick with tension, eased. He had talked to Ed and me as if the doctor was not even in the room. I bet he'd been there to examine us in a way that wouldn't seem suspicious. That, or he wanted to get some of that miracle hangover cure Phil had given me. *This stuff is amazing*, I thought. *I'm still going.*

The door closed with a light click. You could see his shadow and the obviously hired muscle join him while their footsteps disappeared down the hallway.

Ed turned to Dr. Freeman. "Right, I think we need to have a little chat." As he spoke, Ed pulled out a small silver disk from his pocket, laying it down on the desk. He followed with a murmur of "*Scroto.*" There was a quick snap as an invisible bubble engulfed the desk and area around us. Ed inspected it and smiled. "No one will be able to hear us talk while we're in here."

Looking at Dr. Freeman, I could tell he was unfazed. For a non-Mage, he was very comfortable with this world. Dr. Freeman put his hands on the desk and let out a breath, at the same time easing the tension out of his posture. It was obvious he hadn't been comfortable with Marlow in his office. I cut Ed off before he could talk.

"Did you know Marlow was coming by today?" I asked, leaning back in my chair and also letting my shoulders relax, mirroring the man sitting behind the desk.

Dr. Freeman was a typical old-school professor, unlike the newer teachers who thought it was hip to dress like the kids in their class. He was wearing a button-down beige shirt with nonmatching slacks. I could almost feel the presence of a pair of slip-on loafers under the desk. His hair was brown and clearly lacking on the top of his head—he had the classic comb-over in full effect. The hair had, by the looks of his thick mustache, retreated from the top of his head and gone to his upper lip. He had an old, fragile-looking pair of round glasses on.

Looking closer, I could see he was a small man who, if I were to guess, had to be around a hundred and fifty pounds. His frame wasn't full of muscle, but you could tell by his eyes that he was full of knowledge. He wore lines on his face that told the story of travel and a little adventure.

Dr. Freeman was an interesting man who seemed at home at Flagler College. The smell of pipe tobacco coming from the room added to his persona. I'd bet you a beer he didn't smoke.

Ed was apparently going to ask the same question I had about Goolsby. He seemed to be slightly impatient as he sat in his chair and tapped his chin.

"I have no clue why he came by. His name was the only reason I knew how serious the visit was. Tom warned me he might come looking for information on the project. So, when he showed up, I figured it had something to do with the Vale Project," Dr. Freeman explained as he clasped his hands in his lap.

Ed looked up, letting a small breath out after a momentary silence. I think Ed had been trying to read him.

"I'm going to cut right to the chase. Let's call it what it is. I know you were working with Tom on the Fountain of Youth," Ed declared.

Dr. Freeman cracked a huge smile that went to his eyes. "Yes," he replied in an excited voice. He sat up a little straighter as he smiled. Dr. Freeman was proud of his work. "I helped Tom with a project called the Vale, a team assembled by the Council to find the Fountain of Youth or, as they named it, the Genesis. Tom was the lead for that team. In reality, I wasn't part of it being that I'm, well, normal, but he gave me explicit instructions, and I followed them with no deviation," Dr. Freeman said as he looked at the both of us, still smiling. He had accomplished something no one else had.

"So, I have to ask. What did Tom tell you, and what can you tell us about the Vale Project?" Ed inquired.

He was going into lawyer mode, where he had an order about things. Ed was after the five Ws: what, when, where, who, and why. He didn't always want to know the information directly but what the information meant. It was like watching a professional surgeon work.

"Ah, the Vale Project. There are pieces of this I'm not completely aware of. Tom kept it close to his chest. There were six members on the team, including Tom. As I stated, I didn't really count, and I was off the books. I realize there are only a couple left," Dr. Freeman trailed off, letting his smile recede, realizing that several members of the team had taken an early trip to the Over and Under, as Petro called it.

"So you know about the deaths?" Ed asked.

"Yes. I just found out about Circes. The last two days, I've been confirming the information he gave me. It's right. As soon as I tried to call him back, I found out he's dead. Almost everyone now. Ezra and Old Penny. Jamison was also on the team, and some really weird guy named Belm. Tom said we could trust him, but he was an odd one. I'm not like them; I can't do much, but I know things. They would come to me with the information they found, and I would see if I could dig anything up. I wasn't as close to this as they were." He paused. "Looks like that's changed now," Dr. Freeman finished, reflecting on the loss of the others.

Ed, who had been tapping on his chin again, leaned forward. "Dr. Freeman, I know why Tom involved you. You and I have worked together before, and I know you're good at what you do and also have a very strict set of guidelines when it comes to historical artifacts. What were Tom's exact instructions?" Ed asked.

"Ah, that's the interesting part. Max, I've heard a lot about you, believe it or not. You were part of his instructions. I didn't write them down—Tom gave me some type of memory voodoo. They were very simple. If he ever disappeared, I was to continue searching for the Fountain and talk to no one about it. That includes you, Mr. Rose.

"I think he was worried about having too many people involved. He got scared about it. The next thing he told me was that if his grandson showed up, I was to let you know everything and where I'd found it. No sooner. I wanted to contact you earlier, but I couldn't, if you know what I mean. He also left me the letter I dropped off at your office. It's as if he knew all this bad stuff was going to happen," Dr. Freeman said, looking down at his hands and shuffling his thumbs.

When Ed opened his mouth to talk, Dr. Freeman started back up.

"I'm not a superhero like a lot of you. I'm a normal guy. I know a lot of things and have a few tricks up my sleeve, but I'm a little freaked out," Dr. Freeman confided.

I decided to get Dr. Freeman back on track and spoke up. "What was Marlow asking you about?" I inquired, looking at Ed for support.

"Mr. Goolsby? He's not the only guy who has stopped by over the last two weeks, by the way. He wanted to know what I knew about the Vale Project. It was kind of odd, but it appeared he didn't know too much about it. He just kept asking me about it. Who else was involved in the project? Had we found anything? Then he rattled off the names of a few artifacts, even mentioning the Genesis, our nickname for the Fountain. He started to get impatient when I told him I didn't know much about it. You see, I wouldn't be able to tell him anyway," the professor said as Ed leaned back, smiling.

"Tom put an enchantment on you, didn't he? You couldn't talk to us about the details even if you tried," Ed deduced.

"That's right," Dr. Freeman burst out. "A little voodoo, some words, I drank a potion, and that's all she wrote. You would have to pull my brain out to get the information," Dr. Freeman unfortunately declared as Ed and I looked at each other, not wanting to say a word about the Eater.

I could feel Ed working to read my thoughts. Oddly, I could feel the echo of his mind bouncing off mine like a radar. Dr. Freeman had no idea how the others had died.

"Right." Ed cleared his throat as he looked up. "Who else stopped by?"

"That's the interesting part. I don't really know who the guy was. He was tall, well dressed. Said his name was Vestulie, and he worked with Ezra. Even showed me some credentials. He asked a bunch of the same questions. Tom never mentioned the guy, so he got the same treatment Mr. Goolsby got. But while Mr. Goolsby seemed to understand I was not going to tell him anything, this Vestulie guy wasn't buying anything I was telling him. He kept looking at me. His questions were more interesting, that's for sure," the professor said.

"Interesting how?" I asked, lifting an eyebrow and taking a breath.

"Well," Dr. Freeman started back up. "He knew a lot more than Mr. Goolsby did. He knew the names of some of the people on the team, and asked if I knew where any of them were. When I asked why, he simply stated he was closing out Ezra's affairs and this had come up while doing so. He got up and left shortly after that."

Ed looked at the professor, and I could tell he was about to get the prize behind door number one. "You've been busy. Why did these gentlemen come to visit you, and why now?"

Dr. Freeman's face lit up and a smile stretched to his eyes. He was a proud man and knew something no one else did. "Ah…that's the million-dollar question."

For some reason, the pieces started to fit together, and I blurted out, "You found the Fountain, or at least where it is, didn't you?" Like Ed often did, I said this as a statement, not a question. I think the old grouch was rubbing off on me.

"Bingo!" the professor exclaimed excitedly. "As a matter of fact, I had to wait until I saw you two in order to work the final piece of this. Did you bring the journal? Whatever Tom did to my memory, I keep remembering things when triggered. I'll be glad when that's over."

I reached into my blazer and pulled out the small leather-bound book, setting it in front of him. "As requested," I breathed out.

"After hearing how you handled your guests, I see Tom was smart to trust you. Lay this all out for us," Ed followed up, relaxing slightly.

"Well, first you need to understand how we found it. You see, Circes was cross-referencing some old artifact inventories. You know, the old Ethereal ones from the crossover. When the first Ethereals and Fae came over to Earth from the Plane after the old wars, they brought a bunch of artifacts. Since a description usually doesn't do, they depicted them with drawings and a little note. A few weeks ago, we found a symbol that is shown in the back of his journal," Dr. Freeman said as he patted it, pulling out a piece of paper and unfolding it to show us an old coin-like symbol.

"Here is where it gets a little weird," the professor continued, not giving us a chance to speak. "The notes under the symbol in the inventory simply state, 'path to eternity,' followed by the word 'key' written in some old Fae language. It was tough to figure out. In the back of his Fountain journal there is a symbol, which, while seeming identical, isn't. Look here."

He laid out the paper opening the journal to the last page. "We cross-referenced the picture in the back of the book like many of the others, and nothing came up. You know, where you scan the image on the Internet and the results pop up if there is a match. Anyways, as soon as we popped this picture in the regular internet, we had immediate and obvious results."

I was starting to realize that even though this all seemed to be going on in the background, someone else still had to know they had found this information. The look on Ed's face reflected the same realization.

"The symbol in the inventory list is an exact match for one engraved on the left front drawbridge turret on the Bridge of Lions leading to Anastasia Island. Over the years, the bridge has been rebuilt and worked on. I was able to find some interesting information on those lions. I think they were put there to protect the place. Even without anyone knowing."

"Wait. So, the Fountain is located somewhere on the bridge?" I asked.

"Not exactly. I'll show you in a minute. You need to understand that as soon as we made the connection, Circes was, well…killed. Which is when I went to your office," the professor said, looking Ed squarely in the eyes.

"Dr. Freeman, for your peace of mind, you are coming with us and will be staying at the Atheneum. We will make sure nothing happens to you. Continue, please," Ed prompted, realizing that most of his babbling was nerves.

"Thank you," the professor exhaled, relieved that he was

going to be safe. "I was going to ask. Anyway, so the last thing that Circes told me was that the inventory book was for a shipment sent to the St. Augustine area thousands of years prior to its formal habitation. I am sure, Max, you understand that the history books like to leave a lot to the imagination. When Ponce de Leon came to Florida, the Native Americans told him about the Fountain. Well, guess where they heard it from?

"The journal on this desk is not what you think. It's thousands of years old, and was the property of the guard, the Keeper, put in place to protect the Fountain. Something made him come out of that hole and give this journal to someone. From what I understand, it happened sometime around World War II. The Germans were looking for all this stuff." Dr. Freeman paused glancing at both Ed and me. We nodded for him to continue, not wanting to interrupt.

"They've even made movies about it. He came out every so often and interacted with the natives. After he left this journal, the Keeper was never heard from again. He's the only reason the story stuck that the Fountain of Youth was here in this city. The journal has been in Tom's hands for decades. I think he got it after the war. He told me all of this when he gave that letter to me."

Ed cut off the professor again. "That's right; I've seen this before, and Tom used to talk about looking for the Fountain. It was a hobby of his. Kind of like looking for Bigfoot."

Did Ed just crack a joke? I thought, seeing him smile slightly. I think this was getting him excited. I was literally on the edge of my seat as the professor spoke. Ever had to take a piss while at the movie theatre? You don't want to miss the movie you paid twenty bucks to see, so you wait it out for a boring part or just hold it, finally leading to the best bathroom break ever. There's actually a website that tells you at what times you can take a bathroom break and not miss anything.

Genius. That's where I was.

Dr. Freeman started to speak again in finality. "So I went out to the bridge and made this etching over the engraving. It's the exact size of the one in the Journal. From what I understand, in the journal the markings are different on this symbol. You apparently need to read the inscription in the journal, which I didn't have, with it closed, placing an image of the etching inside. The symbol in the book has a note that says, 'Gate.' Put the two together—gate key. We already knew this journal was more than just a bunch of notes and drawings. Tom had already figured out that somehow this journal is the key to the Fountain's location. Oh, and one more thing, you can't access the gate until the full moon comes around. That's in two days. I'm not sure about any other paths to the Fountain. And I'm pretty sure you can only use the Fountain during the full moon."

"Right," Ed started in his normal cadence, tapping his chin. "Two things. First, I'm pretty sure someone saw you on that bridge. Second, let's see what this does and get back to figuring out our next steps. Max, what's on your mind? I can see you have a thought."

"Well, my mom used to tell me stories about things like this. I remember her telling me one about the Fountain of Youth. Probably because of Gramps. Something about it being underwater, and you could get to it by hook or crook. Some funny rhyme. I'm thinking that now that everyone knows where it is, we aren't going to be the only ones out during the full moon on that bridge. I wonder if this is the only way in?" I reached over and opened the journal, placing it in front of Ed as he started to look at the writing.

"You're right. I think it's time we go on the offense. Someone was waiting for you to turn thirty, and I'll even take it one step further—someone knew only you could open the box with the journal. But I'm not sure that whoever knows about this recognizes all the other details we just discussed. Maybe the big rocks but not the little ones." Ed put the paper in the back of the book, closing the leather clasp and saying, "*Manifestum*," followed by the inscription from both symbols.

As Ed opened the book, a puff of ozone came out of the journal, dropping a solid gold coin from the burnt pages. I could see that each side of it represented a side of the symbols.

"Ah...a gate key. A really nice gate key," Ed admired before he looked down at the now slightly burnt back pages of the journal.

"Was that important?" I asked Ed as a smile flowed onto his face.

"Oh my God," the professor said. "Wow, this is amazing. The journal is the gate key. Someone went to lengths to hide this thing."

He grabbed the coin out of Ed's hand. It wasn't a greedy grab, and you could tell Ed knew it. It was one of educational amazement. The same feeling you got when kissing that really hot girl way out of your league and pulling back for a second, thinking in amazement *this is really happening*. After a minute of examining the coin, he handed it back to Ed, letting out a breath of air.

"Right. So now we know the when, the where, and the how. We just don't know who. We need to go back and form a plan. I'm sure Phil's found our friends by now, and we may be able to use tomorrow to make that trip up to Jacksonville. I have a feeling we are still missing something here," Ed said as he placed the coin in a holder and into the breast pocket of his blazer. It was the same as mine and could hold a little more than it showed to the outside world. "Let's not discuss this until we get back to the Atheneum."

Ed snapped his fingers, and the bubble around us popped just the same as a soap bubble. It even discharged a haze of liquid residue. The noises of the building came back to life, and Dr. Freeman was standing up. He surprisingly already had a bag packed. I don't think he was planning on being stationary for long.

CHAPTER 17

Treaties and the Knives that Make Them Stick

On the ride home, Ed and I discussed the treaty arrangements for the evening. Meanwhile, Dr. Freeman sat in the back seat trying to act calm over the evening's events while we pulled onto trusty old Highway 16.

"So..." Ed started, getting into the details of how important the treaty actually was. "Do you know what he's offering? If a Pixie wants to have a truce, he will always offer something. I think I know what I can put on the table."

"No, I never asked," I replied, looking at Ed with a slight grin. "I sent him a text that it was going to be tonight, and he sent back an emoji of a cat. Not too sure he has the texting thing figured out yet. I'll check on him when we get back."

Ed snickered lightly. "Hopefully, it's not a pet cat. I think it will be a huge asset to have our little friend on the team. I'm going to offer him a job and maybe a little something extra. I also sent everyone a note to be ready thirty minutes after we get back."

Most of the trip was spent listening to the professor discussing Pixie ceremonies and how he had never met a Pixie from the Plane.

"And that is how they usually end up working for others," Freeman concluded his speech about Pixies.

"Makes some sort of sense, I guess," I said, countering the ridiculousness of the entire process. "So I have to ask, how long have you two known each other?"

Ed spoke up first. "Twenty years, I believe. Sounds about right, professor?"

"Correct. I will say, though, I was much younger back then, and these guys used to take me on all kinds of odd adventures. I can't keep up with them as well these days. You know, the whole thing about aging," Dr. Freeman said.

I could feel him looking directly at me from the back seat.

Ed replied before I could get a word out. "You know Jenny has offered you some rejuvenation potion. Maybe it's time you took her up on it."

"We'll see. I think I just need to make it through the week first. That stuff freaks me out. I've seen too many things go wrong. Everything has a price," the professor retorted, leaning back in obvious reflection as he let out a sigh.

Driving through the gate, we noticed that all the lights were on in the front of the house. As we got closer, I could see Chloe standing outside talking with Phil while he smoked a cigarette.

"Hey, honey, hope you had a good day. Supper went and got cold," Phil joked, looking at Ed and leaning back to watch Dr. Freeman as he stepped out of the back of my truck.

"Good to see you too. Hello, Chloe, I see you got my text. I'm glad you're here," Ed greeted, glancing at me. Probably to see if I was going to behave myself. I wasn't.

"Chloe, good to see you again," I said, reaching out and shaking her hand, smiling like a school kid and running my fingers through my hair.

Chloe turned the smile on and gave Ed a side-glance. "I can't stay away from this bloody place. Maybe this time if we go out, Max, we can avoid having someone slinging spells at us."

"All right, enough of the pleasantries. Everyone, this is Dr. Freeman," Ed introduced. "He will be staying with us for a while. Phil, what did you find out?"

"Bruther. This Jamison guy hangs out at the Blue House every Thursday for drinks. Go figure. Even after the deaths, he is still a creature of habit. If this is correct, he will be there tomorrow," Phil informed as he spit out the rest of his cigarette and looked over at me. "Road trip time. Maybe we can get some food and a few drinks while we're there. I hear it's great. Oh, and that Belm guy. I found nothing on him."

"We'll make plans later. I think I would like to send Chloe and Max in. Phil, I'm not saying you stick out in a crowd; however, you stick out in a crowd. I'll fill everyone in on what is going on later this evening. I need to go get ready for the treaty," Ed said as he walked past the group, indicating to the professor to follow him.

"This will be exciting," Chloe commented. "Everyone's here. Jenny even has her two Pixies, Lacey and Macey, in the dining room. They're all decked out."

"I thought they hated Petro," I said, then looking at Phil, "It's going to be a busy two days," I shifted topics in the same sentence.

Phil took a deep breath. "Nah, Pixies always stand up for each other even if they don't like someone. I think you lot have found something."

I left Phil and Chloe so I could catch up with Petro. Since

I was outside, I took the front door into Gramps's old place for a change. While I was entering, Petro came rushing down landing on my hand as I held it up.

Petro was in his armor and had cleaned himself up. Without the red paint, you could actually see his armor was scarred and had seen more than its fair share of fights.

"Hey, boss. I'm about ready. Did you hear the smart lady's Pixies are walking me to the table? This is great! I think I still have a chance," Petro gushed as I dropped my hand, watching him hover in the air. I decided I would give Petro the talk on the birds and the bees, or the bees and the bees, or whatever combination was the flavor of the month.

"Petro, looking very sharp. Hey, what are you offering Ed tonight?" I asked, trying to play off the fact that I knew very little about the proceedings.

"I am going to offer him my services at the house and protection of everything therein," Petro declared, resting his palm on the hilt of his sword.

"So what are you asking for in return?" I continued, actually curious by this point.

"An apology," Petro replied with an air of finality.

People often ignore the value of an honest apology, I thought. I remembered reading in one of those leadership books that it showed weakness. My take was to always err on the side of apologizing. For me, this was mainly due to the fact that I would more than likely gracefully mess something up again.

"Fair enough, Petro. I think he will be pleased, and I'm sure he will offer an apology," I assured. "You ready to get going?"

"Give me a few more minutes, boss. Oh yeah...remember that thing you wanted for your sword? Go look on your bed.

While you do that, I can finish getting ready." Petro winked taking off up the stairs past the fountain at a blurring speed.

I climbed upstairs through the office over to my living quarters to see my sword and a three-inch-long leather scabbard sitting beside it on the bed. The scabbard was made of burnt dark leather with silver inlays throughout its short length. It looked old and new at the same time. Petro and I had talked about a way for me to carry the sword around without it looking too out of place. He had come up with the idea of a sword scabbard that would hide the blade. He had blown my expectations out of the water.

Leaning down, I picked up the sword and started to slide it into the scabbard. As soon as the blade passed the three-inch length, it disappeared, nothing coming out of the other side while I kept feeding the blade into the opening. "No shit," I exhaled out loud as I slid the final couple of inches in with a click.

I clipped the scabbard on my belt and put my hand directly under where the blade should be; there was nothing but air. This was insane. The sword itself, while large, when tucked in this holder was not much bigger than having a service pistol or radio on your hip. Just to make sure I wasn't crazy, I pulled it out, watching it come back to life, light shining on the muted steel.

"Petro!" I yelled. He came zipping around the corner with a small stack of Post-it notes. "Come here, little fella. Give me a hug and a kiss," I said as I acted out trying to give him just that. Pixies were fast, and he was not having it, laughing as he dodged me.

"Thought you would like that, boss. I wish I could say it was all me. I ran into Leshya earlier and started talking to her. I figured this sword had to have a scabbard. Twenty minutes later, she dropped this off. That's some serious old magic. I would even bet it predates the first Ethereals coming over to

Earth from the Plane. Anyway, are you ready to go?"

I texted Ed and gave him a heads-up on what Petro was bringing to the table. "Yeah, let's do this," I agreed as Petro landed on my shoulder. I leaned over, blowing him fake kisses while I put my sword back into its new home and let my blazer fall over it, watching him grimace.

"I like you better when you've been drinking," Petro told me before we both started to chuckle walking down the hall.

"Me too," I replied.

Walking into the main house, we could hear everyone in the dining room before seeing them. As soon as we got to the bottom of the stairs, Lacey and Macey came buzzing up to my shoulder, taking Petro by either arm. "I'll be back. I have to make an entrance and all," Petro said as he nodded for me to go into the dining room, throwing in a wink as he raised his eyebrows looking at Lacey subtly so she couldn't see.

Everyone was there: Frank, Angel, Dr. Freeman, Jenny, Phil, and Ed. Ed had cleaned himself up some. As if he needed it—he had yet to ever look disheveled. He wore a dark purple sash around his shoulder with a large royal brooch on it. I could recall seeing those in books showing pictures of royalty. I asked Chloe later that night, and she said it was an officer's sash from the Council. A big deal, apparently.

Sitting down, I sat between Phil and Dr. Freeman. Chloe took her seat across from me with Ed at the head of the table flanked by Frank and Jenny. Angel was sitting beside Chloe, looking bored out of her mind.

After I had walked in, Lacey and Macey had closed the doors. There was now a light knock on it, followed by Ed stating, "All parties are welcome at the table."

The doors swung open, as Petro glided in with his hand on the hilt of his sword, Lacey and Macey taking up position on either side of him. He looked elegant. When he landed, he did so with one foot first, looking as if he was stepping down to the ground, and stood in front of me looking directly at Ed.

Petro spoke up in a voice louder than it should have been. I guess it was some type of potion or charm. "Edward Rose, or, as I call you, the Mind Wiz. I am here to seek a truce with you over my imprisonment. Will you listen to my terms and accept what is asked no matter the consequences?"

"I will," Ed stated as he sat down. There was a small table and three chairs that looked to be from a dollhouse in front of him.

"Then I ask my party to please stand. Max Abaddon Sand and Phil Eces, you are both witnesses and saviors of not only myself but my brothers as well. You have proven your loyalty to me. Will you accept my request for escort?"

Phil and I both let out grunts of approval and stood up. The funny thing was that Petro only had to walk a few feet, so we both just stood in place.

Ed stood up too and did the same. "Jenny, Frank, will you represent me as sponsors?" The two responded with a simple, "Yes."

As the whole group stood, Petro walked forward and asked everyone to be seated. Petro unrolled the Post-it notes and unstuck the first two pages, handing them to Macey to take over to Ed.

"Mr. Rose, for the deplorable act of imprisoning myself and my brother in the freeze prison, we ask for the following reparation. An apology given in front of this group of sponsors without reservation. In return, I will offer my service as a guardian of the realm of the Atheneum and those who flourish here. I will also help with potions when requested," Petro listed before rolling up the yellow paper in his hand and sat down.

This was all a little melodramatic for a simple apology, I thought.

"Petron, or as I call you, Little Warrior. I accept your proposal. I offer my apologies for the deplorable act of false imprisonment. I also have three other gifts to offer. First, a title. Petron, Warrior of the Freeze and Sergeant at Arms," Ed spoke, as you could see the excitement building in Petro. "Second, as an officer of the Council, I offer you full and open employment on our team working at the Atheneum under the NCTS. This offer includes all the benefits therein. Third, please accept this bottle of Honey Mead as a gift for you to celebrate our truce."

Petro stood up, taking flight. Ed held his palm out as Petro landed on it, pulling out his sword and looking up. Surprisingly enough, instead of poking Ed's eyes out, he laid his sword on the palm of Ed's hand. Petro flew back down to his papers and brought them up, also placing them in Ed's hand before picking up his sword putting it away.

"I accept your apology and your terms. Under the condition that I may continue my life debt to Max," Petro said, looking over at me.

"Agreed," Ed replied as he clapped his hands.

The group started clapping and cheering as Petro rose, zipping around the room and landing on people's hands, formally introducing himself.

Once Petro landed on my shoulder, he leaned into my ear and whispered, "I think I still got a chance with those two ladies." This was followed by him taking back off to finish talking with everyone.

Overall, it was probably the weirdest thing I had witnessed, but it felt like a celebration. Even so, all the while, the thoughts of the evening's previous conversation loomed heavily in the back of my mind as I wrapped my hand around the hilt of Durundle.

Chloe was looking at me with her head tilted, smiling. I could see the glint of the dull background light on her lips. As she walked closer, Ed spoke up.

"All right, now that we have this past us, we have a few things to discuss," Ed said, killing any chance I had to chat Chloe up. I think Phil was feeling the same, since he let out a breath and swore something about having a bottle somewhere that needed tending to.

Angel looked up, still wearing her bored face. "I have to go. I think you all can handle this one without me." With that, she walked out the door, not leaving room for a response.

Frank shrugged. "She was close to Circes," was all he said, sitting down.

"Right. The next two days are going to flush all this out. Petro, you are welcome to join our meeting," Ed offered, knowing that what he was about to reveal would be dangerous.

For the next hour, Ed, Dr. Freeman, and I laid out everything that we had learned today. The meeting with Marlow and all the information the professor had to offer. Sitting there, you could see the look of amazement on everyone's face. Frank even cracked and raised his eyebrows a few times. Petro had decided to sit on the table between Phil and me, letting dust fall periodically. Jenny, for once, didn't have her nose buried in her laptop, and Chloe was leaning back, not giving away her thoughts on what she had just heard.

The plan was simple. At least it was supposed to be. Chloe and I would go to the Blue House and see about Jamison. Phil and Kim would be close in case something crazy happened. Ed wanted us to bring Jamison back to the Atheneum for protection as we had done with Dr. Freeman.

Ed, Jenny, Frank, and our newly appointed team

member, Petro, were to make preparations for Friday night and the trip to the Bridge of Lions. Dr. Freeman would remain in the crucible room like I had done in the past and help direct traffic in case of an emergency with Kim. Ed didn't want to get her involved directly.

Kim had shown up after the ceremony and left just as soon as Ed was done, but meanwhile, Kim had, as usual, made sure to meet me with skeptical disapproval while I stood there with the hilt of the sword hanging out of the front of my blazer. I guess it didn't work for all the ladies.

Ed's last request was for me to go to the Postern and grab a gate key from the Evergate. This was our "get out of jail free" card. He also wanted me to go to the evidence room and grab an item called the rope. He described it as well…a rope. Apparently, if we all grabbed it and bonded with it, whoever held the rope could pull everyone simultaneously through a designated gate, that being the gate from the key I was to get first.

Saying our goodbyes, Chloe gave me a firm handshake. "You want to go to the evidence room?" I asked as we stood there.

"You know I'm a diviner and can see what would happen if I went down there with you?" Chloe replied with a wry smile. "I think I need you to take me out for a drink first," she finished as she walked off swinging her hips.

Hell, she knew that if we went down to the evidence room together, I would have made a pass at her. But I was so nervous I don't think I would have. *Or would she have?* I asked myself. Dating in the Magical community was complicated. Maybe it was a good thing she couldn't read my mind, at least. *She would probably have me arrested*, I thought, laughing to myself, much to Phil's chagrin as he stood there observing me.

"Come on, lover boy, let's grab a drink. I'll go with you.

You may need to relieve some pressure from that castor of yours," Phil said as he patted me on the back and started marching out of the room.

Petro jumped up and flew over to my shoulder. "Hey, boss, think it would be an issue if Lacey and Macey came over for the afternoon?"

"Sure thing, partner," I agreed, flexing my shoulder and forcing him to take flight. He let off a light trail of dust.

"Bruther, I think they're going to have a little chat with him tonight. Poor bugger. Oh well, all's fair in love and war," Phil commented as we headed to my office for a drink, watching Jenny and Ed walking Dr. Freeman toward the guest rooms.

Frank decided to join us and fell in step with an eerie silence. I never really spent much time with Frank other than the normal pleasantries, and the guy wanted a drink.

Entering the office, Phil headed straight to the bar, setting up glasses and grabbing a light green bottle without a label. Frank looked over approvingly. "Frank? How do you think this is going to shake out?" I asked, genuinely wanting to hear his opinion.

Frank seemed relaxed. If I didn't know he was a V, I would think he was just a normal guy. What is normal these days, right? When I'd first met him, I thought he was just having a bad day.

"Now that I hear Goolsby and Vestulie are involved, I'm not sure. Did you know that Ezra and Marlow are stepbrothers? Well, they share the same mother. One had the gift, the other didn't. Or at least we don't think so," Frank commented, sipping his drink.

"Phil, what the hell is this? It's amazing," I said, taking a neat pull from my glass and looking at the smudge mark Phil had left on it.

"Elf Juice," Phil let out in the same cadence as the "ahhhh" that followed. "It's made of Plane's berry and Elf mash. About four thousand a bottle."

Almost spitting my drink, I looked at a smiling Phil. "No wonder your asses are always in my house. Gramps had a fortune in this crazy liquor stored here. Either way, this stuff is amazing. It's like Midori made out with Chambord then hooked up with some Ye Old Blackstrap Rum, resulting in a baby," I noted, watching the smile creep over Frank's face.

"You nailed it," Frank agreed. "However, I don't think you would be drinking that if you knew what Elf mash was."

"At this point, I don't want to know," I said, taking my pulls a little lighter. "Anyway, back to Marlow and Ezra, Ed said they were related but didn't get into any detail. This means he had a motive, if he inherited his brother's fortune and position," I noted, forgetting about the old adage that blood is thicker than water.

"Actually," Frank interjected. "We heard that when Marlow showed up to meet his brother's attorney, he turned everything over to a trust until they found who did this. I believe his exact words were, *'I am going to kill this person, then I'll worry about all that.'* Mr. Goolsby is not someone to cross. He is the head of the Order Society. As much of a piece of shit as he is, it has been well documented that he is brutally loyal to blood. Ezra disowned him after an incident in Africa pertaining their mother about ten years ago. According to all reports, Marlow never forgave himself either. From what I heard, their mother was killed, and Marlow was with her at the time.

"Directly after, a field recorder for the Council said something about Ezra in front of Mr. Goolsby. The next day, they found the field recorder's body hollowed out without any signs that someone had cut him. Not inside out like his skin. I mean his organs were found on the outside of his body in a bucket. All of them. That's some pretty serious magic to get that to happen. They tried to pin it on a Fae who works for him, but no luck," Frank said, finishing off his drink.

Frank was actually quite the talker, I noted as Phil and I stood there listening. "Vestulie is the enigma in this situation, being completely cooperative while having no reason to do so. I get he is probably working on the company's behalf, but he seems to keep popping up."

"He was at the professor's office, and he apparently knew a great deal about everything. I think Ed wants to have another chat with him," I added as I took another pull.

"I believe the Eater is an Ethereal or Fae from the Plane. Too sloppy for an Earthborn Mage. Or hell, who knows? Maybe they are doing that to throw everyone off. Earthborns are usually more subtle," Frank said, shaking his head in thought.

It was clear that while I had visions of him out sucking blood under the moonlight, he was actually out working his connections in the V community. Frank still had an edge to him.

Phil looked over, gumming an unlit cigarette. "I think it's time to head down to the Postern and the evidence room."

"Don't get lost down there or take something you shouldn't," Frank warned, grinning, then headed out the doors, throwing up a peace sign on his way out.

"Are all Vamps like this?" I asked Phil.

"Yup, pretty much. Except the really scary ones. Just wait until you get a load of one of those." Phil shook off a chill as he obviously thought about it.

The trip to the Postern was fairly uneventful minus the discovery of one missing gate key. The ten keys were inlaid in the door and were all different. Some were in the shape of keys with a few in the shape of coins with a handful looking like rocks. I grabbed the coin-shaped one and put it in the inside pocket of my blazer.

Phil and I spent most of our time speculating on whether or not Jamison was on the bad side of all this. Phil believed that Jamison was important because of his ties to his father, Ned, the high-ranking Fae from my rebirthday party.

"He's not dead yet, or at least he hasn't popped up. To me, that means he might be a suspect here," Phil established about Jamison.

"I'm not disagreeing; I just don't see anyone on that team being a plant," I countered, looking at Phil as if defending my Gramps's judgment of people.

"Look, bruther, I'll tell you this once. If you haven't figured it out yet, people on this side of things are not always what they appear to be. That magic Ed says the Eater is using could just as well be used to make someone appear to be someone else. Even enough to fool Tom."

The conversation was getting too serious, so I switched topics.

As with any good operation, you had to give your target a nickname. For Jamison, we had landed on Assface One. If we found Belm…yup, you guessed it, Assface Two. Elf Juice put you in a good mood. We'd see how that goes over the radios. Jenny had insisted we switch to the synced communicators in the morning.

"You figure any of these other gates out yet?" Phil asked, looking around the room and shuffling some papers on the desk in the middle.

"A little. I found a book that has all kinds of information on them, but it's more of a design-type manuscript. Nothing really solid on what they do. Just a bunch of funny pictures around sketches of the doors. Petro looked at it and said it looked like a bunch of doodles," I replied as we started out the door, closing it behind us. I turned to look at the dragon smiling back at me. For some reason, I always felt like it was watching me. Hell, it probably was.

The evidence room was down by the range and Jenny's lab. Looking at the door, I assumed there would be a secret magic lock or code. But nope, it was secured with a good old-fashioned key and lock followed by two full minutes of internal clicking and clanking inside the door, releasing a multilevel locking mechanism. That was a lot of drama for a simple key lock. As the door opened, my perception of a sterile evidence room vanished.

For starters, the room smelled old and musty with the thick scent of old, burnt papers and an undertone of freshly cut grass. It almost smelled like someone had walked by with a gas-powered lawn mower. It made the smoky scent level out.

The air was cool and not as damp feeling as the other rooms under the house. The ceiling was roughly ten feet tall. To the right was a small booth with a door and a meshed window, much like you would see in an old police movie or show. The booth, however, was old.

The lighting was dull and moody. On the booth's counter sat an old piece of parchment and the back of a fairly new computer that looked out of place. To the left was a small sitting area with a place to hang your coat and two small couches. The walls were stone, same as the rest of the foundation to the house; however, they were brownish gray, lending to the belief that this was a very, very old room. Ten feet past the entrance were shelves leading down a long hallway filled with odd-looking items and cardboard boxes obviously filled with evidence. You could see the hallway take a turn about thirty feet down.

I glanced at Phil. "What the hell is this place? It's kind of a mess," I said, staring at the shelves.

"It's the evidence room. They haven't really had anyone work down here in a long time; things had been quiet. Since the recent uptake in activity, there has been limited time, and evidence has just been dropped off and loosely cataloged. Kim also brings all her findings down here if it relates to OTN cases. If you can think about it being used for no good, it's probably down here somewhere. Also, there is something you need to know: always turn right; never take a left in here—it may lead to a few days' long detour," Phil warned, stepping closer to the computer and looking up the item Ed had sent us down here for.

"Ah, here it is. Six rights, and it should be to our right in a loose box labeled 'gate ropes.' Gate ropes are used when a group of people are up to no good and need to leave at the same time no matter where they are. They got outlawed by the Council. More specifically, by the NCTS in the US. It has something to do with how they are made, as well as the application."

"So there are many halls like this down here?" I asked, starting to pick up items off the shelves and study them.

"Oh yes, bruther. Tom once told me that no one has been to the center in over a hundred years. Apparently, you couldn't find it anyway. I heard he tried with a few Pixies a while back; he was looking for a special charmed mirror. It was not a blended item, but rather, it was supposed to be enchanted with the essence of an old Fae. It could change you into anyone if you looked at it and wished it. No clue why he wanted it, but he never could find it."

"Once again, I'm in another room that obviously doesn't fit into this building. Jenny explained it as if it was normal, at least for this building. She said half of it isn't really here?" I inquired as we kept going, taking the prescribed amount of rights.

"Who knows?" Phil replied. "It's some type of field. This place is old. Rumor has it, it came from the Plane centuries ago and has been built on ever since, but a piece of the Plane still remains in the center. Old magic. And—here it is." Phil leaned over, picking up a piece of rope coiled like a lasso. "These things are amazing. I wonder if we can keep it out or if we have to bring it back down here. If we got audited by the Council and it was found to be gone, that would be problematic."

"No way they could figure this all out?" I asked, looking at Phil.

"They could. You have just met our little team, but there are people who specialize in this type of stuff. If they are looking for something, they'll find it," Phil declared, looking at the shelves and gazing quizzically upon a purple box with a dragon crest like the one on the door to the Postern.

"That's curious," Phil murmured as he picked up and opened the box. Holding it in front of us, I could see a small glass globe and two small gems. The gems looked like glass eyes of some sort, while the globe had a translucent liquid resembling a duller version of mercury.

"You know, the dragon on the door of the Postern has two hollow spaces for eyes," Phil said, raising an eyebrow. Putting an unlit cigarette in his mouth, he chewed on it.

"Hey, man, isn't its mouth open and could hold something like that globe?" I joined Phil's interest.

"Damn right," Phil agreed. "I've been this far in here before and never seen this box. Notice how it doesn't have any dust on it?"

"You're right. It would at least have a layer of dust. That thing looks like it was just put there. Look at where you picked it up from. There is dust under the box. You think someone, or something, put it there for us to find?" I asked, tilting my head back.

"Max, this whole place feels alive sometimes. Hell, the house probably put it there or something. It's probably been in the room for a little bit, but I'm with you. It was purposefully placed here for us to find," Phil said, putting the lid back on tucking it under his arm. "I'll check it out of the computer. If we can't find it, I'll just sign it out in that old roster on the counter; that's for things not in the computer. You know the people who have been coming to catalog the books and digitize them? I don't think they are allowed down here, so that rules them out. When this is wrapped up, we should see if this does anything. Maybe get Jenny to look at it first."

Phil and I left the evidence room but not before I had a chance to see several other items I wanted to learn more about. I'd have to talk to Ed about coming back down here.

When we walked back into the main house, Jenny and Ed were standing in the offices talking to Petro.

"Here it is," Phil spoke up as he handed over the rope.

"Perfect. I'm glad it was still down there. You never know," Ed said as he looked over at Jenny. "You want to give them the good news?"

"Well, gents, it looks like the Council is concerned about us keeping this quiet. They're having a meeting with several civilian world leaders about the Balance in one week and have given us till then to resolve the murders or this city is going to become subject to a natural problem," Jenny informed.

"What do you mean by that? Are they coming here?" I asked.

"Not precisely," Ed spoke. "That means the Council will quarantine this area until they can get their hands on whatever it is everyone is looking for. Which, for us, is good—they don't really know what it is yet. Or they know more than they are letting us in on, in which case, we may be about to be put through a meat grinder. Either way, they don't want any interference in the meetings. The vote is coming soon. They don't want any loose ends. It wouldn't be good press if a demon was cut loose in New York the day of the meetings, if you get my drift."

Phil just rolled his eyes. "Politics. Max, last time this happened in Florida, they brewed up a damn hurricane and shut down the whole coast to address the issue."

"You mean they can make a hurricane just happen?" I asked, stunned.

"Yup. That's not the half of it," Phil said, tucking the purple box tighter under his arm.

"Right, I think it's time to get ready for tomorrow. There is still some more work to be done." Ed dismissed us as Petro flew over to my shoulder.

"Hey, boss. Lacey and Macey stopped by for a few. I need to talk to you about something," Petro murmured in a low voice meant not to be heard.

"Sure, buddy, can it wait till morning?" I was fearing the conversation about the birds and the bees. Petro agreed.

As the group broke off, I headed back to my room, wanting nothing more than to go to FA's for a drink. Per Jenny's recommendation, I spent the rest of the evening practicing casting words instead. She had supplied a list of phrases commonly used for fire magic and a handful for water casting. I had a hunch these would come in handy, deciding to spend the next hour in the shower figuring out how to manipulate the water.

Needless to say, things got interesting.

CHAPTER 18

First Coast Riot

After a morning breakfast with Petro in the kitchen and a minor counseling session, the day started out well. Petro had become an honorary brother to Lacey and Macey, bound to protect them and thus no longer a love interest. Well played, I thought after listening to the story.

"Hey, boss?" Petro asked while crunching on a handful of Golden Grahams. "You sure I can't go with you today?"

"Nope," I replied, looking over and sipping my quickly cooling coffee. "From the sound of it, you're going with us tomorrow on the big score. Ed wanted you to stay here and work on refreshing a few blended items he wants to take, whatever that means. I think they are a little old and need some attention."

"Ahh, kids' work. They just need a little dust, that's all. Not like they are enchanted or anything; just some old charmed junk," Petro said, smacking his hands together.

Petro and I wrapped up breakfast, followed by heading up to my room and got the essentials for the day. Magic blazer, sword, service pistol, and communicator. While the blazer could hold some extra things, it still weighed the same. I had to sacrifice one magazine to balance out the sword.

Last night, I'd fashioned a hook putting it on a shoulder holster that Phil had given me. Since I hooked the small pistol on my belt, it gave my pants some much needed relief and freed me up to move and pull it out a little faster, making the sword almost completely unnoticeable.

"Good morning, everyone," I greeted, walking into the offices with a yawn.

"Right, Max," Ed grunted as he walked out of his office toward the crucible room. Phil, Chloe, and Jenny were in there looking at the screen. Kim's face was in a corner of the monitor. "Kim, thanks for the update. If anything changes, let us know. For now, we will move forward as planned." Kim's picture clicked off as Chloe turned to me.

"Morning, sunshine. Looks like all's quiet on the western front. We are a go." Chloe smiled, holding a cup of Trish's finest from FA's and nodding her head toward a carton holding one last drink. *Thank God*, I thought to myself, hoping I didn't wake him up either.

The moment I picked up the cup and took a sip, I let the mouthful shoot out onto the floor, seeing Phil walk up and post pictures of our targets labeled "Assface 1" and "Assface 2." He turned around with a grin on his face. Something was going on today, and he liked the fact that things were moving forward.

"Very funny, boys," Jenny drawled as she shook her head, walking over to the pictures. She lifted a sharpie and wrote "AF1" and "AF2" under the names, not breaking a sweat. Phil was so red trying not to laugh that the colors of the tattoo on his neck were changing. Me? I was wiping coffee spit off my shirt. So she had a sense of humor. Ed, on the other hand—no, none at all this morning.

Once the rest of the group showed up, Ed went back over the day's plan. He seemed intent on us finding Jamison. I had a feeling that Ed was a few steps in front of the rest of us.

Chloe was dressed in a black pair of working pants with a blouse and a midsize jacket obviously trying to hide the fact she was carrying a pistol with little success. Her hair was straightened in a sleek ponytail, and as I walked closer, I could smell a mix of lavender and honeysuckle.

"Thanks for the coffee. I uh…spilled a little bit," I said, looking at her with my head tilted.

"That's all right. You can make it up to me later by buying me a drink," she flirted, strolling out of the room and leaving nothing to the imagination in her walk.

"Spilled a little bit…uhhh…thanks for the coffee… dumbass," I chided myself under my breath.

Jenny and Ed were standing by one of the desks, talking to each other. When you stood back and observed them, you could tell that one of them liked the other. Maybe they both liked each other. Either way, there was something there that I think they had yet to figure out. And maybe I was just reading into things.

After a few hours of going over plans for the next day, we decided to show up thirty minutes after shift change at the Blue House. Five thirty on a Thursday was a fairly straight shot into town with little traffic, since we had decided to drive the Black Beast. Phil would gate to Kim's office, and the rest of the crew would be able to head that way if needed quickly and would stay behind in the offices prepping for tomorrow.

Okay…so I had explained the cereal test earlier. But there happens to be one more test that stood above all others. This test was so ancient and important that it could change the course of history, start and stop love stories, change minds, and make enemies friends and friends enemies. What's this test, you ask? It's the "do you like what I am going to crank up on my radio during a drive" test. Or "are you going to ask if something else is on the radio" test.

Since this was my first real time alone with Chloe after London, I had settled on the ever-faithful ballad by Planes Drifter, "To the Edge of Hell." Often imitated, never duplicated. I had once been asked what the song sounded like by one of my army buddies. I said something like this: "Take 'Pictures of You' by the Cure, turn the amp up to eleven, and rock out so hard your liver may fall out." I think I nailed the description.

Long story short, you touch my radio, we may have a problem.

I met Chloe in the lobby with Petro in tow. He was giving me a lecture on getting back safe and reminding me that he had important work to do while I was gone. She was wearing the same clothes from earlier; however, it looked like she had put on some makeup and spent a little extra time on getting ready. Maybe it was the fact that she had put on some nicer high-heeled shoes. *Does that mean anything?* I thought, trying not to get too distracted from the evening ahead.

Full disclosure, I had actually combed my hair and thrown on some more respectable clothes. My blazer, dark jeans, and a navy-blue short-sleeve polo. I hadn't forgotten the main reason we were going out, though, and was loaded down with everything I needed in case trouble came looking for us.

"Ready to go?" I asked her as Petro finally stopped talking and took off down the main hall toward the offices.

"Ready as I'll ever be," Chloe replied, turning off the phone she had been messaging on. "Jenny just gave me a communicator."

"Gods and graves, she got you one too, huh?" I said, remembering to pull mine out. I pushed it in my ear, activating the device and instantly hearing Jenny talking to Phil.

"Hey, guys, it's me. Copy?" I radioed, looking over at

Chloe who had already turned hers on without guidance. She was a pro.

"*Loud and clear, bruther,*" Phil responded once he finished telling Jenny he had made it to Kim's office sober. I could hear her in the background laughing at Phil as he obviously made a face or rude gesture.

Ed chirped in. "*Right, we are a go. We don't expect any trouble at this time, so we're getting back to work here. Let me know as soon as you see the target.*"

"Roger. AF1 mission is a go," I replied, having a hunch Ed was calling me an ass under his breath.

Chloe and I climbed into the Black Beast as I started the war machine up. "Nice truck, Max. Compensating for something?" Chloe laughingly asked, passing judgment on all Americans for driving big trucks.

I opted to start the radio test immediately after that blow to my ego. I was proud of the Black Beast. As she roared to life, Planes Drifter came pouring out of the speakers. Not too loud to not be able to talk, but loud enough to make the person in the vehicle take notice.

Chloe glanced at me, smiled, and threw up some devil horns. "Oh, this is one of my favorites," she said, singing along to the first verse as we pulled out onto Highway 16 heading to I-95 North.

Love. It happens. Is it real or just a feeling you get when you haven't had a girl in your car for a while? She passed the test on my first attempt. She even turned it up during the chorus. As the song stopped, we pulled onto I-95, and I turned the radio down. Hell, maybe she was testing me. I bet she was.

"So what do you think we are going to find?" I asked Chloe as she settled in for the forty-minute drive.

"I'm not sure. I hear this place is nice. If it's uneventful, hopefully dinner," Chloe answered. "I think everyone is focused on tomorrow and getting us out of their way. You know, Phil is going to Jacksonville to brief Kim. I doubt he will be paying much attention to us."

"Figured as much. I'm hoping to get some time to relax. If we find Jamison, I plan on getting him back to the Atheneum and going for a drink later at FA. You game?" I offered.

"It's a date," Chloe replied as she took out her service pistol and checked the chamber. That was her: always friendly but with an edge. *Did I check my breath before leaving?*

While driving, Ed came over the radio to tell us to try and be back by 9:00 p.m. If we had to gate back, we could leave my truck and come back to get it in a few days.

As we arrived to Jacksonville, Riverplace Tower stood tall and white with black windows striping the building. There was a parking garage attached to its side, and since it was quitting time, it had emptied out minus a handful of cars.

Chloe and I parked, wandering in through the main entrance. The directions were easy. Go to the main elevator bank and push the up button, putting a little effort into it. On cue, the arrow dinged, and the far-right elevator opened up. The inside was dark and trimmed in wood. Looking at the button panel, Chloe quickly tapped in the code. The digital readout registered all zeroes as it lurched to life, taking us to our floor.

We hadn't really figured out what floor we were going to. Ed said most buildings had the thirteenth floor reserved for Magical or Ethereal business, but we were going much higher up than that. The elevator lurched to a stop, and the doors slid open to reveal the Blue House.

How to describe it? For starters, the face of a gorgeous hostess stared at you, making sure you were in the right place. The restaurant was huge, occupying the entire floor. The first thing that stood out was the blue tint to everything, giving you the feeling of being underwater. After doing a quick scan around, I saw the color was coming from a mix of oddly tinted windows and some fancy decorative art-deco ambient lighting.

Stepping out of the elevator to the left, we saw the main seating area, a large room with tables set neatly in rows. You could see from one side of the building to the other. To the right was the kitchen and service area, both separated in the middle by a large bar that faced the seating area with a waist-high wall divided by glass the rest the way to the ceiling.

It was the type of bar that people went to while either waiting for a seat or to conduct business. To the virgin eye, the place looked like any other boutique high-end establishment. I had learned over the past weeks to look closer, and I could see hints of the Mage and Ethereal worlds woven throughout. It wasn't like the Fallen Angel, where you knew you were either in the wrong place or at home. A rich executive probably wouldn't be able to tell the difference.

The floor was filled, much to my surprise, with a mix of crafts and people, crafts being the magical equivalent of a representative of someone else. Ed had mentioned that Mages often did business this way to avoid being seen. You could tell a craft by their slightly gray-tinted skin and their mildly clouded eyes, again being only noticeable to those who knew the difference.

Chloe glanced at me as we walked up to the hostess.

"Chloe and Max Abaddon Sand. We're just here for a drink," Chloe said as she cracked a disingenuous smile, the first I had seen on her face.

The hostess typed something into her tablet and looked up with a mirrored smile of indifference. "Ah, you are good. Mr. Goolsby sends his regards. Take this card with you to the bar. Drinks are on the house," she informed, her demeanor changing after reading the note. "You two must be special. I don't see Mr. Goolsby having guests like this too often. Please help yourselves. If there is anything you need, please let me know," the young lady finished as she ushered us over to the bar.

The bar was directly behind the hostess stand. We couldn't see the patrons, just the wall separating the dining area from the rest of the space. There was enough room for us to enter and not be overly obvious. Walking to the side, we could clearly see a handful of people at the bar, including the bartender.

He was at least seven feet tall and looked half Asian, half black. He had a solid smile on his face and was wiping off wine glasses, something bartenders did when they were bored or didn't want to talk to the patrons.

What caught our attention was Assface 1 sitting at the bar. He was hard to miss, with fire-red hair, pale skin, and a pointy nose. Jamison was talking to some type of greaser crackhead wearing all leather, looking very out of place. AF1 was dressed, well…normally. Since he was Ned's son, I was expecting a guy in a suit similar to the rest of the Fae I had met, which at this point, had been all of one.

"I think that's our mark," Chloe whispered as she gestured me over to the bar, looking at the smiling bartender.

"Gods and graves, this is going to be interesting," I muttered, observing the assorted crew sitting at the bar. For a nice place, it was an eclectic scene.

As we approached the bar, Jamison and the greaser turned around almost as if they knew we were heading over to talk to them.

"About time," Jamison said in a thick voice not matching his appearance. AF1 and Phil could have a man-off to see who had the deeper voice. "Pull up a seat. Rex, a round of drinks for our friends here. I think two Vamp Ambers will do."

I liked the guy instantly after that. I didn't think he could do any wrong. "You two scream authority. Think you could tone it down a notch?" Jamison asked as he scooted over so Chloe and me sat between him and his friend. "Name's Jamison. You must be Max and Chloe. I believe we've met before," he told her, lifting an eyebrow and smiling.

"We have," Chloe agreed, taking a seat next to him to avoid having to sit next to the greaser. "Three years ago at the annual ball. We didn't talk to each other. Thanks for the drink."

I looked over at Jamison, ignoring the greaser sitting next to me. He smelled like pepper and was making less than appealing noises. He could tell I was sizing him up as Rex handed me a beer, raising his eyebrows, making it a point to tell me without talking not to push the guy. I whispered into thin air, "AF1 located." I figured the team was listening.

"Jamison, nice to meet you. I met your father, Ned, a week ago. Nice guy," I started, trying to set some type of level conversation before we got to the weird stuff.

"Yup. I don't hear him being called a nice guy too often. Belm, if you're done freaking out our company. Anyway, I think your timing is perfect joining us here," Jamison said.

I looked at the greaser and said to the air, "Ahh, AF2." The smell should have given it away; he smelled like Devin. Not nearly as put together though; he was a mess with a razor-sharp aura.

"Belm, nice to meet you. I've heard a lot about you from Devin." I was hoping to get him to stop making the rasping, breathing noise. He didn't.

His voice came out low and stressed, as if he was trying not to yell what he was saying. "Yes. Father. Seems like everyone here has a famous relative. We are rejects, the next generation," Belm spoke, rasping out a laughing cough that caught Jamison's attention at the same time. He also let out a snicker.

"What about the timing is so good?" I asked, again having the feeling I was a few steps behind everyone else.

Belm glanced at Chloe. "Hey, pretty lady. You're a diviner. How far can you see?"

"Far enough to know what the hell you are. Jesus, you're a demon," Chloe accused as she stood up, pulling her ears back and taking a defensive posture.

"Relax. I'm not here to cause trouble. Actually, I'm here to help. Though that's all a matter of opinion, isn't it?" Belm mused.

Rex the bartender walked up leaning on the bar, talking to our group. "I know why you're here, and I don't really have anything to say. I think your friends here can tell you everything you need to know. I highly recommend you all take your conversation outside."

"Rude," Jamison said as he took a pull off his beer. "I guess we can leave after this drink."

Chloe was turning pale as she stared at Belm. I guess a demon was a big deal. Hell, I had no idea what that really meant. All I knew was that these two were supposed to be the good guys.

"Hey, Max. You smell that?" Belm asked, looking at the two men sitting at the opposite side of the bar. "That's charred flesh burned by magic that hasn't healed yet."

"I'm confused. What do you mean by—" I stopped midsentence, getting a closer look at the men sitting at the opposite side of the bar. As the larger one took a drink of his cocktail, I saw a bandage on his wrist under the cuff of his shirt. I looked over to Chloe as the large, bulking man smiled.

"Let's get out of here. Everyone go..." Chloe trailed off; it was obvious her divination had picked up on something unexpected.

Combat happens quickly. It's violent and unpredictable. A second seems like a minute, a minute seems like an hour, and an hour seems like an eternity. Several things happened all at once.

The men at the opposite side of the bar stood up, and the taller man's hands started to glow green. Once I saw the green glow, I knew it was the same team from London, and he was putting together the same nasty mess he had thrown at us before. The other shorter man was obviously the same man Chloe had shot. He started reaching into his coat, but it was too late.

Chloe had already started moving toward her service pistol. Rex pushed a button, closing off the dining section of the restaurant with a thud as a solid metal wall appeared, covering the glass. The only people left were our team, the men on the opposite side of the bar, and about ten other pale-looking crafts sitting at the high-top tables scattered around the bar.

The entrance behind us and route to the elevator was still clear; however, the rest of the room was cut off. Rex, sensing trouble, dove out of sight.

This is where things got a little crazy. Jamison kept sipping his beer, squatting down, as Belm jumped up on the bar. Belm then proceeded to turn pitch-black and rip through his clothes, releasing an eight-foot-long spiked, spear-like tail, turning into, well...a demon.

Two glowing, hissing green spheres flew over our heads, slamming into the metal wall with a pronounced thump and whoosh, splashing the acid-like matter on the floor behind us.

Belm's eyes flared and his hands turned to claws; his transformation happened in the blink of an eye. He dropped to the ground on all fours as his tail ripped through three of the crafts sitting behind our group in a spray of gore and gray sludge. The apparent telltale sign of a craft.

When I went to talk into my communicator, I realized that it had been eerily silent and the cool feeling it brought to my ear wasn't present. Someone or something was jamming the signal. I bet it was one of the two jackasses trying to kill us. Ed had said it was nearly impossible for the signal to be blocked; however, I was learning quickly that *impossible* was more of a suggestion.

By the time I fully realized what Belm was doing to howls of enjoyment, I felt several thumps on my blazer before Chloe pulled me down under our side of the bar.

The smell of gunpowder and sulfur filled the air among the sounds of cracking bones accompanied by splintering wood.

I could still clearly see Belm violently ripping through the crafts that had obviously been sent there to deal with us, feeling a searing pain in my right arm when my patience ran out.

As Chloe rose up to let out a small barking *pat, pat, pat* from her service pistol, I noticed five other crafts coming around the entrance straight toward us at full speed. Jamison was still crouching down and smiling.

It's amazing what you can do when you feel your life's in danger.

"Enough," I said out loud, my words drowned out by the noises of fighting and gagging coming from Belm's work on the crafts. I reached into my jacket and pulled out Durundle, blindly yelling, "*Ignis!*"

Hellfire engulfed the blade, lighting up the side of the room we were on. Two blasts of green plasma slammed into the bar above us, shattering the marble.

I turned to the crafts, taking a leading swipe at the first two as they came within touching distance, instantly engulfing them in fire while cutting off their legs at the knees, spraying gray gore on us. It was like slicing through butter and not bone, leaving the scent of burnt rubber behind. The sword sang as it flew through the air. I stood up from my crouching position, pointing the sword at the other three crafts, and without thinking, yelled, *"Bellos,"* making the sword shoot a stream of hellfire toward the other three crafts.

The crafts on fire turned and ran toward the entrance, colliding with the others who were trying to leave the room at the same time, setting several of them on fire in the process. It was true chaos. I guess hellfire was a little sticky.

As the last craft in the room expired, the sprinkler system went off, dousing the room in a light foam that put out most the flames minus my blazing sword. Chloe backed up due to the amount of castings chipping away at the bar, and was behind me when I turned to look her in the face.

From what I could tell, Belm was working his way over to the men. Chloe spun to face me with her service pistol pointed directly at my chest. Shocked, my heart stopped for a beat. As Chloe squeezed the trigger, I heard her voice in my head screaming, *"Get down!"* and I immediately dropped to the ground, extinguishing the sword and slipping on the foam.

The cadence of her service pistol released the trademark three-round burst that I had grown used to. Before I could fully look, I again heard the distinct sound of three quick muffled impacts, followed by another burst of fire.

Turning around, I watched as the demon jumped over the hulking figure, lancing both him and his partner through the chest with his tail in one fell swoop. Belm landed on the other side and slowly removed his tail from the men with a crunching, wet sound. The move was almost poetic, as it was so violent and efficient.

It was over. Jamison was still squatting down, holding his hand over his beer with an eyebrow raised. It was at that moment I realized that in all the fighting, Chloe saw a chance to land several rounds in our attackers while Belm kept them distracted. Hey, like the paperwork said, a bullet is still a bullet. Plus, I bet Chloe's had a little extra kick to them.

In the silence after the firefight, everyone took stock of their body parts. Me? I had been shot in the shoulder by the smaller of the two attackers. The blazer, as it had been designed, stopped the bullet, but it allowed the tip of the round to lodge into my skin, only making the wound superficial but still hurting like hell.

As I pulled the blazer from the impact area, the bullets tinkled to the floor, muffled by the foam. Chloe, Jamison, and the now crackhead version of Belm all stood there staring at me. I put the sword back under my arm.

The room looked like something out of a gothic horror winter fairy tale. White foam and gray splatter covered the walls and bottles. I'd have to ask later what that stuff was called.

Where the two men had fallen was a pool of distinctly different red blood spreading out.

"Stand back," Belm indicated. "The big one has not taken the trip yet." He walked to the other side of the bar, naked, to retrieve his clothes.

Looking at the men on the floor, I saw they were almost fully covered in foam. I held out my hand, whispering, "*Aquas.*" A light steam covered the bodies, rinsing off the foam to fully expose the two men. *Hey, you can only learn so much water control in a shower.* I had graduated to steam so far. Chloe and Jamison stared at me as Belm stood there, chuckling in his raspy voice.

"Nice trick. I wish I could stay and help clean this up, but I don't think finding a demon here will help anyone," Belm said before he disappeared in some type of blur. I guess demons could do that. Jamison looked unfazed. Rex had obviously disappeared. As we walked up to the bodies, the communicators chirped back to life, and I heard Ed's voice.

"*Nearly there.*" He sounded out of breath. I responded with a simple, "Sure."

Chloe still had her pistol drawn. "That was the craziest shit I've ever seen," Chloe exhaled as she turned to look at the mess Belm had left the men in. Her rounds had landed in the large man's side under his arm, going through his chest.

"He's somehow still alive," Jamison noted, finally setting his beer down, the bottle landing on what was left of the bar.

Ed, Kim, and Phil came rushing into the room. Phil slipped and landed on the foam floor right where I had taken out the first two crafts, leaving him covered in a mix of everything that was on the floor. Ed had gated in somewhere while Phil and Kim rushed over, taking the elevator here, evident by its ding.

A handful of heavy hitters who looked to be employees of Mr. Goolsby also came rushing in directly after with Rex. He had made it out somehow. Hey, never doubt a bartender.

Kim stood at the entrance, cutting them off. She pulled out her badge and politely asked them to piss off. I kept my eyes on her. The cavalry had finally arrived—late, but they were here.

"What the hell?" Ed muttered as he looked around. The hellfire I had shot had charred the entrance and the accompanying wall.

"Bruther, this is a mess," Phil said, finally on his feet, shotgun at the ready. The new additions to the party were still trying to take in everything they were seeing. The incident later that evening became known as the First Coast Riot.

Jamison looked up, nodding at Ed. "That big one is still alive. He's so packed full of Etherium that I can smell it. It's the only thing keeping his lights on."

Ed marched over, taking off his blazer, and pulled out a smooth, flat, rounded stone, placing it on my previous attackers forehead.

"What are you doing?" Chloe asked as she holstered her pistol walking closer to the two men.

"Trying to concentrate," Ed replied before starting to mumble under his breath. Chloe looked anxious as she stepped a little closer. This guy had tried to kill not only her but me as well—twice. With a pop of ozone, the man gasped and settled back down, coughing blood from his filled lungs.

"Why are you here?" Ed asked.

The man was obviously under a spell. He started gargling an answer. "To collect the Fae and read his memory, and…" He was moving slightly on the floor, obviously coming to terms with his impending death. I had seen this before, when I was deployed.

Ed leaned over and poured the contents of a small vial into the man's gasping mouth. "Did you kill the other people on the Vale team?" Ed continued, rushing his questions since he knew time was running out.

"Yes. Just doing my job, and…" The man let out a breath that was nearing finality.

"Damn, I'm losing him. I'm going silent. No one talk." Ed was clearly drilling into his memories, mumbling something under his breath as the man writhed in pain and, with a twitch of his hand, disappeared into nothing with a pop and blast of air, pushing Ed to the wet ground.

"Bloody hell!" Phil exclaimed. "He just gated. How the hell?"

Phil went closer, bending over, picking up a small device from the floor, similar to a pen with a clicker on the end. "A peer gate. Where did he get that?"

Ed was sitting there staring at the space that the body used to occupy. "Something familiar. Are we sure his partner is dead? I saw a few things, but something shut me out and caused the gate to activate." Ed stood straight and looked around, then down at the other man.

"He's gone," Jamison said. "Trust me on that one."

Ed nodded his head. "Well, we found the Eater. That was him, no doubt. Just a damn puppet working for a puppet master. Wherever he is, he's dead, that much is for sure. That gate was an insurance policy," Ed spoke, talking to no one in particular. Almost as if he was trying to convince himself of something.

"Chloe, bring Jamison and Max downstairs. I need to talk to Kim and make a call," Ed indicated, gesturing for Kim and Phil to walk over to him, letting the other men in as well.

Marlow Goolsby stood in the hallway. He was in a gray suit with a glowing white button-down shirt, the top few buttons undone, and not wearing a tie. Marlow had an aggravated look on his face, the look you gave a kid when you were dropping them off at school and they told you they had forgotten to do an important homework assignment due today.

Marlow was looking around the scene with his arms crossed. One of his men approached him to talk just as his eyes landed on me, and he put up a single finger, waving off the man.

"Max," Marlow said in a calm, level voice. "Mind telling me about your little party? Seems like we have a little issue on our hands, and needless to say, I need to understand why my bar is destroyed."

I was still running on adrenaline, so I decided to just tell him. "We got him. The man who killed Ezra." I was letting him know I understood the connection.

Chloe eyed both of us, still anxious from the fight.

Marlow stood there for about thirty seconds before he finally spoke. "I'll speak with Edward. If this is the case, consider yourself free of my statement yesterday. If you still need to talk to Rex, please do so. He's at your disposal. However, if you ever step foot in here again or attempt to, we will be talking again but not on such common terms," Marlow warned as he dropped his arms and started to walk past.

"Hey, you mean that as a threat?" I asked.

"Precisely that," Marlow replied, marching past us into the room to talk to Kim.

I stood there for a second, letting everything sink in. As I looked around, I could see char marks where the burning crafts had evaporated. I guess burning crafts didn't leave as much of a mess as ones taken out by other means. *Thing is*, I thought to myself, *someone was driving those.*

Chloe, Jamison, and I walked into the car park. "You're coming back with us; we have a few things to sort out. Dr. Freeman is with us," I told Jamison, hoping the name would build some trust.

It did. Jamison immediately lit up. "That's great. I was worried about him. Look, thanks for that. And I know they're going to figure out soon enough that we had some help in there, but I would prefer to explain Belm to everyone later," Jamison requested as we reached the Black Beast.

Phil came over the communicator. *"Hey, get back to the Atheneum. Mr. Goolsby Grouchypants is being rather cooperative. Kim is going to stay here and get this cleaned up. We will still be a while. Ed wants us to meet in a few hours."*

Jenny also spoke. I could hear Petro in the background asking questions. *"Thank the stars everyone is okay. Petro is about to go crazy."*

In all the excitement, I had forgotten I had been slightly shot and was bleeding under my blazer. "You any good with stiches?" I asked Jenny.

"Just get back. I think we all need to figure out what just happened. I heard your conversation. You got him?" Jenny asked as I heard Petro buzzing right by her ear.

"Yes, we did. We'll be home soon," I replied.

Phil chirped in, *"You called it home. You're stuck with us now, bruther."*

I was going home for a shower, a few stiff drinks, and to let Petro give me an earful about what he would have done if he was with us.

We looked like a bunch of zombie extras for a cheesy movie, covered in mess and wet from the foam.

Chloe smiled at me as we loaded up into the truck. "I guess that's going to be another rain check on that drink?"

CHAPTER 19

Fae Drunk

"I'm exhausted," I proclaimed to the group as we pulled back onto the highway after a few minutes of reflective silence.

"Look at your castor. I noticed it when we were in the car park," Chloe said in her British accent, pointing at my wrist. The watch was no longer deep bloodred, but rather a cooling blue-silver mix. "You used up everything you had in you. Or at least it got pulled from you when all those fireworks went off. That was something else." She raised an eyebrow as Jamison chuckled from the back seat. "What's so funny, Red?"

"Ha, that sword. I know what it is. It's enchanted—old Fae magic; not charmed or blended. And you just showed up with the gas for it. Let me ask you," Jamison paused as he leaned forward to poke his head between the two of us in the front seat. "Do you actually know what you did back there? I don't think you do. A new junior Mage yelling *Ignis* while pulling out a sword would have melted it. That sword likes you. And the fact that you had it and not some other weapon probably just saved your hands from turning into a snack for Belm."

I glanced at Chloe. "He's right. What I did back there just came out of me. I lost control of myself for a minute. I wanted something to happen, and it did. Looks like Jenny will be wanting to spend more time in the lab with me," I sighed, focusing on the road.

Jamison reached in his bag and handed me a small potion bottle. "Here, drink this. It will get you back to normal until you get some rest."

"What is it?" I asked, pulling the cork out of the top and releasing a waft of honey.

"It's a potion to settle the Etherium in your body. Nothing too magical, just some minerals with a little extra kick to get them into your system. Not as good as a cup of coffee, but it will prevent you from feeling drained. Take it," Jamison explained as he sat back in his seat.

I turned up the bottle, taking a pull and letting out a sigh. While it wasn't as aggressive as the anti-hangover potion Phil had given me, it had a soothing sensation that did just as promised. I needed to set aside some time with Petro to learn more about potions. Jenny had explained that some potions didn't mix well, and that having too many in my body could have catastrophic effects. I was still in the "ask for forgiveness" phase of figuring these things out, like a teenager getting drunk for the first time.

"Chloe, what are your plans for the rest of the evening?" I asked, starting to level out my thoughts.

"Well, if you haven't noticed, I'm a mess. I need to gate to the Dunn and get cleaned up, then grab a few things for tomorrow. Unless there are any changes to the plan, I'll be back in the early morning. If it wasn't for this mess, I'd say you still owe me a drink," she proclaimed, closing all chances of an evening together. "Oh, I noticed the journal sitting in the back seat. Looks and smells like you got what you needed out of it. Can I take a look? I'll make sure it's taken care of and will give it back to you in the morning. I'm interested about what's in it after everything I've heard today."

I considered for a second if Ed would be upset. After retrieving the key and other information from it, he hadn't mentioned the journal again. "Sure. Old uptight will be fine. I don't think there's anything else we need in it. I do want to take it with us, though, just in case."

Jamison spoke up. "Well, Max, looks like you will have to settle for a few drinks with me. I'm not planning on going on whatever it is you have planned for tomorrow; I work with information, not my body."

"You're a full-blooded Fae. You could have taken out those two men with a snap of your fingers," Chloe accused with a slight edge of agitation, holding the journal in her lap.

"True. However, that's not my style. My father, Ned, is on the Council, and that kind of thing is frowned upon," Jamison said with finality. He was telling us the truth. While I knew there was more to him, Jamison and Dr. Freeman were on the nice list.

The rest of the drive was fairly normal. Jamison and I planned on meeting in Tom's old office at about 9:00 p.m. to have a drink and go over any details that we might need to know. Chloe was leaving as soon as we got back against Ed's recommendations, and this time I made sure to let Phil know we would save a few cold ones for him while he griped about his cleanup duties.

"Good night, Max," Chloe said as she leaned over and kissed my cheek, leaving me blushing.

"Good night. Drive safe," I replied as she walked through the gate in the main entrance.

"Drive safe?" Jamison chuckled. "Classy. Don't get kissed much on the cheek by pretty girls?"

"Look, it's not like that. I think it's a European or

British thing," I denied, not hiding my excitement and also embarrassment. "What do you say? Gate safe?"

"It's a start," Jamison allowed. His chuckles always came across as earned arrogance. With his mix of fire-red hair and rich looks, he actually pulled it off without pissing me off.

I headed toward the house calling for Petro. On cue, he came flying up as I entered the kitchen.

"Hey, boss. We've been worried sick. Here, take this," Petro urged as he handed me a ziplock bag of what looked like gray clay. "Jenny made this for you. She said to put it on your shoulder before you get in the shower, then rinse it off after five minutes. It should make that smelly wound of yours heal up faster." Petro held his nose, letting me know he had a great sense of smell.

By the sound of things, the smell of blood made him queasy. Petro continued spilling out a jumble of words, making up for lost time. "Jenny would put it on herself, but Ed just gated back, and they are in her office discussing something. Not sure what, but it's something big. Oh yeah, another thing! Apparently, Dr. Freeman had more beans to spill after you left. Not sure what, but it got Ed all kinds of excited. Whatever spell your Gramps put on him was good; probably time released or situational. Freeman was alone with Ed for one minute, and he started singing like a bird."

"Great, something else to throw into the pot," I said as I trudged into my room, taking off my blazer and exposing my shoulder and blood-encrusted shirt. Petro zipped off.

After thirty minutes of self-examination for other injuries and finally taking off the clay, I was feeling good. My shoulder would be sore for a few days and had already started turning purple, but the wound itself looked to be completely healed.

I had given Jamison directions to the office and left the

back door unlocked. Leshya had stopped by and dropped off a bag for tomorrow containing a black combat outfit and a full-on dragon armor kit. This was starting to look like another day of getting shot at. It seemed to be happening a lot lately.

By the time Jamison arrived, I had already poured us two of my all-time favorite cocktails, the not-yet-but-soon-to-be-classic vodka and sprite with extra lemons. It's what I called the redneck vodka tonic. Jamison looked at it, raising an eyebrow, before finally clinking glasses and taking a sip.

"Mmm...this is oddly good. Great vodka as well," Jamison complimented as he sat down in the chair facing my desk. I took my seat in the leather throne and kicked my feet up.

"Glad you like it. I used to have a girlfriend from Austin who got me hooked on these. Nothing fancy; simple and to the point. So tell me what you were doing at the Blue House tonight. I'm not buying this story about you being there every Thursday. I didn't want to say anything, but I believe tonight was orchestrated," I started, letting out my thoughts on the evening.

"Just like Tom—smart. Yes, your friend Phil was searching for me, so I obliged. I knew the cat was out of the bag about Dr. Freeman finding the Fountain, so we can skip all that. Belm and I decided to go fishing. Looks like we caught our fish," Jamison said, leaning back and taking another eager sip.

"Bait. You used us as bait," I realized, raising an eyebrow. "You knew that if you put the information out there and someone was looking, the right people would find out and be there."

"Bingo," Jamison admitted, finishing his drink quickly and forcing me to immediately slam the rest of mine. I stood up, still listening, to mix another round of drinks. "You see, we figured that if Belm and I were the only ones left and other parties knew that tomorrow was a special night, they would, without a doubt, play their hand. Which they did. Plus, we knew your team would not be far behind. I can tell you this whole thing proves one major point."

"What's that?" I asked, handing Jamison another drink. This time, I had made them in taller glasses.

"The Eater, as I hear you call him, is nothing more than a thug. A hired puppet just doing the work for someone we have yet to see. You know my father is a powerful Fae, as am I...to a point. The fact that we still don't know who is behind this is what's truly scary," Jamison said before immediately slamming his second drink, again forcing me to follow suit.

Petro showed up momentarily and helped himself to a small cap of vodka before buzzing away. I think he was just making sure I was still there.

"True. What's your take on the Balance?" I asked, cutting to the chase.

"Oh...that." Jamison stood up, this time pouring our rounds of drinks and making them perfectly. "I wish they would go ahead and vote to get it started. Look, I'm a pure Fae living on Earth, so I have nothing to gain or lose here. Most people living on Earth are in the same situation. But there is more to gain than lose here. Fae such as myself choose to live here for different reasons. In some cases, because we are not welcome on the Plane. Politics knows no boundaries."

"Fair enough. So what about the others who live on the Plane?" I asked.

"They look at this as negative for the most part. I can go to the Plane, but I choose not to. My father's love for mankind made that certain. Don't fool yourself, Max. He's still a Fae. There are others who travel between the two, mostly Ethereals and Fae. Those are the ones who think the Balance is a chance to take more control. You know, over Earth. You might think that's weird, but wait till you have more time to settle into your new surroundings. It's not that far-fetched. A thousand years is nothing to some of them.

"Those parties think if the human race and everything else living here combined forces and resources, the chances of that ever happening are either gone or significantly harder to obtain. You saw it tonight. A bullet can take down a powerful Mage, and the same applies to Fae and many Ethereals. I call Ethereal something or someone that doesn't fall into any real category and includes many of your deities or gods."

"That's probably the best way I've had it explained to me," I said, starting to warm up to the libations.

After thirty more minutes of talking and discussing the night, Ed's voice came over the communicator that I hadn't realized was still in my ear. He set a meeting for the early morning; apparently, something important had presented itself. I knew Ed was with Jenny working on something. Phil was heading our way to join us. I made sure to let him know that he had some catching up to do and to grab some of those antihangover potions or he wasn't allowed to join. Trusty Phil promised not to let us down.

By the time we decided we needed to stretch our legs, Jamison and I were pretty much smashed.

"Hey, let's go look at that Postern room I've heard so much about," Jamison suggested, sounding much more comfortable than before.

Hell, why not? I thought, *maybe he could help me figure some of it out.*

Plus, I needed to get up and walk.

We trekked through the house joking about everything, from girls to our favorite food on FA's menu. I liked Jamison. He was not in the Phil category, but I could see why Gramps liked him. He was honest and direct.

Walking up to the entrance to the Postern, I stopped and looked at the door. "You know what that dragon means?" I asked.

"It's there for protection," Jamison replied, leaving it at that, seeing my drunk satisfaction with his answer.

Walking into the room, Jamison let out a whistle. "Max, there's so much Etherium in here, it's making my hair stand up on the back of my neck."

I commented on the fact that he didn't have any hair on his neck, causing us both to laugh.

It was about 10:30 p.m. when Phil finally sent a text saying he was home and asking where the hell we were. After a round of name-calling, Phil said he would be there in twenty minutes.

Jamison looked over after examining one of the gate doors. "This place is amazing. Have you figured any of these out yet?"

"Only the one on the far left. You take one of those keys embedded on the frame, and wherever you are, it gates you back here. I think if you have a key somewhere, it will take you there as well," I said, walking closer to the middle table.

"I can see that coming in handy. I bet some of these go to very specific places," Jamison mused, smelling the air.

"Gods and graves, who knows?" I replied. The gate in the middle of the far wall shimmered to life.

"Holy shit," Jamison exclaimed as he marched over to it. "Say that again."

"Gods and graves?" I mumbled in the form of a question. The words made the gate glow.

This gate was an older-looking door that was one of the

more normal openings in the room. It was cherrywood and set with pentagrams that seemed to be crafted in pure silver. The doorjamb was solid iron housing intricate details carved throughout.

"Where did you hear that phrase?" Jamison asked.

"It's carved in Gramps's desk," I replied. "We have to see where this goes. Hey, are you good enough to bring us back here?"

Jamison glanced at me, smiling. "Only one way to find out." He stepped through the gate. Thinking on my feet, I pocketed a round key from the Evergate, just in case. After a second of hesitation, I followed behind, letting the alcohol erase the responsibilities ahead.

Arriving on the other side, we both took a second to take in the scene. The gate opened into a large, cavernous room. What was more striking was the vast amount of other gates in the room. There were gates as far as the eye could see. It was like the Postern on steroids, and sitting in the middle of the room in front of us was an old man hunched over at a desk with a stack of papers looming in front of him.

"This is crazy," I whispered, looking at Jamison.

"Let's go talk to the old man," Jamison said as he sidestepped, obviously feeling as good as I did.

The man seemed to be roughly eighty years old. He was small and slender, wearing small, round, gold-rimmed glasses. He had a black robe that had seen better days draped over him. As we drew closer, he looked up with raised eyebrows without moving the rest of this body.

Once we got up to the small oak desk, we both took a step back. The old man's finger moved, letting off a cloud of dust and cracking noise. He hadn't moved in what could have been no less than ten years. He smelled like a musty, damp book;

however, his eyes were as sharp as razor blades.

Jamison spoke up, realizing that I was in awe looking at him. "Hello...Whom may we have the pleasure of greeting? We seem to be slightly lost. Where are we?"

"I am the Messenger. It has been some time since I have seen anyone. As you can see behind you, your gate is still open, and you have a friend walking through it as we speak. Who do you want me to send a message to?" the old man finished in a rather calm voice still wearing its age.

By then, Phil had reached us. "What the feck is this, bruthers?" he let out in a loud bellow.

I looked at the two. "Well, since we are in front of the Messenger, and he asked us to send a message to someone, let's get one out," I said as Phil glanced at Jamison, sizing up how much drinking he had to do in order to catch up. In Phil's defense, he was cradling a Vamp Amber and a pistol in his other hand.

The Messenger moved slowly, creating clouds of dust, and pushed a piece of blank parchment and a quill in front of me. *Hell*, I thought, *who is this going to?*

"Sir, who was the last person who sent a message?" I asked.

"Let me see," he croaked, looking over at the one-paper-high stack to his right. "Icupiousous. Many of these gates are no longer used or have been abandoned. I believe his is still active."

I reached down and scribbled a note.

Dear kind sir,

Please read the following out loud to a group of people: I. C. U. P.

Love,

Max, Phil, and Assface 1

"Here you go. Please make sure Icupiousous gets this note," I requested, turning on my heel and heading back toward the gate while holding back the laughter.

Jamison and Phil followed suit, as we walked back into the Postern, the gate closing behind us. Phil was chugging his beer; he had already started on another one from the six pack he had brought with him.

We all immediately started laughing.

"Holy hell. I've actually heard of that place. I thought it was a myth," Jamison said, still smiling. "I know of the Messenger and his realm. It was a story my nanny would tell trying to get me to sleep. I also heard it was destroyed during the war—not the one you gents are probably thinking about. Story goes that the Messenger was exiled thousands of years ago to a realm that was like a passageway for every gate that went through the Plane. As time passed and gates were forgotten, the way in and out of the realm was too."

"Guess it's not lost anymore. All I had to do was read that note carved into my desk. Whelp. Two down, eight more to go," I huffed in reference to figuring out the gates in the room.

"We have to tell the boss about this one, Max. So that was written on the desk? Do you know who used to own that?" Phil asked, letting out a cloud of smoke from his nose.

"Thinking Pottery Barn," I retorted, getting another chuckle out of the group.

"It was supposedly Arthur's. You know, King Arthur, and it was a gift from Merlin, if you believe all that rubbish," Phil proclaimed as Jamison looked over.

"Rubbish, you say? How quaint," Jamison responded, clicking his teeth. I decided the mystery of the desk would have to wait for another time.

We spent the next thirty minutes hearing about the aftereffects of our evening at the Blue House. Marlow Goolsby had been in a relatively good mood, considering the guy who had killed his brother had just been killed in his establishment. He even had a few Mages and cleaning crew show up to ensure the facility was ready for business the next day. Rex said the place would be like new by morning.

Kim had taken the other body for identification, and it would more than likely end up in our morgue at some point.

Phil was mostly interested in the video footage from the scene. Mr. Goolsby had supplied the tapes for review on-site, but had refused to turn them over for various legal reasons. No one had seemed to want to push the issue.

They now knew about Belm and, upon Jamison's request, would discuss it in the morning, as he was not an immediate threat to the operation. Oddly, both men seemed very interested in the steam trick I had used. As for me, I had questions about the demon.

For now, though, it was time to drink and tell war stories.

CHAPTER 20

The Bridge of Lions

Waking up the next morning, I leaned over and downed Phil's magical cure-all "snake oil," as I had branded it. I could see Phil two hundred years ago selling this stuff from a suitcase out of a wagon. Phil wasn't that old, but frankly, he could still pull it off even today.

I could hear Petro in the office going through something, finally deciding to take a shower before starting the day. I put on my castor for good measure, and it turned the familiar bloodred I was used to. The tank was full.

Over my time here, I had grown fond of my small living quarters. The space was simple yet functional. Everything I needed. The bathroom was my favorite, not so big that you couldn't steam the room up but also not so small one was always walking into something.

Leshya had dropped off my new kit bag, and I set it on the bed for later. No use getting ready now. I had figured that was what Petro was probably up to.

The bathroom was starting to fill with steam due to the seemingly endless supply of hot water the building held. Looking in the mirror, I pointed my right index finger in the air and whispered, "*Ignis*." The tip of my finger lit up like a cheap lighter, the small, hovering flame above my finger enough to light a candle. I was thinking about the steam I'd let out at the Blue House.

Lifting my other hand and pointing my left index finger, I whispered, "*Aquas*." A small, swirling mist of water about the size of the flame on my other finger swam in the air.

Up until now, I had simply been working on keeping the water off my body and moving it. I think it was time to go to step two. I slowly married my two index fingers together, letting out a stream of steam that further misted out the small room.

After about a minute, the steam was so thick I could see my reflection again in the mirror, as water was beading up and sliding off. The moisture in the room was becoming overwhelming, as a shower of small droplets started falling on my head from the ceiling.

Well, I thought to myself, *I guess that's where the steam came from.* I separated my hands and shook the water out of my hair, putting out the flame and water casting.

I got ready with the normal accoutrement of dark jeans and a T-shirt. I'd get ready for the night's mission later. Which was another thing. Did it really matter if we went at night? Why was it always at night when this stuff happened? Maybe people just thought it was the way things were supposed to be.

"Morning, boss," Petro greeted before heading off to head to the dining room.

"Morning, Petro. Man, you look like you are ready to win the war single-handedly," I noted, admiring the miniature scale armor Petro was wearing.

"This stuff is great," Petro said excitedly as he flew over to me. "Check these out. Mini grenades. Some of them are blended items—I think a few are sleep charms and a couple are electric. Cool stuff. Oh yeah…and check this out." He pulled out a small rifle with a magazine full of arrows. "This thing shoots stabilizers and sleeping potions. If you're spelled, all I have to do is shoot you with one of the stabilizers and whoosh, you're back to normal. We used to make these on the Plane for money. I heard they are expensive here. Oh, and your girlfriend dropped the journal off this morning."

"She's not my girlfriend," I replied, looking at Petro's miniature armor closely. "This stuff is great. Badass, Petro. I think we're going to rock it tonight. Let's head down. Ed wants us all downstairs by 8:00 a.m.," I said, looking at him as he strutted off to put down the rifle.

***

The dining room was loud. The entire crew was there, including Inspector Holder, Kim, and the normal suspects. Apparently, Chloe had convinced him somehow to fly over.

Everyone at the table had tan folders in front of them stamped "TOP SECRET OTN" on the covers with individual people's names on them.

The inspector, as always, was cramming a bagel in his mouth as he walked up to me. "Oy, sounds like you might be a proper copper after all. Good work on taking down that Eater fellow," he said as crumbs fell on his shirt and tie. He wrapped up with a hardy pat on my back. I wondered what the hell Chloe had told him. I'm guessing she had skipped the demon part.

"Morning," I greeted, sitting next to Chloe as she closed her folder.

"Morning. You look bright-eyed and bushy-tailed. Have a fun night with the boys?" Chloe asked, smiling.

"A little. We didn't stay up too long, with it being go time today. It was good to get to know Jamison better. Thanks for dropping the journal off. Hey, sorry we didn't get that drink last night. If things go well tonight...tomorrow, you, me, and the Fallen Angel?" I suggested, sounding levelheaded for once in my banter with Chloe.

"Things go well, I'll take you up on that date," Chloe replied, smiling as Ed cleared his throat.

"Right, everyone, take a seat," Ed indicated, walking to the head of the table to stand beside Jenny as her Pixies flew over to check out Petro's armor. The group took their respective seats, which I was starting to realize were more like assigned spots.

"As you can tell by the folders, the Council is now involved in the operation. While they won't have a direct involvement, just know that Big Brother is watching. We don't plan on any major trouble; however, we need to be ready. Kim, has the evacuation of the area around the Bridge of Lions started?" Ed asked, looking at her.

"Yes, the 'gas leak' started before sunrise. It should be clear by 3:00 p.m. at the latest. Surprisingly, many people cleared out on first notice. Our teams will be posted at the entrance and exit points," Kim replied, looking at me. "As long as nothing gets set on fire, I think we'll be okay."

"Right," Ed started in his normal cadence. "There's not been many changes since yesterday. We go to the bridge gate from the drawbridge control house. Get the Fountain and gate out using the rope and the Evergate key Max has. Before we leave, we'll bind with the rope to make sure we all get out in case of any trouble.

"Everyone, after looking at their folders, now knows that the Fountain is just that—a fountain. It's imperative that we secure it. Phil should be able to handle its weight. Chloe and Frank will stay at the gatehouse to make sure we aren't followed. Jenny, Phil, Max, Petro, and myself will gate in and secure the target. If we run into any trouble, use minimum force unless your life or that of others is in danger. Inspector Holder will stay in the crucible room with Ned, Jamison, and Dr. Freeman. Ned has been assigned as the Council representative on this operation. Any questions?"

Jenny looked around the group while the team waited for Ed to continue.

"Everyone needs to be prepped and in the main garage at 8:00 p.m. We'll be driving to the bridge to avoid anyone gating along with us. We will gate back. Everyone has their gear and will be debriefed on what we can expect to find in the Sanctuary, as we are calling it. The journal we have gave us a good amount of information. Chloe, it'll be critical for you to make sure that the team is safe before we gate into the Sanctuary."

"Sure thing," Chloe agreed, tapping a finger on her folder. She had a concerned look on her face.

The group talked out the rest of the details over the next hour with the typical dumb questions. My favorite part was Jamison's explanation for Belm and the fact that his best friend and drinking confidant was an honest-to-God demon. The general consensus from the group had been that they wanted to meet Belm on neutral ground in the very near future.

As everyone went off to prep for the night's mission, Ed pulled me to the side, out of earshot of everyone else.

"Max, I don't think tonight's going to be as easy as it sounds, and I know you get that," Ed confided as he made solid eye contact. "Look, we think that whomever we have been dealing with is using a heavy-hitting diviner. Chloe is good at what she does, but she is limited to the near future, mainly actions. A real diviner can see hours, if not days, out if the conditions are right."

"Fair enough," I said. "Why are you telling me this?"

"You see, Dr. Freeman had a little more to relay. Let's just say it was a small yet major detail. The issue is that the more people know, the more they will act on the information they have been given, which can give a good diviner a clear path to see what is going to happen. I'm a little different; I can bury what I know. The point is, Max, you need to be ready. You're not used to being out with me, so I want you to know that if I do something that seems out of sorts, there is probably a reason for it. The rest of the team is used to it," Ed explained, tilting his head.

"Understood. I always like a good surprise." I smiled. "I know yesterday evening was a setup, and I also know that it was a little too easy. My gut is telling me it's going to be a long night as well."

Ed returned the smile, approving of my response, and let out a breath. "Looks like you figured it out. I think whoever sent those two and all the crafts to the Blue House was trying to tie loose ends, as they already had what they needed. You know, get rid of the deadweight."

For the next several minutes, I filled Ed in our little trip in the Postern and the Desk in Gramps's office.

"That's amazing," Ed said as I wrapped up telling him about our night in the Postern and meeting the Messenger. "Tom never mentioned what that gate did. To be honest, I don't think he knew."

Ed wanted to pay the Messenger a visit when we got back. He also followed up with an explanation on who used to own the desk. Like Phil, he seemed proud of it, so I just let him run with it.

When I got back to Gramps's office, Petro was standing there looking over the gear that I had moved to the desk. It was a little after lunch, and I had decided to squeeze in some time with Petro in the lab.

"Do you think there's anything else we should take?" I asked Petro, talking about the potion or casting side of things. I padded over and released the catch to open the door down to the lab behind the bar.

"I don't know boss. We already have a good amount of stuff. There is one thing, though," Petro spoke as we started down to the lab.

I looked over, pointing my hand at the fireplace whispering, "*Ignis*." The wood ignited.

Petro went over to one of the shelves and retrieved two bracelets. "These are pretty neat. Folks use these all the time on the Plane. All you do is put one on and give the other to someone else. If someone is lost in a field or hidden, it will link the both of you. They use these like an Ethereal walkie-talkie so you can always have a connection with the other person. They can come in handy. Give the other to someone you want to be connected to, and you will be able to get to them. They don't even have to wear it, just accept it," Petro said. "It will be a cool gift for your girlfriend."

"She's not my girlfriend, but if it can help her out, I'll give Chloe one before we go," I replied, looking around the room.

"How cute," Petro gushed as he took flight. "Boss, I think we have about everything we need. Besides, you wouldn't know how to use some of the stuff in here yet anyways. Likely to blow us all up or turn us into rats or something."

After a few minutes of poking around, we left the lab, and I did the one thing I had been putting off for days: I called my mother.

"Hey, Mom," I greeted, putting some strain in my voice to justify my lack of calling.

"*Oh, Max, your father was just saying we needed to call you. I told him you were just busy with your new job*," she said, putting me on speaker. Old people. They loved to put you on speaker phone in the middle of a conversation so they could say "what" more.

"Sorry about not calling. It's been busy, but I wanted to catch you before it got too late," I replied.

My dad spoke up in the background in his usual monotone voice. *"You caught up in the gas leak down there?"* he asked, referencing the evacuation of the downtown area.

"Close. That's actually what I'm working on later," I told him.

"I see," Mom said, hesitating a moment too long. *"Max, I think you need to come over for supper Sunday so we can talk."* There it was. She knew. I knew it. And she was offering to break the ice. *"Be careful tonight. I hear gas leaks can be dangerous."*

"I will be," I promised. "And I'll be there on Sunday. Mom, we do need to talk. I just can't now."

"Well, stay dry and bring laundry with you." With that, she ended the call. *Shit*, I thought to myself. *She did it again.* If I was still alive come Sunday, I was going to lay it all out and see what she said.

After a five-hour nap, it was go time. I called Petro, and we kitted up together. It was like one of those cheesy '80s TV shows. We listened to Planes Drifter while putting on our body armor and loaded our gear, sizing ourselves up in the mirror and telling each other how badass we looked.

Phil messaged me, obviously antsy, and came over to walk down to the garage with us. He had literally made the trek all the way from the garage only to walk right back. Phil was nervous, and ready to go. I knew the feeling.

"Bruther, you look proper in that. A little fresh off the shelf but ready to go," Phil complimented, gumming an unlit cigarette as he often did when things were in motion. I noticed he had a hammer slung over his back. It looked like a sledgehammer, but slightly smaller; something you could handle without it being too bulky.

"Phil, what's with the hammer? You trying to get your Thor on?" I joked as we made our way toward the main house.

"That ass. No…well, kind of. Its name is Plan B. For tonight's purposes, it's just that," Phil said, strutting as Petro led the way, letting off dust.

"Ed wants you to destroy the Fountain if we can't get it, doesn't he," I asked in the form of a statement.

"Yup," Phil let out in a grunt.

This was another part of the plan that Ed had decided to keep to himself and whomever else he deemed needed to know. I was starting to wonder if everyone had a separate piece that no one else knew about. Maybe I was the only one who knew that Ed thought a diviner was involved.

Entering the garage, we saw three black SUVs sitting there, along with the rest of the group. Everyone was in their kits and ready to go. Jenny handed out FM radios so we could communicate with the local authorities if things went south and as a backup. Jenny also handed out the other communicators, even having one for Petro. I noticed she didn't give one to Chloe. She would be staying at the gatehouse on the bridge, so I supposed it was to keep down radio traffic. Jenny clarified she had to take one and shrink it to fit Petro, so Frank would be our only contact up top, leaving us one short.

I stepped up to Chloe and smiled. "Ready for the big night?" I asked, handing her one of the bracelets.

"We'll see," she replied, taking the bracelet and inspecting it. "Good luck charm?"

"Not for luck. See." I raised my sleeve to show her mine. "Least I can do if I can't get you out for a drink is give you a promise bracelet," I said, actually playing off that I wanted to have a way to reach out to her if needed.

"You're sweet, Max. Thanks. I'll keep it as a good luck charm for tonight. It matches my outfit," she teased as she spun around in a uniform obviously from the Dunn and not the standard NCTS issue.

Just as we were getting into a good rhythm in the conversation, Ed spoke up, splitting the teams up into the two back vehicles. The front SUV was obviously muscle from Kim's side of things to lead us downtown.

I looked over to see Chloe occupied with slipping the bracelet into a pocket on her vest. *Better luck next time*, I thought. Petro buzzed over and whispered in my ear, "Hey, boss, as long as she has it with her—and I heard her, she accepted it—all you have to do it push some will into yours and you should be able to link with her." He flew off afterward making kissing noises, claiming shotgun as he flew into the SUV and decided to take the cup holder in the center console as his own personal throne. Must be nice being a small guy.

We pulled out of the gates and headed downtown. It took a few minutes to get Petro to calm down and stop pushing buttons. By the time he stopped, we had gone through all four seasons temperature-wise and were listening to Whitney Houston on the radio.

As soon as we flew past the first roadblock, all the relative ease settled into silence as the team got their game faces on. Ed, Jenny, Petro, and I rode in the last vehicle while Chloe, Frank, and Phil rode in the other.

The radio was alight with chatter about clearing lanes before finally settling on an all-clear call from Kim.

St. Augustine in the early fall was muggy at night. A light mist hung in the air, lending to the odd quiet of the deserted city center. Once we passed the fort, we could see the bridge. The lead vehicle pulled off as the caravan stopped at the entrance to the Bridge of Lions.

I leaned forward in my seat. "Hey, guys...isn't there supposed to be two lions on the Bridge of Lions?" I asked, getting a sinking feeling in my stomach.

"Damn," Ed cursed before taking a deep breath. "Remember, Max, in the journal, those lions are there to protect what the bridge contains. Someone may have already taken a shot at it and had a little run-in with its guardians."

"Not likely," Jenny suggested. "I think they know we are coming, and I think the lions know we have the gate key. It may be some type of trigger. Did we check to see if they were here after you made the gate key? No. Plus, that's not always a bad thing. Especially since we are coming in the proper way."

The teams in front of us must have also noticed the lack of lions, since no one got out of the vehicles.

"Right. We are a go. We walk from here," Ed indicated, as all the doors opened at the same time.

I came out with my service pistol drawn. I had decided to leave the Judge at home after my last experience with an enchanted weapon, instead settling on the one I sort of knew how to use. The rest of the team did the same.

Chloe and I had our service pistols out, Ed held a sharp-tipped staff, and Jenny had an honest-to-God wand. *See, I knew they used those*, I thought to myself, letting out a little chuckle, much to the chagrin of the group. Phil—well, he'd decided on a street sweeper, a fully automatic shotgun. Petro was content with his sword in hand, leaving his rifle in the truck. Frank just stood there looking razor-sharp. I didn't think he needed a weapon.

Kim came over the radio, telling us the area was *clear*. On that note, the group started to diplomatically shuffle up the bridge. I think we were all expecting two concrete lions to jump out at any moment. Petro was hovering a few inches behind my shoulder and had actually been quiet for five whole minutes while the group moved up to the gatehouse.

The mood was still, as no one wanted to talk. The air was thick and smelled like the ocean. You could hear the waves splashing on the pylons below as the moon lit up the mist in the air, lending an eerie glow to the night.

And there it stood. The main gatehouse had red-and-green navigation lights blinking, and it made me wonder if the waterways had been shut down too. Jenny walked up to the door and tapped it with her wand, generating a small clanking sound and unlocking the door.

The room was filled with various control panels and was small enough to fit about four people, from what I could see from my angle. I decided to hang back as Chloe and Ed walked in with Jenny, leaving the rest of us to put our backs to the structure looking for any movement.

Phil was already chewing on a new unlit cigarette. Petro had landed on my shoulder, and Frank was staring blankly at the water.

I could hear Ed talking to Chloe. "Right, here is the gate key. What do you see if we go through it?"

"It looks clear," Chloe answered with a slight hesitation. "Everyone gets through. That's all."

"That's it. Let's go," Jenny said before I heard the click of metal on concrete. She had activated the gate.

Frank came over to me. "Be careful. I don't feel good about this."

"Thanks?" I replied. One thing Frank didn't have was tact. He meant it, though. Phil just looked over and shrugged.

"Man, he gives me the willies," Petro murmured under

his breath.

"Let's go in order as practiced," Ed called out.

I stood in the doorway as I watched Ed walk through the gate, then Jenny, followed by Phil, and lastly, me with Petro in tow. I turned to Chloe before going. "See you in a few. Keep supper on the stove," I joked as she smirked.

"I'll see you in a little bit." She winked at me, looking around before motioning Frank to come in so they could close the door.

The gate was oddly set in the back wall, making it look like we were walking through the window. As we gated through, I could feel the cool breeze of Petro's wings on my neck.

CHAPTER 21

Sinners and Sanctuaries

I stepped through the gate, feeling the cool, damp air. The team was standing in a semicircle looking around at what appeared to be an entrance hall. Ed had lit the oil lamps that hung from the ceilings, letting off a dull, yellow glow.

The room was roughly the size of a large classroom. The structure had been cut from the earth, but in a designed and manicured manner. Light trickles of water ran down the walls, pretty much proving that we were, in fact, underwater. The ceiling was thirty feet up, and the lamps hung down from slightly corroded chains, likely due to the saltwater. The room smelled of ocean and dirt with a hint of mold. The briny smell actually gave it a refreshing tang that you could taste in the air. The floor was solid and cut from stone.

Jenny was leaning over a small pad showing our location. "We are directly under the bridge," she informed, looking around.

"How under, lass?" Phil asked.

"Ah, well, that's up for debate. I would say a mile?" Jenny responded, making the point that we were well below the water table, which accounted for the change in temperature.

Ed looked over, raising an eyebrow. "Well, that explains

why Ezra's scans didn't pick this place up. From what I gathered from Dr. Freeman, they scanned the area, but only so far down. Jenny, is there anything on the e-meter?"

"No. I don't expect to get anything until it's triggered. And before you say it, I know the lions are missing," she said, putting up her pad and pulling her wand back out.

"Right," Ed started. "We looked at the layout. From what we found in the journal, we need to move toward the far end."

We had spent some time over the past two days looking at a rough sketch of the Sanctuary. Jenny had even transferred it to digital 3D, showing us it had been designed with various sections all leading to the main room. Dr. Freeman had said there would probably be several different wards in place to stop people who shouldn't be down there. As he'd said, there was more than one way down, and only going through the front door would be safe.

"Frank, you copy?" I asked into my communicator. Nothing, just silence. It was so silent, I could hear Petro hovering over my shoulder. He seemed to like that spot.

"Max, I think this place is a little too warded for that to work. I may be wrong, but I wouldn't count on that working," Ed said as he started to walk toward the one door in the room.

Phil cocked his shotgun. I was with him; either the communicator or the radio should be working. As the team stepped into the next room, Ed lit the torches, exposing a long, wide room the length of a bus with a solid sealed door with several markings at the other end. Ed pulled a sheet from the journal and put his hand out, murmuring something under his breath.

Phil lit up a cigarette, saying, "To hell with it," to the group. As soon as the smell of tobacco filled the air, gunfire erupted from the other side of the door. Not just a little but several different cadences of rapid automatic small caliber gunfire, followed by shouts of orders.

"We're not alone, boss," Petro said as he flew in front of me with his sword.

The team stopped and looked inward at each other. "Against the side walls," Ed ordered as the door groaned under not gunfire but brute force, releasing dust from the ceiling. "I knew it," Ed huffed. The gunfire on the other side of the door was loud enough to cover our actions. "That other way in must have triggered the defenses. We are not alone."

"Shit," Phil cursed, rolling his lit smoke in his mouth. "It's game time." An odd smile smoothed over his face, showing his mild enjoyment of justified violence.

Ed gave the signal for us to stand in place as we heard the sounds of gunfire trailing off, growing less prominent. Either the group was on the move or getting thinned out. I was betting on the latter. After a few minutes of waiting, the noise completely stopped. Even the scuffling sounds went away, making way to an eerie silence.

Ed stood up and looked around before walking back to the door. This guy had some guts. He was going in come hell or high water. A minute later, the door started to come to life, grinding open and exposing the room on the other side. It was massive, the size of an indoor football field. A dozen or so highly armed and suited up bodies lay on the floor. Many were ripped open or had various limbs missing. These had been professionals. All of them wore matching dark gray uniforms and had gear close to what I had on. The weapons were all top of the line.

The team entered and surveyed the dimly lit room. Whomever these folks were, they had dropped several flares in the room, covering it in a shimmering red.

Jenny whispered to the group, "These people are not Mages."

I guessed that was important; however, I was focused on what the hell had done this. Petro flew into the room, much to our surprise, before flicking around the walls and out of sight.

"That bugger is brave," Phil said.

Ed kneeled over one of the bodies. "Right. These are more than your normal hired muscle. Jenny, do you see what I'm seeing?"

"Yeah," Jenny replied, not taking her eyes off the far end of the room. "Mags-Tech security."

From what I gathered, the other team had come in through another location and set off the wards in the room. Ed lit the hanging torches with a flick of his wrist, noting that he could not get the ones further down the hall to start.

"Something is keeping things dampened down here," Ed said as he stepped forward.

"You hear that?" Phil asked, squinting his eyes toward the dark end of the room. "Look at that."

Petro came flying through the air, letting out a trail of dust behind him with his sword drawn. "They're coming, and they are nasty," he barked, taking position overhead in front of the group.

"Everyone, get set. Put your guns away and let's take a go at this the old-fashioned way," Ed yelled, obviously understanding the guys with guns hadn't seemed to fare well.

The team started pulling out various items: Jenny her wand, Phil his hammer, and Ed some type of staff with the end falling down, exposing a glowing chain. *Shit, glowing sword time*, I thought as the first of the creatures creating the noise showed themselves roughly twenty-five yards away.

As I pulled out Durundle, I barked, "*Ignis*." The sword sprang to life, not as it had at the Blue House but rather in a dull, glowing amber. It looked like it had just been pulled out of an iron forge. No flames this time around.

What was coming at us was the thing of nightmares. Let me put this into perspective: a small, inch-long scorpion was enough to send me off screaming like a child. When my brain finally computed that the scorpions in front of us were the size of a fully-grown adult with stingers as long as a human leg, it was too late. The crusted, snapping wall of creatures started swarming the group, the sound of their encased legs clicking and multiplying as they got closer. They had claws and two deeply set, shining black eyes.

Jenny put a green shield around Phil, who was the first to make contact, charging the group in front of him with a deafening crash of his hammer, generating a crackle of breaking shell and bone. Ed was swinging his staff, knocking over the creatures as they finally reached my blade's range.

I lifted the glowing sword over my head, swinging down with the hiss of heat, making contact and cutting through the scorpion in front of me as if it were cardboard. I was so focused on the stinger that I had forgotten about the lower claws, feeling the burn of a surface cut on my leg. Yeah...they never trained you to fight life-size scorpions in the army.

Lesson learned. I started to take lower swings at the creatures, seeing Ed do the same. I lost sight of Phil, but I could hear the rhythm of his persistent crushing blows.

The swarm was too much, and I was doing everything I could to stay on my feet, not to mention not running away.

There was a noise at the end of the dark hall that stopped the onslaught long enough for me to look around at the pile of shells and pieces lying around. "Shit...Petro," I yelled.

Petro came screaming out of the darkness, talking into his communicator breathlessly. I guess they still worked in close quarters. "Hey, boss. It's the sound and light they're drawn to, and let me tell you, they keep pouring in through an opening on the other end of the room."

"Right," Ed spoke up. "Petro, can you create a diversion long enough for us to maneuver along the side of the room? Is there a way out?"

"There's a door at the end like the one we came through. Guys, they are stacked two high down there. I have three detonators. I'll get these creatures away from you then circle back here. Better hurry," Petro urged, starting to sound desperate.

On Petro's word, the team disengaged all the lit-up devices, including my sword. Phil and Jenny came running over as the scorpions' attention started to drift back to us.

Just as I was about to pull the sword back out, there was a loud bang and flash at the end of the hall, along with the torches being lit in order. Man, Petro was going to get all the Golden Grahams he ever wanted if we made it out of here.

The team ran to the side wall and started moving at a brisk pace. Not so fast as to draw attention but fast enough to make up ground.

"Petro, if we get any closer, they'll be on us. Set off the other detonator," Ed indicated, directing Petro to let off a distraction at the location we had come from.

On cue, Petro did as requested, letting off the other charge. The sight took my breath away as the whole group gasped, watching the mass of scorpions crawling over each other to get to the side of the room we had come from.

Phil turned, holding up a finger to his lips to remind us all to be quiet. After thirty seconds of shuffling with a few stragglers, we made it to the door. Ed started working on the symbol as he had done on the prior door. This one had a moon on it, while the other had a sun chiseled into the stone.

Petro's plan had called off the monsters, but it had also

lit up the entire area we were now standing in. We could see across the room to the other side; however, there was still a black void in the middle of the elongated room.

Just as I had settled in on looking around, Petro chirped in our earpieces again. *"Hey, guys, better hurry up. I got one more of these things left, and they are losing interest fast..."*

"Ed?" Jenny prompted.

"I know, I'm almost there. Someone came through this door and shut it with a little extra bravado," Ed said, not taking his hand or eyes off the door. The etching on the door was as complex as the other.

As with all bad situations, things started getting worse. Half the creatures had peeled off from the pack and were starting to head in our direction.

"Now, Petro!" I shouted as Phil and Jenny went to work as they had before, making contact with a small group of the scorpions; however, I was stuck on watching Petro. The creatures had started crawling on top of each other and were close to the ceiling in a few areas.

"Got it!" Ed shouted as the grind of rock and stone started. "Be ready. Whoever did make it through may still be on the other side."

I turned to see Phil lighting a cigarette right before smashing the head of the last scorpion in the group in front of us. "I hate bugs," he grumbled as he walked over to the door. Soon, I was the only member of the group still on this side of the door waiting for Petro.

"Hey, buddy, we got to go," I urged. I could see his trail of Pixie dust racing toward us.

"Max!" Ed called out. "The door is closing!"

I took off through the door, not taking my eyes off Petro. With about two feet to spare, the little warrior came spiraling in through the door and slammed into my chest, landing on my hands where I had cupped them.

Looking down, I could see his left wing had been damaged by what looked like an acid burn. "You okay?" I asked, trying to stay calm.

"Hey, boss. Yeah…I think so. I'm not going to be flying anytime soon, though. I hear chicks dig scars," Petro said as he let out a light chuckle, trying to cover up the pain he was obviously in.

I pulled the radio out of the holder that he had jumped in earlier, letting it clatter on the floor, and sat him in it. He stood up and gave me a thumbs-up, pulling his sword back out.

"Game on, buddy," I said, realizing the room was stone-cold quiet. Guess it was time for me to turn around.

The scene in front of us was just as odd as the last.

"Found your lions, bruther," Phil drawled as he spit his second cigarette on the floor, letting it burn itself out.

"And, if I'm not mistaken, the Keeper too. I don't know what happened here, but it doesn't look good," Ed noted as he stepped in front of the group.

The room was about the size of a large movie theater and was divided by a fifteen-foot-long bridge crossing over a deep chasm in the floor. The space was lit by torches, this time sitting on posts. At the other end of the room was another door with the lions sitting on either side, unmoving. They looked as if they were carved out of the rock walls.

There, propped up between them and leaning on the door, was a large older man dressed in classic leather armor. He was covered in blood and looking at Ed.

Ed moved a little closer, slowly reaching the wooden bridge. The wounded man at the other side lifted his arm and motioned for Ed to cross in a peaceful gesture, even putting a slight smile on his face. Ed crossed the bridge and kneeled next to the man. They appeared to be talking, and after about two minutes, Ed stood up and motioned us over.

As we walked up, Ed looked over at the man. "Team, this is Ordius, the Keeper. He's dying and needs our help," Ed said emphatically.

With a light cough, the man started to speak. "I'm beyond help." Ordius again coughed. "Whatever it is they hit me with has taken what I am. I don't think you are here for the same reason as the others. They plan on taking the Fountain. The Fountain cannot leave the Sanctuary. Do you understand?"

"Sure," I replied, glancing at Ed.

"Young man," Ordius spoke up again. "You look familiar to me." Drawing closer, I could see the aged strength in his build. He was a proud and old warrior at the end of his days. I knew the type.

"I get that a lot these days," I said. He chuckled lightly, letting out a spatter of blood on his chest.

"I can stay here with him and see if I can do anything," Jenny offered, looking concerned.

"No, you're needed on the other side of this door, young lady," Ordius coughed out. "I'm done here. I'll open it for you, then I have to go." He reached for Ed to pull him up to face the door.

Ed obliged, and as the door started to grind open, Ordius reached over and leaned on one of the lions, letting his blood drip on its back. Within a matter of seconds, Ordius started to dissolve into the lion like mist fading away into the concrete beast.

The sanctuary in front of us was a round, dome-shaped room the size of a large basketball court. The area was lit by iridescent rock at the top streaming a dull yellow light around the cone, fading to near darkness as it met the floor. The room had four columns spread out around the space to support the structure.

What stood out the most was the glowing blue field in the middle of the room surrounding a fountain, which consisted of a column holding a stone-carved human head at the top and a small pool beneath. Standing in the field were Vestulie, Jayal, and Chloe.

Before my brain could compute what I was seeing, I stepped forward. "Chloe! Thank God." As the last word left my mouth, I had the startling realization that she was, in fact, there by choice.

"Max, I don't think this is a rescue," Ed said as he stepped forward. The door behind us slid shut, and in the blink of an eye, the two lions appeared at the far end of the room, resolute and unmoving. The team by the Fountain hadn't noticed their presence and kept turned facing us.

The look on Chloe's face was one of defiant determination. She no longer wore the happy-go-lucky glowing smile that I had grown attached to.

"Hey, Max, you always have been a little late to the party," she mocked, looking over at Vestulie as he set up four small triangles around the Fountain. There was no water flowing from it yet; we had gathered it only did so at certain times. Jayal stood there looking at us with no real emotion on his face.

"Chloe, you don't have to do this. I'm not sure why you are doing this, but we can help," Ed pleaded, stepping closer.

"Ed, you always seem to think you have the answers. This isn't some cheesy movie where you waste my time getting me to talk while you wait for backup to arrive. That's not going to happen," Chloe jeered, looking at the watch on her wrist. "As a matter of fact, we have some company to keep you busy while we wait for the Fountain. Oh, and Frank is otherwise preoccupied. Probably ripping apart your friends trying to get himself back together."

"You bitch, if you hurt him, I'll personally extinguish you," Jenny belted out of nowhere.

"Everyone, calm down," Ed told the group. You could hear Phil's knuckles and leather bracelets tightening under his fists. He was not in a good mood.

"Jayal?" Ed prompted, looking at him.

"Don't talk to him," Vestulie finally spoke, standing up.

It was obvious that while Vestulie thought he was the one in charge, it was in fact Chloe who was the leader of the pack as she looked over at him.

"You always treated me as if I wasn't good enough to be a part of the group. Well, I am now," Jayal sneered as a green field shot to life surrounding the Fountain's blue field that Jayal had obviously put in place.

"You all are not going anywhere, and Jayal, you should keep your mouth shut," Chloe scolded as she raised her service pistol and released the familiar bark of her pistol into Jayal's head. *Pat, pat, pat.*

Jayal's field blinked out of existence, replaced by the new green glowing field that Vestulie had set up.

I looked away as Jayal's body crumpled to the ground. Senseless violence not in the heat of combat made you sick to your stomach no matter the pain you had inflicted on people to protect yourself and others. Chloe was rotten to the core.

"You'll pay for this, Chloe," Ed warned with hate in his eyes.

"Damn…a reverse field," Jenny cursed.

"That's right. Your little plan to gate out of here…well,

let's just say we came prepared. You will all die down here. Minus Max. I think someone wants to talk to you," Chloe informed. She looked at the Fountain as a small trickle of water came out of the stone eyes.

"Lilith," Ed said out of nowhere. "The Thule Society is back up and running, I see."

The shock on Vestulie's and Chloe's faces was evident. Ed knew. Hell, he probably knew coming down here what was going to happen.

"Ahh...right on time," Chloe noted as three gates opened in the room.

The one in front of Phil winked out of existence before whoever was coming through could exit. Phil had lifted his shotgun and unloaded ten rounds into the opening, his shotgun letting off successive *ka-chuck, ka-chunk* noises before falling silent as the team darted behind the pillars.

Make that two gates.

Ed's staff came to life while I pulled out Durundle, lighting its blade. Jenny put her shield back up around her and Phil. I wondered if she could use it for all of us, but figured it could only stretch so far. I could feel Petro flexing his good wing, and I put my hand on top of the radio holder to let him know to get down.

Two hooded figures walked out of the other gates. As they did so, the one closest to Ed and me dropped their hoods and let out a wall of lightning.

The man under the hood was albino white with no hair and deep, solid black eyes.

"Shit," Ed cursed as the other hooded figure let out a round of fireballs at the column Jenny and Phil were behind. "Pearl."

"Pearl?" I asked, moving closer to Ed to get out of the

line of fire. The two figures were still across the room, and Jenny was letting off small laser beams as if she were shooting some type of gun from a sci-fi movie. Ed threw a silver marble, attracting the lightning to the foot of the field Vestulie had put up.

"Well, look at him. It's an old nickname; everyone used to call him Pearl. I'll tell you the rest later. Well…maybe. He's bad news," Ed snapped quickly.

Our team was pinned down, and I could see Chloe and Vestulie in the bubble watching the water slowly start to flow out of the Fountain.

"You think they are going to take it?" I asked Ed as a chunk of wall blew out behind us.

"I think they are going to try. Remember what Ordius said. I think he was being literal—the Fountain can't leave this place," Ed replied as the lightning started to take pieces out of the large column as well.

"I have an idea," Ed stated, surprisingly calm as he handed me the gate key. "Take this to the lions on the other side of the room while we distract Chloe and Vestulie. See if there is a way to open a gate over there, anywhere. That reverse gate will make it hard, but even if it opens in the middle of the room or the gatehouse, it's worth a shot. You have the rope. If you can gate inside the reverse field, we have a chance. If there is a way in, there is a way out."

Ed leaned away from cover, slinging a round of white bolts from his staff much like Jenny's at Pearl. At the same time, Phil came running around the other side of the room ripping out rounds from his shotgun, putting the Mages on the defense.

A quick glance at the Fountain showed Vestulie and Chloe appeared to be arguing over something, a slight look of concern on their faces.

"Will you listen to me, jackass?!" I finally heard Petro yell over the sounds of fighting.

Fights in real life weren't like the movies where music was playing in the background. It's all bangs, screams, and things getting tossed around. Hell, I could use a little Planes Drifter right about now, I though.

"What?" I huffed, looking down, not realizing he had been trying to get my attention.

"You still got that ball Trish gave you for your re-birthday? You know, the 'break glass in case of emergency' one?" Petro asked, showing off his newfound knowledge of Earth slang. I needed to cut down on his TV time.

I pulled out the small, smooth stone and looked at Petro. "She said to get it wet. I dropped my water at some point fighting those things, and my mouth is dry as a desert," I told him as Petro hefted himself up on the rim of the radio holder, slapping the stone out of my hand while unbuttoning his pants. Before I could react, he started pissing on the stone.

"Ahh...I needed to do that since the encounter with the crawly things," he let out, winking at me as I accidently took a glance at him. "Gazer. I'm telling Phil." It was odd how he still had his sense of humor after everything that had happened.

The stone started to let out a cloud of fog so thick I couldn't see my hand in front of my face. Except that after a second, I could see my hand in front of my face, and surprisingly, I could see everyone else in the room. The space went silent as everyone looked around. It was like they had a wall in front of them. Everyone was blinded by the fog except me. *Game on.*

The two hooded figures stopped casting spells, as did our team. Everyone was trying to get their bearings and figure out what had just happened.

I concentrated and let out a simple message. "Fog. Max did it. I see."

Ed came back with a simple, "Right."

It was my chance to move. I put out the flame on my sword and skirted along the rounded back wall over to the lions. The one space that the fog didn't cover was inside the circle, but while they still couldn't see me, I could. From the looks of it, they were in the middle of the process and were becoming impatient.

I leaned against the closest lion and started looking around the room. As Ed had recommended, I held the gate key in my hand and concentrated. Nothing happened. While I was sitting there, the two Mages started firing off lightning and firebolts in random directions, hoping to hit someone. Or more than likely, they were getting their bearings. Was the fog dissipating?

I looked back at Chloe and Vestulie as a concrete tongue licked the side of my head. In shock, I turned to see the lion with Ordius's blood was licking my head and had its paw out. Whatever they were doing in the circle had his attention.

The air was starting to thin out as Pearl slung lightning through the air to charge it. I didn't have enough time to steam up the room, never mind that I didn't think I could.

Once again, I realized Petro was screaming at me. "You still got that bracelet, boss?"

"Shit," I whispered under my breath, lifting my arm and looking at it. "Yeah, buddy. I hope she still has her half of it. It should be in that bag inside the circle."

"Good enough. You should be able to get to her or something," Petro said just as I heard a thump and Phil starting to curse. He had been hit by a fire casting, and the shield Jenny had up was starting to fade.

I looked over at the lion as something came over me. I took off the bracelet, just as the lion extended a claw, signaling for me to put it on him. Petro stared in astonishment. Like me, he had no idea what was going on. As I placed it on its claw, it retracted, and the stone lion smacked my other hand holding the gate key. I dropped it on the ground, as he placed a concrete paw down on it, dissolving it into its concrete body.

Looking around the room, it was clear that Ed had gained ground on the lightning-flinging Mage, but Phil and Jenny were in trouble. Vestulie had put on the backpack, and in his hand was the same device the Eater had used at the Blue House.

Without warning, the lion sprang to life and launched itself through the field, ripping through Vestulie as if he was paper. The gore was so intense, it turned the field red on the inside as parts of what was left spread around the bubble. The sound was nauseating.

Chloe, now covered in blood and parts of Vestulie, let out a howl of anger as she started shooting blindly in my direction. I was in the shadows, and there was still a light fog in the air. It looked like closing time in a smoky bar.

Everyone in the room stopped and stared as Chloe kept firing. I rolled to the left as several bullets landed on the other lion, bringing it to life.

That was when the Fire Mage made a tactical mistake. She launched a round of fireballs from the corner of the field at the other lion still standing by me. The violence that followed was just as extreme. Ordius's lion again sat resolute in the field, staring blankly at the battle covered in blood, watching his partner the same as he watched over the bridge.

"Shit," Ed barked as Pearl launched a barrage of concentrated lightning at the center of the dome, opening up a gate and leaving. I had a feeling they had danced before.

Click, click, click, was the only sound you could hear as Chloe kept pulling the trigger of her pistol to no effect. I guess the lions didn't see her as a threat. She looked around the room and screamed, "This doesn't change anything! You'll die down here."

The ceiling that Pearl had damaged started to crumble. This led to the far column falling to the ground in a loud, dusty thud. I watched as several stones hit the field and bounced off.

"Don't," Ed yelled at Chloe as she leaned over the Fountain placing a portable gate on it.

Ordius the lion came to life. He didn't attack Chloe immediately but instead knocked over the portable field Vestulie had set up, extinguishing the green barrier with a final pop of ozone.

Chloe picked up her bag, and before I could reach her, blinked out of existence. Ordius, too, had been charging at her and landed on the spot she had occupied.

"Ed!" Jenny shouted as the column he was standing by started to crumble. By then, I was on the other side of the Fountain and had reached the rest of our team. There was a cloud of dust and a moment of hesitation before Ed finally came out of the gloom.

"Thank God," Jenny let out with a sigh.

"Bruther, it's time to go," Phil declared. As I went to pull out the gate key for the Postern, I looked in my hand seeing the coin that I had given Ordius.

"What the hell," I exhaled to no one, turning around to see that both lions were gone. I squeezed the coin in my hand, tapped my heels together, and said, "There's no place like home," holding the rope in my other fist.

Once the gate activated, I walked through, feeling the rope pull the others along without any effort, dumping us all on the floor of the gatehouse in a pile of stiff bones, groans, and dust as the Sanctuary we left behind crumbled in on itself.

Phil was the first to talk—well, laugh. "That was a ride," he said as the team looked around.

Jenny turned to Ed, concerned. "Frank?"

The radios barked to life. Kim came bursting into the room, looking at the pile of us on the floor surrounded by the remains of what looked like one of the Mags-Tech security guards painting the walls.

"Looks like things are normal here, as always," Kim said as she lowered her pistol, shaking her head in disbelief.

Walking out into the humid, sticky night, Ed debriefed Kim on the status of the Fountain and Chloe. Petro was asleep in my pouch, and Phil was walking beside me. He handed me a smoke.

"I don't smoke," I told him. He cocked his head.

"You do tonight, bruther," he declared. I took it and lit it leading to a flurry of coughs.

Between coughs, I overheard Kim telling Jenny and Ed that Frank was okay for now. Apparently, when Chloe's team had left him there to die, he'd grabbed the last guard to pass the secondary gate and...well, the rest was a fairly graphic description of what a dying Vampire did to stay alive. They had to put him in confinement till he calmed down, and it would be a day or two. Angel was heading over to help out.

At the foot of the bridge stood the two resolute lions. Ordius was on the left, with a handprint marking him in blood. Walking by, we slowed down for a bit while Kim gave us all confused glances. I reached over, petting his paw and nodding as Phil nodded his head approvingly.

The crowd of agents had grown, and there were three people obviously from the Council, including Ned. You could tell they had handled getting Frank out of there by the various marks on their clothing.

We all decided not to gate back, having our fill and feeling drained from the night's use of our powers. The team all piled into the black SUV to drive back to the Atheneum—I mean, home.

The team was silent for a minute before I spoke up. "Did we win?"

"The battle? Yes, I think so. The war? No," Ed answered reflectively. "I'll explain when we get back. I don't think anyone will be seeing the Fountain again. You all want to know what Dr. Freeman and Ordius said to me?"

Jenny leaned over, punching Ed in his apparently injured arm. Ed winced before smiling at Jenny, who returned the grin. "We get to hear it now?" she asked in a smug, silky voice, picking on Ed for holding back information before the mission. Which was, as Ed had stated himself, "common practice."

"Whatever they took tonight will not do them much good. The Fountain has to fully charge before its powers can really be used. You see, it's true that you can only use it on the full moon, then it starts its cycle again. The moon was truly full this morning. It drained all its water and was in the process of resetting when we arrived tonight. That was the reason it was dry and just starting up. It was also the reason we went to the Blue House last night. As a distraction. Tom knew that if he let that information out too early, it would blow this whole thing. He had this operation timed down to the hour when the location of the Fountain was found."

"You sneaky son of a bitch," Phil said, laughing. "You can only take a true swig from that thing the moment of the full moon."

"Yes; however, what Chloe took could still cause issues,"

Ed warned, looking at me.

"Gods and graves, you knew. You knew about Chloe last night," I huffed, getting aggravated.

"Max, calm down. Remember when we talked about diviners? The more people know about what is going on, the easier it is for a diviner to figure out a solution based off decisions that have already been made. There is a reason she is the only one still alive other than Pearl from that group. The field Vestulie set up interfered with her ability to see beyond it. I'm not sure they were expecting that, or maybe he was planning on it.

"The incident at the Blue House was to tie up loose ends. Max, you were a loose end. Chloe didn't expect you to be as powerful as you are and backed off when we all arrived. When the Eater was dying, I caught a glimpse of Chloe. She gave herself away trying to shut off his mind. Like I said about minds or blocks, they all have their own distinct signature. I happen to know the one she and the Eater used."

I took a deep, calming breath, too tired to be upset about being the reason this all happened. The journal, the timing, everything. If I hadn't agreed to bind with the will, none of this would have happened. People died. It felt like I had blood on my hands.

"Your trip to London was probably a test. Chloe was working with the Eater all along, getting as much information as they could on the Fountain. I don't think they believed someone would connect the dots as fast as we did. There's more we can talk about later. It's not important right now," Ed sighed, leaning back in his seat, clearly exhausted. I turned the radio on, finding it playing an old Genesis song.

CHAPTER 22

The Fallen Angel

After I crashed in bed as soon as we got back, the next day was full of activity and interviews. The Atheneum was overflowing with Mages and civilian authorities alike. There had been an "earthquake" last night caused by an underground gas line explosion that helped sell the evacuation. The Sanctuary had imploded, destroying the Fountain and everything inside.

I actually learned some more information about our trip to the Blue House. Word that I used hellfire was spreading and getting some attention. I had been cleared of any wrongdoing in the destruction of several prominent Mages' and Fae's crafts. But the kicker was Marlow being set to take control of the Mags-Tech board of directors next week. He had called Ed that morning, reassuring him that he would weed out any issues that might still be present.

The Council also decided to set the date for the Balance to one year to the day. This last attempt had convinced both groups it was necessary at this point. The civilian governments had agreed to a set of guidelines that the Magical community would have to put in place. Jenny stated we would be hearing soon enough what role we would have to play.

I stopped to talk to Jamison, who worked with often

unofficial information. Jamison said that this had been only "one of a handful of attempted plots to cause issues." What those issues could be, I had no clue, but I was determined to find out.

As Ed had alluded to earlier, a group called the Thule Society was to blame. Ned and a few of the older Council members confirmed this. The group was a Nazi cult that collected magical and religious items of significant power in order to gain standing, or as Phil put it, "Take over the world."

The Eater's name was Timothy Powell from Huntsville, Alabama. He was a necromancer who specialized in taking over people's bodies for those about to die and set them up in a new, plush, and younger body. Highly illegal, though very sought after in certain circles. The team concluded that he had been hired, and when he found out who he was truly working for, he couldn't back out. Funny thing was, the body of his gun-wielding friend who had been shot on several occasions went missing last night with no trace while in transport to the morgue at the Atheneum.

Chloe had become number one on the most wanted list. Frank would be fine and was set to come home next week; however, we wouldn't be seeing him for a few days.

Dick, as he now allowed me to call him, made sure to talk to me on his way out.

"Hey, Max," Inspector Holder greeted as he was leaving for the airport. "That was good policing. You have friends in London when you need them. Keep the voodoo stuff to a minimum when you come, though. I'll get to the bottom of this Chloe thing, mark my words." He finished off with a firm handshake that ended with the man pulling me in for a hug. I think Chloe's betrayal had gotten to him, if not the embarrassment.

We met in the dining room after the last few authority

figures or, as Phil called them, "regulars" left.

"So what now?" I asked, looking around the room at the whole team, including Kim. By the looks of her, she hadn't gotten the rest that our team was forced by nature to take. Petro was sitting at the small table that I had found for him on the main tabletop with the rest of his Pixie crew.

"We go for a drink," Phil replied, addressing the whole group. "I know just the place."

"Yeah!" Petro exclaimed. "Lacey and Macey have a friend coming into town tonight. You know, a lady friend." Even with a bum wing, he was still up for the challenges of dating.

"Right," Ed said as he sat, still looking tired. "I have a few things to wrap up, and I think after we decompress, we could use some more rest. The NCTS is sending a few more people over tomorrow to wrap up the report. Let's all meet at FA's around six?"

Jenny, who was sitting next to Ed rewrapping a bandage on his upper arm, answered "I'm in," with a smile. Her touch was light on Ed. She glanced at me and gestured toward Kim.

"Kim, you joining us?" I asked.

"Sure, why not. Shit can't get any weirder than last night." She smiled at me. I had a feeling Jenny was trying to take my mind off Chloe and play matchmaker. For now, I was not in the mood to pay it any attention.

"It's settled," Phil declared as he stood up and walked out of the room.

"Where are you going?" I asked.

"I need to clean my guns. You never know." He started whistling on his way out.

"Max, can we talk in private?" Ed requested as the rest of the group split up. Ed and I walked back to Gramps's old office.

I sat behind the desk, pouring us both a light drink.

"What's up?" I looked at him with genuine interest.

"Lilith. She's your grandmother," Ed informed without hesitation, waiting on my response. His shoulders were up to his ears, fraught with tension. I decided to take it easy on him regarding this news, as I knew there was nothing I could do about it now.

"After last night, nothing would surprise me," I said lightly. He released the tension in his body. "Look, Ed, some of this I get, but most of it I don't. I'm winging it here. I'll take what you are telling me and figure out what to do with it."

"You need to keep this to yourself for now," Ed began. "Tom was ashamed of many things, but Lilith was, at the time, not one of them. Something happened to her and got into her mind. Max, your mother knows about this. Lilith is her mother. I can feel the questions going through your mind, and yes, this means your mother is special. Not completely like you, but she is a former witch, and she used to be a damn good one."

It was my turn to let out some tension as I blew out some air. "Ed, I need a few hours."

"Sure, make sure you're back by six. I think it will be good for the team to take a break tonight. If there is such a thing when you start to grow old. Max, you're a good man and you're going to be one hell of a Mage." With that, Ed stood up. I swear I saw a little tear coming out of his eye as he turned and walked out.

I picked up the phone and dialed Mom, telling her I would be over in a little bit.

*　*　*

Pulling up to the one-story rancher, I took a calming breath. The last few days had left my body in need of some rest and time to recuperate. The issue was my mind wasn't letting that happen.

My mother stood at the door with two cups of coffee in her hands and smiling. "Here you go. You look like you could use a strong cup of the good stuff," she said as she handed me the mug.

I immediately recognized the faint smell of Fae honey coming from it. We sat at the kitchen table in silence, both taking a sip of our drinks before my mother spoke up first.

"I know what's been going on and, yes, I am a witch. Well used to be," she confirmed as she grabbed my hand, squeezing it tightly.

For some reason, I froze. Actually hearing the words come from her mouth rocked me. It's not like she ever lied to me. She just never told me. Funny thing was, it didn't feel like a lie of omission either. It was something different.

"I know. For some reason, when all this craziness started, everything just fell into place. It felt normal. I felt normal," I said as a smile that would light up the night filled her face. It suddenly shifted to something else as she spoke again.

"This has been in front of you your entire life. You just chose to ignore it, so it ignored you." For the first time in my life, I looked in her face and saw regret and the years all collapsing on her at the same time.

"What's wrong?" I asked. "By the way, where's Dad?"

"Max, your father..." she trailed off.

I smiled at her, holding her hand, as she started to smile again, wiping off her face.

"Your father was once very integrated into the Mage way of life, marrying me without a care in the world while knowing full well what he was getting into. He was even given a civilian job working on Mage history. One night, someone came to the house before you were born and almost killed us. I was pregnant with you at the time. As your father tried to protect me, he was almost killed and lost most of his memory. Your father fought off a Battle Mage with his bare hands. The attacker was someone after Tom and was going through our family to get to him," my mother told me, the painful event replaying in her memory before being put back.

"So what happened to the Mage?" I asked, wanting to go after them.

Mom never said what Gramps did about it, but she suggested the situation had been handled with finality. "What about Dad? What happened?"

"You see, he isn't really all there with his past and has always known it. For some reason, he started shunning the community, and I stopped practicing. He's a great man who saved our lives," she said, standing up to get the door for my dad, who was back. "You better get going, dear."

As soon as I saw my father, I perceived him in a different light. I walked up after all these years of not knowing and gave him the biggest hug I think I had given since Santa gave me my first Nintendo. I didn't have to look. I could feel the smile on his face.

"Hey, Dad. I was just leaving. What do you say we get out on the water next weekend?" I asked.

"That would be great, Max. It's been too long since we did. Good to see you. Hope you're staying out of trouble. I'll check on the boat, and lunch is on me," he said. Saying our goodbyes, I walked out the door, looking back in time to see my mother put her arm around him.

You ever watched the end of *Toy Story 3*? That's how I felt driving home. I left the radio off and rolled the windows down, staring at the road and not blinking the whole way.

The rest of the afternoon was more upbeat. We arrived at FA's as a group, and we ran into more of the team from the previous day's excitement. Petro had gotten everyone's phone number and now had a thing for texting people.

As we walked in, Trish ushered us toward the bar, pushing down the chairs she had reserved for us. She informed us that they'd shut down the other locations for the evening. There were a few people in the bar, but Trish didn't seem to mind them.

Dr. Freeman and Jamison showed up with none other than Belm. Kim and Ned arrived next, as they had been working on the report together. Trish served drinks with a fury unlike any I had seen, talking to everyone and finally landing on me.

"Hey, Max, I hear you're kind of a hero," she said.

"I guess. I just showed up for work today," I replied, smiling as I took a pull off the Vamp Amber she set before me. "Hey, by the way, that 'get out of jail free' card you gave me… worked out just fine."

I proceeded to tell her the story of Petro's heroic piss break during the battle to activate it as she took pulls of her beer, laughing through my explanation. She explained that stone was something that had gotten her out of a lot of tight spots, and she came by them every now and then. She would grab another one for me when one showed up. I guess they were rare.

Belm had quite the crowd around him. I didn't think most of the crew had ever met a real demon before, at least not one who wasn't trying to eat them. I walked over to Belm on my way to the restroom. "Hey, man, eaten anyone lately?" I joked, trying to figure out if demons did, in fact, have a sense of humor.

"Not yet," he replied as he grossly licked his lips. "The

night is young." He stared at my eyes, unmoving. "I'm just shitting you. I would rather stay out of trouble. If others knew I was here, it would be bad for my reputation back home," he rasped. "Plus, there are some rules I do have to follow."

I stood there, taking a gulp of air, trying to calm my nerves.

"Oh yeah, that reminds me...I have a message for you: Debt paid and enjoy the purple box. Use it with caution," Belm relayed as he took a drink.

I blinked at Belm and the others staring. "Good. I'll write it down in my book," I said. Apparently, my comment nailed the demon humor because he laughed out loud, spitting on the back of Jamison's head. I had a feeling that wasn't the first time, watching the two interact after that.

Finally heading to the bathroom, a young woman walked out of the lady's room and stopped in front of me. It was Sarah.

"Hey, Sarah," I greeted, looking at her in confusion and interest.

"Max, long time no see," she replied, looking up at me. "I heard you were having a party a while back and showed up to say hi, but as luck would have it, I couldn't find you anywhere, and my car got towed. Crazy night."

"Yeah, I saw you briefly. Anyway, what are you doing here tonight?" I asked.

"Max, you don't remember our night together, do you?" she asked right back.

"No, and that is something I wanted to talk to you about," I started before she cut me off, knowing I was going to make sure I had behaved myself.

"Someone sent me to visit you that night. The whole point was to give you some information to see how you would react. If you took it in stride, then I was to help you forget the evening and let the rest unfold as it has. If not, well...you would probably be in your apartment right now or, hell, maybe still at the bar," Sarah said. I started to see where this was going.

"Who?" I asked.

"Here, drink this, and you'll remember. It's a simple potion. Let your Pixie friend check it first if you want. You know what they say—never drink potions from a strange girl you meet at the bar." She winked as she handed me a small tube.

Once I took it in my hand, she turned around and walked back through the women's bathroom door where she had just come from. "Hey, let's get a drink," I called out as she went inside and Kim walked out.

"Who are you talking to, fire boy?" Kim said, obviously much looser than before.

"You didn't see her?" I asked in surprise.

"Easy there, lover boy. You're batting zero in the love department and, by the sounds of it, the drink department."

I downplayed it. "I just really have to go to the bathroom. It's been a long few days. I think I'm seeing things." I squeezed the vial in my hand. "I'm still not used to the new drinks."

Entering and standing in front of the urinal, I took out the vial and, without hesitation, drank it all in one gulp. It took a minute, but I began to see the events of that night in my thoughts. Sarah had come over and, as she mentioned, started talking about magic, followed by...

"Shit," I said out loud as I remembered Gramps walking into my apartment, drinking the last of my coffee, and cleaning up my dishes while we talked. He was alive. He'd come to visit me from wherever he was hiding and was going back after he left my apartment. Gramps didn't want me to go looking for him. He informed me he was safe, and when the time was right, he would make his way back. He also told me to trust Sarah if I was ever to see her.

I must have been standing there for ten minutes just staring at the wall. I snapped out of it when the flash from Phil's camera went off. "Look at this nosh. You done playing or want to grab another drink?" he goaded as he stood there with Jamison and Petro riding shotgun on his shoulder, doubling over laughing. I couldn't help it; I joined in.

After a few more minutes of talking, I walked back to the bar knowing about Gramps and trying to figure out the best way to talk to Ed about it. Later. *Yes, later*, I thought to myself.

"Right, everyone, listen up. I have great, stupendous news. In light of recent events, the Council has decided to punish us by hosting the annual mixer ball at the Atheneum," Ed informed us, obviously joking about the punishment part. "We have the honor of coming up with the theme. Better yet, the final talks over the Balance will occur afterward."

He slammed his glass of Magnus, polishing it off. Jenny just looked over and shook her head as she put her hand on Ed's, laughing at the drops he had spilled on his immaculate shirt.

Ned came over holding a glass of red wine and sat down beside me. "Max, you all have done a great service for the Council. It will not go unnoticed."

I could see Ed looking at us, moving his head in a positive manner.

"I have an offer to make you," Ned started. "You don't have to accept it today, but I want you to think about it. Jamison and everyone else tells me how great of a person and Mage you are and will become. I was also made aware that Ed is not going to sponsor you for an apprenticeship."

I interrupted. "Why is it every time you hear a story about magic there is always an apprentice?"

He ignored me. "As I was saying, I would like to offer my services as your sponsor. If you accept, we can arrange the details. It's not often a Fae and a Mage partner up. I think it will send a good message," Ned finished.

A politician. He is, after all, a politician, I thought to myself, trying not to roll my eyes. I liked him, though, and his son was, from what I'd gathered, a good guy.

"Let me think about it," I replied while he smiled and stood up, being replaced by Phil and Jamison. Those two were becoming fast friends. Phil handed me Petro, then they started laughing. It took me a minute to figure out they had put something in Dr. Freeman's pocket, who let out a whelp, followed by a flurry of educated curse words.

"Petro, you having a good night?" I asked. He looked over at the new Pixie at the bar with Lacey and Macey.

"You betcha, boss. Casey likes me. I'm in love. Lacey said Casey wants to get married and have kids and move in and…" Petro gushed before I cut him off, still confused by the speed at which Pixies went through the stages of a relationship.

"All right, just remember what we talked about… manners," I reminded him, letting out a huge smile as I set him back down and watched him strut over to the little table.

My phone rang as I sat back down. On instinct, I picked it up. "Hello?" I said, pretty much smashed at this point.

"*Is this Max Abaddon Sand?*" a rough, tight voice spoke.

"Yup, that's me. I'm not in right now. If you leave—" He cut me off.

"*This is Icupiousous. I got your little message and think we need to have a little chat. You and your friends,*" the voice threatened, as the line went dead on the other end.

"Shit," I cursed out loud. "Jamison, Phil, you're never going to guess who that was. They sounded pissed. Icupiousous is a real person, and they got our message," I said as we all started to laugh, watching the others in the group look as if they were missing out on the joke.

Yup, that's my life now. Magic is real, and I think I saved the world. Well, at least our little part of it.

EPILOGUE

Chloe flashed into the room, the dust from the Sanctuary following her through the gate. She was in a large room with windows facing a gray sky and a dark blue-gray ocean.

"Ah, Chloe," a voice came out of the shadows before Lilith walked out.

"Master." Chloe kneeled down, holding out the bag and handing it over.

"Where is Vestulie?" Lilith asked in a tone that could cut through metal.

"He's dead. The Keeper was there. It got complicated," Chloe replied with a shake in her voice. Three men and another woman wearing all red had walked into the room.

"That's unfortunate. He was a valuable, well-placed asset. Let me guess— Max?" Lilith inquired, getting close and putting her index finger on Chloe's chin, forcing her to stand up.

"Yes."

Lilith quickly slapped Chloe, hard, making her fall on the rigid floor. "No matter," Lilith continued as she pulled the container out of the bag and inspected it. "You didn't wait until the Fountain was full, did you? Why am I asking…this will still work, but maybe not as intended. We can use this for another purpose."

The tall man walked closer. He was wearing black leather and had a scar from the top of his face to his chin, as well as a neat scar across his throat. Mengele, better known as the Angel of Death, stood there, eyeing the container as he motioned Pearl over to Chloe. "Take her to the chamber. We will figure out what to do with her soon enough. She may just need some time to reflect."

"You're not killing me?" Chloe asked with a desperation used only by people at death's door.

"No, we have lost enough on this endeavor. You will live, but not comfortably…for now. You will serve a purpose again," Mengele replied in a deep, soothing German tone.

Pearl walked Chloe out of the room. Screams could be heard as the door to the room shut.

"So Lilith, Max is proving to be an issue, as are his friends. I don't think we can let this stand. We need to talk to the Thule governance," Mengele told her as Lilith put her finger on his lips.

"Soon. We need to deliver this. I'll deal with Max soon enough. He's a weak, starstruck drunk," Lilith said in her silky voice.

"He's strong," Mengele countered. "He will be a roadblock in the near future. We need to go into phase two of our plan. This water will suffice for now to get what we want from our patriot on the Council."

Lilith turned around, walking out the door, the echoes of Chloe's screams filling the room.

ACKNOWLEDGEMENTS

Special thanks go out to all my family, friends, and the authors who have inspired me to do more. Years spent reading in Afghanistan, needing a getaway from the harsh realities of the world around us, and the things we as people call a needed escape. Years spent driving to and from work, escaping the labors of traffic in the worlds built by others' minds on audiobook. This book exists because of the inspiration of so many others.

To my friends who dealt with and worked with me through this process. You have been my inspiration to keep moving. Asking for more to read and letting me know your thoughts on my world. Thank you all for sharing this with me.

To my family. My wife and two sons. This book is part of my legacy to you. When I am but a memory in time, you will always be able to pick this book up and remember what a nerd I really was.

BOOKS BY THIS AUTHOR

Max Abaddon And The Will : A Max Abaddon Urban Fantasy Novel

Max Abaddon And The Purity Law: A Max Abaddon Urban Fantasy

Max Abaddon And The Ghost And The Grave: A Max Abaddon Short Story

Max Abaddon And The Gate To Everwhere: A Max Abaddon Urban Fantasy Novel

Max Abaddon And The Dark Carnival: A Max Abaddon Urban Fantasy Novel

Sheltered: Part 1 Of The Sinking Man Series

Awakened: Part 2 Of The Sinking Man Series

Released: Part 3 Of The Sinking Man Series

Simple Deeds: A Collection Of Urban Fantasy Short Stories

Printed in Great Britain
by Amazon